aunty lee's
deadly specials

Also by Ovidia Yu

Aunty Lee's Delights

aunty lee's deadly specials

OVIDIA YU

wm
WILLIAM MORROW
An Imprint of HarperCollinsPublishers

HarperCollins books may be purchased for educational, business, or sales promotional use. For information please e-mail the Special Markets Department at SPsales@harpercollins.com.

FIRST EDITION

Designed by Diahann Sturge

Library of Congress Cataloging-in-Publication Data has been applied for.

ISBN 978-0-06-233832-7

14 15 16 17 18   OV/RRD   10 9 8 7 6 5 4 3 2 1

For Richard, PP, and H

aunty lee's
deadly specials

Prologue

TGIF Morning Drive Time News:

Though several residents of the Ang Mo Kio Housing Development Board block of flats heard a loud crash sometime after midnight early Friday morning, none of them made their way downstairs to investigate.

Our reporter spoke to Mr. Toh Kang, 78, who said, "I thought it is car crash. Car crash what for rush downstairs to see? So late. Car will still be there tomorrow, what."

But it was the body of a young People's Republic of China woman that two students found at the foot of Ang Mo Kio Block 352 on their way to the bus stop just before 6 A.M. this morning.

"There was blood everywhere," Tristan Tan, 14, told reporters. "She was just lying there wearing a lacy white dress all covered with blood. It was so shocking I almost fainted and I couldn't go for band practice and my mum had to call my teachers and say it was because of the trauma so that I wouldn't lose points."

The *Straits Times Online:*

Police traced the dead woman to an illegally sublet ninth-floor flat in the block. Seven other PRC women renting beds there said they did not know her well. She had arrived only a few days before and kept to herself. They gave the police a note the woman left before climbing over the barrier at the lift lobby and dropping into the night.

My beloved husband-to-be, you came to Singapore for the sake of our future together. Because of me, you were willing to sacrifice part of your own body. Because of wanting life with me, you lost your own life. I followed you to Singapore to die where you died and be with you forever. But I can find no sign of you. I pray that when I am dead we will be together in the next life. (*Translated from Chinese*)

The *Lianhe Wanbao* (Singapore's Chinese evening tabloid, known for covering movie-star scandals and government gossip):

The dead woman was Bi Xiao Mei, 24, a factory worker from Xixiang Village in Shandong province. (*Translated from Chinese*)

Bi Xiao Mei and her coworker Zhao Liang, aged 23, had been dating for several months when Bi found she was pregnant. Zhao arranged to come to Singapore to sell a kidney. They calculated the money would be enough to pay for a wedding and an apartment and seemed their best chance to start a life together with their child. A family member who did not want to be named said that Zhao was a responsible and devoted son.

"He knew such transactions are illegal. But his intention was to save a stranger's life and at the same time gain enough money to provide for his wife and child."

Unfortunately the operation went wrong. Zhao Liang's family was informed he had not survived the procedure. They were offered compensation money if Zhao Liang was cremated in Singapore. Alternatively, if they were willing to pay for tickets, they could go to Singapore to collect his body. Zhao's family accepted the compensation money. In life, Zhao Liang had always wanted to travel, so they decided to let their son's ashes rest in Singapore. They saw no reason to provide for Zhao Liang's pregnant girlfriend. They blamed her for their son's death and said there was no proof her baby was his.

Bi Xiao Mei came to Singapore intending to kill herself and her unborn child in front of Zhao Liang's funeral niche. But with her limited English, she could find no record of his death or remains. It appears she killed herself as publicly as she could, hoping to be cremated and her ashes left with his.

It is not yet clear whether this will be permitted under Singapore government regulations.

1

Aunty Lee's Delights

"Madam, you will kill anybody who eats that!" Nina said.

Aunty Lee continued shaking drops of chili oil into the spicy peanut sauce she was stirring. "Just a bit more. Just for flavoring," she said. "This oil is not too hot. Read me some more about the dead woman." Aunty Lee was working on a new line of chili oils to go with Aunty Lee's Shiok Sambal and Aunty Lee's Amazing Achar. Glass jars containing a variety of thinly sliced chili peppers fried in different oils lined the kitchen counters.

"Finish already, madam. No more."

"If you want hot, you should try the one I made with my naga king chili," Aunty Lee said. She had started growing imported chili plants in the garden of her Binjai Park house to see how they did in Singapore. The hot, humid climate seemed to suit the naga king chili, reputed to be the hottest chili in the world, and Aunty Lee had just bottled her first harvest. "The naga king chili is so hot the Indian army is trying to use it as a weapon! In tear gas and hand grenades!"

"And you want to feed that to customers? If they all die, who will buy your food?"

"Hot country you need hot food. Besides, if it is so hot, you only need to use a few drops each time, one bottle will last a long time, good value for money!"

"Good for the customers. Not for you. How are you going to make money if you sell them one bottle and they no need to come back for years? You should be like the iPhone, iPad, like that. Every year must upgrade!"

Aunty Lee could launch an iCook device, Cherril Lim-Peters thought. She smiled to herself in the dining area separated from the small but airy kitchen of Aunty Lee's Delights. She was packing freshly cut fruit into huge plastic containers. At first Cherril had been taken aback by how Aunty Lee and her maid, Nina, talked to each other. But she had soon realized it was a game for them. Like children playing *chatek*, a rubber disk topped with rooster feathers; the goal was to keep the "dialogue" going rather than score points. When Nina was not around, Aunty would talk to one of the photos of her late husband.

Aunty Lee's Delights was a little Peranakan café in Binjai Park, less than five minutes' walk from Dunearn Road. Binjai Park, one of Singapore's oldest elite residential districts, was

rapidly becoming known, especially among wealthy local
foodies, for the *achar* and *sambals* and good traditional Peranakan food available at Aunty Lee's Delights.

Cherril Lim-Peters was new there. And so were the blender
and juicer health drinks she was introducing to the menu.
But that morning, as she peeled and sliced and diced at the
long stainless-steel table (that had supported the cooking
demos and wine dining events that had first brought Cherril to Aunty Lee's Delights), the former flight attendant felt
she had found her new vocation. Her husband, lawyer and
nominated member of Parliament Mycroft Peters, was a
much pleasanter man in private than many would allow. But
Mycroft had insisted Cherril give up her job with Singapore's
national airline after their marriage. Cherril might have
fought this (having been a Singapore Stewardess, she was
trained to fight all manner of battles with a smile), but the
man had won her over with a simple "I need to see you after
a tough day. Even if you're already asleep in bed. Just seeing
you makes me feel that everything is worthwhile."

Mycroft Peters admitting he needed her still gave Cherril
a shiver of pleasure. And Aunty Lee had said she needed her
too, that she cheered up the shop. Cherril had never known
anyone like Aunty Lee before. Her plump Peranakan boss
was an overprotective grandmother, inspiring teacher, and
gossipy girlfriend all rolled up into a *kaypoh* (meddling) *kiasu*
(competitive) *pohpiah* (spring roll).

Cherril was planning to buy the wine business Aunty Lee's
stepson had set up to complement her food business. After
the café had been involved with a couple of murders and a

gay marriage (which Mark and his wife, Selina, considered even worse), Mark decided that the catering business did not really suit him.

Aunty Lee approved wholeheartedly. Mark would never have helped cater any event where plastic cups were used, as Cherril was doing that morning. Also Cherril had got her husband, Mycroft, to agree to finance her new venture while Aunty Lee had had to finance Mark. Mycroft hadn't liked the idea of his wife working in a café. But at least Cherril would be on the ground.

Aunty Lee worked on the principle of doing what she could to make others happy and letting them know how they, in turn, could make her happy. She thought people who tried to earn virtue points by being martyrs just ended up making everybody unhappy. Aunty Lee had realized Cherril could learn almost anything she applied herself to but still had trouble fitting into her husband's world. Aunty Lee had taken her on (against the wishes of Mark, his wife, Selina, and Mark's sister, Mathilda, who lived in London) because after thirty years of marriage she had learned that fitting in was a matter of deciding what made you comfortable. She was more comfortable working with Cherril than with Mark.

Cherril turned her attention back to the mounds of freshly chopped watermelon, papaya, pineapple, and guava. There were also chopped apples, pears, and carrots that had spent the night in the freezer.

"We can call these drinks 'doctails.'"

"Why you want to call them duck's tails? What have they got to do with ducks?"

"Not ducks, Aunty Lee. You know, like cocktails and mocktails, only these are healthy, like a doctor would recommend, so we call them doctails. I'm using green tea, barley water, soy milk, and brown rice tea as bases for the freshly juiced fruits."

Aunty Lee liked the idea enough to wish she had come up with it herself. "You can bring the juicer with us. Then you can ask people what they want and then add fresh fruit juice, like in the food court."

Mark had objected to Aunty Lee serving her homemade barley water, soy milk, and tap water instead of pointing people to his wine list. His wine dining events had been his attempt to cultivate like-minded people who shared his love of fine wines. Cherril, like Aunty Lee, preferred that people simply ate and were happy—and healthy.

Rosie "Aunty" Lee was a plump Peranakan supercook who divided her energies between fixing meals for people and helping them fix their lives (whether they liked it or not). As far as Aunty Lee was concerned, the two were different sides of the same coin. How could you feed someone well unless you understood them? And how could people appreciate her food if the rest of their lives was out of balance? It was no use simply letting people decide what they wanted to eat because Aunty Lee had long ago realized most people had no idea what foods suited them. They remembered dishes prepared by loving grannies or shared in the first flush of romance and spent the rest of their lives complaining that nothing tasted the way it used to. Aunty Lee also believed Peranakan food was the best food in Singapore, possibly the best food in the world. Her definition of Peranakan food had got her into trouble with Peranakan purists, because as far as Aunty Lee was concerned, "I am Peranakan. So all food I prepare is Peranakan food!"

Aunty Lee was the archetypal petite, slightly plump, and very precise Peranakan lady of a certain age. She was familiar to most Singaporeans because her *kebaya*-clad image beamed brightly from jars of Aunty Lee's Amazing Achar and Aunty Lee's Shiok Sambal. But today Aunty Lee was wearing her work outfit—a bright yellow *kebaya* top with pink and green embroidery over a lime-green T-shirt and dark green tai chi trousers. She was also wearing a batik apron with multiple pockets she had designed herself and had her maid, Nina, sew for her. Aunty Lee's sneakers that afternoon were yellow and white and worn over bright green socks. Aunty Lee believed in tradition but she believed even more in comfort.

Her Filipina domestic helper, Nina Balignasay, was the opposite of Aunty Lee. Nina was slim, dark, and minded her own business. But in Singapore it was Nina's business to keep Aunty Lee happy. Her already considerable powers of observation had sharpened considerably in her time with this busybody aunty. She had also learned not to worry that her employer would lose a finger or eye as she speed-sliced, diced, and waved her chopper around to emphasize her points. After all, Nina, who had been trained as a nurse, was nothing if not adaptable. Even if her nursing degree was not recognized in Singapore, she would have been able to stanch the bleeding should Aunty Lee have a slip of the knife. And she had learned it was dangerous—and pretty much impossible—to stop Aunty Lee from doing what she wanted to.

Aunty Lee's Delights kept Aunty Lee occupied after ML Lee's death left her a (relatively) young widow. Of course Aunty Lee always grumbled about the amount of work she had to do on whatever budget her clients gave her. Cherril noticed that if a client increased the budget, Aunty Lee simply upgraded her menu and went on complaining. Aunty Lee's grumbles were a way for her to disguise how much she enjoyed cooking for people. When there were no clients, she cooked for free. She had managed fine on her own but she seemed glad to have Cherril around.

Mark had not paid back the money Aunty Lee lent him to finance the wine business, so the handover of the business should not have been a problem. But Mark still had not signed the transfer papers or returned his keys. It was almost as though he was reluctant to let go. Aunty Lee had given Cherril keys to the shop's front entrance, but there were no extra keys to the service entrances connecting the kitchen and wine room to the alley behind the shop. Aunty Lee had hung the keys to these doors on hooks beside them.

"And don't forget that today's people have not paid you yet, madam," Nina reminded Aunty Lee. "You must ask them right away or else later they will say, 'I'm sure I paid already.'"

Nina sounded uncannily like Niyati Fornell, who had given that excuse the previous week. Aunty Lee gave a cackle of delighted appreciation but Cherril's laugh was a little weak. Nina was a skilled mimic. The thick Filipino accent she spoke with most of the time was a token of subservience, designed to keep her invisible. Cherril was very conscious of this because of the difficulties she was having with her own accent and with standard English. The Hokkien-Teochew infused with Malay and English "loanwords" Cherril had picked up from her parents was as despised by speakers of pure Amoy Hokkien as her neighborhood-school "Singlish" was by her husband's mission-school-educated friends. Many of Mycroft's friends affected British, American, or Australian accents depending on where they had gone to study, and several had laughed at Cherril's pronunciation and grammar mistakes. One (who Cherril suspected had wanted Mycroft for herself) had given her a link to the "Speak Good English" campaign website. Cherril, too practical to be proud, had found the site very helpful. But the ease with which Nina adopted voices and accents made her wonder if Nina mimicked Cherril's "gahmen" school accent when she was not around. And when Nina so mimicked her, did Aunty Lee cackle with laughter as she was laughing now? Nina grinned at Cherril as she carried some food out to the car. Cherril smiled back.

Nina Balignasay knew the wealthiest employers and clients could be the meanest and stingiest when it came to not paying up. At least, thanks to her, Aunty Lee now collected a down payment when taking on a job. Aunty Lee was too easily distracted by stories and menus. It was a good thing she had Nina by her side and on her side. It was good for Nina too. Though she had not known how to cook or drive when she arrived in Singapore, she had since learned to do both proficiently. Aunty Lee considered her one of the best investments she had ever made, one that had paid off hand-

somely. From the start it had been Nina who kept the business grounded and the accounts balanced. If Aunty Lee had
a gift for making food, Nina had a gift for managing money.
And, if unleashed, she went after late payments like a loan
shark.

That bright September Saturday morning Aunty Lee was
happy as she followed Nina out to the car. She had a catering
job to occupy her and the prospect of looking over an unfamiliar house to entertain her. Could life get much better
than this? But of course she was too much a *kiasu* Singaporean to tempt fate by saying so.

"Looks like it's going to rain," Aunty Lee said, looking up
at the brilliant blue sky with only a few light, white clouds.
"Sure to spoil the food. Don't know why these people with
big houses always want outdoor parties. You said it's a big
house, right?"

"A very big house, according to Google Maps," Cherril
said, joining them. "It's not going to rain. It looks like it's
going to be a beautiful day."

"Then sure to be too hot to eat outside," Aunty Lee said
firmly. "Nina, better get more dry ice."

"Did you read in the papers about the Mainland Chinese
woman that committed suicide?" Cherril threw this in to distract Aunty Lee from imagining possible weather disasters.
Nothing tickled Aunty Lee's mental taste buds so much as a
strange death.

"Of course! But the newspapers never say everything. I can
tell there's some funny business there!"

"Madam, the woman write a letter and say she is going

to jump off the balcony and then she go and jump off the balcony. Even you cannot say there is funny business there!" Nina said firmly. Catholic Nina did not approve of suicides any more than she approved of the murders Aunty Lee had a tendency to get herself involved in.

"The Chinese papers said her boyfriend phoned her right before the operation to tell her that everything was going to be all right. She said she already knew something was wrong because even over the phone she had heard angels singing."

"The English papers didn't report that." Aunty Lee looked put out. "Nina, I wish you would learn to read Chinese. Chinese news is much more interesting than English news. What else did the Chinese paper say?"

"The Chinese papers interviewed one of the women staying in the one-room flat where Bi Xiao Mei stayed. She said they pay five dollars a day to sleep there. Bi Xiao Mei went out to search for her fiancé all day, then went back and cried all night. She could not find any record of his death or of the operation. Because the operation was illegal, she was afraid the people who did it did not bother to properly dispose of his body but just dumped it somewhere.

"Anyway, the woman said that that night before she died they went to Bukit Timah Plaza and Bi Xiao Mei said she heard the same angels singing as she did over the phone. And then she died."

"Did the woman also hear angels singing?"

"She only heard the *getai* people playing their music outside. There is an uncle at BTP with Alzheimer's. When people play *getai* music he will sit in his chair there and sing."

"You don't really know that China man is really dead," Nina said. "Probably the guy is not really dead. He didn't want to go home, didn't want to marry her, so got people here to tell people back home he's dead." Nina's previous experiences with men had not left her with a very high opinion of them.

Aunty Lee's lips pursed appreciatively. There was nothing she liked more than a good gossip based on romance, betrayal, and death.

"The Chinese papers also said the fiancé Zhao's father told reporters his son said he was going to Singapore to work and save to pay for his wedding. The father was sure his son would never have come here for an illegal operation."

"That boy wanted to come here to work and earn enough to save money for his wedding? He must be crazy! Here, every time you earn one dollar you spend two dollars on food, three dollars on housing!"

"Not really, Nina," Cherril said. She handed each of them a banana (so full of necessary potassium, healthy fiber, manganese, and vitamins C and B_6). "Eat this to keep up your energy. I know this PRC guy who came over less than five years ago. He rented an HDB flat—yes, illegally—then subrented rooms out. He did the cleaning for them once a week when he collected the rent. Then he got a second apartment and a third apartment . . . now he's a millionaire!" Singapore's Housing Development Board had strict rules on the renting and subletting of the HDB flats, especially where noncitizens were concerned. But new arrivals from the People's Republic of China seemed able to get around anything.

"I wonder how much you get paid for a kidney," Aunty Lee

said. She looked thoughtfully at the portable food chiller Nina was filling with crab cakes and prawn patties, ready to go onto the grill.

"Not worth the risk," Nina said sharply. "That is illegal."

"The girl's family said she had been depressed since news of his death. And with the baby coming, it must have made things worse. One of the letters they found was from Zhao's family telling her not to make any more trouble because they had accepted the rest of the payment promised to Zhao for his kidney. Apparently the advance he got was only enough to pay for his ticket to Singapore. That shows his family must have known what he was going to do."

"What we are going to do is serve food. Come," said Nina firmly. The last of the food and equipment in the car, she turned the sign to CLOSED and locked the door, wishing she had the time to go at the kitchen with a scrubbing brush and mop after all the food preparation. People who came in and said how beautifully organized everything in the shop was did not realize how much constant work it took to maintain everything dust-free and functioning despite the stream of people passing through.

"Isn't that Mark's car?" Cherril asked as they drove off.

"I already told him the shop is not open today," Nina said firmly. "If he can't remember, too bad. He will have to come back."

Aunty Lee was torn. Her *kiasu* (fear of losing out) side dictated that she leave immediately in order to arrive at least thirty minutes early for the catering project, but her *kaypoh* side that made everybody else's business her own wanted to stay and find out whether it was indeed Mark Lee in the car and what it was that he wanted.

"Maybe he came to talk to me about the handover," Cherril said.

"Sir Mark just wants to come and look at his wine bottles," Nina said. "His precious babies. He will stand there and talk to them, his precious wine bottles."

2

Sung Office Law

GraceFaith Ang knew she was looking beautiful that Saturday morning. She always looked good, but her new green dress with its flared skirt and bright blue and white stars made her stand out even more than usual. As always, her hair and makeup were perfect and she was aware of appreciative glances from her fellow Mass Rapid Transit commuters. The best were the ones tinged with envy. GraceFaith found envy the best monitor of her progress; as long as others wanted what she had, she had to be doing all right.

Of course, these days GraceFaith knew how well she was doing even without the envy, but she still enjoyed it. The Caucasian man who had stood up to let GraceFaith have his seat caught her eyes and smiled at her. GraceFaith returned the smile but lowered her eyes modestly, blocking off further contact. As far as GraceFaith was concerned, no man traveling on public transport was worth smiling at unless he was the Minister of Transport (who was, incidentally, one of the better-looking ministers). Still, she was not going to burn any bridges unnecessarily. Her eye fell on the newspaper the man was carrying: another woman had committed suicide for love, apparently. Such losers did not interest her. Grace-Faith could well understand being driven to kill in desperation. But it was not herself she would kill.

When GraceFaith found the main door to the Sung Law office unlocked, she was only mildly surprised. The cleaners were in, she supposed. Or whoever had been the last to leave last night had been careless. GraceFaith felt a small tremor of pleasure thinking how angry Mabel Sung would be when she told her. Mabel, founder and big boss at Sung Law, was obsessive about security and privacy. GraceFaith thought it was a lawyerly trait. Mabel's daughter, Sharon, also a lawyer in the firm, was the same way. GraceFaith herself had become a legal assistant intending to become a lawyer's wife. That had been almost two years ago, and until certain recent events GraceFaith had been beginning to think it was time to move on. Mabel's husband, Henry, and son, Leonard, were the only men she encountered regularly at Sung Law. The Sung money and connections had made Leonard Sung look like a possible option for a while. But there was a limit to what GraceFaith was willing to put up with. Leonard Sung had not even managed to pass his O levels in Singapore. If he had come from a poor family, the boy would have been shunted into vocational training. Instead he had been sent to America. GraceFaith had heard such stories about what he had got up to there—even all that family money had not managed to buy him a degree—but she still liked Leonard better than Sharon. GraceFaith generally preferred men to women. Things were in her favor at Sung Law now and she might as well put away as much cash as she could till something better showed up.

The door to Mabel's office stood slightly ajar. If the cleaners were in there unsupervised, Mabel Sung would really freak out. At least a Mabel Sung tantrum would be more interesting than the utterly dull and pointless brunch party at the Sungs' house was going to be, GraceFaith thought. Perhaps she should call and let Mabel know that the door had been left open and the cleaners were in there unsupervised. Mabel had been boringly subdued over the past couple of weeks. Her making her daughter Sharon a full partner in the firm had not surprised anyone.

GraceFaith did not like Sharon Sung. Despite a drab wardrobe and a loser haircut, Sharon Sung showed no sign of even noticing GraceFaith's superior appearance. Sharon Sung was a spoiled rich girl who thought she was so smart when all she had done was pick up what was handed to her on a plate. GraceFaith resented this and resented giving up her Saturday morning to go all the way out to Bukit Timah to celebrate something no one cared about. Still, she had dressed carefully. No one could call her silky vintage-looking dress revealing. But the way it fell open at the neckline and clung to her hips emphasized GraceFaith's best assets. And why not? She had paid for them and it was time they worked for her. But until they paid off, she had other work to do . . .

GraceFaith pushed open the door of Mabel's office and stopped, taken aback.

Sharon Sung was sitting behind her mother's enormous desk, reading. GraceFaith felt a sudden urge to turn and run. But why? Just because Sharon was in Mabel's office didn't mean she knew anything. After all Mabel herself had no idea what GraceFaith was doing . . .

"You're here so early?" GraceFaith said brightly.

"Still here."

"You mean since yesterday? You spent the whole of last night in the office?"

Sharon did not answer.

GraceFaith knew her first duty at Sung Law was to play personal assistant to Mabel Sung and keep her happy. Keeping Mabel Sung happy was top priority for everyone at Sung Law except perhaps Sharon. Sharon seemed to go out of her way to provoke Mabel. She was not a typical spoiled second-generation money brat, which Mabel might have found easier to handle. No, Sharon prided herself on being a good lawyer, good enough to point out flaws in Mabel Sung's own work.

"You should be getting home. Isn't your big partnership party this morning?"

Sharon didn't bother to answer this. Her head hurt and her eyes hurt and she had a crick in her neck. But what hurt most of all was that she had spent all night in the office and no one from her family had been worried enough to call.

"Did Mabel send you to get me?"

"No. I just came in to look up something—"

"I could have died here and they wouldn't care," Sharon said.

"What?"

Sharon thought GraceFaith a miserable excuse for a legal assistant. In her opinion, no one who put so much time and effort into makeup and manicures could be of any real value. Sharon was proud of how little time she spent on her own appearance. It was a matter of being organized. Sharon had worn her hair in the same bob since her school days. Every year she bought herself five new sets of shirts and suits for work and three black dresses and one blue or green dress for Chinese New Year. This was a compromise. Though a fervent Christian, Mabel Sung would have preferred her daughter wear red for New Year fortune, but had only succeeded in weaning her off black.

"Shouldn't you be at home preparing for the party? After all, it's your big day!" GraceFaith tried again.

"It's not a big day. It's a big responsibility. That's what I've been trying to prepare for." Sharon slammed shut the ring binder she had been staring at. Misaligned papers muted the impact, spoiling the effect. "It's not as though dressing up for some fancy party is going to get the job done."

"How can you not be excited about your own party? Mabel will be so disappointed. She organized it just for you, you know. She's so proud of you."

"She called some stupid friend of hers to bring Peranakan food. She should know I can't stand Peranakan food."

"How can you say that? Everybody loves Peranakan food. Besides, once you've tried Aunty Lee's *otak*—remember even you said it was so *shiok*."

"Grace, you are such an idiot sometimes. You and all the other idiots that make such a big deal about the kind of food that makes you fat and unhealthy!"

Sharon collected the folders on the desk and returned them to a shelf in the cabinet, which she pointedly locked, taking the key with her before leaving the room. Perhaps she expected to shock GraceFaith. After all, Mabel Sung's locked file cabinets were even more sacrosanct than her locked office door.

GraceFaith looked suitably taken aback. She also remembered to look hurt by the "fat" epithet thrown in her direction. Why not, if it made Sharon Sung happy?

After Sharon stepped into the elevator, GraceFaith got down to work. She would have to hurry, but she would still manage to do what she had to and get to the Sungs' place by eleven.

And GraceFaith had her own keys to Mabel's private cabinets.

Mabel Sung was a woman with a great ability to impress people. She had complete belief in her own powers of organization and sufficient force of personality to convince others to believe in them too. The truth was that Mabel crashed into situations, stirred them up, and let the pieces fall down into new patterns. This was very often enough to break a stalemate and open new channels. When it worked, Mabel took all the credit, and when it did not, she found someone else to blame. GraceFaith had survived longer than any other assistant in Sung Law largely because she had mastered the art of serving up other people for Mabel to blame. And because GraceFaith believed anything was worth putting up with if the goal was big enough. In this case, her goal was definitely big enough.

3

Good-Class People

Number 8 King Albert Rise was a GCB or "Good-Class Bungalow." What this meant to someone familiar with Singapore real estate guidelines laid down by the Urban Redevelopment Authority was that the gently sloping land the two-and-a-half-story bungalow perched on had a plot width of at least 18.5 meters, a plot depth of at least 30 meters, and a plot size of at least 1,400 square meters in a desirable residential neighborhood (this being Singapore, rules clearly defined not only what constituted a luxury bungalow but where such bungalows were permitted to be built). And of course it also meant those able to afford it were good-class people

Henry Sung liked the idea of the King Albert Rise house. It was the right size and in the right location to send all the right signals to the right people. It was expensive enough to show everyone that his family had made it, that they had enough money to be a force to be reckoned with in Singapore. At least that was what his wife, Mabel, said and he believed her. Mabel was right about most things. It was her financial investments that had paid for most of what they had. And even when Mabel wasn't right, life was more comfortable when he agreed with her. So he did. Henry liked things to be comfortable. Who didn't? And that was the problem Henry Sung had with the house. It had been designed by an award-winning architect and furnished by a world-renowned interior designer. It had also been featured in two lifestyle magazines in articles about Mabel Sung, first female dean of the law faculty at the National University of Singapore and founder of Sung Law, a top-tier firm in Singapore.

But 8 King Albert Rise was not a very comfortable house.

On the camera monitor he watched the caterer outside the back gate talking and laughing with her assistants. Rosie Lee had been a second wife. Maybe one day . . . he smiled as he thought of someone. Someone other than the woman who shared the house with him. Even thinking of her felt slightly clandestine, though they had been doing nothing wrong. Anyway his wife was in their son's room, and once in there she could stay there for hours, oblivious to everything going on outside.

"Not long now."

But he knows they are bound to live for eternity in this beautiful prison. No escape unless he acts. Finally there is a person who is both his reason for wanting to break away from Mabel and the one who has been urging him to stay and be patient, telling him things will work out for them if he just waits a little longer. No one who has seen Mabel Sung crushing all opposition in court or at home (and Henry has witnessed both) can believe there is any hope. But he is willing to dream a little longer because he knows that once Mabel feels challenged, it will be a battle to the death.

"Where's Sharon?" Mabel demanded accusingly from the doorway.

"Maybe she went to the office," Henry said without turning to look at her.

"Don't be ridiculous. Why would she go to the office today? Guests will be coming soon. Find her and tell her to get ready! I think somebody is here already!"

A buzzer sounded, but not from the gate. Since their son, Leonard, became too weak to get around on his own, Mabel had installed a buzzer call system as well as a camera monitor in his bedroom. And Henry knew she had planned many more things that would involve wiring and foreign workers walking all over his house, and he winced at the prospect. The buzzer sounded twice more, followed by their son's voice: "Mum! Nobody came to change my sheets!"

"Maybe Lennie would be more comfortable in the hospital—or in a nursing home," Henry said, not for the first time. He did not like being around bad smells and soiled sheets. It had been bad enough when the children were babies, even though he and Mabel had had servants to do the actual work. It was far worse now that his son was making bigger messes and bigger fusses. "He'll have trained professionals looking after him there—"

"You're just trying to get rid of him—your own son, and all you can think about is shipping him off somewhere you don't have to bother with him. What kind of father are you?" Mabel could go on for hours, but Leonard's buzzer was sounding and she started toward the stairs. "Go and find Sharon. She should be helping. This is all for her and she can't even be bothered to help!"

The office phone rang. GraceFaith ignored it. She had more important things to do than answer phones. And thanks to Sharon seeing her there, she would have to come up with something to justify her presence in the office that morning.

Aunty Lee's Delights had been commissioned to cater a brunch for fifty people to celebrate Sharon Sung being made partner in Sung Law, the law firm founded by her mother, Mabel Sung. Even though this made it almost a family affair, Aunty Lee had been surprised that a company function was being held at the Sungs' residence rather than a hotel or country club. Didn't lawyers usually go to expensive restaurants and celebrate with expensive wines and liquors? But Mabel Sung, the founder of Sung Law, was also said to be very Christian. Aunty Lee had thought perhaps Mabel Sung believed in giving money to the poor rather than spending it on alcohol and restaurants for herself. But once Aunty Lee saw Number 8 King Albert Rise, it was clear to her that the Sungs did not mind spending money on themselves.

There was no one at the back gate Aunty Lee had been directed to bring the food around to, but the gate was not locked, and looking through it, Aunty Lee could see the pool and patio area with several long tables and stacked-up chairs. That would be where the party was going to be. Aunty Lee told Nina to park the bright yellow Ford Focus on the side of the road by the entrance. There was a white line indicating no parking at all times on both sides of the road, but it was unlikely the Land Transport Authority would act unless residents complained. This was probably the entrance that service and tradespeople used. From here, the residence looked far grander than Aunty Lee's own house. She had heard rumors that the Sungs' fortune was not as stable as her late husband's, but Aunty Lee knew most of the time rumors only meant other people were envious of what you had.

Aunty Lee had been more intrigued to learn that Leonard, the Sungs' *havoc* (an untranslatable Singlish term used to describe an uncontrollable or promiscuous child, but with indulgent overtones) son had recently returned from the United States and moved back in with his parents. Leonard Sung was said to be a drug addict, an AIDS victim, a cancer patient, or all of the above. But none of the people who fed Aunty Lee these delicious news nuggets had actually seen the boy since his return. Not having children herself, Aunty Lee loved hearing details about problem children. But what interested her most about Leonard Sung was her stepdaughter, Mathilda, telling her Mabel Sung had once tried to matchmake Mathilda and Leonard.

"She's not good at taking no for an answer," Mathilda had

said wryly when Aunty Lee told her who her latest catering job was for. Aunty Lee had continued the weekly long-distance phone calls to Mathilda in London after her father's death. She wanted Mathilda to remember her roots in Singapore, and besides, she liked the girl.

"You didn't marry the boy, so you must have said no, right?"

"Why do you think I'm staying out of Singapore until she's married him off to someone else? Actually she never talked to me. She was bugging my parents and implying that unless they accepted her offer, they would never find a nice Chinese boy willing to marry me after sending me away to become all Westernized."

Naturally Aunty Lee was curious to see what Leonard Sung looked like. But there was no one in sight as she pushed the gate open.

"Hello. Hello." Nina spoke into the gate intercom but there was no answer.

"The gate's not locked. Why don't we just go in and start setting up?" Cherril suggested.

Nina started to say they ought to try calling first but Aunty Lee was already pushing the gate open, eager as a little girl to start the day's catering adventure.

Once inside the gate, Aunty Lee looked around with interest. Did the Sungs really have a private chapel and baptismal pool on the grounds? People said they had turned to religion after their son got sick. But the only pool she could see was the small, blue-tiled swimming pool, along one side of which the line of buffet tables was standing. And the small building on the other side of the pool . . . could that be the famous chapel?

The house itself was clearly a luxury mansion. Aunty Lee herself lived in a good but somewhat lower-class bungalow. Built on the sloping inner reaches of King Albert Park, the main Sung residence was on the highest level, while the architect had made the most of the sloping land behind the house by creating a series of living spaces linked by external sheltered stairs as well as what looked like a chairlift. An outdoor kitchen complete with cooker, barbecue pits, and an enormous freezer was located on the stone patio by the swimming pool on the lowest level, where the back gate was located. Across the pool the front of the smaller building (which looked more like a guesthouse than a chapel) had French windows facing the pool and patio. These were coated with silver reflective film, so Aunty Lee looking in saw only a distorted version of herself. A sheltered stone staircase linked the guesthouse and small circular gravel driveway leading from the back gate to the main building and there was also the chairlift. Aunty Lee wondered whether it was intended as a granny flat—you were close enough to have dinner with your family and have grandchildren dropping in but you had your own toilet and space for mah-jongg games. Aunty Lee did not miss having children, given all the exam worries that came with them, but she would have liked to have had grandchildren to spoil . . .

Despite these pleasant thoughts, something about the little pool house made Aunty Lee uneasy. Was it because she could not see what was going on inside? She knew some people valued privacy above everything else. But too much privacy also meant that no one could look in to make sure nothing was wrong. A fall, for example, could mean lying there helpless for hours or more.

Cherril came to Aunty Lee's side, snapping her out of her daydream. "Should we bring down the extension cables for the blender and chillers or wait and see if they provided them? They said they would, right?"

"Better to bring everything." It was not that Aunty Lee did not trust people who didn't do their own cooking—she just trusted her own instincts and equipment more.

It was still early. A few guests appeared, making their way down the stone staircase and admiring the landscaping in little clusters. Cherril supplied them with drinks (tea, coffee, fruit juices, and her mocktails) while Aunty Lee and Nina spread out the tablecloths and plugged in the food warmers.

"It's going well, isn't it? Isn't it fun?" Cherril said so happily that even Aunty Lee did not have the heart to remind her that the hungry (or just greedy) hordes had not yet descended with their demands. "I'm just going to bring in the rest of the coffee flavoring syrups."

Aunty Lee was steadying the chafing pan that Nina was plugging in under the table ("Madam, a lot of rubbish underneath here. All their cleaners and bottles of everything they just push underneath the table!") when she saw the electric gates slowly open as Cherril returned with two bags of syrup bottles looped over her shoulders. Cherril looked surprised but pleased. Of course there would be a remote control for the gate somewhere, Aunty Lee thought, most likely in the family cars. She was just going to warn Cherril to watch out, a vehicle might be coming, when a black car turned sharply off the road and charged through the gates. The car's passenger mirror caught on the handle of one of Cherril's bags, pulling it taut against her shoulder and dragging her after the car at a stumbling run.

"Don't fall under the wheels!" Aunty Lee shouted. "Stop! Stop the car! Stop!" She dropped the chafing pan and started to run toward the car, desperately waving her arms and wishing she had spent more time with her Active Elders exercise group. Cherril had dropped the other bags and was frantically trying to loosen her arm. Fortunately the bag handle snapped. The car continued up the side slope to the house, leaving a trail of broken glass and syrup stains and a shaken Cherril in a heap on the drive.

By the time Nina and the other guests reached her, Cherril was sitting up and saying she was all right. There were red welts on her arm from the bag strap and painful-looking scrapes and bruises on her legs but nothing worse. The electric gate slowly swung shut.

"Do you want to go home?" Aunty Lee asked. "Nina can drive you back. You should rest."

"Of course not. This is my first big job. But all my coffee syrups are smashed!"

"I don't think the driver even saw you," one of the guests said. "Nowadays, with tinted windows, with stereo system and shock absorber and noise cancellation system, you hit something, also you don't know until you get home and find your car dented."

Or bloody, thought Aunty Lee. That was another disadvantage of too much privacy. Sometimes you didn't know what damage you were doing. Or perhaps you didn't care.

4

Preparing the Buffet

The food looked and smelled good, laid out on the heating pans. The early guests had been calmed down and, drinks in hand, were chatting in little clusters. Aunty Lee, Nina, and Cherril set to work clearing up the mess of broken glass and syrup concentrate on the driveway.

"It's nothing compared to what we used to get during in-flight turbulence," Cherril said lightly. "Once you get used to clearing up coffee and cake smears on the cabin ceiling and broken glass and vomit on the cabin floor without spoiling your makeup and manicure, nothing on the ground is too much to handle. Since this is a driveway and they don't have a dog or children, we don't worry about the glass dust, okay?"

Even Nina could not fault Cherril's cleanup. If Aunty Lee had had any lingering doubts about working with Cherril, this dismissed them. It was important that a team be able to handle disasters together, but this was seldom tested till it was too late. Perhaps, Aunty Lee thought, it would be a good idea for all restaurants to plan a disaster as part of the staff screening process. Perhaps she could come up with a restaurant staff training guide and take on apprentices at Aunty Lee's Delights. Perhaps this could become the next big reality-TV hit that everybody looked down on in public and watched in secret . . .

"What are you thinking, madam?" Nina asked suspiciously. Nina believed they should only take on jobs they knew they could do and knew they would make a profit on.

"Nothing," Aunty Lee said. "Can you believe we were afraid Cherril couldn't do real work?"

"What's that?" Cherril asked.

It was Nina's turn to say, "Nothing," She tied up the final bag of stained newspaper and glass shards and took it out to the bin.

"You look so delicate, Nina thought you are not strong enough to do real work," Aunty Lee explained. "And I thought you look so thin, how can you work in a restaurant if you don't like to eat?"

"Oh, I eat a lot but I never get fat," Cherril said.

"You are lucky. I have a Budai figure,"

"Budai?"

"Laughing Buddha. The fat, happy Chinese Buddha, not the thin, sad Indian one. You rub his tummy, it is sup- posed to bring money and good luck. But I don't have to rub his tummy, I got my own." Aunty Lee rubbed a hand over her own middle section, making Cherril laugh. "Healthy, wealthy, and wise."

"Well, it seems to work!"

Aunty Lee, with all the energy she put into her curiosity and cooking, was one of the happiest people Cherril had met in her new life.

Things were not as happy up in the grand Sung house.

Mabel came out of her son's room and slammed the door hard. Yet another maid had said she wanted to leave. It was the third one since Leonard's return. They were supposed to take care of the housework but they all gave Leonard as their reason for leaving. The girls said he shouted at them, threw things at them, and tried to "hug and kiss" them. Mabel had tried to talk to Leonard, who said only that the stupid sluts deserved it. Even as a boy, Leonard had always had his moods and what Mabel thought of as his indulgences, but he had always kept them out of sight. Mabel knew, of course. She had paid his bills and settled charges with compensation money. And she had been careful not to give her husband the details. Leonard was a strong and charming personality, full of talent and potential. It was not his fault he didn't fit into Singapore's strict academic system or America's moralistic, politically correct system. Mabel knew that after her son had sown his wild oats he would settle down. And with her support he would make her proud of him.

But that had not yet happened. Now the poor boy was so weak she could not be angry with him. Instead she was angry with her husband for not doing more to save their son.

Henry was the doctor but Mabel was the one fighting to save Leonard's life. Mabel would do whatever it took to give Leonard back his health. She knew her son was not perfect but he was her son.

Mabel looked at her phone screen. She had persuaded Henry, who was paranoid about security, to install monitoring cameras all over the house. This way she could make sure Leonard was cared for when she was at the office. Leonard, propped up on a chair and cackling gleefully, was throwing something at the maid who was changing his bedsheets. Mabel looked more closely. Leonard was tearing pages out of a book. He crumpled and smeared the papers in his soiled adult diaper before throwing them at the crying girl. Mabel knew that despite the pay raise she had just offered, the girl would be leaving. But at least Leonard was laughing.

Mabel switched cameras to see how many people had arrived. She needed a decent number of classy-looking people present. Aunty Lee, the caterer, was there too. The stupid, fat old woman was chatting with Mabel's guests as though she was one of them. Mabel Sung and her husband had been acquainted with the late ML Lee. ML had gone to the right schools, worked with the right people, and lived in the right district. At one time Mabel Sung had considered the Lee children worthy matches for her own. If only they had had a mother who understood the importance of good connections, Mabel was sure something could have been worked out, but Rosie Lee had been no help at all. "Leave them to work it out themselves," she had said irresponsibly. As though children knew more than their parents. But at least she was

supposed to be a good cook. Leonard had complained that
their Filipina maids didn't prepare real Singapore food. He
was too weak to eat out and he didn't like reheated dishes.
If Mabel hurried, she had time before the meeting to bring
Leonard something from the buffet, just to make him happy
and keep him quiet for a while.

"Mabel, I have to talk to you." Sharon caught Mabel as she
came down the stairs.

"Not now. I'm busy." It still jarred Mabel when Sharon
called her "Mabel." At Sung Law it was a rite of passage when
she graciously gave new staff permission to "call me Mabel,"
though few took advantage of the honor. When Sharon confronted her with "Do I have to go on calling you 'Mrs. Sung'
forever?" she had simply said "Of course not" and Sharon
had started calling her "Mabel."

"Mabel—"

Mabel winced again. Sharon had been offended when reminded to address her as "Mrs. Sung" instead of "Mum" at
the office and this was payback. Mabel was careful not to
show she minded or noticed.

"Mabel, this is important. It's about the firm and it's not
just important. It's serious and it's urgent. There are big
problems!"

"Then you go and take care of them. That's what I made
you partner for."

"Mabel, it's serious. It looks like there's money missing.
Will you please listen to me for once? This is more important
than some stupid party."

"I have to get your brother something to eat before the food gets cold. There's no money missing, don't say things like that and frighten people. It's all just paperwork, this account or that account. Probably GraceFaith just put something in the wrong place."

"Or maybe GraceFaith is the one who took it. I don't know why you trust her so much. If you were running the company properly, you would get a trained lawyer or at least a trained accountant."

Mabel Sung did not bother to defend her assistant. "Ask GraceFaith to explain everything to you. I don't know why she isn't here yet. I told her to come early and help set up. Give her a call and tell her to hurry up but don't bother her with your questions until Monday."

"She's probably still in the office." Sharon knew she was in the right and her mother was being stupid. But she still seethed at the suggestion that GraceFaith could explain anything to her.

"Don't be ridiculous. Why would GraceFaith go to the office today?"

Mabel headed toward the covered stone stairs to the pool patio.

Sharon's questions had not been answered. But she had seen GraceFaith at the Sung Law office that morning and now she knew Mabel had not sent her there.

"Are you sure this is the right house? Why don't they let us in? Why do we have to wait outside?" the woman asked in nasal, tongue-curling Mandarin that marked her as coming from Beijing or one of the northeast provinces of Mainland China.

"Of course it's the right house. I am here every day. I told you I am the doctor that looks after the son of the house." The man had grown up speaking Mandarin at home in Malaysia, but all his education since moving to Singapore had been in English. He suspected the woman looked down on his Mandarin much as Singaporeans looked down on his English—but not as much as they looked down on the inability of PRCs—as recent arrivals from the People's Republic of China like his companion were tagged—to understand any English outside a textbook. But no matter. He was on the verge of making his big break. He was going to be rich and more important, he was going to be powerful. And then everyone would be forced to respect him.

"If you are the doctor, why do we have to take taxi here? Why don't you have a big car? And why do we have to wait outside the front gate like poor people?"

"I told you I arranged the meeting for eleven thirty, we are still early."

"Either I go inside now or I'm leaving."

5

Mabel Sung

Aunty Lee was always happiest when she was serving food. And she especially loved buffets like this. Laying out the stacks of clean plates and utensils, setting up the decorations (edible in this case), the dishes of *achar* and *sambal* and spicy fried anchovies and peanuts, the baskets of *keropok,* and of course the food. The steaming tubs of white rice, yellow rice, and coconut rice and the aromas that rose from the warm food all promised comfort, satisfaction, and fulfillment . . . for a while at least. Aunty Lee wanted to make people happy. That was at the root of what some saw as her busybody meddling. She was not always successful because some people seemed determined to live unhappy, uncomfortable lives. Still, when they came to her table to be fed, Aunty Lee did her best to remind them what contentment felt like—a little spicy stimulation, sweet and sour sensations, and the age-old comfort of steaming rice and rich, clear soup.

"Yes, it is traditional *nasi lemak,* coconut rice," Aunty Lee said to a couple of curious guests. "My own traditional version of traditional *nasi lemak.* The rice is cooked with coconut cream and flavored with *pandan*"—screw pine—"leaves grown in my own garden. That's why the smell is so fragrant. There's also *nasi kunyit*—yellow rice—to go with the chicken *buah keluak,* and white rice because some people prefer white rice. This is my own anchovy *sambal* paste, if you want you can buy from my shop. One bottle, keep in the fridge, can last you four weeks, but you're sure to finish before then. I make it using tamarind juice, dried chilies, anchovies, garlic, and onions, very *shiok.* These are hard-boiled quails' eggs, easier to eat than chicken eggs. And more *sambals*—today I brought my cockle *sambal* and cuttlefish *sambal* also. These I'm not selling in bottles, if you want, you must come to the shop. You can try them with the roasted peanuts or put on the fried chicken."

There was also stir-fried *kangkong* (water spinach), *achar* (pickles), and generous portions of Aunty Lee's favorite garnishes: sun-dried anchovies fried to a rich savory crunchiness and crunchy peanuts roasted in golden-brown rice-paper-crisp skins.

Aunty Lee stepped back to let the guests pick their own food. That was another thing she liked about buffets—you could learn so much about people by watching how they picked food items off the buffet table. At the last family outing to the Ritz-Carlton buffet, Mark's wife, Selina, had persisted in taking large portions for everyone at the table despite their saying that they wanted to help themselves. She had eaten hardly anything herself, piling her food onto Mark's plate and saying, "Eat it, don't waste," more like a mother than a wife.

Selina needed to have children quickly, Aunty Lee thought, then she could focus her energy and attention on looking after them. And Mark? Mark helped himself to what he liked best. Three oysters, perhaps, with a wedge of lemon and capers. Aunty Lee wondered whether Selina had been trying to get Mark to serve her. She would bring it up with Mark another time, along with the suggestion that it was time to start a family. Nina would call this interfering, but if Aunty Lee did not talk to Mark, who would? Wasn't this her responsibility as a mother substitute? (Aunty Lee conveniently forgot both ML's children had been grown up when she married their father. They had been welcoming but hardly in need of mothering.)

But Selina already thought Aunty Lee was a *kaypoh* busybody, so it would hardly make any difference. Aunty Lee was glad Mark was married, even if his wife made it clear she didn't trust her. Married men were always easier to handle. And as for Selina? With life as with food, a little sourness often brought out the best in the rest of the meal.

Mark would never have helped to cater a celebration buffet like today's, especially if they were being paid to do so. More familiar with inheriting than earning money, Mark Lee had been trying on and discarding careers since dropping out of two different Ph.D. programs because he lost interest in

them partway through. Though supportive of his last venture, Aunty Lee had suspected from the start it would only
be a matter of time before Mark tired of the wine business.
The best thing that had come out of it was Cherril. Cherril
had been one of the regulars at Mark's wine-tasting sessions
and her husband's sister had been one of the women whose
murders Aunty Lee had solved. Cherril had time on her
hands until the children started showing up. And after that?
Aunty Lee was sure she could persuade Cherril that it would
be good for her children to have a working mother as a role
model. Perhaps they could help create a children's menu for
Aunty Lee's Delights . . .

The two women were very different. Cherril, an expert
in food and beverage service, could greet and seat customers in nine different languages and handle potentially life-
threatening emergencies in high heels. Aunty Lee talked
to customers in Singlish, treated them as guests in her own
home, and only wore shoes that made her feet happy. But the
two women bonded over a common love of current gossip—
what Aunty Lee called "caring about people" and Cherril described as grassroots culture.

The only problem now was Mark's reluctance to formalize
the handover of the business to Cherril. Was it the contents
of the specially constructed wine room he found it difficult
to let go of? Or was it Cherril's eagerness to take over? Was
Aunty Lee's stepson one of those people who only valued
what someone else wanted, the archetypal Singaporean who
joined lines because anything worth queuing up for must be
worth having?

Aunty Lee shook herself. Mark and Cherril had already agreed to the handover and would sort things out between them. It must be so nice to be someone like Mabel Sung, Aunty Lee thought. You founded your own successful law firm and when you wanted to make your daughter a partner you just did it, without having to worry what your son thought about it. Aunty Lee looked around for Mabel Sung and her daughter, but neither seemed to be in the vicinity.

Aunty Lee did not cope well with spare time on her hands (the buffet was already set up and there was nothing more to be done till people started eating seriously and top-ups were needed). Aunty Lee looked to see whether Cherril and Nina could use her help but they were standing together by the giant drinks coolers, equally idle and unemployed.

Aunty Lee decided it would be wrong not to take the opportunity to explore the way that rich people lived—in particular that little pool house that might be a guesthouse or private chapel.

Aunty Lee's late husband used to tease her for her *kiasu, kaypoh, em zai see* approach to all food and all life. *Kiasu* in Singaporese meant "scared to lose," a very Singaporean trait that induced citizens to take excessive precautions against being left out or left behind. Aunty Lee went further, going out of her way not only to be the first one in on whatever was happening but doing her best to make sure no one else was left out. As for being *kaypoh,* or busybody-like, as far as Aunty Lee was concerned what everyone else did was of great interest to her . . . which therefore made it her business. And her being *em zao see,* or not afraid to die, especially when following her nose or her instincts, probably explained why she usually got what she wanted. Right then she wanted to find out more about how people lived in this place.

Because the little building on the other side of the swimming pool looked oddly out of place. Unlike the graceful (though modernized for air-conditioning) pseudo-Grecian colonial look of the main house, this obviously new construction was all brown brick and red trim with something greenish on the walls. It made Aunty Lee think of a factory-packed moon cake that had begun to turn moldy.

It triggered Aunty Lee's "Other People's Place" response: Can I live there? How would I decorate it if I lived there? Size- and location-wise, it made a very pretty little dower house or granny flat. She could happily live (with Nina of course) in something that size if either Mark or Mathilda decided to move *en famille* into the Binjai Park bungalow. Entertaining and major celebrations would of course continue to be held at the main house and Aunty Lee would continue to be in charge of the kitchen operations . . . But the decoration would definitely need to be seen to . . .

Aunty Lee peered at the wall for a closer look (if she had had a scraper at hand, she would have cleaned it up) and saw that what she had thought was mold was really thick paint. Green dots were painted on the wall—in fact, standing back, she saw that what she'd taken to be a creeper was actually a mural painted on the side of the building, cleverly seeming to send tendrils around the pipes. Aunty Lee prodded at a painted leaf with a tentative finger. It had a slightly spongy texture, as though the paint had puffed up after settling on the brick. Or as though it was cake icing. Aunty Lee wondered whether the artist who had done this would be willing to decorate cakes . . . he or she had real talent. Aunty Lee might make Singapore's softest sponge cakes but her decorating skills stopped at arranging peach slices on them. She could not resist scratching at the paint with her fingernail just to see how firmly it was anchored to the painted wall . . . Suddenly a hand grasped her wrist firmly and pulled her away from the building.

"Rosie Lee! How lovely to see you! Your food all looks so good!" Mabel Sung said chattily to Aunty Lee as she linked an arm through Aunty Lee's and led her back toward the buffet table. Mabel sounded slightly breathless, as though she had been running. Aunty Lee wondered whether to feel flattered by her welcome. Most clients, however friendly or concerned, did not expect her to be anchored to the food display.

"It looks so professional. I mean like a restaurant or hotel caterer would do."

Aunty Lee agreed. It was not enough for food to taste good (which her food definitely did), and the range of the heated food display trays now gracing Mabel Sung's poolside tables would not have looked out of place on any four-star hotel buffet counter.

Mabel was wearing a pink-and-white floral-print dress. She looked older in person than in her photographs— somewhere in her late sixties, Aunty Lee thought. Her broad face still showed scars of adolescent acne and her assertive, commanding manner made her high, breathy little-girl voice a surprise.

"I'm sure everybody going to love it. My assistant says your *otak* is the best in Singapore! If you want to hand out cards for your café, I don't mind. You can treat this like a chance for free advertising. I'm sure your business will go up. All the people coming today are big fans of local food and they don't mind spending if it's as good as yours!"

Mabel paused, giving Aunty Lee the chance to bond with her by offering to waive the cost of the brunch. Such a generous gesture, it was implied, was enough to transfer her from paid caterer to old family friend. But Aunty Lee had already inherited far too many family friends from her late husband to take the bait.

"Your assistant already sent me the ten percent deposit. Can I pass you today's bill?"

"Oh, today's party is all company expenses. If you just send an itemized bill to the company, somebody there will take care of it."

"If your company people are here today, maybe I can pass the bill to one of them?"

Rich people, Aunty Lee thought, were the hardest to pin down when it came to money matters. They thought nothing of writing a check for a twenty-thousand-dollar donation if it got their name up on a wall but they never had enough change to leave a tip at the café.

"Henry, look who's here—"

Henry Sung had already spoken to Aunty Lee. In fact it was he who had shown her where to connect the power supply for the chafing dishes and had unlocked the garden tap ("Can't have the gardener using water without supervision") for her.

"Hello, Rosie."

"Did you see all the food? Doesn't it all look wonderful? Rosie, you're so clever. You must think about running classes for young women. Nowadays none of this younger generation knows how to cook," Mabel said.

"Mum, if she teaches the young women to cook for themselves, she'll lose all her business, ha ha!"

Aunty Lee beamed genially at Henry Sung. His wife ignored him.

"Or shall I just pass the bill to Mr. Sung?" Aunty Lee asked.

"Oh, Henry doesn't have anything to do with this. Today's party is hosted by my law firm. My husband is the medical side of the family. He has nothing to do with the law side of the family. We girls run the law business by ourselves. This is real feminism, you know. You know Sharon was in school with your husband's girl . . . what was her name—Maureen? Maria? That one never came back from studying in England, right? Children grow up so fast. One day they are in school and the next day they are taking over the family business."

"This is Cherril, my new partner, who is taking care of the beverages side of the business for me." Aunty Lee waved Cherril over to join them.

"Hello, Mrs. Sung, Mr. Sung." Cherril Lim-Peters smiled. "Would you like to try our new ginger–honey–almond milk freeze?" Henry accepted a glass, but Mabel Sung did not believe in wasting time on unimportant things or people.

"I'm just going to put together a plate for Leonard. My son is not feeling well enough to join us today but he doesn't want to miss your wonderful food. He's been so looking forward to it. That's your famous chicken *buah keluak,* right? I must take some of that for him."

Watching Mabel ladle huge servings onto plates her husband was commandeered to carry, Aunty Lee offered her a tray, which was graciously accepted, along with porcelain ramekins for *achar* and *sambal.*

"I'll be right back after I bring these up to him."

"These drinks are good—try one!"

"Don't be stupid, Henry. You know Lennie can't take cold drinks."

There was definitely some underlying tension and resentment there, Aunty Lee thought. But with long-married couples, long-held resentments were sometimes the only thing that kept them together. She watched as Mabel Sung and her tray of food were stopped at the foot of the stairs by a slim, brown-skinned Chinese man.

"What?" Mabel demanded. "Not now! Can't you see I'm busy?"

The man said something in a low voice that Aunty Lee could not catch despite her best eavesdropping skills. However, she had no difficulty hearing Mabel's response.

"I don't see what for. None of the other guests are going up to the house, why should you bring her there?"

Perhaps to use the toilet, Aunty Lee thought. Sometimes rich people overlooked the most obvious things. And it was obvious from everything she saw around her that the Sungs were rich people.

The man looked insistent. Again he said something Aunty Lee could not make out. Aunty Lee reminded herself to dig out ML's old hearing aid with its adjustable volume. Aunty Lee could still hear what she was supposed to hear but she needed artificial assistance to listen to everything else. She grabbed several *ondeh-ondeh* and headed toward them.

Mabel Sung's lips set in a grim line and she shook her head but said, "Okay, okay, okay," to the thin dark man, who looked annoyed as Aunty Lee joined them.

"Mabel, you must take some of my *ondeh-ondeh* for your son to try. Very fresh, I made specially this morning. Sir, you want to try? You take one bite, the *gula melaka* inside will burst out in your mouth!"

"This is Edmond Yong," Mabel Sung said. "He's a doctor and he's helping to look after my son. Edmond, of course you recognize our famous Aunty Lee?"

"I'm Dr. Yong, pleased to meet you. I am the doctor in residence responsible for Leonard Sung's health."

"Is something wrong with your son?" Aunty Lee asked with hopeful interest.

"Oh no. Please don't be alarmed. Nothing whatsoever is wrong. I just need you to excuse our charming hostess for a moment."

Aunty Lee thought Dr. Yong looked more like a poor relative than a guest or resident doctor. He was obviously familiar with the place and people but seemed socially awkward. Aunty Lee could tell his English, rather like Cherril's, had been learned in school rather than "absorbed with mother's milk." He was not one of those who had coasted through school thanks to tutors and connections to emerge with an impressive degree and even more impressive sense of entitlement. Aunty Lee was fond of such characters. She liked Mabel Sung more for hiring him.

Aunt Lee watched as the young doctor introduced Mabel Sung to a young woman with long hair. Now his manner reminded Aunty Lee of an irritatingly ingratiating insurance agent. And the woman? Aunty Lee's first impression was that she looked like a match for Mabel Sung. She was probably in her thirties, but the makeup she was wearing made her look older. She was dressed for a business meeting rather than a brunch party and was clearly unfamiliar with her surroundings. Moreover, she was looking around with a mixture of impatience and contempt designed to show that she was not impressed. Aunty Lee could not hear most of the conversation but could tell that the three were talking in Mandarin. It was the woman's Mandarin accent that marked her as coming from China rather than Singapore or Malaysia. In addition to English and Malay, Aunty Lee could shop, gossip, and eavesdrop in Hokkien, Teochew, and Cantonese. Surely she should be able to follow a simple Mandarin conversation? But no. All Aunty Lee could tell was that the woman was the dominant party in the dialogue and Edmond Yong was deferring to her. Indeed, even Mabel Sung was deferring to the woman, which Aunty Lee found very strange. Mabel Sung looked like she was eager to please, and even a little afraid of, the long-haired woman.

Aunty Lee looked around for Cherril and found her staring in the same direction as she was. "I can't believe it! What's that guy doing here?"

Aunty Lee said, "He is here looking after the Sung boy. You know him, ah?"

"Like a bodyguard?"

"He said he's a doctor, so I suppose like a medical bodyguard. The Sung boy is supposed to be sick," Aunty Lee said. "How do you know that man?" All her Aunty senses were tingling and she was picking up discomfort, awkward memories, embarrassment . . . this was no mere acquaintance of Cherril's. "Ex-boyfriend, ah?"

"No way!"

"But he's a doctor, right?" Aunty Lee pointed out, even more intrigued. On the Singaporean marriage scale, doctors generally outranked lawyers like Cherril's husband. Even if Cherril found this particular doctor personally unappealing, she would not have dismissed him so vehemently unless there was a story there. Aunty Lee was always ready to hear a good story. To be on the safe side, she took the tray of celery and watermelon shooters Cherril was carrying and put it on the table beside them.

"His name is Edmond Yong. He used to have a clinic at Bukit Timah Plaza," Cherril said. She pulled out an insulated carrier from where it had been concealed under the overhanging tablecloth and emptied crushed ice into a large glass bowl. Thanks to her years as a flight attendant on Singapore's premier airline, Cherril could lift weights like a bodybuilder while looking like a ballerina.

"Is he good?" Aunty Lee thought you could never know too many doctors.

"I don't know. I didn't go through with it. It was some time ago, before I married Mycroft."

"You were having health problems?"

"No—I was thinking about getting enhancements. Some enhancements, some reductions, some adjustments . . . just the basic package. But in the end I decided against doing it at Dr. Yong's clinic."

"You weren't comfortable with Dr. Yong?"

"My friends said it's a lot cheaper in Korea." Cherril did not look up from arranging the little glasses of juice in the bowl of ice.

Aunty Lee studied Cherril with new curiosity. Even her sharp eyes told her nothing about whether the younger woman had received her assets from God or a plastic surgeon. But Aunty Lee would have plenty of time to find out more about her new partner. Now she had a party full of interesting people to examine. Mabel Sung herself, for example. Studying Mabel Sung's appearance with some attention, Aunty Lee could not see any signs of either enhancement or reduction, not even where these procedures might most usefully be applied. Mabel's whole look said, "I am more powerful and important than you, fear and respect me!" yet she was nodding docilely as she listened to the long-haired woman.

"That PRC woman with your Dr. Yong. Do you know who she is?"

"Sorry, never saw her before. And he's not *my* Dr. Yong."

Aunty Lee felt something about the tall, long-haired woman was out of place. It was not wrong or even unpleasant, just not quite right. This was not any kind of supernatural intuition. Consciously cooking to please others had conditioned Aunty Lee to register the tiniest variations in how people (and their food) looked, sounded, and smelled. Though not always aware of what triggered it, she could sense when something was out of place. Like sweet tapioca paste that had been stored in a jar formerly containing clove or garlic oil, there was something about Dr. Yong's woman friend that didn't fit here. Or perhaps it was Dr. Yong himself who was out of place . . . ?

Mabel Sung left them, waving a vague "I'll be right back" at all her guests before heading toward the stairs to the main house. Edmond Yong and the PRC woman continued talking in low voices. Aunty Lee edged closer to the pair in much the same way she would have turned up the volume on her television at home. Where was Nina when she needed her?

Another young woman walked up and joined them, grabbing and squeezing Dr. Yong's arm in a playful greeting.

"Drinks? Edmond? What about your friend? Hi, I don't think we've been introduced. My name is GraceFaith Ang. I work with Mabel and Sharon and I'm also a member of Never Say Die, so you could say I've got a double reason for being here today!"

The woman said something to Edmond Yong and walked away, ignoring GraceFaith, who made a humorous moue.

"She doesn't like other people talking to you? Who is she?"

"She's just a business contact," Edmond Yong said. "Nobody important."

"Important enough for you to invite to a private party,"

GraceFaith said, her playful manner dropped. "Does Mabel know you brought a stranger to her house?"

"Wen Ling is not a stranger. In fact she came to meet Mabel. It's a potential business arrangement, but right now it's still confidential," Dr. Yong said.

GraceFaith immediately switched into coy girlish mode and shrieked demands for information but Edmond Yong walked away. At least Aunt Lee had learned the long-haired woman's name.

GraceFaith was the carefully turned-out young woman who had come to Aunty Lee's Delights on Mabel Sung's behalf to commission the brunch buffet. Despite Aunty Lee's attempts to push her superspicy *sotong* balls and *unagi otak,* they had settled on a fairly conventional menu.

"Some of the guests are not so adventurous when it comes to seafood." GraceFaith explained.

"Vegetarian?" Aunty Lee guessed. Inspired by an American vegetarian acquaintance, she had recently started experimenting with vegetarian versions of traditional Peranakan dishes.

"No, of course not! All the people coming are Christians!"

Aunty Lee was always open to learning new things about her customers' beliefs.

"Some Hindus and Buddhists are vegetarian for religious reasons but there are vegetarian Christians too, right?"

"Oh, I daresay there are some weirdos. But don't worry, you can prepare normal food. Lennie would scream if anybody tried to make him eat vegetarian!"

"And Lennie is . . ."

"Leonard is Mabel's son." GraceFaith lowered her voice slightly. "He is having some health issues, so praying for him is the main focus of Never Say Die now."

Aunty Lee had heard of Never Say Die, a group that conducted focused prayer and active healing sessions. Indeed her late husband had been invited to join the group after his cancer was diagnosed but had dismissed them as "rich camels."

"I remember you, you came to my shop to make the booking for Mabel," Aunty Lee said to GraceFaith. "You look very nice, by the way. So many young girls these days don't bother to dress up nicely. Just now you said you are part of that Never Die group. What is wrong with you?"

"Never Say Die. It's a prayer and healing group that Mabel joined when her son got sick. She got the staff at the law firm to join too, to pray for him." GraceFaith's eyes roamed the growing number of guests as she spoke till they settled on Henry Sung, who was talking to an older woman at the foot of the stairs. Henry was still holding the tray of food his wife had prepared for their son. Mabel was nowhere to be seen.

"Excuse me."

As she watched GraceFaith heading toward them Aunty Lee wondered why the woman Henry Sung was talking to looked so familiar. The woman caught Aunty Lee's eye and waved at her with apparent delight, gesturing for her to join them. Aunty Lee waved back but stayed put and tried to look busy. She would try to recall the woman's name before they met up.

6

Sudden Death

Looking back on events later, Aunty Lee decided the real excitement of the day had begun with the commotion at the back gate. There was shouting followed by a painful crash as Henry Sung dropped the tray of food he was balancing on the stair rail. Aunty Lee winced for her dishes but hurried away to the gate which Edmond Yong was trying to slide shut despite the man's arm caught in its heavy metal frame.

GraceFaith ran up and pulled him away. "Stop it. Edmond, are you mad? Stop it!"

"He's a troublemaker," Edmond Yong said.

"You're going to break his arm! Stop it!" GraceFaith pushed Edmond Yong away and released the man's arm. "What do you want? This is a private function."

The newcomer also looked familiar to Aunty Lee. Was this

the beginning of Alzheimer's? Aunty Lee put the thought aside as she pushed her way through the murmuring guests to get a better look at him. Yes, the man definitely looked familiar, but unlike the woman with Henry Sung, he did not seem to recognize her.

"I need to speak to Mr. or Mrs. Sung," the man said. "I tried calling their offices but I couldn't get through to them. It's about a friend of mine who's missing. He was working on a project here. His name is Benjamin Ng."

"No one here by that name," Edmond Yong said. He sounded like a schoolboy bully. Aunty Lee thought he had probably been bullied in school and was getting his own back. "You are trespassing. You better just get out of here before we call the police!"

"Wait. Please," the man said. "I know he was here working on something. Is he still here? I just need to reach him. Or can they get a message to him at least?"

"What is the message?" Aunty Lee asked helpfully and hopefully. She had no idea who Benjamin Ng might be but she intended to find out.

The man turned to her, but before he could answer, Grace-Faith pushed him out and shut and locked the gate.

"Come on, the food will get cold and then everything will be wasted," she said, sounding like a bossy school prefect.

Sharon said, "I don't believe it. She's got the key to the back gate but I've got to phone the house if I want to drive in. Can you believe that? Anybody would think she's the daughter of the house! You know, GraceFaith got Mabel all worked up before the party because there was algae in the pool. I told Mabel nobody was going to swim, but of course she didn't listen to me. Now look. After all that fuss nobody is swimming and nobody is eating."

It was obvious to Aunty Lee that people had, in fact, been eating. Her buffet was already looking tired in parts. The *nasi lemak* had been a great hit. The advantage of a *nasi lemak* buffet was that as long as the rice was kept steaming hot, everything else—crunchy anchovies and peanuts, folded omelets, *otak*, fried chicken chops, and fried fish fillets—could be kept warm on heaters. Aunty Lee took pride in her rice soaked in coconut cream before it was steamed with knotted bundles of her homegrown *pandan* (screw pine) leaves and crushed stalks of lemongrass. For today's buffet, Aunty Lee had included chicken frankfurters, fried fish cakes, and luncheon meat as well as a vegetable curry that food purists would have objected to. Still, these side dishes had come to be part of the Singapore *nasi lemak* experience and Aunty Lee believed the best menu was one that suited dishes to the tastes of the eaters. And though it was not part of *nasi lemak*, guests were clearly enjoying Aunty Lee's special chicken *buah keluak*.

"We should let Mabel and Henry know somebody is looking for them," Aunty Lee said.

"Why?" Sharon asked. "Why should they be bothered just because some nutcase is bugging them?" she added as Grace-Faith joined them.

"Sharon's always so intense," GraceFaith said. "I'm not criticizing you, of course. That's what Mabel always says: 'Sharon is so intense.' The problem with some clients is they have no respect for boundaries."

"I have to get something else for Lennie," Henry Sung said, looking helplessly at the buffet spread. He picked up a fried chicken wing and looked at it, then put it back on the warmer. The tray he was holding was smeared with food and there were splashes of gravy on his trousers. Aunty Lee saw Nina and Cherril cleaning up the rest of the mess by the steps.

"I'll take care of that, Dad. Go and change before Mabel sees you." Sharon Sung took the tray from her father.

"Let me do that for you," GraceFaith said.

Sharon snatched the tray back from her without answering.

About the same height as GraceFaith, Sharon looked much thinner in a black dress and pumps. Yet GraceFaith seemed more comfortable in her body than Sharon was as she smiled, shrugged, and moved away.

Sharon arranged several bowls on her tray and saw Aunty Lee watching her.

"I don't suppose you remember me. I'm Sharon Sung. I was in school with Mathilda."

Sharon Sung had red bloodshot eyes. Aunty Lee hoped that Mathilda, her stepdaughter, was getting more sleep than this young woman.

"Will he eat chicken *buah keluak*? It's my special dish."

"He asked for it, apparently. I don't know if he wants to eat it or throw it at the maids."

Aunty Lee watched as Sharon ladled chicken *buah keluak* into a bowl and added it to her tray along with a plate of rice with fried chicken drumsticks and fried anchovies. She would have made a good cook, Aunty Lee thought, seeing how she instinctively arranged the food to its advantage. Too many cooks forgot that presentation was part of preparation.

"I don't see why everybody makes such a big fuss about *buah keluak*. People only think it's so special because they have to make an effort to dig it out of the shell, which means they have to slow down and taste what they're eating. Otherwise they just shovel the food in without tasting it!"

Sharon spoke fast. She made Aunty Lee think of a student trying to get attention by making smart-aleck comments. "I don't know why I'm bothering. Once when he didn't like the dinner the maid prepared, he phoned KFC to come and deliver. Dad scolded him for wasting money and Len said Dad should take it out of the maids' salary because if they cooked better he wouldn't have had to order in!" Sharon laughed awkwardly.

Mathilda had already been away at Warwick University when Aunty Lee married her father, but home on vacation, she had hosted a school gathering at the Binjai Park house. Aunty Lee remembered one of the girls saying loudly, "Just wait until that woman has a baby and your dad leaves everything to it instead of you!" followed by that same awkward laugh. Aunty Lee had not been hurt by the girl's words. She knew other people were probably thinking far worse things.

In fact she liked Sharon Sung for saying what others didn't.

"This is supposed to be a law-firm party, right? I mean this is supposed to be to celebrate me becoming partner, right? So I thought I should dress like a law partner. I don't know why some people seem to think that just because a party is held in somebody's home, it must be supercasual. Maybe we should have put down a dress code on the invitation. But then if it's a law-firm party, you assume that people are going to know how to dress, right?"

Sharon might be trying to make her colleagues feel uncomfortable about dressing up, but GraceFaith, the only one in hearing range, smiled serenely and fluffed out her hair.

While talking, Sharon kept one arm folded protectively across her stomach, palm cupping the elbow of her other arm as she emphasized her words with jerks of the plate. Her defensive body language reminded Aunty Lee of her domestic helper, Nina, when she had first came to work for her. At that time Nina's previous experiences had taught her to be afraid of everything and everyone in Singapore. Now, of course, Nina was not afraid of anyone or anything, even telling off her employer when she felt the need.

Sharon scooped up some of the *buah keluak* gravy in a spoon and tasted it.

"Why did you do that? Isn't that for Lennie?" GraceFaith stepped up.

"I always taste food I'm serving," Sharon said. "It's a personal rule. Then nobody can blame me if something's wrong with it."

"I do the same thing!" Aunty Lee said.

"That's what makes you a good cook."

Aunty Lee could also tell that Sharon was trying to be "nice." And it was obvious from her body language that this unfamiliar behavior made her uncomfortable. Her voice had the high artificial note people adopt to talk to strange babies, her shoulders were tense, and her smile was almost a grimace.

"I hope your brother likes it."

At a safe distance, Aunty Lee followed Sharon up the steps to the main house. If anyone asked she would say she was looking for the toilet. But it was curiosity about Leonard Sung that was really driving her.

"Oh, Rosie, so nice to see you again. You don't remember me? It's Doreen, lah."

It was the familiar-looking woman. Of course Aunty Lee knew Doreen Choo. They were not close friends. But as their generation started dropping off, the survivors drew closer naturally. But—

"I had a little work done," Doreen said. "Looks good, doesn't it?"

"You mean plastic surgery? I heard it's dangerous, right? Didn't some famous writer go for chin tuck and then die of heart attack?"

"I also go for tai chi meditation. No need to do anything, just imagine the moves. Can do it while watching k-drama." (Aunty Lee nodded agreeably though she did not understand why women like Doreen were so fond of Korean TV miniseries. Wasn't real life far more fun even if the characters were not as good looking?) "Are you going up to the main house?"

"Well, I was looking for the—"

"Me too. Let's take the lift. Just one person; I always feel bad, so you come with me."

The little chairlift ran up the slope alongside the stone

steps and into the house, not stopping till it reached the second floor.

"We should have pressed 'one.'"

"The toilet up here is nicer. Got real flowers instead of plastic like downstairs."

"Shh—" Aunty Lee heard something.

"Dad, you have to do something about Mabel!" It was Sharon's voice, coming from one of the rooms. It was harder to make out Henry's mumbled response.

It was interesting, Aunty Lee thought, that while Mabel's daughter addressed her by name, her husband called her "Mum." Aunty Lee would not like to be called "Mum" by a man who had to be at least seventy.

"We shouldn't stand here listening," Doreen said.

"Then how will we hear anything?" Aunty Lee asked reasonably and very quietly.

"I can't hear anything anyway. I got my eyes fixed, so now I can see better, but I still cannot hear properly."

"What did you do to your eyes?" Aunty Lee asked. "Cataract removal, is it?"

"Cataract and some kind of corny transplant. Henry got that young doctor of his to do it for me."

"That Dr. Yong that's looking after his son? I thought Henry Sung is a doctor, right? Why can't he take care of his own son?"

"Henry is a very good doctor but we are all getting on a bit, so they have that boy here to take care of the daily things. And also he is in Mabel's prayer and healing group, so she can keep an eye on him and everybody is happy."

"He prays while operating, ah? Like that's how to concentrate? Must be like talking to God on mobile phone while
driving, right?"

"No lah! Other people pray while he operates, lor. And it is
not just praying, they are very scientific. Last time Mabel told
us about this man in America who was cured of stage-four
liver cancer by Plácido."

"Plácido Domingo?" Aunty Lee hazarded a guess. "One of
those man singers who sings Christmas songs?"

"Maybe. Oh, I don't know. My ears are not yet fixed to hear
properly. I was supposed to have some hearing thing put in,
then the clinic at BTP burned down so it was postponed until
I don't know when. Ah, GraceFaith. Come here. You must tell
my friend Rosie about that man cured by Plácido. You know,
that one Mabel was talking about. I must stay up here in the
air-con for a while. I can't stand the heat. I don't see why
people have parties outside in Singapore. Even Lee Kuan
Yew uses air-con." It being a truth acknowledged among Singaporeans if not universally that their country's first prime
minister could do no wrong.

"It's not that hot, Doreen," GraceFaith said. She put a
hand on the older woman's arm and propelled her firmly
toward the chairlift. "And it was placebos Mabel was talking
about, prayer and placebos. I'll switch on the chairlift for
you, okay?"

"Oh!" Doreen stumbled and almost fell. "My legs not so
good, can't walk so fast. Ow! Girl, you are hurting my arm! I
think I'm going to faint, let me sit down quietly for a while.
I need some warm water. Rosie, if I don't make it, please tell

Henry and Mabel it's not their fault. I am an old woman and not well.

"We can sit here comfortably for a while," Doreen Choo said to Aunty Lee once GraceFaith had found them chairs and gone in search of warm water.

Aunty Lee was impressed.

"You mentioned a fire at Bukit Timah Plaza?" Aunty Lee was always interested in fires. "How come I didn't hear about this?"

"Small fire only. I think only one foreigner died but nobody knows who. You wouldn't be interested."

"Are you waiting to see my father?" Sharon came out of the room looking sulkier than usual.

"I want a word with your mother. She arranged my eye operation for me. I was supposed to get follow-up checkups, but then after that fire at the Bukit Timah Plaza clinic, I never heard anything more from them. Checkups are supposed to be part of the package. Now you are a partner you can go and check for me."

"Aunty Doreen, Sung Law and Never Say Die are totally separate—" but Doreen was not to be stopped.

"And then somebody phoned me after that, you know. Did I want to go through with the ear operation? he asked. And have I don't know what cartilage injections? Only I was out with some friends at the time and I didn't get the number. I was telling Rosie about the operation. She's also interested."

"I'm sure someone will get back to you," Sharon said dismissively. "I don't have anything to do with Mabel's healing stuff. It doesn't have anything to do with Sung Law."

"It's very expensive." Edmond Yong appeared from the room next to the one Sharon had come out of. Aunty Lee guessed he had been listening while Sharon shouted at her father.

"Don't worry. My friend Rosie is very rich," Doreen said dismissively.

"I'll go see if I can find Mabel," Edmond offered.

"If you find Mabel tell her she should be at the party with her guests. This is supposed to be her party for me. Why isn't she even at it?"

"Sharon, calm down. There are people here." Edmond Yong smiled at Aunty Lee and Doreen as he spoke, giving the impression of a nanny trying to ward off a childish tantrum.

"Who are you to tell me to calm down? Who are you afraid they are going to tell?"

Aunty Lee wanted to say she was not at all the sort to tell tales. Finding out things about people was a hobby of hers, and if only Sharon explained what she didn't want told, Aunty Lee wouldn't tell it. She turned to Doreen to back her up but Doreen had gone. Doreen claimed to be a feeble old woman when it suited her but could move fast when she wanted.

It was definitely turning out to be a very interesting party, Aunty Lee thought.

GraceFaith returned. Nobody paid much attention at first because GraceFaith was not someone people generally took notice of. She rushed a few steps into the room, then stopped abruptly. There was a strange frozen look on her face. Aunty Lee thought she looked like someone trapped on a roller-coaster ride—incredulous, terrified, and about to be sick.

She was breathing with fast, shallow little whimpers, her eyes panicked and pleading. Alarmed, Aunty Lee moved toward her. For once she was driven by concern rather than curiosity, but GraceFaith shuddered at Aunty Lee's light touch on her arm and looked right through her.

Even Sharon and Edmond noticed something.

"Is something wrong with Lennie?" Sharon sounded prepared to be bored. "Again? What's he done now?"

"Your mother and Leonard are dead," GraceFaith said. Her voice was dead calm. She might have said they were watching television.

Aunty Lee gasped. She was dying to ask what had happened but held herself back as the other two processed the information.

"Leonard? And Mabel? Both of them?" Sharon asked in disbelief. GraceFaith nodded, the frenzied look still frozen on her face.

"Are you sure?" Edmond said. He gave a little laugh or cleared his throat. "You must have made a mistake. Or it's another of Lennie's stupid jokes. He's probably just playing a trick on you." He looked around for support but none of the women responded. GraceFaith and Sharon had their eyes fixed on each other and Aunty Lee was watching them both.

"Where's Henry?" Sharon asked. Then, as though realizing her mother was not there to be annoyed about her using her father's first name, "Where's my father?"

"I don't know. I didn't see him. Your mother and Len are on Len's bed. There's food everywhere. I couldn't wake them up. I know they are dead."

For a moment Sharon didn't move. Then, as Aunty Lee thought later, she seemed to shift into gear, or rather into her mother's role.

"We should save the food in the room," Sharon said in a voice that echoed Mabel's bossy tone. "So it can be tested. GraceFaith, call the police. We shouldn't touch anything until the police get here. They should examine everything. And we should make sure nobody leaves."

"This is not some kind of TV mystery," Edmond snapped at her. "Don't drag the police here for nothing. I'm going to check on them first."

"Dad, where were you? Do you know what happened?"

Henry Sung came through the passage looking dazed. Doreen was with him.

"I thought they were praying," Henry Sung said. "I went to get Mabel, to tell her Doreen needed to talk to her. They were so quiet in there. Mabel is never quiet unless she is praying. I was sure they were praying."

"There are *buah keluak* shells all over the floor," Doreen said. "As though somebody was throwing them."

"For goodness' sake!" Sharon Sung snapped. "GraceFaith, go and call the police and tell them two people are dead. Tell them it's Mabel Sung and her son. That should make them come more quickly. And say they were probably poisoned by *buah keluak*."

"No!" Aunty Lee said. "It could not have been the *buah keluak*!"

7

Inspector Salim

Inspector Salim Mawar, officer-in-charge of the Bukit Tinggi Neighborhood Police Post, was in his office when the calls came in. This was not surprising. Salim, whose recent awards and promotion to inspector should have catapulted him from this apparently dead-end posting onto the main administrative track, was almost always in his office.

"Sir, I think you better take line two. It's the commissioner's assistant, calling on site with DB."

"Thanks, Neha."

"And there was another call but the woman couldn't wait and gave me a message to pass to you—" Staff Sergeant Neha Panchal hesitated. This was a new posting for her and she was still getting used to the casual way residents called or dropped in on the station.

"The message?" Salim picked up his phone and pressed 2.

"She said to tell you it couldn't have been the *buah keluak*. I asked her what she meant but she said she couldn't talk now. She sounded a bit funny, frankly, but I thought I better tell you just in case—"

Salim got his connection and gestured to her to exit and close the door. Panchal was not sure whether her boss had heard her message. Or whether he had heard her and thought her a fool for bothering to convey it. But Panchal had already been told off last week for telling a Filipina maid she could not see Inspector Salim without filling in a request form and having a woman officer present. She was not going to give him another excuse to embarrass her. And just in case, Panchal was keeping a strict record of all regulations she had observed Inspector Salim flouting. When he got into trouble for treating this jurisdiction as his own personal domain, Panchal was not going down with him, unlike the other officers in the station, who worshiped their boss. If she handled things right she might even come out of it with a promotion, like her predecessor Timothy Pang, now in a dream posting in International Affairs. Panchal knew Pang must have discovered something on Salim (or someone even higher up) to have leveraged such a promotion.

Staff Sergeant Panchal had researched Inspector Salim thoroughly even before starting her current posting. Inspector Salim Mawar was a lucky man. Thanks to subsidized education, he had graduated from the National University of Singapore with a basic degree in Social Studies and then thanks to a Singapore Police Force Scholarship, acquired his master's in Management in Science. With these credentials, Salim should have been rising through the public service ranks as an example of how meritocracy benefited minorities. So why wasn't he?

"You got a body?"

"Two—"

Inspector Salim took down the address he was given. "Fast response vehicle?"

"Three on the way. But CP is here and asked for you."

Salim, on his feet and moving to the door, had already sent their destination and a message to his driver to meet him by the car.

"You know who they are?"

"Mabel Sung and her son, Leonard. Apparently there was some kind of party at the house and it may have been food poisoning."

"*Kanasai!* How many guests present? Anybody else sick? Who provided the food?"

"No indication. The caterer is Aunty Lee's Delights."

"Ah."

Salim knew Aunty Lee's Delights well. The small café in Binjai Park was within walking distance of Bukit Tinggi NPP.

Salim remembered the message Panchal had given him. He thought he knew who had sent it.

"With me, Panchal."

Though she should have expected to accompany him,

Salim had to wait while she retrieved her phone from its charger, locked her desk, and shut down her computer. All according to regulations, of course.

It was at times like this that Salim missed Timothy Pang most. Timothy would already have called up all available information on his phone and by the time they arrived at the crime scene would know the ages, educational qualifications, declared and undeclared income, and Pinterest loves of the people involved. Plus the way his new aide watched him made Salim uncomfortable. He reminded himself that change was good. Panchal reminded him to put on his seat belt.

There were other eyes on Inspector Salim Mawar. He might believe it was by his own decision that he was still at the Bukit Tinggi Neighborhood Police Post. In fact his being allowed to decline several offers of promotion and transfer was part of an as yet unnamed Ministry of Home Affairs experiment. If all went well it would be hailed as a successful step forward. If not, then all there was to see was an efficiently run police post in an important residential area. Salim had declined to be promoted to a higher level in a larger machine. His salary, power, and prospects would all have improved, but it was made clear he would be a very small cog. At the moment he was running things very well in his little kingdom. Crime rates were low and harmony and goodwill were high. The idea was to gradually expand and replicate this success. Like the Regional Public Libraries and Regional Post Offices set up following the same principle that had combined individual voter constituencies so successfully into Group Representation Constituencies or GRCs. Regional Police Hubs, starting with the Bukit Tinggi Regional Police Hub, would be small enough for residents to feel a connection with the officers but large enough that new officers could ride on the coattails of their experienced seniors.

As things stood, calling Bukit Tinggi a "neighborhood" post was a misnomer, as its jurisdiction stretched some way beyond Bukit Tinggi. And Inspector Salim had already solved cases beyond the Bukit Tinggi district. Just weeks ago he had exposed and arrested a group of international con artists in Chinatown, thanks to a *tai tai* in his district who told him about a wise man there who offered to bless her jewelry and money to ward off bad luck. Most *tai tais* were idle wealthy women, but Aunty Lee, though wealthy, was anything but idle.

In any case it was not quite an official project. If anything went wrong it would still be possible for top officials to deny the whole experiment. But if successful, it could provide a template for things to come. Among the unknown factors was how much the experiment's success depended on Salim and his relationship with residents in the area.

"What do we know so far?" Salim asked as they waited for the front gates of 8 King Albert Rise to slide open for them. "Background on the victims, who found them, anything?"

Panchal looked at him blankly. "Do you want me to find out?"

8

Staff Sergeant Panchal

"This way, sir." Salim's men were already on the wide front driveway. Salim paused for a moment, looking at the front of the enormous house and then turning to look at what could be seen of the neighbors, which was not much other than high walls and privacy shrubbery.

"Shouldn't we go inside?" Staff Sergeant Panchal prompted.

Salim did not answer.

"Sir, shouldn't we—"

"Security? Cameras?" Salim asked the officer who had let them in.

"Four cameras in the house, sir. Front and back gates, pool area, and the son's room, where the bodies were found. I'll send someone round to ask the neighbors."

Salim missed having Timothy Pang by his side at a crime

scene. Or rather, Tim Pang would not have stuck to his side. Panchal was acting like an eager dog on a leash. Tim would have wandered off collecting impressions of people who didn't notice him and confidences from people who did. Being mistaken for an actor or model had embarrassed Officer Pang but his good looks and open manner inclined people to trust him. Officer Panchal, glaring suspiciously at everyone in sight, was not proving as helpful.

Inside the house, people looked at one another uncertainly and whispered but no one said anything out loud. Commissioner Raja had arrived late and meant to slip away early once he had congratulated the new partner of Sung Law. However, he had been detained by the death of the old partner, and now as he watched his fellow guests he was reminded of mission school boys waiting for the punch line to an off-color joke. They knew something was coming but were afraid to guess exactly what in case it revealed their ignorance, or worse—their knowledge.

"Commissioner?"

Commissioner Raja turned to see Inspector Salim with Staff Sergeant Panchal. Panchal saluted him smartly and he responded with a nod.

"I'm here for the party, not for the murder," Commissioner Raja said to explain his green-and-brown batik shirt. "The Sungs are old friends. I got here right after the bodies were found. Must have been just before noon. Thanks for coming down."

"You are a friend of the Sungs?" Salim asked. He seemed surprised.

"You could say that," Commissioner Raja said grimly. He had not liked Mabel Sung. The woman had been good at manipulating people into supporting her causes, making her both a powerful ally and a dangerous person to cross. "With some people it is better to be friends than enemies.

"Anyway, this is your case, Salim. I can give you my statement but I want you to handle the investigation. By the way, you'll find some familiar faces here. I tell you, any funny business in this district they are sure to be somewhere around."

Familiar faces? Salim looked around and saw Aunty Lee, Cherril—and yes, Nina. Thank goodness that aggressive Carla Saito woman had finally left Singapore. Salim had heard she had gone on to China. Good luck to the Chinese, he thought.

"I saw them!" Aunty Lee said, waving to catch their attention. "I saw the bodies!"

"Can I see your IC, ma'am?" Panchal took out her notebook and recorder.

"You know who I am! I am Aunty Lee, from Aunty Lee's Delights! Yesterday I brought the *kueh dadar* to the station, remember? That was because I made extra for the party here today!"

"You saw them?" Salim said. "You saw Mabel and Leonard upstairs after they died? How come?"

"I heard they were dead so I went in to see to make sure," Aunty Lee said. "Sometimes people shout somebody died, everybody gets worked up and calls the police, then they only fainted. So *susah*, right?

"Anyway I can describe for you. The son, Leonard, was

lying in his bed. He had been eating off a folding table on his bed and it looked as though he just leaned back and went to sleep and didn't wake up. Mabel looked as though she was crouching on the floor beside his bed. But GraceFaith said that when she went into the room to call Mabel, she thought she was asleep in the armchair by the bed. So she touched her on the shoulder and she was so startled when Mabel did not move that she jerked her arm back and knocked her onto the floor. And there was another plate on the coffee table next to the armchair. So it looks as though Mabel was also eating there. Then her son died in bed and she died in the chair next to him."

Nina and Cherril, looking worried, came to join Aunty Lee.

"Thank you. Staff Sergeant Panchal will take down your statements." Salim smiled encouragingly. "I'm going to have a word with the family."

Panchal could tell she was being fobbed off with unimportant witnesses. But Commissioner Raja Kumar was there and this was her chance to make a good impression. She turned to the three women and addressed Aunty Lee clearly and loudly enough for her exemplary interview technique to be heard by the senior officer.

"You said you saw the plates. What were they eating before they died, did you see?"

"My chicken *buah keluak*. But that had nothing to do with what happened to them."

"Have you been friends with Mabel Sung for long? How well did you know her?" Staff Sergeant Panchal glanced between Aunty Lee and Cherril.

"No," said Cherril, "I didn't know her at all."

"That's hard to say," Aunty Lee said brightly. Nina groaned.

"Would you care to explain that, Mrs. Lee?"

"I knew who she was, of course. Her husband, Henry, was a friend of my late husband's and we used to run into each other at social events and other people's houses. Their daughter was in school with my stepdaughter and I think they still keep in touch. But I wouldn't say we were friends. We move in totally different circles. She was a high-powered lawyer and I am a cook. When my husband was still alive she invited us to join her prayer group, but my husband said better not because he knew she was praying to find somebody's daughter to marry her useless son and somebody's son to marry her scary daughter and he didn't want to put his children at risk."

To her credit, Staff Sergeant Panchal recorded all this without any sign of confusion. But she lowered her voice as she continued, "Why did Mabel Sung choose you to cater the party at her house?"

"Actually it was her assistant who came to place the order. She said Mabel Sung wanted a *nasi lemak* buffet at her house and made all the arrangements. You should talk to her. She was upstairs today too. Her name is GraceFaith Ang, I have her card somewhere . . ."

"I can get Miss Ang's contact myself. Can you recall if anything else significant happened earlier? And you, Mrs. Lim-Peters? Can I have your identity card as well?"

"It's in my purse, locked in the car. I'll get it for you," Cherril said. "I don't remember anything unusual. I set up the drinks table. I put out all the glasses and the napkins and I served drinks—orange juice, mango juice, aloe vera juice, and green tea. They asked for two bottles of champagne but we never got round to opening them. I didn't know most of the people there."

Staff Sergeant Panchal noted this.

"What specifically do you want to know?" Aunty Lee asked.

"Everything you can remember. We will put together all your individual statements to get a complete picture of what happened."

"There is a very interesting building next to the swimming pool," Aunty Lee said. "Or rather it had a very interesting mural painted on it. I remember wondering who did it. It's where Mabel's son was staying and I wondered whether he had painted it himself. Sometimes these young people who go overseas to study become all artistic when they come back—*if* they come back. At least Mabel's son came back. So many of them don't, you know. Like my stepdaughter, for example. But of course even though he came back he's gone for good now, so maybe that was not such a good thing . . ."

Nina glanced curiously at the policewoman to see how she was taking all this. To her credit, SS Panchal was writing steadily, occasionally nodding to encourage Aunty Lee's narrative. Nina was impressed.

"And what time did you arrive here this morning?" SS Panchal continued the interview.

"I think it was around eleven something . . . or just before eleven. Or ten something. They said their guests were arriving at eleven A.M., so I was going to set up the food before that. It was supposed to be a morning brunch but substantial enough to carry everyone through to lunch as well—"

"After eleven A.M.?"

"We arrived here at nine forty-eight A.M.," Cherril interrupted. "I texted my husband when we got here, to say I was turning off my phone volume. That's the time on the message."

Panchal noted this and turned her attention to Cherril.

"And you are working for Mrs. Lee? "Can you spell out your full name for me, please? And your IC number?"

Cherril spelled out her name and recited her number, looking intimidated. Like most second- and third-generation Singaporeans, she had never questioned the need to carry personal identification. But being asked to verify her number made her feel as though she was checking into a hospital or being stopped for a traffic violation.

"You do not have your identity card with you. Are you aware that if you fail to produce identification we can detain you until such identification is produced in person or by proxy?"

"Cherril is my new business partner," Aunty Lee answered for her. "She came to help me with the buffet and drinks." Aunty Lee was cross with Panchal's officiousness but managed not to show it. There was no point antagonizing people you wanted information from—something this police would do well to realize. "Cherril will show you her IC afterward. But there was another woman here just now you should talk to. She won't be on the guest list because Mabel didn't know her. Long-haired, Mandarin-speaking. Do you know who she is yet?"

"All in good time. Mrs. Lee, can you tell me why did you include the *buah keluak* dish in the buffet if Mabel Sung ordered a *nasi lemak* buffet? *Buah keluak* is not a dish that usually comes with *nasi lemak*."

"Mabel asked specially for my chicken *buah keluak*."

"Mabel Sung came to your café to make the order?"

"GraceFaith Ang told me that was what Mabel Sung wanted when she made the order," Aunty Lee said. "I remember quite clearly. A *nasi lemak* buffet with yellow chicken curry and chicken *buah keluak* on the side."

The policewoman made a note on her pad.

Aunty Lee saw the implication. If Mabel had been planning to kill herself and her son, there would have been no better way of concealing the taste of poison than by putting it in the *buah keluak*. Mabel ordering the dish seemed to suggest that she had planned the deaths from the start. Aunty Lee hoped the police would pick up on that point but this officer did not seem very bright.

"Can you give us anything to substantiate that?"

"You can ask GraceFaith. She is the one who said Mabel requested it specially. Don't you see?" Aunty Lee burst out. "It's premeditation on her part!" *Buah keluak* definitely indicated premeditation, given the amount of preparation time it needed. But the police officer looked politely noncommittal.

"It may be premeditation," Staff Sergeant Panchal said, as though to herself, "or just food poisoning."

"You can't think—" Cherril burst out indignantly.

"They have to suspect everybody first, " Aunty Lee said genially, though she was equally cross. It was always the easiest solution to blame it on the cook and food poisoning. Well, on behalf of all the cooks in the world, Aunty Lee was going to make sure they did not settle for the easiest solution. Aunty Lee remembered the young man at the gate. He had seemed so certain that Mabel Sung or someone else there would know where his friend was. There had been something so familiar about him but she still could not put her finger on what it was. She had not met him before, of that she was certain. So why was he so familiar?

"There was a man shouting at the gate. He tried to get in to look for his friend Benjamin Ng and they shut the gate on him. Do you know who he is yet?"

"I'm sure someone is looking into it," Staff Sergeant Panchal said. Her tone was polite but Aunty Lee could tell she didn't know or care if it wasn't part of her assignment.

"You should really pay more attention to details and strange people if you want to rise through the ranks," Aunty Lee told her kindly. Panchal ignored this.

"Mrs. Lee, can you sum up how well you knew Mabel Sung?"

"I suppose I knew her as well as I can know somebody who I have got nothing in common with except race, language, and finances. She and her husband were acquaintances of my late husband. We ran into each other a few times at the Island Club and those fund-raising dinners where people donate a lot of money to get invited to eat expensive food with other people who donated a lot of money. She would say, 'How is your restaurant doing?' and I would say, 'It's not really a restaurant' and she would say she really had to come with friends one day. But she never did. That's why I was quite surprised when she asked me to cater the buffet at her house."

"Do you have any idea why she called on you to cater this function if she had never eaten at your café before?"

"I think it was because she didn't want to spend too much. My catered meals cost a lot less than the places she usually goes to. And she was having her prayer-group people over, so she probably didn't want them to think she spends a lot on food. I know what you are thinking right now."

Panchal was just thinking that old Chinese aunties were just as nosy as old Indian aunties.

"You are thinking I'm an old busybody. But can you help an old busybody by just looking and telling me whether you have a Benjamin Ng on your guest list? That is the name the man at the gate was shouting. They must have given you Mabel's guest list, right? You tell me yes or no and then later after you have checked everything here you can come to my shop in Binjai Park and look through everything in my kitchen and all my *buah keluak* ingredients and leftovers and put samples in plastic bags to take back and show them how thorough you are. That would impress them, right?"

It would, Panchal supposed. Inspector Salim might be impressed. Panchal was always polite and proper in procedure and felt Inspector Salim's standards were somewhat lower than hers. But still, he was a senior officer. And he would be impressed by her going through Aunty Lee's kitchen and cooking equipment on her own initiative. She guessed that Inspector Salim was a little afraid of Aunty Lee. Some single men were uncomfortable around women, especially women like this Aunty Lee, who could move from planning your meal to planning your life and before you knew it you were settled down with a wife and she was picking the best possible names for your children. Well, Panchal was only too happy to take the heat off Inspector Salim and be nice to Aunty Lee if it meant getting ahead in the investigation.

"There's no Benjamin Ng on the guest list. One or two other guests mentioned seeing the man at the gate but no one has identified him. However since he did not actually get into the grounds he is not on our list of suspects."

"He didn't get in through the back gate. But what is there to stop him from going round to the front gate after they didn't let him in? And that would be nearer to the main house, where Mabel and her son died. I could tell that young man was very anxious to get in to see her. After getting himself there and knowing she was home, I'm sure he wouldn't just have given up and gone away."

Staff Sergeant Panchal barely acknowledged this. She was busy thumb-texting a message into her mobile. Aunty Lee was pleased by what she had learned. She did not believe the anonymous young man had had anything to do with Mabel's death but his showing up when he did made him relevant to why she had died. These days computer cooks believed success came from following online recipe measurements to the precise second and centigram. Real cooks knew that a successful meal came from taking everything into consideration, right down to the color of the plate you served it on.

Cherril was also texting on her phone, presumably to her husband, because it rang a moment later and she answered it with "Mykie, you'll never believe what just happened! Mabel Sung and her son are dead, poisoned, and the police are here talking to us. We're part of a murder investigation!"

As she listened to what her husband said, her face changed.

"Mycroft says we may be in big trouble. We shouldn't say anything until he gets here."

9

Family and Partners

Despite the best efforts of Mycroft Peters and Commissioner Raja, the guests (and caterers) of the ill-fated brunch party did not get home till after dark that Saturday.

However, Aunty Lee (with Nina in tow) was at Aunty Lee's Delights before nine the next morning. The café and shop did not open till eleven but there was a catering job that evening to prepare for and Mark had texted Aunty Lee and Cherril saying he would be over to discuss something important with them. Aunty Lee hoped this meant the handover would finally be completed and was preparing a celebratory breakfast—*chwee kueh,* or little steamed rice-flour cakes with savory preserved radish topping. She was still buzzing with excitement from the previous day's happenings, and stirring boiling water into sifted and salted rice and tapioca powder to form a smooth batter was as good an outlet for her energy as anything. And of course she did her best to keep up with the news. For this she now needed only Nina's good eyesight and an iPad2 (on the kitchen counter) but so far there had been nothing new.

Running the café had kept Aunty Lee blessedly busy after her husband's death. She felt he watched over her there, not least of all because one of the last portrait photos of the late ML Lee, taken with him in his wheelchair, hung by the door of the café. That was where he used to sit in his wheelchair, when walking, even from their house up the road, became too tiring. There was at least one photograph of him in each room of the house and shop so that Aunty Lee could talk to him wherever she was. He did not answer, but then he had seldom answered even when he was alive. He had always said his energetic little wife talked enough for them both. In this photograph ML was wearing a blue-and-white golf shirt and squinting a little against the sun.

Aunty Lee loved the little café kitchen. It was small enough to get around quickly but there was space to fit in friends. She always felt that bonds formed while cooking together ran deeper than those formed merely eating together.

"Smells good." Cherril came into the shop and joined them in the kitchen.

Aunty Lee said, "Mark likes *chwee kueh*. I made the traditional topping but also *gula melaka* banana sauce to pour on top."

"Good." Cherril looked haggard and stressed.

Despite the excitement Aunty Lee had gone to sleep fast

and slept well. She had mastered the technique during her husband's last illness (turn air-conditioning to very cold, take a very hot shower, turn off phone and all lights, and repeat "wake up at six A.M., wake up at six A.M." to herself till she did) or she might have been up all night going over the events too. She felt sorry for Cherril, who looked as though she had not slept at all the night before.

"You better go home and rest after settling everything with Mark. I can manage tonight myself with Nina's help."

"I have to go home by eleven anyway. The police are coming to the house to talk to me."

"Why not come and talk to you here? We are all here; they can talk to us all together!"

"The police already listen to you talk too much yesterday, madam," Nina pointed out. Nina was worried about repercussions her boss seemed to have missed. After all, wasn't the caterer always the first suspect in a food poisoning case?

"Mycroft thinks Mabel Sung killed her son because he was not going to recover and she didn't want him to suffer, and she couldn't bear to live with the thought, so she killed herself as well."

"Mabel Sung didn't kill herself," Aunty Lee said firmly. "She wasn't the type. And she wouldn't have killed her son. You tell me she killed her husband, I say maybe. But not her son. And no way she would kill herself."

"Hello, Aunty Lee." Mark came in, followed by Selina.

"Aunty Lee, lucky for you more people didn't eat your *buah keluak* yesterday!" Selina said.

Though Mark had comfortably addressed his stepmother

as "Aunty Lee" since before she married his father, it sounded strange to Aunty Lee when Selina called her that. But then perhaps it only felt strange because Selina seemed to be enjoying it so much as she continued, "Aunty Lee, you could have poisoned everybody at the party. It could have been a mass murder. Aunty Lee, we could be coming to visit you in Changi Prison now!" Selina laughed and nudged Mark to share the joke. But Mark only said, "Hello, Cherril, how's things?"

"Cherril, you look tired. Are you sick? You look like you've put on weight. Are you pregnant?" Even the thought of her stepmother-in-law in prison could not distract Selina for long from the threat of other women.

"That's the first thing people always say. Food poisoning," Aunty Lee said to the photograph of ML Lee on the wall by the wine room door.

"Let people say what they want. As long as they don't come and make a lawsuit," Nina said in the same direction.

"If it wasn't food poisoning, then what? You're not going to say there's another murderer around?" Mark laughed.

"I heard Sharon Sung tell the police it was probably suicide," Aunty Lee said. "She said her brother was depressed from being sick and a burden and he talked about killing himself before. And then she said maybe her mother killed her brother because she couldn't bear to watch him suffering, but then Dr. Yong said no way because Mabel knew that Leonard was going to be completely healed soon."

"Must be one of the praying healing people said that, madam." Nina wiped down an already clean counter.

"No, it was the slimy little doctor," Aunty Lee said eagerly. "And I saw Sharon give him such a nasty look and he stopped talking."

"I still don't understand why anyone would risk eating something that smells funny and could kill them!" Mark laughed again.

"Some people eat fugu fish," Cherril snapped. She flashed a glare at Mark that came and went so quickly Mark was not sure he hadn't imagined it. He had recently shared photos of his first taste of fugu fish (350 Singapore dollars for a few translucent slices) at a top restaurant in Japan.

"Some people like taking funny risks," Selina said, looking around the café meaningfully.

Cherril felt this was directed at her. But she was in no mood to spar with Selina. "Look, Mark, you said we could settle the handover today?"

"It's not a handover," Selina said quickly. "It's a buyout. You're buying out the business from Mark."

The others looked at Mark but he only gave an exaggerated "Don't ask me, she's the boss" shrug. It was clear he had been instructed to let Selina do the talking.

"We have an estimate of how much the business is worth. That's not including the profits that come with the wine dining program. We are not including wine dining as part of the deal because Mark is willing to come in and help with that, for a consultation fee, of course."

"Frankly put, you need me," Mark said. "I know every bottle of wine in the wine room with my eyes closed."

A police car slowly drove past the road in front of Aunty

Lee's Delights, going deeper into the estate where their houses were. Cherril watched it, distracted. "I should be going."

"I hope you're not going to back out just because of this business. You had a verbal agreement with Mark," Selina said. "It was as good as settled."

"It's a bit more complicated than that." Cherril pulled her attention back. "It seems a good part of the wine stock here is on consignment."

"That's how these things are done," Mark said. "Of course it only works when the suppliers know you well enough. But they all know me, so it won't be a problem."

"You can't just use Mark's name," Selina said quickly. "The wine is here on consignment to Mark. So he will sell the bottles to you and pay the suppliers after he takes his cut. That's only fair because he's the one who arranged to have the bottles brought in and he's the one who made sure that they were kept in the right conditions. This way it's easiest for everybody. You pay Mark and he'll take care of everything. Then you can go ahead and run the business however you want to."

"But I don't want to buy the wine from Mark," Cherril said. "This is great, actually. We can return all the bottles and nobody will have to pay for them!"

"Cherril, listen to me. If you don't take the wine, how are you going to run a wine business?" Selina said with the sarcastic precision of a teacher facing a particularly slow student.

"It's not going to be a wine business. It's going to be a

drinks business. That's what it says on the contract, right? Aunty Lee showed me her copy."

That was indeed what the contract said. Mark had focused on wines because Mark always focused on what he was interested in.

"I can come and help you if you're afraid you don't know enough about the wines," he said kindly. "For example, in Singapore you have to be careful of room temperature wines." His wife might look down on Cherril for not having a university degree, but Mark had always found a willing listener in her. "The French recommend serving their reds *à chambre* but the temperatures of French *chambres* are probably around eighteen to twenty degrees Celsius. Here room temperatures can go up to thirty degrees Celsius and anything you store and serve at that temperature is going to taste heavy, hard, and very bitter. That's why the wine room is so important. And it's even worse for sweet dessert wines. But there you have to be careful not to overchill them, especially the more complex and vibrant ones. I'll point out to you the ones you should take special care with. Not just because they are more expensive, which they are, but because you don't want to damage their vibrancy . . ."

Mark rose, intending to walk Cherril round his precious wine room yet again. But Cherril shook her head. "Not now, Mark. Thank you. I've already learned so much about wine from you, Mark. But that's not what I want to focus on. I'm going to serve all kinds of hot and cold drinks to go with all the food. Maybe there will be some wine and some beer, but that's not what I will be focusing on."

Mark looked flabbergasted. Selina stepped in. "Well, what are you going to do with the wine room, then? It cost a lot of money, you know."

Aunty Lee knew that. She had paid for the construction of the wine room because, as Selina had pointed out, it was installed in her café. And she loved it. The inch of high-density, rigid foam insulation was discreetly covered with unfinished oak, the sophisticated Breezaire system worked almost silently, and Mark had chosen a double pane of dark-tinted glass for the door that hinted at joys within without revealing too much.

Despite being widely seen as the sweet old aunty championing traditional foods and cooking methods, Aunty Lee loved modern electronic gadgets and systems. She might have an enormous charcoal brazier standing in the back alleyway, but she also had Certis CISCO Integrated Operations round-the-clock burglar and fire alarms, which Nina had linked to the nearest neighborhood police station. And though Aunty Lee swore by the superior quality of spices hand-pounded in the heavy granite mortar and pestle (never to be washed with soap), she also owned the latest models in blender mixers (for catering) and took no chances with her API Food Poison Detection Kits and a GHM-01 Detector for Common Heavy Metals that covered possible food contaminants from rusty water pipes to arsenic.

She had been less happy about the room's exit to the rear alley, a legacy of its origin as a toilet. "If you don't lock the door properly, alcoholics can come through the back door and steal my kitchen equipment."

"Alcoholics are hardly likely to steal your kitchen equipment, Aunty Lee," Selina had pointed out sarcastically.

"You think just because they like to drink they don't like to cook?"

"I'll make sure Mark locks the door properly," Selina had said.

Now Aunty Lee had the temperature-controlled walk-in storeroom every Singaporean cook dreamed of. It would be perfect for store-at-room-temperature goods like soy sauce and sesame oil once they got rid of the wine bottles. "I could make kimchi," Aunty Lee said dreamily. "Part *achar*, part kimchi. It will be like a fusion pickle."

"We will serve wine of course," Cherril said. "After all, it would be a waste not to when we have the wine license. But it's not going to be our main focus. We're also going to serve cocktails, mocktails, and doctails. Doctails . . ." Forestalling the question: "Doctails are the medicinal drinks. The drinks that TCM and folk remedies recommend as healing. Honey drinks and aloe vera and wolfberry teas as well as energy drinks."

"That's actually a good idea!" Selina said. "Traditional Chinese medicine is a growing market today. Mark, are you sure you don't want to do this? You haven't signed the papers yet. This could work. You take care of the wine, I take care of everything else. You—this to Aunty Lee—"you must agree not to sell any kind of cold drinks or desserts so that people are forced to buy from us . . ."

Mark had intended to cultivate a Singapore-based wine

appreciation platform. Making money from the business had never been a priority for him. And now even the people he had been trying to help didn't appreciate him.

"I don't want to," he said sulkily.

Aunty Lee wondered how this would influence his next career step. ML had been wise, she thought, to set a limit on how much of his inheritance Mark could tap into during her lifetime. Though both he and Mathilda had been left well off by their father and would be wealthy by Singapore standards after her death, Mark had already drawn substantial loans on his future inheritance.

The shop phone rang just then. Nina answered, "Aunty Lee's Delights, good morning," brightly enough, but as she listened to the voice at the other end her expression changed. "But it is not a problem, ma'am. You want to postpone until tomorrow or another day? No? But you should speak to Aunty Lee first. She is here, I will pass the phone to her, you wait—"

"This evening's client canceled?"

Nina nodded. "She said there is some family emergency, they have to cancel the party."

"I already ordered dry ice for the drinks chiller—and what about all the food!" Cherril said. "I'm sure they're lying. Family emergency, my foot. They are going to order in Pizza Hut or Kentucky Fried Chicken. I hope they all end up with food poisoning. They deserve it!"

"Don't say that," Aunty Lee said. "Nobody deserves food poisoning."

Even a rumor of food poisoning could haunt a café for

years. Aunty Lee hoped this would not happen to hers. She turned for assurance to ML Lee's portrait. ML was smiling with his usual charm but Cherril, standing in front of the frame, looked really upset.

"It's just one booking," Aunty Lee said briskly. The deposit on the canceled meal would cover what she had spent on ingredients. "Come help me experiment how to package cooked food for the freezer. I want to make two-person servings of yellow chicken curry and rice with *achar* separate. Like they sell at the petrol station to heat up in the microwave. Only mine will be nicer."

10

Home Interrogation

The Peters family home was a large bungalow off Binjai Crescent, deep in the Binjai housing estate and closer to the hilly center of Singapore island. Mycroft Peters had grown up in this house. Now he and his wife, Cherril, lived in a newly added two-story wing with its own pebbled path leading from the driveway.

"So this is how the rich people live," Staff Sergeant Panchal said snidely. Salim could tell she was intimidated and made no comment.

Salim buzzed the gate intercom. Mycroft appeared at the front door of the main house.

"You shouldn't park there," Mycroft said, looking at the police Subaru. Though parking opposite the continuous white line outside was illegal, it was an offense for which drivers seldom got fined, especially here in Binjai Park, where people were rich and roads were wide. Since Singaporeans did not understand the concept of bribery, it just meant paperwork and bad karma for the traffic officer. Warning people off worked much better for all concerned and cleared the road faster, which was the point of the whole exercise.

But few people challenged the police on where they, the police themselves, left their cars.

"I'll give myself a warning," Salim said.

Mycroft laughed. "Come in."

Mycroft was not usually home at noon. But Cherril had phoned him to say the police were coming to speak to her at home and he had postponed two meetings, canceled a lunch, and got back to the house before the police arrived for their appointment.

"They already talked to you yesterday, why should they want to question you again? And why here if they were at the shop earlier?"

"Mykie, I don't know!" She looked frightened.

Mycroft looked at his wife fondly. He knew some people thought he had married beneath him, that he had been seduced into this marriage or had chosen her to spite his parents. In fact it was Cherril's addiction to learning that had caught his attention. Her curiosity about how systems worked matched his own. He had fallen in love with her when they started learning Japanese together. And now he meant to protect her.

"Mother is out to lunch. We'll talk to them in the big house."

Cherril, who had taken some time to get used to living in a house larger than the three apartments in her old housing block combined, knew that Mycroft was deliberately trying to intimidate the police visitors with his lawyer side.

"But why? Do you think they suspect me of having something to do with it? Is that why you rushed home?"

"I think they want to talk to you and Aunty Lee separately, that's all. But I would like to hear what they have to say."

After Mycroft settled them into a living room that seemed to the police officers the size of a community center recreation basketball court, Staff Sergeant Panchal started to ask questions. Speaking with Cherril apart from Aunty Lee had been her idea and she wanted to make sure any evidence she extracted was credited to her.

"Someone heard you saying, 'I hope it wasn't the chicken *buah keluak*,' after Mrs. Sung and her son were found dead. Can you explain why you said that?"

"Because—well, you know they can be poisonous if not prepared properly. But nobody ever had any problems with Aunty Lee's *buah keluak* before." Cherril glanced at her husband and Inspector Salim as she spoke. Mycroft remained impassive but Salim nodded slightly.

"Did you mention your concern to the police you gave a statement to?"

"No. I didn't. It was just a thought. A joke, in fact."

"I understand you were helping with food preparations yesterday."

"Actually I was taking care of the drinks."

"So you did not touch any of the food? You did not help with any of the preparations?"

"Well, of course I did help a bit. There are only three of us, Aunty Lee, Nina, and myself—"

"What qualifications do you have in food preparation, Mrs. Peters?"

"I—well, I'm sort of learning on the job."

"Yet you were helping with the food preparations for the party yesterday. Did you help with preparing the chicken *buah keluak*?"

"No."

"You were formerly working as an air stewardess, am I correct? "And you left your job as a stewardess after some complaints were made against you, is that correct? Did these complaints have anything to do with your food service?"

"No."

"Are you sure? There is a copy of the complaints made and the passenger, one Mr. Scott Barber—"

"The passenger said that he wanted the chicken main dish but he didn't want to eat halal chicken because he was not Muslim. I explained to him all the chicken on board was halal and he got angry. Actually he was very drunk. But I didn't leave my job because of that. I left because I got married."

"And do you cook at home, Mrs. Peters?"

"I don't see what that has to do with anything," Cherril said. "Why are you asking such stupid questions?"

She turned to Mycroft but he was watching as Staff Sergeant Panchal pointedly wrote down "uncooperative" on her pad.

"I think you should leave now," Mycroft said.

"Are you sure you want to go through with this?" he asked after the police had left. "Why not just go for cooking classes? We can do up the kitchen here if you like."

"Of course I want to go through with it. What happened has got nothing to do with Aunty Lee. We just happened to be there when it happened, that's all."

"Aunty Lee manages to be around a lot whenever something happens. I don't want her dragging you into trouble. You know they'll probably decide it's food poisoning and drop it, right? And you know that's going to have an effect on her business. Are you sure you want to go into it now? Just think about it."

"Who else would take me on without any experience? Besides, you don't know who else might have had a motive to do away with the Sungs. Maybe Mabel's daughter had a boyfriend." Mycroft snorted at this. "Or her husband had a mistress. Any of those people might have had something to do with it. And you said yourself, isn't it possible that Mabel killed herself and her son rather than watch him die slowly?"

Cherril was already starting to sound a little like her culinary mentor, Mycroft thought. Whatever she wanted to do was fine with him as long as she was happy. But now it struck him that it might also be very tiring—for him.

11

Buah Keluak

"We should get back to the guest list," Salim said as they got back into the car.

"We are wasting our time questioning people on the guest list," Staff Sergeant Panchal said. "Why would anybody purposely kill people like that? They got poisoned by the *buah keluak*, we should bring in the catering people. They would have been arrested already if you weren't so friendly with them."

"I'm sure there's more to it than that."

"You are biased."

"I have previous info. Personal experience."

"What are we waiting for now?"

"More info."

Back at the station, general opinion was on Panchal's side. The risk of eating *buah keluak* was a well-known urban legend, even though none of the officers knew anyone who had died from eating it. Even Salim would probably have blamed the deaths on the *buah keluak* if the caterer had been anyone other than Aunty Lee.

"Anything more from the Sung house?"

"There were canisters of Algae Bomb and rat poison stored in the pool area, brands banned in Singapore. Neither the husband nor daughter can say where they came from. They both said Mabel Sung couldn't stand any kind of dirt or pests around. She was afraid of infection getting to her son. Apparently she used to get friends to bring pesticides in from Malaysia because she said the safe ones sold here are not effective," Corporal Chan said. She and Corporal Ismail were on a three-month training posting and still new enough to be excited about lab and interview reports.

"Anything on that other death? The jumper?"

"She told people her fiancé came here to sell a kidney to pay for their wedding and died during the illegal transplant op. But there's no record of his death or a body. What happened to the guy? Mysterious, right?"

"Fishy story. The guy probably just ran out on her," Corporal Ismail said with the worldly-wise air of a twenty-two-year-old. "If he came here for an illegal transplant, he's not going to come forward. The last time those guys got caught coming to donate kidneys to Singaporeans, they could not prove they were related to each other, so they got prison time and caning." To deter profiteering off organ trafficking, transplants were illegal unless a family relationship could be proved.

Back in his own office, Salim went over the notes he'd taken at the Sung house. No results had come in yet from the tests he had ordered. It was only on television dramas that results came so quickly. On his instructions, his team had recorded not only the answers to their questions but everything they observed yesterday. Salim knew that you could learn more about people from what they did than from what they chose to tell you. According to the investigators who had been at the Sung house that day, Henry Sung had spent all day at his computer watching what was going on in the rest of the house via security camera feeds. He had agreed to supply the police with recordings from the cameras, only to find that the live feeds had not been recorded. Yes, he had been cooperative enough but he was an old man who did not seem to know much about how the house was run or about what his wife had been doing. At the hospital where he had worked for almost forty years, he had an office and the title of "advising consultant" but no duties.

Sharon Sung had spent the rest of the evening at the Sung Law office, immersed in Mabel's files and paperwork. Dr. Edmond Yong and GraceFaith Ang had showed up and spent some time with her, the officer who escorted Sharon had written said. Salim called him to his office.

"Edmond Yong was looking after Leonard Sung's health at the Sungs' place, right? What was he doing at Sung Law?"

Sergeant Bong, the young officer assigned to observe/

protect Sharon Sung the previous day, had no idea. He had watched everything but wondered about nothing and found the whole assignment very boring. Bong was a stolid Candy Crush addict who found most of real life very boring.

"He went there to talk to Miss Ang, sir. Miss Sung got angry with them for talking without her. She said they should not keep secrets from her because she is in charge of everything now. Then they went inside her office to talk and closed the door, so I didn't hear what they said."

"In charge of what, that's the real question," Staff Sergeant Panchal said from the doorway. "Bong, you're useless. Why didn't you say you had to stay in the room with her and listen?"

For once, Salim agreed with her. The two young corporals were tense with excitement, hoping he would give them a chance to do better. But Salim knew it would be no use. Sharon Sung had decisively dismissed Sergeant Bong and the idea she needed protection. Salim could sense she had information she was not sharing and they would have to get it some other way. And he knew someone who would do the job better than corporals Chan and Ismail.

Salim announced he would be out of the office for a while and left, ignoring the surprised looks of his staff.

Less than fifteen minutes later Inspector Salim pushed open the door to Aunty Lee's Delights.

"Aunty Lee," he said, "can you tell me everything you know about *buah keluak*?"

"What are you doing here?" Nina asked. "We are very

busy here, you know. Shouldn't you be busy doing your own work, questioning people in their own homes and things like that?" Though Nina was always busy, this time she looked genuinely cross. Salim guessed Cherril had told them about the visit to the Peterses'. But this time he was there because he was busy too. And getting information from someone who knew both the subject and what he needed to understand was faster than sifting through material online.

"I want to do my work. But I need to understand more about the background first." He looked past Nina to Aunty Lee, who nodded. He hoped she would understand. After all it was something he had learned from her as well as from his mother . . . you had to understand a process inside out before you could find out where it had gone wrong. "I'm not here to question anybody, just to learn. I've been eating *buah keluak* all my life, I just don't know much about it."

"Get Salim a drink, Nina." Aunty Lee waved him to take one of the bar stools by the kitchen counter. She was always ready to talk about food, especially traditional foods that modern young people risked losing touch with.

"I still remember in the old days, if you wanted to find *buah keluak*, you looked for where the older wild pigs went to eat. Those *babirusa* always knew where to find kepayang trees with ripe *buah keluak*. Nowadays Singapore has no space for old pigs any more than for old people. I usually go and buy my *buah keluak* nuts from the sellers in Tekka Market.

"When we were children we used to go and collect them ourselves. In those days no matter how poor you are, no money too, you could find food. Tapioca, *kang kong*, chicken, fish . . . as long as you got space you can grow your own. Nowadays no money means no food. And they say we are better off.

"The women collect nuts and bring them over from Indonesia. There they still have many wild trees, so they gather them and treat them first to remove the poison before selling them. But to be safe I always soak my *buah keluak* at least overnight in water before cooking. See? Like these ones. I don't need them until next week but I'm soaking them already."

Salim looked into the large tub of water. The (dangerous?) dark nuts looked like misshapen golf balls. He wondered whether Aunty Lee was trying to convince herself she could not have made such a terrible mistake. Nina had looked cross when he came in, but now she brought them glasses of cold lemongrass tea. She did not even pretend to be listening to her boss. Salim guessed she had heard it all before.

"I am very careful! All the people who come and eat my *ayam buah keluak* and *nasi rawon,* they don't know that *buah keluak* seeds contain cyanide. Even the wood and the leaves of the tree are poisonous. People crush raw *buah keluak* kernels to poison lizards, insects, and animal ticks. If you eat even a small amount you get trouble breathing, you get dizziness and headaches and seizures. If you eat too much you get heart attack and die. People don't know that but I know. That's why I am always very careful!"

Salim thought this did not sound too different from what had happened to Mabel Sung and her son. He knew *ayam buah keluak* was chicken stewed with *buah keluak* seeds and *nasi rawon* was an Indonesian rice dish cooked with the same.

Because of its distinctive rich, oily bitterness, *buah keluak* was an acquired taste not everyone shared.

"Of course you are careful," he said soothingly. "But you know the police have to suspect everybody who was there when it happened."

"They should be suspecting everybody who was there, but it is easier for them if they decide to blame my cooking and close the case and never eat *buah keluak* again. At least they will never eat my *buah keluak* again. I might as well close shop now, nobody will ever come here to eat again," Aunty Lee said dramatically.

"But you said eating *buah keluak* isn't really a risk if it's properly prepared, right? How is that done, Aunty Lee?"

"To make sure all the poison is removed, the seeds are removed from the fruits and boiled and then buried in ash pits lined with banana leaves and covered with earth for over a month. At the beginning the seeds are hard and yellow, but by the time they are dug up they are dark brown, almost black color, and after fermentation the insides are soft like lumpy tar. Some people say they smell like opium. Then they have to be washed because fermentation releases the hydrogen cyanide, which is water-soluble.

"I usually get them from dried food stalls in Tekka Market or Geylang Serai Market. The sellers already do the whole poison removal process, but to be on the safe side I always soak them again. In fact I leave in the water until I need them, up to four or five days. Nina changes the water twice a day, so no mosquitoes. Not just because of the poison but to get rid of the taste of mud—most of the time the trees grow in the mangrove swamps, very muddy there—and to make the shells soft enough to crack."

"Sounds like a lot of work."

"That's only the beginning!" Aunty Lee crowed, the current sad state of affairs pushed aside by the thought of work.

"After that, you have to scrub every nut one by one and then chop off one end and dig out all the flesh inside. You combine all the insides and pound it and season it. Sometimes you must use a small cutter to trim smooth the opening you chopped into the nut so that when people eat it they won't cut their mouths. And then you stuff the flesh back in, along with all the other ingredients, and cook on a low fire for a few hours until the soup is thick and everything has the flavor. Now, that is a lot of work!"

"It is." Salim found himself wondering what could be worth all that effort.

"It's delicious when you get used to it." Aunty Lee smiled. "And even if you don't like the taste, when you know how much work went into making it, you'll eat it."

12

Evenings at Home

Having already announced that Aunty Lee's Delights was closing early that day because of the (now canceled) catering job, Aunty Lee and Nina took advantage of a night off and went home early after Salim left. It had been a long time since they had had a quiet night with no one to cook for but themselves.

In the smaller home kitchen, Nina made *arroz caldo* like she had done so many times at home in the Philippines. The thick, savory chicken rice porridge reminded Aunty Lee of Chinese chicken congee and Korean ginseng rice chicken soup. When it came to finding comfort in food, different peoples were often far more alike than they realized. And the love of similar comforts went far beyond food.

They ate together at the dining table instead of in front of the television because Aunty Lee needed space to spread out all her notes.

"I'm seeing so many reasons why Mabel might have killed herself and her son. Leonard became a drug addict while studying in America and had heart and lung problems and was on the waiting list for a heart transplant."

"Madam, if he is already on the waiting list, then what would she kill him for? Why not just wait?" Nina asked dully, more because it was expected of her than because she wanted to know.

"Because that is almost a hopeless case. The donor has to be a healthy person who dies quickly in a way that doesn't damage the heart. You must rush him or her to be kept alive in hospital while they prepare you for the operation. Plus he or she must have signed the donor consent form or the relatives must sign it and the police must be satisfied there is no funny business because organ trading is illegal. Surely all these things cannot happen together without some kind of funny business, right?"

"Why is organ trading illegal in Singapore? I thought in Singapore people can sell everything. As long as can make money, it is all right."

"We have got to protect people who are desperate for money. There are medical risks and things like that."

"If people are desperate for money they need money, not protection."

Something in Nina's tone made Aunty Lee really look at her for the first time since sitting down. Nina looked tense and worried. She had barely touched her dinner. Aunty Lee, gulping down delicious spoonfuls of creamy rice broth with chunks of delicately flavored chicken as she leafed with equal relish through the notes that she had spread across most of the dining table, had already finished her second bowl.

"Can I get you some more porridge, madam?"

"First tell me what's wrong, Nina."

Nina looked at the papers with notes and excited arrows and sticky tabs all over them and said nothing.

"Nina, are you upset because you think they killed themselves?" Nina was Catholic and Aunty Lee had a vague idea that Catholics considered suicide and birth control far worse than murders and miscarriages. Ordinarily this might have been the beginning of a very interesting discussion. But at the moment Nina had more pressing worries.

"Madam, you don't understand. This is serious. The police went to Madam Cherril's house because they want to make trouble for you—"

"Nina, I'm sure Salim won't—"

"Madam, people think it is because of your *buah keluak* that those people die. Maybe they will make you close down the shop. Maybe even if they don't close down the shop, people won't come anymore. Today already somebody canceled. Think about what is going to happen if everybody also cancels?"

Nina was not worried for herself, Aunty Lee realized. She had sent home enough money for her mother and sisters to buy farmland in her name and was already the biggest landowner in their village. She could stop work now and live a very comfortable life back home. Nina was still in Singapore and worried because she cared about what happened to Aunty Lee. And maybe because she cared about someone else she wouldn't admit to.

"I have thought about it, Nina. That's why it is so important that we find out what really happened."

"That is the policeman's job."

"But we have an advantage over the police, even your Salim. They have to consider the possibility that Mabel and her son were accidentally poisoned by our *buah keluak*. You and I know very well that could not have happened. So it is up to us to find out whether they poisoned themselves or were poisoned by someone else. Okay?"

Nina nodded. "He's not 'my' Salim," she said. But just saying the name made her smile. Though she really did not know what that man was up to, or what she thought of it.

Salim had been trying to get Nina to take an online prelaw class with him. He knew that with Aunty Lee's full encouragement Nina had invested her spare hours in Singapore studying. So why not law? But Nina was trying to learn all she could about cooking, hairdressing, and massage—practical skills that could be practiced anywhere in the world for pay. Nina knew she could never be a lawyer in Singapore. To her, working toward an impossible goal like studying law was as much a waste of time as not working. And it seemed as impossible for Salim as for herself. Salim could not or would not see that. Much as he loved his work, he felt the system he was part of could be improved. And the only way he could improve it was from within because throwing complaints and criticisms from outside was about as effective as bird shit landing on a car.

As a favor to Salim, Nina had agreed to look at the syllabus and online material he had printed out. Perhaps she could help him study, he had said shyly. Her friends with male friends in Singapore were taken on picnics and out dancing and on movie dates. Nina and Salim went to the library study rooms and discussed points of law while walking along the Parks Connector green routes that crossed the island.

To her surprise Nina enjoyed their discussions. But when Salim brought online registration forms for both of them, she had balked. It was a nice dream, that was all. And Aunty Lee needed her in real life.

"Nina." Aunty Lee's voice cut into her thoughts.

"Yes, madam."

"The big woman with the little-girl voice, do you know if she was one of the lawyers or one of the Christians?"

"I don't know, madam."

Then again, life with Aunty Lee was not most people's idea of "real life."

With her eyes half closed, Aunty Lee was trying to match the people she had seen at the party to the names on her list. She had not seen Leonard Sung while he was still alive. Nina had found photographs of the young man online that showed his progression from a smug, plump schoolboy to a painfully thin, sneering man. Tributes from friends suggested most of his friends from school had not seen him for years but remembered his "crazy sense of humor" and missed laughing at his "wild pranks."

And Mabel Sung? According to the newspapers, she was seventy-four years old but she had managed to appear younger despite the stress and worry in her life. A handsome rather than a beautiful woman, Aunty Lee thought. Mabel Sung looked as though she was used to taking the lead and standing out in a crowd. She reminded Aunty Lee of someone—oh yes, her old mathematics teacher who had been so inflexible she had turned a generation of schoolgirls off math forever. Why was it so much easier these days to remember people from twenty, thirty, or even forty years ago than someone she might have met last week? But wait—Aunty Lee returned to Mabel Sung. Had Mabel really seemed stressed and worried? Aunty Lee remembered her short, unpainted fingernails drumming on the buffet table, the barely covered irritation that caused her to lash out at her husband and daughter . . . and the strange expression that crossed Mabel's face when she first caught sight of Edmond Yong's long-haired woman. Yes, Mabel had definitely been on edge. And for some reason she had been anxious to please the PRC woman, had looked almost afraid of displeasing her.

Mabel Sung and her son were found dead in the boy's bedroom. Her husband had been in his office, farther along the corridor. Aunty Lee had seen Henry Sung several times but the man left no lasting impression, unlike his wife. He looked like a successful man, the sort whose funeral wake would be attended by former ministers of state and whose idea of exercise was being driven around golf courses. But then, what was the connection between Henry Sung and Doreen Choo? Aunty Lee had only seen them together for a moment but it had been enough for her to see that the two were definitely not strangers. Strangers, even friends and acquaintances, greeted and talked to each other. Henry Sung was familiar enough to go up Doreen Choo and stand by her side without a word. And she had reached out and steadied his tray on the railing post with an automatic familiarity that told Aunty Lee as much as catching them in flagrante delicto would have.

Aunty Lee paused. She had known Doreen Choo for many years. Doreen and her late husband had not been particularly close friends of hers. But at their age even mere acquaintances from the old days became a precious link to who they had once been. She said as much to Nina.

"I didn't recognize her at first. Then afterward I couldn't believe I hadn't recognized her."

"She was your old school friend, ma'am?"

"No. She came from that girls' school with blue sleeveless uniforms. My father would never have let any of his wives or daughters wear sleeveless dresses. He thought it was immodest. But we ended up running around like little ruffians in our sailor suits and bloomers while they grew into ladylike girls who shaved their armpits and legs."

Aunty Lee did not say anything about Henry and Doreen. She knew she was not mistaken, but even the faithful Nina might doubt the evidence of words not said. And even if Henry Sung was having some kind of relationship with Doreen, it might not mean anything. She would talk to Doreen Choo herself first.

Who else had been there? Several assistants from the office had come early, then left before the bodies were found. Two other lawyers had been invited but had not bothered to show up. It seemed that things were definitely starting to fall apart at the seams at Sung Law. All the other guests had been friends or members of Mabel's Never Say Die prayer and healing group. None of them had gone up to the big house. Apparently there was a toilet on the far side of the little pool house that Aunty Lee (fortunately enough) had not noticed.

Sharon Sung had been up at the house, of course. And Mabel's assistant, that fair girl with a complexion so perfect it had to be standard theater makeup—

"GraceFaith Ang," Nina said.

"That's right. GraceFaith Ang. She must have very Christian parents. I wonder whether she has a sister called Joy-Hope or maybe CharityPeace. It must be very difficult for a child to go through school with a name like CharityPeace. Just think of the teasing."

Nina's ability to ignore Aunty Lee's less relevant digressions played a big part in how well the two women worked together.

"GraceFaith told the police that Sharon spent the whole night before the party in the office going through her mother's work folders that her mother had passed her. I think she is lying. Why would anybody stay in the office and read old files all night?"

"Maybe she fell asleep in the office and told the girl she was working all night. Or maybe there was a deadline." Aunty Lee knew this was unlikely even as she said it. She had heard GraceFaith say there were no cases pending; in fact Mabel had stopped taking on new clients since Leonard's return to Singapore. And the office was closed the next day for Sharon's partnership party. How long could a law firm survive without taking on new clients? Well, if the old clients were satisfactory, Aunty Lee supposed it could continue indefinitely. Perhaps Mycroft would know.

"Or maybe Sharon went to meet a boyfriend her parents disapprove of. Then GraceFaith told her parents and they scolded her and she got angry and killed her mother."

"I don't think so—and if that was the case, wouldn't she have tried to kill her mother and father instead of her brother?" Aunty Lee thought back to what she had seen of Sharon Sung. She did not look like a girl who had a secret boyfriend. Of course different girls reacted differently to boyfriends. Some took more pride in their appearance; both triumphant hunter and trophy. Others dressed in their boyfriend's old shirts and settled down to grow fat and happy. No, Aunty Lee was sure Sharon Sung did not have a secret boyfriend.

"And the day after her mother died, this Sharon went back to the office to work some more. Can you believe that?"

Aunty Lee could believe it all too well. The day after ML's death she had also gone straight from his deathbed in the hospital to work in her kitchen. In her case, making labor-intensive *orh kueh* or yam cake. The amount of work and mindless focus needed to soak, slice, and chop dried mush-rooms and dried prawns had got her through that terrible day. She felt she could understand Sharon Sung and she felt sorry for her. Keeping her mother's law firm going was her way of paying tribute to her mother.

"It wasn't an accident. That means either suicide or murder. Or suicide murder. But why choose to do it like that? And why—"

In Aunty Lee's opinion there were different kinds of murder. The quick flash sparked by sudden rage and the slow stew, the boil that finally bubbled over. But which was this?

The answer had to lie with the people involved. People were drawn to certain ways of committing murder the same way they were drawn to certain foods. That was where she had to start, Aunty Lee thought. Often what people ate was not even a matter of conscious choice. They were drawn to a taste or a texture because on first encounter (even if they hated it then) it had impressed itself on them as how the world was and how it should forever be.

"I forgot to tell the police about the long-haired China woman," Aunty Lee said. "I don't think she was a guest be-cause she didn't know Mabel Sung. I saw Dr. Yong introduc-ing them. I think they were talking about money. She wanted money from Mabel to finance something or because Mabel owed her for financing something . . . I couldn't understand very much."

"Madam, how do you know? You cannot understand Mandarin. You are imagining things again." Even Nina had picked up more Mandarin during her years in Singapore than Aunty Lee had done during her whole life on the island.

"Mabel Sung's Chinese is almost as lousy as mine. Edmond Yong translated for her, so I could understand those parts. The woman sounded like a PRC, she had that posh *shwa-shew-shoo* accent that the local Mandarin speakers don't have. Does your Salim know who she is yet?"

"She is from the People's Republic of China, here on a visitor's pass."

"I got the feeling Dr. Yong was trying to impress the long-haired woman. Men always have that slightly off-center look when they are trying to impress someone and trying to look as though they don't care, don't you think so? And he was very nervous about something."

Or the man was anxious by nature or had not been worried about anything in particular that day. That was the difficulty in figuring out things about people you didn't know well. The only solution was to find out more about them.

And there was a name Aunty Lee knew would not be on the list. The vaguely familiar young man at the gate looking for his friend had not been expected. He said his missing friend had been doing some work for Mabel Sung. Aunty Lee did not know what the young man's name was but the friend he was looking for was named Benjamin Ng. That was a start.

"Benjamin Ng," Aunty Lee said. "Why did his friend go there to look for him? Did he think his friend would be at the party?"

Nina had nothing to suggest.

Aunty Lee thought back. "I don't think he even knew there

was a party. He wanted to talk to Mabel Sung and he couldn't get in to see her at her office, so he went to her house. For a moment I thought he was an undercover policeman, can you believe it?"

"Why, madam?"

"Timmy Pang. The handsome staff sergeant who used to be here . . ."

"Tim Pang got big promotion already, not here anymore. Madam, what's wrong?"

"I remember Timmy Pang very well."

The phone rang, it was Cherril. Could she and Mycroft come over for a moment? Of course Aunty Lee said yes. She was only surprised they had called to ask first. Neighbors usually just shouted from the gate if they wanted to drop in. Aunty Lee hoped Mycroft was not pressuring Cherril to drop the catering business. This was not purely selfish on her part. Aunty Lee thought Cherril and Mycroft were a good match but how many careers would Cherril think worth sacrificing for this marriage? And Aunty Lee was glad to have a chance to ask Mycroft about the running of law firms.

Inspector Salim was also thinking over the people Mabel Sung and her son had left behind as he drove himself home. From observing Henry Sung's body language when he took a phone call, Salim suspected the older man already had someone on the side. It might not be relevant of course. And there had been tension between Sharon and Mabel's assistant GraceFaith. But what had Edmond Yong been doing at the Sung Law office?

The easiest solution for everyone would be if this turned out to be an accidental *buah keluak* poisoning. The newspapers would run articles on the dangers of *buah keluak* alongside photos of Mabel Sung, new restrictions on importing it would be set up, and the whole business would be forgotten . . . along with Aunty Lee's Delights.

At Aunty Lee's house, Mycroft Peters was saying much the same thing to Aunty Lee.

She had served a dessert soup; rice-flour balls stuffed with peanut paste served in hot, sweet ginger broth that was both stimulating and soothing.

"You can't tell that the rice balls came out of the freezer, can you?" Aunty Lee asked.

Instead of answering, Mycroft got straight to the point.

"You may be in trouble because of this *buah keluak* business."

"I tell you, my chicken *buah keluak* had nothing to do with what happened to Mabel and her son. So many people ate it, I ate it myself, why nobody else got sick?"

"That's not relevant. The Sungs are important people. Mabel Sung was a real pain but she had connections. If these people decide to make trouble for you, it could be very messy."

"I thought they were supposed to be so Christian," Cherril said sullenly. "Aren't they supposed to forgive and forget?"

"People like them crush whatever they don't like, so there is nothing left to forgive or forget."

But he didn't say anything about Cherril leaving the partnership. Aunty Lee guessed that had already been discussed and dismissed.

"My mother knew Mabel from school. She didn't like her. Used to call her 'porridge face,'" Mycroft said. "Mum said Mabel Sung had a dangerously elevated sense of her own importance and entitlement. Dad said as a lawyer she would bend the law to get what she wanted. I just don't like the idea of you people coming up against her. You are nice people. You don't know how people in her league fight."

"Mykie, she's already dead. There's no reason for us to be scared of her now."

"She's dead but you don't know what someone like her left behind. And this is confidential." He lowered his voice, "But Mabel Sung cashed out her personal insurance some months before she died. So she can't have been killed for that."

"She could have, if the killer didn't know Mabel cashed it out and still hoped to get the money," Cherril persisted.

"If you're going through all the trouble of planning a murder, I'm sure you would check up on that," Mycroft said genially. It was clear he didn't take his wife's murder-solving hobby very seriously. But it was also obvious that he was very fond of her. In Aunty Lee's mind, that made up for a multitude of defects.

"How do you know Mabel Sung cashed out her personal insurance?"

Mycroft shook his head. Aunty Lee knew there was no use pushing him further.

"Okay, you don't have to tell me how you know. But I heard Mabel Sung stopped taking on new cases and clients after her son came back to Singapore. Like that can also do business, ah?"

"If the firm has strong retainers—sure it's possible. But Sung Law . . . let's just say that it wasn't in very good shape. They weren't taking on cases because all the lawyers who could find anything else have jumped ship. There's even talk of them filing claims that Mabel was financing her religious group with company money. Not that they're going to get anything. Sung Law is verging on bankruptcy. Maybe Sharon Sung can pull things together, but if I were in her position I wouldn't bother."

Salim smelled his mother's cooking as he got out of the lift. It reminded him it was "cook a pot of curry" day. This year was the first time Aunty Lee had missed coming round to the station with a pot (or several) of her curries in various degrees of chili heat.

At his mother's flat there were several neighbors sitting around the table and they called out greetings to Salim as he took off his shoes at the door.

"Quick, go and wash and come and *makan*. Mrs. Kumar brought mutton curry and Vera brought *petai*." Salim also saw his mother's *ayam masak merah,* the golden-brown pieces of fried chicken in spicy tomato sauce that made him look around for—

"Yes, here is your tomato rice. In the kitchen because no space on the table. Go and wash, quick." His mother was already setting out a plate with a mound of his favorite rice.

They were laughing affectionately at him, these old neighbors who had become an extended family.

It felt good to be hungry knowing there was good food to come. Money was not everything. Salim thought of the Sungs in their grand empty house and was grateful for his humble family home. His mother would cook for him as long as she lived. All she wanted was for him to marry and have children before she died. He was the only child left at home now. He put the rich, dead people out of his mind as he washed himself. There were unvoiced problems at home too. The subject of his marriage and future, for one. But that could wait. At least till after the curry dinner.

Then his cell phone rang. His hands dirty, he let it go directly to voice mail: "I know who that man trying to get in the gate at the Sungs' house reminds me of!"

13

Police HQ

At Aunty Lee's Delights

"Are you going to the service for Mabel Sung? I suppose they haven't asked you to cater it—ha ha."

"Are you and Mark going?" Aunty Lee asked Selina. She suspected Mark and Selina happened to "just drop by" the shop to find out whether she had been closed down.

"I don't think so. I don't think Mabel Sung would remember me," Selina said. Aunty Lee managed not to interrupt to say that the dead Mabel Sung would not remember anybody. Unless of course she was looking back from the beyond with all her memories intact, in which case she was as likely to remember Selina as anyone else.

"Anyway, I heard Sharon is planning everything. You know how people always put 'No Donations' when they announce such things, or 'All donations will go to . . . whatever abandoned-cats or lame-dogs or sick-babies charity the dead person supported? Apparently Sharon didn't. She's just going to let her mother's friends pay for her mother's funeral."

"Poor girl," Aunty Lee said. "Maybe she forgot. It must be so difficult to plan a funeral for somebody who might have been either a murderer or victim. I know there's supposed to be an Order of Service to cover every possible case, but I haven't seen this one yet. Anyway, I'm sure all Mabel's friends will want to help."

"They're a lot of old busybodies who want to see what's happening."

Aunty Lee thought that was probably true and all the more reason for being there.

"I should go. Just to show them there's no hard feelings. After all, we all have to go one day."

Though death was not something people usually prepared for, Aunty Lee liked to be prepared for everything. She was almost sidetracked into wondering what would be served at her own funeral, perhaps she ought to draw up a menu in advance (curry puffs, perhaps; a reminder to take pleasure in life while you still could) just to make things easier for Nina or Mathilda or whoever had to plan that day . . . but she pulled her mind away from this tantalizing thought. Always deal with the current funeral first, she reminded herself. There would be plenty of time to plan her own later.

In Commissioner Raja's Office, New Phoenix Park Police HQ

"Tell them they can go ahead and have whatever services they want but we cannot release the bodies to them until we finish with them."

"Sir, they are not happy about that. In fact they are not happy that we are performing autopsies without their permission and without letting them observe."

"Say whatever you have to, to keep them happy. But we cannot release the bodies to them until we are finished with them."

Commissioner Raja's aide left his room to face the angry Sungs.

Commissioner Raja turned to look at Inspector Salim, who had sat quietly, apparently uninvolved, through the exchange.

"Satisfied?"

"Thank you. We just need to give the labs a bit more time to make us all satisfied."

"That's not the only reason I asked you here today. I hear you paid a visit to an NMP yesterday, Mycroft Peters?"

Commissioner Raja was one of those keeping an eye on Inspector Salim in the Bukit Tinggi Neighborhood Police Post. A great many influential people had homes in the area and it was vital that they felt safe in the hands of Inspector Salim. And now Nominated Member of Parliament Mycroft Peters, one of the most influential of those people, had complained.

"I got the feeling Mr. Peters was not comfortable with his

wife talking to us, sir," Salim said. "But he did not indicate he intended to make a complaint."

"Did you get anything useful from the interview?"

"No, sir."

"Did you expect to?"

Staff Sergeant Panchal had appeared confident she could get something useful from Cherril. Salim, who thought she was following up a hunch and believed it was important to empower his staff, had backed her up. But then back at the station the officer had admitted that her intention had been to record Cherril saying it might have been the *buah keluak* that killed Mabel and Leonard. In Panchal's words, "Mrs. Peters is not a cook. She doesn't know what she's doing. All we had to do is get her to say maybe it was her fault and we can slam a fine on them and wrap up this stupid case. But you saw how her lawyer husband wouldn't let her say anything."

Salim did not say anything either. He would save it for Panchal's assessment report.

But it was as Panchal's supervising officer that Salim now said, "I had to follow up all possible leads, sir."

Fortunately Panchal's clumsy attempt at entrapment had not been too obvious. And the governing party would be pleased to have "nobody is above the law" so plainly and publicly demonstrated. Sometimes it was as important to show they were investigating as to actually investigate. Commissioner Raja waited for Salim to put it in words while Salim waited for Commissioner Raja to acknowledge that some facts were best accepted unspoken.

"What do you suggest I do with the complaint from My-croft Peters that the police have been harassing his wife at her home as well as at her place of work?"

"I will send an apology, sir. But, sir—it was too short a visit to ask questions. Nothing that could be interpreted as ha-rassment."

"Yes, I agree. The fact Mr. Peters took the trouble to file a complaint over this is interesting, but what you make of it is up to you. Putting that aside for the moment I also have a complaint from Staff Sergeant Neha Panchal, currently serving at Bukit Tinggi Police Post. She says that your close friendship and ties with residents in the area is obstructing you from carrying out your duties. She says she repeatedly recommended you shut down the café that provided the food that caused two deaths but you ignored all evidence and refused."

"The forensic evidence is not in yet, sir. Aunty Lee's De-lights has been in operation for almost three years now and we have not received any other complaints about them. And, sir, may I point out Mr. Peters's complaint regarding harass-ment at his wife's place of work contradicts SS Panchal's com-plaint?"

Commissioner Raja sighed. He not only had a law degree from a Singapore university but degrees in criminology and criminal psychology from Cambridge and Harvard. Though most of the time he did his best to conceal the facts of his education, it occasionally proved useful.

"She is an ambitious officer?"

"I believe she is trying to do what she thinks is right."

"You don't agree with her methods?"

"We don't even agree on what's right, sir."

Commissioner Raja allowed himself a wry laugh. "Sorry to haul you down here. But best to get these things out of the way as fast as possible. And it's easier to clear up things face-to-face."

"Not a problem at all, sir. In fact it's good I came by HQ."

"Okay, what else do you have on your mind. I can tell there's something."

"It's a 'who' actually. And she sent you these curry puffs."

Elsewhere in New Phoenix Park

Staff Sergeant Timothy Pang was staring at the computer monitor in his cubicle. Tim Pang was one of very few men who found good looks a disadvantage. He suspected his looks had blocked his boyhood dreams of becoming a detective. His superiors were always joking (at least he hoped they were joking) that SS Timothy Pang was only useful as bait for toilet vice raids. Even now, in International Affairs, colleagues were constantly asking him out for drinks and trying to set him up for dinners with their daughters, their sisters, or themselves. He was still very new to the department—perhaps this was just how they welcomed all new staff?

So it was not surprising that Timothy winced when footsteps approached his cubicle, heralding the interruption of his report writing.

"Tim! How are they treating you in Special Ops?"

"Staff Sergeant! I mean Inspector Salim!" Timothy whirled around and rose to his feet in one smooth move. "Inspector Salim, good to see you, sir. What are you doing here? Can I do anything for you?"

"Are you free? Have you got a couple of minutes to spare?"

These days SS Timothy Pang felt he was never free, yet nothing ever seemed to be achieved or accomplished. Now his biggest frustration with criminals was the amount of administration paperwork they generated. But paperwork, like the poor, would always be with them, and Inspector Salim would not be visiting without reason.

"Buy you a coffee, sir? Not as good as in the old place, unfortunately—"

Timothy Pang had once thought Salim Mawar unambitious and the Bukit Tinggi posting dull. Now he appreciated his former boss's fairness and avoidance of favoritism. And he missed the food in the vicinity of his previous posting!

"You miss the old place?"

"Yes, every day—every lunchtime and break time, to be precise!"

"Someone there misses you too." Salim gestured to the doorway, launching a multicolored whirlwind that had been held back till now.

"Yes! That's who that man at the gate reminded me of! Of course I know it wasn't Timmy Pang. But so much like! Timmy, do you have any brothers? Or any cousins who look like you?"

Staff Sergeant Pang grinned to see the short, stocky

woman who somehow managed to look soignée in an embroidered pink blouse, pink-and-yellow floral sarong skirt,
and pink-and-white sneakers. Aunty Lee had dressed up in
all her finery for this visit to the police headquarters but she
must have left her decorum back at the shop as she flew over
to throw her arms around him.

"Aunty Lee, good to see you again!" Aunty Lee's frequent
treats had been one of the things Timothy Pang missed most
about his previous posting. It was a sign of his sweet nature
that he was as glad to see Aunty Lee as he was to see the
basket Nina carried in her wake. His new colleagues were
already looking up and sniffing.

"Timmy, I must tell you this funny thing that happened.
Last week I was catering a party and a man that looked so
much like you came to the house. He looked so familiar but
at the same time not familiar at all; it was driving me crazy.
But now of course I understand why. Timmy, he looked so
much like you but he was not you!"

"You have a brother who looks like you?" Salim asked.

There were times Timothy Pang wished he did not have
a brother, especially not one like the brother he had. Their
lives ran on strictly separate tracks, but now it seemed his
brother had done a crossover.

"I have one brother. People say we look alike but I don't see
it myself. Why didn't you just ask him?"

"They wouldn't let him in the gate. I thought the doctor
was going to break his arm! Then they found the dead bodies
and I didn't get the chance to go after him."

"The dead bodies?"

Aunty Lee nodded many times, "Yes, yes, yes!"

Inspector Salim nodded once.

"Come with me," said Staff Sergeant Timothy Pang as he headed for another door. "The meeting rooms should be free—Kiruthiga, I'm taking the key to room one—"

"Kiruthiga? Please try some of my special buttery pineapple tarts," Aunty Lee said, pushig the box at her as she followed in Timothy's wake.

"Something about your jaw and forehead is quite distinctive . . ." Aunty Lee said as they settled around the small table, Nina taking a chair by the door.

One of Timothy's new colleagues appeared with cups of coffee and was rewarded with golden pastries and instructions to make sure they were not disturbed.

"I haven't seen much of Patrick since he moved out of our parents' place."

Timothy Pang still lived among his noisy extended family in Queenstown, the Housing Development Board estate they had grown up in. His mother's sisters' families and his father's cousins and children all lived within walking distance. Timothy hoped to get his own flat in the same area someday (on his marriage or thirty-fifth birthday, whichever came first). Patrick had got as far away as possible, as fast as possible.

"Pat was a music teacher for a while but I think most of his money comes from writing songs for other people to record.

He even wrote one of the National Day songs a few years back. Actually he called me last month, said a friend of his was missing. But he didn't want to file a missing persons."

"What did he want you to do?" Salim asked.

Timothy Pang could not shrug his shoulders to a senior officer, no matter how friendly, so he said nothing.

"That friend of his. You didn't think he was missing?"

"He's missing all right. But I don't know whether he's missing on purpose."

"Ah."

"Ben Ng," Aunty Lee supplied.

Timothy nodded. "I think that was the name. Yes."

"Why makes you think he's missing on purpose?"

"No reason. Just that Pat's friends are sometimes . . . no reason."

"Do you know what kind of work his friend was doing for the Sungs?"

"I didn't ask." Timothy saw Salim make a note of this and wished he had paid more attention to his brother.

"Why don't we go and visit your brother?" Aunty Lee proposed brightly.

"What? Now?"

"Why not? I got some extra *kueh* in the car we can bring."

Timothy looked at Inspector Salim. It was Salim's turn to say nothing. Most important, he did not say no.

"All right. But not right away. Let me talk to him first and I'll get back to you."

Pat answered his phone immediately.

"*Kor?*" Timothy automatically used the Chinese honorific for older brother. "It's Tim. Can you meet me?"

"It's Ben. He's dead, isn't he?"

They met downstairs of Patrick's flat in a recently upgraded estate and went to the hawker center food court nearby. It was early for lunch, not quite eleven thirty, but in Singapore a meal is always the best solution to initial awkwardness. Patrick, who knew the area, bought *mee kia* for both of them.

The teasingly rich and tender freshness of perfectly cooked pork liver was the taste of loving nurture, however fleeting. Along with crispy fried cubes of lard and the slightest sheen of vinegar, the enticingly chewy *mee kia* linked the brothers to each other and their shared childhood.

"That time you called you said a friend of yours is missing." Timothy Pang pushed his empty bowl aside. "Still haven't heard from him?"

Patrick shook his head. "He's not just a friend. He's—a very good friend." He took a sip of his plum juice to prepare himself. Timothy Pang suddenly felt an irrational panic rising and had to stop himself from pushing back his stool and shouting, "Don't tell me! I don't want to know!"

Instead he said, "It hasn't been so long, you know."

"Almost two months now."

Timothy shook his head. "Don't worry, that's not long at all. People go away, they forget to tell their friends—it's no big deal."

Patrick sat silently, obviously unconvinced.

"Anyway, it's up to his family to file a missing-persons

report if they are worried. Your friend might just have gone on a holiday or something."

"His family is all in Malaysia. I got in touch with them, they haven't heard from him. I don't think they know he's missing yet. He didn't really stay in touch with them so . . ."

If Patrick disappeared how long would it be before his brother and parents noticed? Timothy wondered. He eyed the hot and cold desserts stall, debating whether a *chendol* or *tau suan* would be most worth the calories. His pork noodles had been satisfying but this difficult conversation needed a sweet touch.

"Wait till the family gets worried. For all you know, your buddy met someone special and isn't ready to tell the rest of you yet. You want *chendol*?"

"No. If Ben met someone else he would have told me. He was very excited about this big job he was doing at the Sungs' place. He said soon he would have enough money to buy us a place together. He didn't tell me much but I know he was designing some end-of-life home-care system. He was doing a special power supply and life-support monitors and everything and he said he was going to get paid a lot. The last time I saw him he was going to do a final system test and collect his check. He told me he would buy champagne on the way back. I bought steaks to grill when he got back. But he never came. And the ceremony was supposed to be last Saturday—"

Staff Sergeant Timothy Pang looked at his brother. Patrick met his gaze, saying nothing till his younger brother asked.

"Ceremony?"

"We were going to exchange vows, have a commitment ceremony. I know it won't be legal here but we wanted to."

There was a long silence. Patrick did not know why he had said so much. Timothy Pang was a police officer, even if he was Patrick's brother.

"How long have you two been together?"

"Five years now."

Was Timothy going to play the police-officer role and cross-examine instead of help him? It was too much, on top of all the friends who he knew assumed Ben had got cold feet and run off. Patrick struggled to his feet, unbalancing his plastic stool so that it tumbled over.

"Wait." Timothy reached across the table and took his brother's wrist in a firm grasp. "*Kor*, I'm sorry."

"Sorry? Sorry about what? What are you going to do?"

"I'm sorry I didn't know. I'm sorry you never told me you found somebody special."

Patrick stared uncertainly, all his panicked bravado melting. He remembered his quiet younger brother again. A year younger, Timothy had somehow managed to be outside Patrick's classroom at recess time every day for two months after class bullies gave him a black eye. They had sensed he was different even then. He didn't know what Timothy had sensed. Timothy had already been a school hero, a Schools Nationals judo champion and captain of the mixed-martial-arts team. Somehow the features that looked so effeminate on Patrick had made Timothy the most handsome boy in school. And every day he had been there on the flimsiest pretexts. "*Kor*, can you explain this maths problem to me?"

"*Kor,* I forgot my money, can you lend me fifty cents?" Timothy's presence had been enough to ensure Patrick was never picked on again.

Suddenly Patrick was close to tears. He could not remember why he had so dreaded telling his brother.

"I thought you would be angry." It was easier to say "angry" than "ashamed" or "disgusted."

"Of course I'm angry with you. I'm furious. You plan to have a commitment ceremony and never tell your only brother. Who wouldn't be furious?

Patrick could not speak.

"Look," Staff Sergeant Timothy Pang said. "We'll find him somehow. But if I find out this guy walked out on you without a word, I'm going to disappear him myself!"

14

Patrick Pang's Flat

"You sure it's okay for them to come here to talk to you?" Timothy looked around the small front room. There was an anniversary photograph of their parents on a side table, next to one of himself receiving a framed commendation. The latter looked as though it had been cut out of the newspaper and slipped into an IKEA frame. Timothy felt moved. He had always assumed Pat thought himself too good for his family and wanted nothing to do with them.

Though there was no good reason, the thought of Aunty Lee and Inspector Salim coming to visit and possibly investigating his brother was making SS Timothy Pang uncomfortable.

"Yes, it's okay. I want to talk to anybody who might help."

"You want to come back for dinner tonight? Ma and Pa would be happy to see you."

No they wouldn't, Patrick thought.

"Not tonight," he said. "Thanks."

Patrick Pang and Benjamin Ng rented a flat on the top floor of one of the older Housing Development Board projects. The weather- and water-stained common space beneath the block and wheezing lift showed their age, but the grime-stained walls concealed higher ceilings and larger rooms than would be found in newer housing projects.

As the lift made its way up slowly, Aunty Lee thought how unfortunate it was that public housing was shrinking as the population grew in size and number. In contrast to the faded gray walls on the ground floor, on the nineteenth floor the wall of the open corridor leading to Patrick and Benjamin's apartment was painted pale peach. As Aunty Lee walked with Inspector Salim toward the unit at the farthest end of the corridor, painted birds and butterflies appeared on the wall, then twining tendrils and leaves and trees leading to an arrangement of potted dwarf palms, bougainvillea, and flowering sweet peas that flanked the dark wooden doorway. There was a pleasant warm breeze carrying a hint of sea salt from the shining waters far away and far below that could just be glimpsed in between the other buildings around them.

Aunty Lee was intrigued. Something about these plants and painted walls signaled an important connection but she could not pin it down yet. One drawback of growing older was how many more memories there were to sift through before you found what you wanted. Aunty Lee had never liked the idea of living on anything higher than the third floor (what if the lifts broke down?) but at the moment, to her surprise, she found it very pleasant being elevated high above the noise and business of city life.

"I'm sure this is illegal," Inspector Salim murmured. "Graffiti is not allowed on public walls without permission. And fire regulations state that common corridors should be left clear."

"But it looks nice," Aunty Lee said.

Salim pressed the doorbell (the belly button of a miniature laughing Buddha statue) and was rewarded by a cacophony of birdsong. He winced. Aunty Lee was delighted.

"Yes! You are the one! I saw you at the Sungs' house trying to get in the gate that day when the people died!"

Patrick had stood up as his brother let the old lady and police inspector in.

"Yes, it was me. But I didn't get in, I didn't see anything. Timothy said you wanted to talk to me about Benjamin?"

"Yes, but I want to talk to you about a lot of other things as well. Can we come in?"

"Yes. Of course. I'm sorry. Please don't take off your shoes," Patrick said with automatic politeness. The young man was genuinely distressed, Aunty Lee thought. The dark circles under his eyes and the weary tension in his shoulders showed he had been under stress for some time. And under stress he was polite.

"Have you found a body? Do you need a sample of his DNA? Benjamin's dead, isn't he? I knew it!"

"We haven't found anyone. This is not an official visit," Salim said calmly. "We just need to ask you a few questions—unofficially."

He bent to unlace his shoes before slowly slipping them off. Aunty Lee, who had slipped off her pink-and-white sneakers in a flash, watched Patrick use the time to take a deep breath.

"If you haven't found him then he's probably still alive, right?"

"We just want to ask you a few questions," Salim repeated. "We should make sure he's really missing and not just gone off on holiday or something without telling you. If he just took off and forgot to let you know, he wouldn't thank you for making a police report."

"He wouldn't do that. But I know what you mean. I did try to make an official police report but I couldn't because I'm not a family member. That was even before I called Timothy. By the time I went to the Sungs' house, I was desperate."

His voice shook slightly. Aunty Lee felt sorry for him.

"This is a very nice apartment. But isn't it hot staying on the top floor?" Aunty Lee asked with genuine interest.

"Ben likes it because there are no ugly pipes in the toilets and kitchen. I'm sorry, please come and sit down. I like it because there are no neighbors above us to stamp on the ceiling or drag things around and no laundry and rubbish dropping into our drying area."

"And in older flats like this, people are less likely to complain about you painting on the wall," Aunty Lee said.

"Oh yes. Ben painted those. He had some exhibitions in

galleries and they liked his stuff. Some Italian magazine even came to take photos of the paintings in the corridor. Of course they couldn't say where it was because it's illegal."

Neither of the police officers appeared to hear this. Aunty Lee carried on.

"He is an artist? Wah! But your friend Benjamin is also an architect and an engineer, right? So multitalented. He used to design buildings and he worked on a project for Mabel Sung?"

"Yes he is." Patrick assumed Aunty Lee was a friend of the Sungs. "Ben still did some architectural design on the side. He was really good at it but he didn't want to work for any of the big companies and he didn't like running a business himself, so he ended up taking on freelance work."

"Why didn't you say so earlier? *Kor*, your friend disappeared after working on a project for two people who end up dead and you don't even mention the fact?"

"He disappeared last month—almost two months ago. Long before anybody ended up dead."

And those people had died right after Patrick tried to force his way into their house. Not good, Salim thought.

"What exactly was the purpose of the building your friend constructed for the Sungs?"

"I don't know. He didn't know, he was just following their specifications. He thought it was some kind of geriatric home-care system. For end-of-life home care."

"They paid him in advance?" Aunty Lee asked. "I hope he got a deposit at least."

"No, he didn't!" Patrick burst out. "And it's not as though they can't afford it. I saw the size of their property. You could build a condo in there. Two condos. With a gym and pool. But they didn't give him an advance, they even didn't pay him for all the planning proposals he drew up for them. They said that since he was overseeing the construction and setup, they would pay him everything in one lump sum at the end. Maybe they never meant to pay him. Maybe they just locked him up somewhere on the grounds—"

Or in the pool house, Aunty Lee thought.

"Maybe we should get you a lawyer," Timothy Pang interrupted, the brother in him overpowering the policeman. "Maybe you shouldn't say too much right now."

But Patrick had a question for Aunty Lee: "Did they tell you Ben designed their building? They were so hypersecretive he had to sign a confidentiality contract even. And that *goondu* went and signed it without getting a written contract. So he didn't have any proof he had done the work, but if he complained about not getting paid they could sue him. Crazy, right?"

Goondu indeed, Aunty Lee thought. But often the innocent and trusting were seen as silly and foolish by the rest of the world. And too often they suffered for it.

Timothy's phone buzzed and he moved away to mutter into it. It sounded to Aunty Lee as though he was trying to get someone to meet him and his brother, but partway through the conversation, another call must have cut in because he switched into an explanation of how stopping to fix a tire on the expressway for an old man had led to a migraine and a messed-up uniform and if there was nothing urgent at the station he was going to head straight home . . .

"Did the Sungs tell you Ben built the home ICU for them?" Patrick said to Aunty Lee, too softly to catch Timothy's attention.

"No."

"Then how did you know?"

"I guessed. The paintings on the walls here and outside," Aunty Lee said. "Your friend painted them, right? I saw the painting on the side of the building at the Sungs' place, by the pool. The creeper with leaves that looked like it was climbing up the wall."

"Oh, that. Yes. Ben showed me photos. His artist side keeps coming up. I've still got them somewhere. He was very proud of how he got the green of the leaves to exactly match the green of the pool."

"The pool wasn't green." Aunty Lee remembered the brilliant blue tiles at the bottom of the swimming pool.

"Yes it was. You can see it in the photos. I'll show you—"

The pool water in the photographs was indeed arrestingly green. Aunty Lee could see why it had caught the artist's eye.

"He's a very striking artist. And trained as an architect?" Aunty Lee said. "Very interesting. I would like to see some more of his work."

"Actually I'm not sure it's very suitable."

"Good. Suitable art is just propaganda. Can you boil some water? I brought some of my homemade chrysanthemum and wolfberry tea sachets. Very good for calming down the

system and giving you energy at the same time. Those cups
will be fine. I'll just give them a quick rinse . . . while the
water is boiling you go and bring me your friend's 'unsuit-
able' work. And if you can find it, I want the address of the
shop where you got the singing-birds doorbell from."

"These folders here are just his artwork. Private artwork."

They were indeed collections of Benjamin's erotic art.
Salim and Timothy turned away, embarrassed, so it was Aunty
Lee who found a folder containing architectural sketches
inside, several e-mails, and extensive notes comparing the
merits of oxygenating blood in gas-filled hollow fibers (effective but short term—best for use in operating theaters)
versus homogeneous membranes (approved for long-term
life support).

And something else.

"I think that's the new device he told me about. Instead
of making the heart beat, it has spinning rotors that circulate the blood. After all, humans don't fly by flapping wings,
humans don't have to circulate blood by heartbeats."

"So which of those things did he install?" Inspector Salim
asked.

"Both." Timothy looked grimly through the receipts. "It
looks as though money was no problem. Though of course
it wasn't his own money he was using. At least we can track
who paid."

"You don't have to track very far." Aunty Lee held up a
receipt signed by GraceFaith.

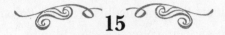

15

Information

The next day Aunty Lee filled Cherril and Nina in on what she had learned at Patrick Pang's flat. Having time to talk was one small advantage of the drop in business at Aunty Lee's Delights.

Benjamin Ng had designed and supervised construction of a home-based life-support system and ICU on the Sungs' property. Patrick Pang thought it likely that Edmond Yong had introduced Benjamin to the Sungs, as Benjamin had also designed Dr. Yong's aesthetic medicine clinic, Beautiful Dreamers, a few years back.

"He said that was also a bit under the table because some of those beauty procedures they are not supposed to do in clinics."

"I've been to the Bukit Timah Plaza clinic," Cherril said.

"I think it got destroyed by fire last year. That's probably why Dr. Yong took the job looking after Leonard Sung. Otherwise it doesn't make sense. He was a very ambitious sort. Always signing up for those get-rich-in-twenty-four-hours and getting-to-know-useful-people courses. He had shelves of those books in his office in the clinic. I would have trusted him more if he had had medical books."

"And Otto called me last night," Aunty Lee said. "He said Patrick Pang got in touch with him and asked him whether I could be trusted." She paused, beaming.

"What did Otto say?" Cherril asked obligingly. Aunty Lee had only met Otto and his partner, Joe, the previous year but after solving murders and family issues together they were closer than most blood relatives.

"Dear Otto. He said he told Patrick I'm wonderful and his favorite aunty and he would totally trust me with his crown jewels." Aunty Lee laughed gleefully. "Anyway, Otto had no idea Benjamin had done a job for the Sungs. He said he would have warned him if he'd known. He had all kinds of stories about Leonard Sung. Apparently this boy was mean and a bully and he could be really nasty."

"Maybe he just don't like gay," Nina suggested. She was not entirely comfortable with homosexuals herself, or with Aunty Lee's lack of discrimination.

"I don't like people who put oysters in *laksa* but I don't pick on them."

"Yes you do, Aunty Lee."

"Okay, maybe I do. But that is such a waste of oysters and *laksa*. Anyway, that's not the point. Otto said Leonard was a troublemaker right from his school days. He didn't just bully the other boys. One time he picked on a trainee teacher that all the other boys liked. He thought it would be a great joke to seduce her and tie her up and take photos. He told all the other boys what he was going to do. Then he went after Miss Rozario. He brought her expensive presents, offered her free weekend getaways on the excuse of tutoring him, told her he would take her to dinner on a no-limit credit card . . . but Miss Rozario told him to get lost. She even reported him to the school for stalking her. Otto said all the rest of the boys thought it was a huge joke. They liked the teacher all the more. But it was a shock for Leonard.

"Otto thought Leonard had a crush on Miss Rozario. But the only way he could relate to a woman was to try to humiliate her. And that was probably the first time he realized money couldn't buy everything. After that Leonard did everything he could to make life hell for Miss Rozario. In the end she left the school and Leonard said driving her away was what he meant to do all along. People thought he was like his dad, just smiling and not bothering with anything. But actually he was like his mum. He had to get what he wanted once he set his mind on it. He didn't care what it cost. He just didn't want the same things as the other boys because he already had them. And he thought it was a huge joke to get people into trouble. Leonard got kicked out of Otto's school after charges were filed against him for beating up a girl he met at a gaming outlet because she wouldn't go back to his room with him. Then in his next school he took photos of schoolmates using recreational drugs and put them online. He called it 'Singapore drug bust.' "

"Leonard disapproved of people using drugs?" Cherril was surprised, given what she knew of the dead boy.

"Otto gave me the impression Leonard disapproved of people using drugs they hadn't bought from him. In fact, by the time he was sixteen Leonard Sung was boasting that he didn't need his parents' money because he was already earning more than they ever would."

It sounded as though Leonard Sung could also have made more enemies than his parents ever did.

"But Leonard was really in bad health, right? He wasn't just pretending, to get away from people?" By now Cherril was ready to believe anything of him.

"Otto thinks he was really sick. Leonard used to say that he would die before going back to Singapore."

"So maybe he's the one who killed himself and his mother?"

Aunty Lee remembered the emaciated figure she had seen dead on his bed. Leonard Sung had been severely underweight, his bones sticking out prominently. His skin was covered with rashes and warts as well as bluish-purple swellings.

"If Leonard poisoned them somebody had to help him. He couldn't have got the poison without help. I don't think he could have got out of bed without help."

"His mother, then."

"That would be the same thing as her doing it. And I don't think Mabel Sung would have. If anybody, I think it was that doctor who was supposed to be looking after him."

Aunty Lee would have liked to pin the blame on Dr. Edmond Yong. She hadn't liked the way he tried to impress people with his importance and connections. But would this doctor have killed a paying patient? Aunty Lee didn't think so, going by how he had devoured her food at the buffet.

Aunty Lee learned as much about people from watching them eat as from listening to them talk. It was not only a matter of what they ate but how they ate that revealed the most about them. This had less to do with table manners than their relationship with food. Because this relationship with the food that nourished them grounded their relationship with themselves and everyone else.

That Saturday Aunty Lee had watched Edmond Yong go for the more expensive dishes, like her chicken *buah keluak*, almost shoveling the food into his mouth with the practiced skill of one who did not know when another chance might come round. It was very hard not to like someone who appreciated her food, but Edmond Yong had not been eating. He had been systematically filling himself up like someone pulling up to a gas station and demanding, "Full tank." And even after he was full Dr. Yong had lurked around the buffet, slyly scraping clumps of juicy (and pricey) crab roe off shrimp patties with his fingers. What was left on the plate had had to be discarded. Aunty Lee was sure that a man capable of such wanton waste was capable of wanton killing. She just did not think Edmond Yong was the kind of man who would murder his own meal ticket.

But who else? Aunty Lee thought back over the eaters at the party that had barely begun before ending so tragically.

Though it was her party, Sharon Sung had eaten hardly anything.

And now it seemed Sharon was already back at work, trying to take over where her mother had left off. Some found this surprising but Aunty Lee did not find it strange at all. Sharon was probably trying to work through her grief like Aunty Lee had done after her husband's death.

During that terrible time (worse even than the time leading up to his death because there was no focus and no hope) the people who kept telling her "Rest" or "Take things easy" had not understood what she needed at all. It was not one's body that needed rest and comfort at such a time. It was one's heart and life that had been terribly amputated, and sitting and brooding over the bloody mess left behind was more torture than comfort.

No, if Sharon could lose herself in taking over her mother's work, then Aunty Lee would leave her to it. But Sharon's discomfort around food had also been painfully obvious even as she prepared food for her brother. Or had it been her brother she disliked? Otto seemed to think Leonard Sung's parents were blind to his dark side, but his sister must have known what he was like. Aunty Lee wondered whether Sharon Sung was one of those people who were so uncomfortable with food that they could only eat when no one was watching. She had put the meal together efficiently enough for Leonard but had not eaten anything herself, beyond taste-checking what she got him. Aunty Lee grabbed on to the thought.

"I saw Sharon Sung tasting the *buah keluak* she took for her brother. So either the poison that killed Mabel Sung and her son was put into the *buah keluak* after Sharon delivered it or it was never in the *buah keluak* at all. They just swallowed pills or something."

"Or Sharon put the poison in after tasting it," Cherril suggested. "Or GraceFaith. I saw her taking the tray from Sharon. I think she just wanted an excuse to go up to the house."

Aunty Lee had seen GraceFaith up in the house herself.

"And speaking of funny business, I want to find out what that Doreen Choo was really doing inside that house and where she went. One minute she was there talking to me and then suddenly she was gone."

"Maybe she slipped off to poison Mabel. Maybe it's your friend Doreen who got Mabel out of the way so that she could get Henry Sung for herself?" Cherril suggested.

Aunty Lee stared at her. "She wouldn't do that," she said.

"Why not?"

"Anyway, Doreen Choo is already seeing Henry Sung," Nina put in.

"Doreen Choo? Never! I don't believe it!" Aunty Lee said with relish. This went with what she had already observed but disbelief usually drew out more information.

"Even when her boring old husband was alive, that woman never had affairs with anybody. Why would she bother to now?"

"She dresses very nicely, ma'am. And she always goes to the hairdresser to make her hair black."

Aunty Lee's lack of dress finesse was a sore point with Nina, who felt it reflected badly on her. Her bringing up Doreen's efforts in an attempt to inspire her boss told Aunty Lee that she was feeling more optimistic about their situation.

"Anyway, Doreen is not going to mess up her black hair and her makeup and her nice dress by having an affair. Who did you get that from?"

"My friend's cousin is working for Doreen Choo's neighbor in the same condo, opposite Botanic Gardens there," Nina said. Aunty Lee would never betray her sources but she had to know who they were before she trusted their information. Nina had been through the same process when buying sun-dried anchovies and fresh tempeh.

"She said almost every night Henry Sung goes to Doreen Choo's house for dinner and he does not leave until eleven something. They go to the healing prayer meetings together."

"Still? But the boy is dead already. And Mabel is dead, so who is running this?"

"Always got other people to pray for, madam. Sometimes his daughter also goes. And her boyfriend."

It did not sound like any kind of affair to Aunty Lee. And did Sharon Sung have a boyfriend? Aunty Lee cast her mind back to what she had seen of the girl. No, Sharon Sung was a young woman with an obsession but it was not for any man.

"Does your friend know where the meetings are?"

"No, ma'am. Doreen Choo's maid is from Myanmar. She only just came to Singapore three months ago and does not speak much English."

"You must have other friends from Myanmar."

"Of course, ma'am."

"You should get one of them to go and talk to Doreen's

maid. The poor girl, so new to Singapore and not knowing anybody. It must be so difficult for her."

"Ma'am, how can? We don't know her. And if she is from Myanmar she will not get Sunday off."

Aunty Lee filed this away to follow up on later. "I want to go to one of those healing meetings. I also want to find out more about what Tim's brother's boyfriend built for Mabel Sung. And what that PRC woman was doing at Mabel Sung's house."

"Maybe she wants to marry a Singapore doctor," Cherril suggested. "Not every Chinese visitor is part of a gang." She had heard Aunty Lee's story about foiling the PRC gang enough times to suspect that was where the old lady's thoughts were going.

"Dr. Yong is Malaysian, not Singaporean. If that girl wanted a Singapore husband she could find a much better one than that. No, she was there to do some funny business."

"Anyway, we don't know someone wanted to kill Mabel. What about her son? From what you said it sounds like plenty of people had reason to dislike him. Maybe someone wanted to kill him and Mabel was just collateral damage."

"There was no reason for anybody to kill Leonard. He was going to die anyway. All they had to do was wait."

"Mabel thought he was going to recover."

"That's only because she was his mother." Aunty Lee looked at Cherril speculatively. "Would you kill yourself for a child?"

"Why are you asking me that?" Cherril looked so startled that for a moment Aunty Lee wondered whether her thoughts had been running along the same lines.

"Just wondering."

"If it is guaranteed the child survives, then of course," Nina said. "But if cannot guarantee, what's the point?"

"But nothing like that can be guaranteed," Cherril said. "Especially if you kill yourself and you're not around to watch out for the kid. I might kill for my child, though. If that's what was at stake."

"Leonard's drug use probably caused the damage to his heart but we can't rule out there may have been a congenital defect to begin with. That may have been what Mabel wanted to believe. He would have been experiencing chest pains and nonfatal arrhythmias for some time, going by the state his heart was in." That's why she was praying for a new heart for him.

"It's not a simple operation." Cherril had read up on the subject after Aunty Lee told her what they had learned at Benjamin Ng's flat.

"For one thing, obtaining a donor heart is very difficult because it must be a heart in good condition, matching his tissue type as closely as possible to reduce the chances of rejection and belonging to someone who is brain-dead and stable on life support.

"His blood would be channeled through a heart-lung bypass machine while the surgeon works on his heart. This machine supplies his body with oxygenated blood during the procedure. To save time the donor heart may be stitched in place on top of his own heart. It's a very complicated procedure. Not something you would risk doing in a fly-by-night clinic. You would need a full operating team and anesthesiologist. You would need equipment and monitors . . ."

Aunty Lee thought of the receipts they had found. "How would you put together a surgical team?" she wondered.

"Nobody would put together a team to operate on Leonard Sung," Nina said. "The boy was already in such bad shape, all the drugs poisoning his body."

That reminded Aunty Lee of another thought chain she had been following. The poison in *buah keluak* was cyanide. If murder in this case was meant to be blamed on the *buah keluak*, then likely that was what had been found in the dish. But though cyanide was also found in almonds, apple seeds, and tobacco products, there was likely to be too small an amount to do any harm. Where else? Insecticides and pesticides, most likely.

Thanks to Nina's online skills, Aunty Lee had been able to find out everything she wanted to know about cyanide except where to get it.

"Did the pool at the Sungs' house look green to you when we were there?" Aunty Lee asked Cherril.

"Wasn't it blue? Water is always blue, right?"

It irritated Aunty Lee when Cherril let what she thought she knew override what she actually saw.

"If it was green that means they had algae bloom." Then again Cherril occasionally came up with gems like this that put everything else into context. Aunty Lee was a rabid autodidact with a bad memory but Cherril went through life picking up nuggets of information without stopping to process them.

"The pond at Mycroft's parents' house got algae bloom last year. The water turned completely green. They kept asking the gardener to change the water but it kept turning back green until they got somebody to come and do an Algae Bomb. I didn't believe it would work. It sounded like one of those lose-weight-without-dieting or whiten-your-skin-without-peeling advertisements, but then it really worked! Just one night and the next day the water was not green anymore. But then of course all the fish died."

"Really, in just one night . . ." But Aunty Lee was not thinking about the fish. "What did they do?"

"They just added the Algae Bomb. I think it came in a tub of powder. They came and added it to the water and warned us not to drink out of the pond . . . not that we would have anyway. It was very effective but they said the algae would come back, it's just how nature works if you have sun and you have oxygen in your water. Actually it means that you have a healthy environment, it just doesn't look very good. I tried to ask what chemicals they used. I'm sure there's a cheaper way to do it on our own. You just need some kind of poison, right? I asked them, can't I just pour in a bottle of Dettol or dump in some cockroach pellets? They said it's more complicated than that. I can understand it's more complicated if you want to kill the algae without killing the fish, but since the fish died anyway I don't see what's the big deal."

Aunty Lee's mind was working furiously. She knew there was something significant here. She couldn't say what it was yet but she knew this was a trail worth following. "Nina?"

"Yes, madam?"

"Nina, can you find out for me who treated the water in the Sungs' pool? And when it was done?"

Nina knew better than to ask Aunty Lee why. But doing anything was better than doing nothing. Since the café kitchen had been closed she had already cleaned the café and the bungalow as thoroughly as she did before Chinese New Year and even waxed all the teak cupboards.

"It's illegal to sell rat poison containing cyanide in Singapore. But people always say it's the only kind that works. They usually get friends to bring it down for them from Malaysia."

"But you can't even buy rat poison in Singapore," Cherril pointed out. "Mycroft's parents had an awful problem with rats one time. None of the traps they bought worked and it's illegal to use rat poison unless you are a licensed exterminator."

It was very unusual to find someone so law-abiding, Aunty Lee thought. She wondered whether it came from being married to an NMP.

"My friend's boss also got rats," Nina said. "She asked her sister to get her rat poison from Malaysia. Just put inside a plastic bag with other shopping things, no problem. They didn't know how many rats they got because they only see them at night. Then sometimes see one or two running past. But then the rats ate the poison in the night, then the next day they went out into the garden to die. Almost twenty of them! Anyway, it was cyanide, probably from rat poison. It would be colorless but come with a bitter taste."

"Can you find out whether the Sungs were using Algae Bombs or rat poison or anything else with cyanide?"

"No need to ask, ma'am. That day underneath the table with the plates and cutlery got the bottles for the pool cleaner. I asked Madam Sung where can I put them and she told me, just leave them there."

"Why didn't you tell me? Anyone could have killed them!"

"How do I know that their pool cleaner got cyanide?"

Aunty Lee amended her thought: Anyone who had known there was cyanide-based powder under the buffet table could have killed them.

And Mabel herself had known the bottle was there—asked Nina to leave it there . . .

The women who thrive in life and business are the ones who know how to make the best of circumstances. More important, they know when a battle is no longer worth fighting. Was that why Mabel Sung had decided to kill herself and her son? Because she did not want him to suffer anymore?

That might work in theory but it did not fit with the impression Aunty Lee had got of Mabel Sung that day and Aunty Lee trusted her own impressions more than other people's clichés. That was the problem.

There was also the question of why Mabel Sung, with all her connections, had not been able to push through a legal transplant for her precious son.

Cherril said Mycroft had already gone through this with her.

In Singapore, the Transplant Ethics Committee must approve living-donor kidney transplants and approval was only given after thorough investigation showed the donor understood and was not being forced into the operation. Otherwise, organ trading was banned in Singapore and in many other countries to prevent the exploitation of "poor and socially disadvantaged" donors who might be forced into selling body parts.

"He said poor people are forced to sell their time and health and self-respect, but they have a chance to earn back these things, but they can never earn back a kidney."

Aunty Lee knew the laws. Middle-class Singaporeans prided themselves on knowing that even the wealthiest and most powerful were subject to laws that protected the poorest and most overlooked. Only a year ago there had been a scandal when the executive chair and head of one of Singapore's top family businesses was fined and publicly shamed in the newspapers and social media for arranging to pay over twenty-two thousand Singapore dollars for a kidney flown into Singapore by its Indonesian donor. Aunty Lee knew the gentle and generous man had been as desperate for a kidney as its would-be donor was for money, and was not sure justice had been served in this case. Though both parties had entered knowingly and willingly into the agreement, they were both fined. And as the poor (in every sense) donor obviously did not have ten thousand Singapore dollars, he spent twelve months in jail, which did not help his own health or family finances. Aunty Lee reflected that laws designed with the best intentions to protect people could hurt them badly if applied inflexibly. It was like someone trying to make *kaya* and blindly stirring coconut cream into their eggs because the recipe said so without noticing one of the eggs was bad.

"To do it properly you must examine every egg," Aunty Lee said out loud. "Egg by egg. That's the only way to do it."

"What's that?"

"They should examine case by case," Aunty Lee said. "Not anyhow say one law fits all."

"Mycroft says one law should apply to everybody."

"But even if you have the organs, how does the law decide who gets them? It's like playing God. Throw a dice, pick at random," Aunty Lee said. "As long as the people can pay."

Cherril started to protest but simultaneously defending the laws of God and Singapore confused her, and Aunty Lee continued: "There's no right way to make some decisions. But if nobody decides, then we are all stuck and everybody suffers. So somebody makes a choice, any choice. And then we all follow. If it was the wrong choice, then somebody else makes another choice. Otherwise we are like people sitting in a restaurant without ordering. Or every time ordering the same white porridge because when you were a baby you were fed white porridge and you know it is safe."

Aunty Lee got up to stir the *tau suan* in the slow cooker. Some people took long, slow walks when trying to work out problems. Aunty Lee preferred to put her problems in the slow cooker. She stirred in a slurry of sweet-potato flour to thicken the sweet soup before ladling out three bowls and topping them with crispy dough balls. Most people used cut-up dough fritters but Aunty Lee preferred to fry up tiny dough puffs that stayed light and crispy longer.

"Eat. Machines and people cannot work without fuel." And money was fuel that someone might kill for. "Maybe I should go and visit Doreen Choo," Aunty Lee said thoughtfully. "We didn't really get to catch up that day and after all I haven't seen her for so long."

16

Doreen Choo's Flat

"Quick, Nina! Go and see what do we have ready that we can bring to give to my friend Doreen. I think her teeth are not very good, so nothing too hard that might make her teeth come out. She is the kind that will make me pay her dentist bill and then go and get extra whitening and straightening and what-not-ing done!"

Aunty Lee had decided to pay a visit to Doreen Choo. But paying uninvited, unannounced visits made her nervous. Nina calmly prepared a *tingkat* of hot herbal chicken soup (defrosted in the microwave but no one would be able to tell).

"You don't have to go, madam."

"Of course I do. Besides, with all these people canceling their bookings, what am I going to do if I just hang around?"

Nina knew very well what Aunty Lee would do. She would

fuss and fret and get in the way of Nina, who was doing her best to prepare and flash-freeze as much of their freshly purchased produce as possible. They had large enough storage freezers and not too much had been wasted yet. But even so, what was the point? Who knew how long people would continue to be afraid of nothing? However things turned out, Nina would get more done without Aunty Lee playing detective in the kitchen.

"But how can I just go and drop in on her and say what—'Hello, I just came to see whether you are having an affair with Henry Sung and can I come to your prayer and healing meeting because I want to find out who took over after Mabel died?'"

"You should go," Nina said decisively. "Give her the soup. Tell her you got nothing to do here because nobody is coming to your shop anymore. Say you miss your husband and pretend to cry a bit. Ask her to pray for you. She will ask you to go to the meeting with her."

"Nina, you are devious."

"You should be happy I am looking out for you, madam. I will go and put the soup in the car. I got the address already, I will drive you there."

Mrs. Doreen Choo lived in an apartment in Taman Serasi, opposite the Singapore Botanic Gardens. If only the Botanic Gardens were air-conditioned, it would have been lovely to walk through them and up to Garden Vista. Instead Aunty Lee enjoyed being driven past the huge old trees and luxuriant greenery and got Nina to drop her, the nourishing herbal chicken soup, and two of Aunty Lee's Tasty Tarts (Pineapple) at the lobby of Doreen Choo's building. Few could resist the buttery pastry encasing Aunty Lee's homemade pineapple-and-coconut jam. Indeed it was the overwhelming number of Chinese New Year orders for her pineapple tarts that had prompted the conversion of Aunty Lee's baking hobby into a business. The tarts still served a very important purpose. Nobody turned away a visitor bearing pineapple tarts.

"When you want me to come and pick you up, madam?"

"I will call for you. If I don't call for you after one hour, then you come and wait outside."

"I keep the doors closed because I'm very afraid of dust," Mrs. Doreen Choo explained when Aunty Lee arrived at her apartment. She opened the front door herself. Aunty Lee noticed a note of smug, querulous martyrdom women adopted when living with a man they wanted to show off.

"I can't get my new maid to come and open the door. She's scared of the doorbell. I thought it was a good idea to get a maid from Myanmar. If she doesn't understand the language here, she can't have boyfriends and get pregnant and forfeit my deposit, right? And she cannot run away because she won't know where to go. At least that's what I thought. But this girl is so stupid she doesn't understand anything I tell her to do. I have to speak so slowly and repeat myself so many times and she still doesn't understand me. Sometimes I just want to throw something at her. But I have to control myself, or afterward *kaypoh* neighbors will report me, and I'll end up in the newspapers holding my handbag in front of my face. I can't even pronounce her name properly and I end up calling her 'Girl' and I feel like one of those slave owners!"

Aunty Lee could tell that Doreen Choo was feeling awkward.

"What is your name?" Aunty Lee asked the shy girl looking round the kitchen door.

"Madam, my name is Hae Mar Hinin Hnin Khine."

"What name does your family call you at home?"

"At home they call me Daisy because I like to learn English."

"Can we call you Daisy?"

"Yes, ma'am."

"Rosie, you're wonderful. I don't know how you do it," Doreen Choo said once the girl had left them, taking the soup and sweets with her. Aunty Lee accepted the tribute as her due and advanced into the apartment.

"Your apartment is beautiful," Aunty Lee said. This at least was honest enough. It was not necessary to add that she did not like it. The furniture was all of good quality and all visible surfaces, including the artificial flowers, were dust-free. The apartment was large but crowded. Aunty Lee knew the Choos had downsized from a huge east-coast mansion when the children went away to university and it looked as though Doreen had crammed as much into it as would fit.

"Your children don't live here with you?"

"No. When my husband sold the old house he bought them one apartment each, and of course there is space here for them if they want to stay here. But my son straightaway went and sold his. He wants to live in some old rented shophouse. This narrow, narrow space and three floors high.

Cannot even put in a lift for me because it is conservation property. What for? I ask him. There is so much room here. What does an old woman like me needs so much room? But that one won't listen. He says he needs his privacy. What privacy? I asked him. I am his mother, okay. There is nothing about you I haven't seen, okay. But what to do. Sheng wants his independence. At least he comes back to see me. The others all cannot be bothered. I have to find ways to look after myself now. Cannot depend on them."

Doreen's vague garrulousness told Aunty Lee there was definitely something on her mind she didn't want to reveal but was dying to tell.

The Myanmar maid brought tea things. A very nice bone-china set with a pattern of light yellow vine leaves over the white of the china and accented by gold filigree highlights. Like Mrs. Choo herself, parts of the pattern and filigree had worn away with time and there were nibbles around the edges of the saucers and rims of the cups.

"Very nice," Aunty Lee said, thinking that one advantage of failing eyesight was that one did not notice signs of decay.

"I got this set in England years ago. It is imperial bone china, you know. Can you believe my children wanted me to sell it? This is something that should remain in the family, don't you think so? Young people these days don't know how to appreciate good things."

"Your children don't want to keep these in the family?"

"They don't care for such things. Now all they want is non-breakable, machine-washable . . ."

"Young children," Aunty Lee guessed. She had to get off

the subject of Doreen's children and find a way to get invited to the prayer and healing session before Nina got there.

Mrs. Choo shook her head. "Noisy, stubborn children. They spoil them. It is my late husband's fault. He spoiled his daughters, now they are spoiling their own children. From the time they were young I could see they were getting spoiled, now look at how they are treating me. Their own mother and I am living here alone and nobody bothers to drop in and see how I am."

"Are they in Singapore?"

"Two of them. One of them went to America to study, next thing you know she got boyfriend, got married, never came back. I warned him, I warned my husband, don't let her go. But that man never listened to me."

Aunty Lee began to get an inkling of why Doreen Choo's children never came by to visit her.

"But at least you can get around on your own, right? And your eyes are still so good. I have so much trouble seeing these days." Aunty Lee blinked confusedly and almost tipped her teacup off the edge of the table. Fortunately Doreen grabbed it in time. And even more fortunately she leaned forward to whisper: "My eyes—same problem. I had cataracts. That stupid family doctor never bothered to warn me this could happen. I thought I was going blind, so what to do? Just pray and see what happens, right? That fool doctor never told me anything. And those children of mine never even bother to find out whether anything can be done. Finally I let Mabel drag me to one of her meetings. Do you know about those meetings?" Doreen's tone was cautious.

Aunty Lee leaned forward and whispered, "Never Say Die? The prayer and healing group?"

"Yes, exactly. You went also? What did you get done?"

Aunty Lee hesitated delicately. "I couldn't make up my mind. Then—well, you know what happened."

Fortunately Doreen was a good jumper-to-conclusions. "Mabel died before you could get it done. I really don't know what those people are thinking. Everybody knows you must have a succession plan. Even Lee Kuan Yew has a succession plan. But that woman just goes and dies and leaves us all in the lurch. But don't worry. Somebody is already looking into it. As long as you are already on the list."

Aunty Lee always tried to appear ignorant with people who wanted to share information. To her this was only polite, like saying you were hungry to a hostess who you knew had spent hours preparing a lavish meal for you. In both cases it took little effort and usually made everyone happy. She looked blankly at Doreen now, and for added effect almost knocked a plate off the table. Doreen Choo steadied it quickly.

"I don't think I'm on the list. I couldn't commit because—I still have so many questions and Mabel . . ."

"Not to speak ill of the dead but poor Mabel was not a patient person. Don't worry; you can ask me anything you want. I decided to just take the plunge and take the leap of faith, and look, I can see!"

"Exactly! Praying aside, are they real doctors or not? And somebody said they don't know whether they go and take parts from pigs and monkeys and transplant them inside you!" Aunty Lee did not think anyone could take that seriously but Doreen smiled, pleased.

"Of course not! Real people. And Chinese people some more! I asked!"

"How can you guarantee? Can you see the body first?"

"Why would you want to see a dead body? Rosie, believe me, you can trust them. They give you a form to fill in, your lawyer can check for you first. On it it gives the race and age of the donor and swears the donor is in good health. I got my Henry to check all the medical details for me."

Oops, thought Aunty Lee. In her school days that would have been called "a slip showing more than your underwear." Thanks to years of playing mah-jongg she knew to take a noncommittal sip of tea as though she had not picked up anything. Doreen was staring at her, watching for a response.

"It's good you got a doctor to check for you," Aunty Lee said, vaguely approving. "Are they real doctors or not?"

"Of course they are proper doctors." Doreen's relief that Aunty Lee had not picked up anything made her even more loquacious. "And Henry supervises everything. You wouldn't believe it to look at the man, but in the hospital world he is a big shot, okay. And when he was in practice he said he made a point to only employ local doctors to work for him. Those foreign grads, not so good. You know why they have to go away to study medicine, right? Because they cannot get into medical school here. Then they come back like so big-time like that. Does not mean they are smart, just means their parents wasted money to send them overseas because they cannot get into university here!"

Aunty Lee remembered Henry Sung's tremor. A rest tremor that disappeared with voluntary movement. If he was in the early stages of Parkinson's he might already have problems with daily tasks such as writing and shaving, and having a young doctor around would be a great help.

"It was one of Henry's young doctors that took care of my eyes. Henry told him what to do, like remote control like that."

"Did you ask who the donor was?"

"I didn't want to know. Must have been a car-accident victim or something. Henry said it's strictly confidential. I can quite understand that." Doreen giggled girlishly. "If I was selling off my relative's body parts I would also want it to be confidential. But why not? After all, they won't be needing them anymore. And it must be very good money for them, given how much they charge us!"

Of course Aunty Lee asked how much the eye operation had cost. The price was high but Doreen said it was worth it. After all, she had been almost blind and depressed and now she could see and had a life and a beau. How could you put a price on that?

"There's something else I should tell you. I sent in a complaint about the hygiene in your kitchen because Henry asked me to. I only did it to make him happy. He still wants to believe it was food poisoning and he says he just wants to make sure nobody else suffers. And anyway, he said if your kitchen is clean you got nothing to worry about. Sorry, ah."

"Don't worry, one letter won't matter so much."

"That's what Henry said. That's why . . ." Doreen trailed off and stopped.

The beautiful but somewhat overcrowded living room looked out through glass sliding doors onto a meticulously maintained patio surrounded by a border of bougainvillea. Aunty Lee wondered how Henry Sung had broached the subject. *Doreen, I want you to write a letter complaining about the hygiene in your friend's café even though you've never been there.*

"Henry brought it up at the prayer and healing meeting actually. He asked all of us to write and complain and to make sure we don't mention that we know him or one anoother. He even gave us sample letters to copy and a list of important people to send them to. You know, same as the letters prayer groups must get together to write when the government wants to support abortion or gays. But we could see it's all part of his healing process. Rosie, I'm so glad you understand. We have to stick together at times like this. I mean everybody knows that Mabel killed herself even if nobody dares to say it out loud. Poor Henry. Mabel only ever cared about her successful lawyer image and her useless son. Mabel's two loves. Both of them rotten at the core. And Sharon is taking over things now. That girl is another one just like her mother. That one is never going to find a husband, you watch and see."

All this sounded incredible to Aunty Lee, who was beginning to despair of being able to bring the conversation back to her Never Say Die invitation. It was seldom she met someone who could outdo her in inconsequential talk. Fortunately the front door opened as Doreen was going into the intricacies of what men really found attractive in women of any age.

The doorbell had not rung so as not to scare the maid. Henry Sung must have his own key, Aunty Lee thought as she watched him enter with all the assurance of familiarity. He looked almost comically dismayed to see her and for a moment Aunty Lee thought he was going to turn and leave. He took a half step backward and bumped into Sharon, who was right behind him.

"I invited Henry and Sharon to stay here for a while," Doreen explained. "Just till things calm down at their place. Come sit down with us and have some tea. Sharon, go and ask the girl to bring hot water and some more cups."

Sharon left the room without answering.

"Too many policemen in the house," Henry Sung grunted. He sat down next to Doreen and helped himself to a drink out of her cup. "Sticking their noses into everything. This is cold. Disgusting."

"I told him he should leave somebody there to watch them. Don't know what those policemen may pinch. They don't get paid very much, you know. I don't know how Henry is going to manage on his own. You know the servants all left? They went back to the agency and refused to return to the house. Mabel was always hopeless at handling servants."

"Poor Mabel," Aunty Lee said, prompting social sighs of agreement from the other two.

"Those whom the gods love die young," Doreen murmured.

"So sad, especially after I heard you put so much into renovating the house for Leonard to move back."

"The pool house was renovated to be Leonard's bachelor pad for after he got better," Henry Sung said.

"It was equipped as an ICU for Len," Sharon said at the same time, coming in with an electric kettle, which she proceeded to plug into a wall socket. Doreen looked disapproving but said nothing. Henry seemed oblivious, and Aunty Lee was sure Sharon had hurried back to monitor what they were saying rather than for the tea.

They should have agreed on a story, Aunty Lee thought. Both explanations were completely credible but side by side they canceled each other out. The difficulty with telling anything other than the truth was that there were so many "others."

Henry cleared his throat. "Well, actually I tried your chicken *buah keluak* that day at the party—"

"How did you find it?" Henry was clearly trying to change the subject but Aunty Lee was always ready to talk about food, especially hers. In her experience people's attitude toward food mirrored their attitude toward life.

"Oh, I thought it was good. Narrow escape, huh! But we're not saying it was the chicken dish that killed them. Just that we should all move on as quickly as possible. Edmond was saying he didn't see the point in people eating all these things that are potentially dangerous. Young people like him, they don't appreciate our traditional foods."

Dr. Yong was a liar. Aunty Lee had seen his platefuls of emptied *buah keluak* casings.

"Edmond Yong is staying at the house while we're here,"

Sharon Sung said as she walked past them toward the corridor beyond.

"Rosie wants to come for the prayer and healing group, Henry," Doreen Choo said. "She needs to do her—what was it, Rosie?"

"Knees," said Aunty Lee as she got to her feet and felt the creak. She had hinted it was her eyes but suddenly she could not bear the thought of Henry Sung looking into her eyeballs with sharp objects at hand. Luckily Doreen Choo had not been paying attention.

"I don't know—" Henry Sung said. "It's a closed group. That means you cannot just go around telling people about it."

"Of course Aunty Doreen's friend can come," Sharon Sung said, pausing in the corridor. "We'll be meeting here on Tuesday night. Six P.M. I'll tell Edmond you will be joining us."

Sharon disappeared into one of the rooms, having made her pronouncement. The three older people looked at one another. It appeared Mabel's mantle had been assumed by her daughter.

"I should be going," Aunty Lee said.

17

Aunty Lee's Delights Closed

The next morning Inspector Salim was summoned to Phoenix Park again.

"The news is good and bad. The *buah keluak* poison is not what killed Mabel Sung and her son. According to forensics, the poison was in the *buah keluak* but it was commercial cyanide—added to the dish, not in it to begin with. It took the lab so long because they wanted to be sure. It is from the same family of poisons but was commercially processed. Probably from the rat poison or anti-algae agent found there. The lab is testing samples to confirm that now."

"So Aunty Lee is officially off the hook?" Salim asked thoughtfully.

"I expected you would be happier to hear that," Commissioner Raja said.

"I suppose the bad news is if it was not a *buah keluak* accident somebody deliberately put the poison in the food?"

"That was supposed to be the good news."

"Sir?"

"Henry Sung's ex-minister friends want us to drop it. They say it's nobody's business but the family's."

"That's what people might call cronyism."

"The old guard sees it as the spirit of sticking together and watching out for one another."

"Watching out for each other against outsiders?"

"The true spirit of Singapore that made us is in these people. They built this country as new immigrants and activists."

"And now their children don't want to take responsibility for anything but feel entitled to a good life just because they were born here."

"The majority is still willing to work hard, Salim. I would call you one of the good examples of that."

"But there is a group of privileged who are realizing how precarious their position is. That's what this is all about, isn't it? These people are fighting to not lose what they think they have even if they are not willing to work to increase it."

"We are not having a political or sociological debate so early in the morning, Inspector Salim. Or at least I'm not."

"You're telling me to drop what should be a murder investigation?"

"I'm telling you this is not officially a murder investigation. Most likely it was a mercy killing and suicide. Mrs. Sung could not bear to watch her son suffer, knew there was no hope for him, and killed him and herself. Henry Sung knows it but cannot admit it because Christians don't commit suicide. They only have Accidents, Misadventures, and While Of Unsound Mind Incidents. Anyway, digging into all that is not going to help anybody. Best to just drop it and let the family get over things quietly.

"And we have received other complaints against Aunty Lee's Delights—the hygiene standards in the shop kitchen, the lack of temperature monitors for the heaters, the domestic helper illegally working at a business location." Commissioner Raja did not enjoy saying this, but he was glad he was not the one who would be saying it to Aunty Lee.

"So you want me to close down the shop even though you know they had nothing to do with Mabel Sung's death?"

"It's not my call. We have to investigate all complaints and in this case letters were sent to the National Environment Agency, a town council leader, and a high court judge who asked us to look into it. The notice has already been forwarded to your people. The closure is temporary pending results of the investigation."

"How many complaints?" Salim asked.

"Four that I know of. This is separate from the poisoning case." Commissioner Raja looked at Salim.

"Four complaints from four different people?" Salim found this hard to believe. "Why now? It has to have something to do with the Sungs."

"I forwarded the NEA report to you with the closure notice. The judge and town council leader had their assistants phone in the investigation request."

"I'll get back and take a look at the notice." Salim had come straight to headquarters after getting the summons at home that morning.

"Your Sergeant Panchal signed for the notice. She said she would see to it."

Outside Aunty Lee's Delights

A woman in the familiar blue uniform of the Singapore Police Force stood in the entryway of Aunty Lee's Delights, triggering the door jangle repeatedly.

Her presence was nothing out of the ordinary. Officers from the nearby Bukit Tinggi Neighborhood Police Post often dropped in for Aunty Lee's treats to take advantage of the "in uniform" discount set up for students and national servicemen. Still, Nina watched the woman suspiciously. Nina was fond of Inspector Salim (who Aunty Lee claimed had turned down a promotion to stay near Nina) and knew most people in Singapore trusted the police. But underneath their uniforms they were still people. When times were good it was easy for people to do the right thing. But if times changed, they were people with the weapons and the power.

"After all the trouble last year I hope that this year is going to be easier," Nina said as Aunty Lee came to join her. "Now looks like this year is going to be even worse."

"Can I help you?" Aunty Lee said pleasantly. "What are you putting on my door?"

"There have been several complaints about your food and

the hygiene of your kitchens," Staff Sergeant Panchal said. "This is a notice of temporary closure pending investigation. If our investigations reveal your food was involved in the poisoning of two people, then we will press charges," Despite the lab results Panchal still had not given up on what she considered the best solution to the deaths.

Aunty Lee looked shocked. "*Aiyoh!* Are you going to arrest me? Are you going to use handcuffs? Can I take my heart medication and my high-blood-pressure medication to prison with me? And my allergy pills and my antiseizure stress pills?"

"Oh no—" Panchal said. "I am not arresting you . . ."

"Are you sure? If you think my food killed those people, why aren't you arresting me?"

"Pending investigation. After investigations are concluded we will get back to you."

"But I am catering a dinner party tonight. I have to get all the food there and ready by six P.M."

"I am afraid that is impossible. You will have to cancel. We will also be taking samples from your kitchen for investigation."

"Who asked you to come and test our food? When did they ask you to come and test? Our kitchen test was already done, you know!"

Since Nina was only a maid, SS Panchal was inclined to ignore her. But Nina was difficult to ignore.

"We got A1 cert. You want to see our A1 cert? Anyway who asked you? You must have documentation before we let you in! Or else how do we know you are not coming here to put poison inside our food and blame us if it kills someone?"

"Everything we used on Saturday has been washed already," Aunty Lee said. "But you can look around the kitchen and test what you want. Nina, you go and show her whatever she wants."

"But, ma'am! She got no search warrant!"

Outside there was a screeching of brakes and a clanging of crushed metal as the red prayer ash bin on the grass verge was knocked over by Salim's Subaru. The car jerked to a stop and Salim leaped across the drain and sprinted across to them. "Thanks, Panchal, I'll take it from here."

"Sir, you didn't close your car door."

Salim pulled the café door shut behind him, cutting off its welcome jangles in midchime. Outside, Staff Sergeant Panchal shrugged and resumed taping the closure notice on the door.

"Aunty Lee, Nina, let me take care of this—Nina put down that chopper—"

"They have to sign this." With another jangle Panchal entered. Salim took the envelope without a word.

"Sir, you want me to close your car door and lock your car for you?"

Salim, waiting for her to leave, did not reply.

"Would you like a cold drink before going?" Aunty Lee asked Panchal cordially.

"Mrs. Lee, I must inform you that while your food and beverage license is suspended pending investigation of your kitchens and premises, you will incur additional fines and or penalties if you contravene the suspension order."

Salim finally spoke. "Panchal. Get out. Now."

Panchal left. Inspector Salim would regret being so rude to her when she filed her complaint about this and all his other breaches of protocol. She stopped to take a phone snap of the badly parked police patrol car her boss had arrived in to add to the list of his misdemeanors.

Salim handed the envelope to Aunty Lee. He already knew what it said. He had been trying to get the order suspended pending investigation when he learned SS Panchal had taken it upon herself to execute it.

"I promise you, this is all just temporary. I can't explain why right now. I need you to sign this to show that you understand you cannot operate out of these premises until the investigation is complete. The restriction includes not selling elsewhere food that has been prepared here. I'm sorry. We have to follow procedure. It's not my female colleague's fault. The orders came from top down. She's new—"

"She is a monster," said Nina. "She enjoy bullying old women and servants."

"So they found poison in the chicken *buah keluak*," Aunty Lee said.

Salim said carefully, "They found poison in the dish. But there's was no confirmation where it came from. This is just a precaution. We received several letters of complaint from the public and we have to respond."

Though it was her café and kitchen he was putting out of business, Aunty Lee felt sorry for him. And now she knew what Henry had done with the letters Doreen had been talking about.

"Let me see. Nina, read it for me and show me where to sign, please. Salim, would you like a glass of tea?" Tea was the last thing on Salim's mind but he recognized and appreciated her gesture of deliberately ignoring Panchal's rudeness.

"Thank you. Not now."

"Hey, what are you doing?" Cherril's voice came from outside. "Stop that!"

With a gentle but firm grip on her arm, Mycroft Peters propelled his wife into the café without waiting for Sergeant Panchal to answer.

"What's that woman putting up on the door?" Cherril demanded, directing the question at everyone in the café. Aunty Lee held up the letter without a word but Nina, taking it from her, held it out to Cherril between thumb and forefinger as though it was something dirty or dangerous.

"Madam, you should not sign it. Madam Cherril, look! Tell her not to sign! This says that there have been complaints that our kitchen is not up to hygiene standards. It says after receiving several complaints of food poisoning from here, they must investigate. Madam, this is all lies!"

"Charges have been made," Salim said. "So we must investigate."

"And if nothing is wrong who is going to pay us back for the money lost? She still has to pay rent here even if we cannot do business. Who made those complaints?" Cherril seized the letter from Nina.

"We should let them get on with their investigation," Aunty

Lee said quietly. "Can you find me a pen? Oh, thank you, Salim. Cherril, give me the paper. Where do I sign?"

"We are investigating Henry Sung also," Salim said to Nina. "With married couples, you don't know what is going on underneath the surface."

"That's why better never to get married!" Nina said.

"No. It's not Henry," Aunty Lee said. "I'm sure he wanted to kill his wife at times but I doubt he would have done it so publicly. And he would not have killed his son."

The problem was Aunty Lee was certain Mabel would not have killed her son either—even as a mercy killing.

"Do something!" Cherril said to her husband. "Can't you stop them? This is police harassment and brutality and all those kinds of things!"

"I'm sorry," Salim said again, glancing at Nina, who was standing, silent, beside Aunty Lee.

"You should know there's nothing wrong with the kitchen here!" Cherril said. "You've been here before. I know, I've seen you here. You've even eaten here. Have you ever seen cockroaches or rats or raw meat on pastry plates or any of the things that people close kitchens for? I've worked in kitchens in far worse conditions and nobody ever bothered to complain. If you don't like it, then don't eat here, lah! As long as nobody dies, what's the problem?"

"But somebody did die," Mycroft Peters said. "This is about Mabel Sung and her son, isn't it?"

"No, sir. This is a separate complaint that was filed," Salim said. "Several complaints."

"If you can't tell us who complained, can you tell us how

many people complained?" Mycroft knew that a single complaint would not have been taken seriously. Too often a customer who felt herself slighted by a waitress would call in and complain.

"Some other people who were there that day have reported feeling unwell after eating food you provided," Salim said.

"So it's all people from that party. That's not true. They're lying. I was there and nobody said anything. Mycroft, do something!"

But Mycroft Peters just put an arm around his wife. "Aunty Lee, if there is anything I can do—"

"Sorry," Inspector Salim said quietly to Nina. "I must follow procedure. If members of the public make a report we must follow up. This is only temporary."

Aunty Lee feared the people in power were not trying to find out what happened. They just wanted to contain the damage and have the incident forgotten as soon as possible. Aunty Lee agreed it was necessary to move on. But you had to find out what the real damage was before you could find the best way to deal with it.

Nina glared at Salim's back but said nothing. This was actually a good sign for Salim. If Nina had written off the police officer she would have put on her perfectly blank foreign-worker image for him—there would have been no anger, no familiarity, no recognition even. But Aunty Lee had other things to worry about than Salim's feelings. She was not even worrying about the café being closed, even temporarily. Aunty Lee could sense a deeper wrong. It was like the smell of decay at the bottom of the fridge that made everything else stink. The problem was she could not tell who it was coming from.

"Madam, I phone the people who made reservations, yes? And next week the catering also must cancel?"

"Yes please, Nina. Save everything you can in the fridge—"

"Freezer better, ma'am. And the fresh vegetables and meat also I will prepare first and then pack into the freezer."

Aunty Lee remembered something else in her freezer.

"I have a sample of the *buah keluak* that I cooked that day. I want you to check that because no one else seemed affected by it."

Aunty Lee always said that the most important thing when it came to cooking for large numbers of people fast was having a big fridge and freezer. Even though she liked to be out shopping early at the wholesale center for the freshest of new produce, she depended on her gigantic freezer to store meal portions of washed and chopped vegetables and meats with basic marinades. These machines had not existed in the days of cooking for households of up to thirty people. The main difference was it had been up to the cook to decide what all those people were going to eat, and they all ate the same thing. Also, there had been the back lot for vegetables and chickens, and amahs and servant girls to help with the multitude of small but necessary tasks involved.

"I am going to the prayer and healing meeting tomorrow night. Why not help me prepare some snacks to bring with me? If I don't charge them it's not counted as business, right?"

"As long as they don't pray until they get sick and blame you!" Nina snapped.

Efficiently operating a host of gadgets, Nina did the work of five kitchen helpers, and the freezer would cut down on wastage during the closure. As long as the closure was really temporary.

That night Aunty Lee was grateful for her own quiet house in a peaceful housing estate. There had been no question of her having to leave the place when ML died. It was just one more thing that she could take for granted, but she was still grateful and said so to ML's living room portrait: "The greatest gift is to realize how lucky you are to have something before you lose it." They had been lucky there and had made the most of their years together. She could have no regrets. But now, almost alone in the silent house (Nina was in her room at the back), in front of the silent, smiling portrait, Aunty Lee was tired enough to be lonely, and at that moment she missed her late husband so much that she felt angry with him for dying and leaving her behind. Maybe it was time for her to take down the pictures and move on. Maybe it was time for her to find a smaller house and move out. What was the point in staying here, close to the shop, if the shop never opened again? She ought to be moving on with her life.

Of course she could still talk to ML. That was why she had photo portraits of him all over the house and café. But he didn't ever talk back. She wished she had some recordings of her late husband's voice. It would be such a comfort now, just to hear his beloved low gravelly tones. It was one of the things she had not known to value till it was lost to her forever.

"I wish—" Aunty Lee said, laying a hand lightly on the phone beside her, then jumped, startled when it rang.

"Yes?" Her voice came out in a strangled squeak.

"I hope I'm not calling too late?" It was Aunty Lee's stepdaughter, Mathilda. "Are you sick?"

"No, of course not. Always good to hear from you. Have you had your lunch yet?"

Aunty Lee always enjoyed Mathilda's phone calls. She had been warned that stepdaughters were much more difficult to handle than stepsons. But she had always gotten along well with Mathilda, who had inherited her late father's good nature and wry equanimity.

"I heard they closed down your café. Are you okay? What's happening?"

Mathilda had already been working in England when her father married Aunty Lee. She had told Aunty Lee how much she appreciated the energy Aunty Lee brought to her father's home and life after Mathilda's mother had been dead for over fifteen years. Mathilda had married an Englishman not long after and settled down in London. Neither Mathilda nor Mark, who had married soon after his younger sister, showed any antagonism toward the plump, fair "aunty" when she began appearing by their father's side at family and social functions. Indeed, they were glad she was there to keep their father company and feed him.

"Who told you?" Aunty Lee asked, wondering for a moment whether the closure had already been on the news.

"Selina sent me an e-mail telling me to call Mark. That woman is one solid lump of stinginess. I found out about Sharon's mum dying online. Can you talk now?"

It was past 11 P.M. in Singapore but Mathilda knew Aunty Lee's habits well. In the old days that hour would have found her father and his second wife side by side in their matching Barcaloungers in front of the television with their drinks (Black Label for ML, sour plum juice for Aunty Lee) and crunchy, dry, fried anchovies on the table between them. With their eyes fixed on the television they would talk about what they had done that day; what they had seen, said, and eaten, what they found funny, sad, or provoking. And this would lead to talk of the past—going over their early days together and filling in gaps in their years apart. And most of all they talked about all the people in their lives, the friends they had in common as well as the many now gone.

Now that ML Lee was gone too, it was the talking that Aunty Lee missed the most. Of course she could (and did) talk to Nina, to all the many people she met over the course of the day, but nothing could match the cozy and intimate camaraderie of those lost conversations.

"Anyway, Mark wants me to tell you to sell the business for whatever you can get. Or rather he started to talk to me and then that Silly-Nah took over because he wasn't saying what she was telling him to say properly. She said your reputation is gone, so you might as well quit now. According to her, since your money is coming to us one day you are cheating us if you lose it all. I said I would talk to you myself. Is the café really closed? Are you all right?"

Aunty Lee did not know what to say. She was "all right" compared to a great many other people. Her health was good, and even if the café never opened again and she lost everything she had invested in it she was not likely to end up selling tissue packets outside MRT stations. But things were definitely not as they should be.

"Aunty Lee? Are you there?" Mathilda sounded worried.

"I'm still here. Yes, I'm all right. Yes, the café is closed. They got some complaints, so they have to investigate but they haven't arrested me or anything, don't worry. I heard they even went around collecting *buah keluak* from the Indonesian women who come to sell them here; they want to test for poison. Didn't even pay for them, the women said. Now nobody will dare to eat *buah keluak* anymore. I wanted to promote our traditional dishes here; instead I end up destroying them!" Aunty Lee laughed wryly.

"It's that Sharon Sung. I'm sure of it. It's the kind of thing she would do. She was also very competitive. I remember she didn't do so well in her PSLE and had to spend two years in the second-best class, and I think she never got over that." The Primary School Leaving Exams were the national exams that sorted twelve-year-olds into science, arts, or technical streams, thus shaping their careers and destinies forever. "The last time we got together she was telling us how much more she earned and wanting to compare with people who had been in the top class. By that time the rest of us had already forgotten what class we were in way back then."

"But it can't have been easy for her. I heard that her brother was in bad shape. Sharon said her mother's feminist talk was all a big lie. Her parents were leaving their house and everything to her brother because he was the boy. But she said it was fair in the end because her brother would never be able to earn his own living, and when he got sick I think she was actually glad."

"Tell me about Sharon's brother. All I know is that he was sick and he died. Did you know him?"

"Everybody knew of Leonard Sung. He got sent off to the U.S. and got into partying and drugs, but even before that he was always in trouble. You know why he had to leave Singapore before his O levels, right? He got in trouble in school for trying to intimidate and blackmail school staff. Crazy, isn't it? The holy Mabel Sung's son! Leonard dropped out of school and became a drug addict and Sharon became a lawyer and joined her mum's law firm. She couldn't stand it that even after all that her brother was still her parents' favorite.

"We were in the same class for several years but I didn't really know Sharon Sung that well in school. I always thought her mother made her invite me to her birthday parties and things like that because of who Dad was rather than because we were friends."

"Poor Sharon," Aunty Lee said.

The problem with favoritism was the rules of the competition were not clear or fixed. They changed to maintain and justify the state of the favorite. But that was not so different from how most things operated.

"She's too good for everybody else but not good enough for her parents."

Aunty Lee could see why Sharon felt unfairly treated. Ordinarily she would have wanted to explore this a little, point out to Sharon that the universe and karma had a way of evening things out (look at how her poor brother had ended up), but right now she had something else on her mind. That two people had died was not as vital as the fact that someone had put poison in her food. This was personal.

"Would you like me to talk to Mark and nag him about making his own money instead of spending more of yours?"

"No! Please don't." Aunty Lee was startled. Such a thing had never occurred to her.

"I'll make sure he knows it didn't come from you. I mean, look, I don't know how you're going to leave your money and everything, but if you decide to split whatever is left between the two of us, then Mark is spending my money too, right? Sometimes I think he's deliberately squandering everything he can, just because he can. Nobody could do so hopelessly at so many businesses unless it was on purpose! And Selina—I think she just wants him to get as much out of you as she can. She got so worked up when you started the café, how you were going to lose all of Mark's and my inheritance and how we would have to come up with the money to support you in your old age. Then you started making a profit and she had to shut up, but now she's started again. And look at how much money Mark's lost so far already! Honestly, I don't know what he sees in her. But then I don't know what she sees in him either."

"Your brother has a very valuable ability."

"You mean how he gets other people to look after him? That may be valuable to him but doesn't add value to anyone else, does it?"

"Mark knows how to enjoy himself. He's enjoying being alive, trying things that catch his fancy, dropping them when he gets bored. He reminds me a bit of a little dog I had when I was a girl. It kept finding things and hiding them away in corners to chew. When it was engrossed in a new toy it didn't even want to come to eat! But once it got tired of it, that was it. No more interest, no more attention. It was looking around for the next thing. I think Mark is still looking out for whatever it is that will hold his attention. I'm sure if he had to he would settle down and find a way to earn enough money to support himself and his family. He's a good boy. But right now, since he doesn't have to, he lives it up and enjoys himself."

"If we all lived like him the economy would collapse."

"That's why we don't all live like him. You can see why it must be very difficult for Selina. By nature she's the sort who is very organized, very systematic, very good at keeping money in the bank."

A small, automatic snort came across the line when Mathilda heard the name "Selina." But she was a fair person, and besides, it was much easier to be charitable about the Selinas of the world from a safe distance. "I'm surprised she's stuck with him. I suspect Selina married dear Marko meaning to make him over and do him some good. And Mark probably went along with her until he got tired of it. Remember they were signing up for all those public-speaking and investment courses together? They were going to be incredibly successful entrepreneurs or something. But Mark couldn't decide what business he wanted to succeed at, so that fell through. Poor Selina. Actually I'm glad Mark stuck with her. It would have been terrible if he was going around changing wives instead of jobs. We have an uncle like that, you know. He's off somewhere in Canada or Australia with wife number four or five now.

"Anyway, has he signed over the wine business to Mycroft's wife yet?"

"The drinks business," Aunty Lee corrected automatically. "No. There's the issue of some wine missing from the wine room. Selina was checking the inventory and she says several of the more expensive bottles are missing. I think she suspects Nina and I go in there and drink it when there are no customers around."

"You know Mark's probably taking them himself, don't you?"

Aunty Lee thought so too. Mark wouldn't see it as stealing. As far as he was concerned, he had selected these wines and they belonged to him even if it was not his money that had paid for them.

"Mark is like a small boy."

"And he's never going to grow up if you and Selina keep treating him like one. But honestly, I don't know that Mycroft's wife is going to be much better."

"Cherril? Why not?"

"She's so skinny, for one thing. I can't see her working in a café if she doesn't like eating."

Aunty Lee knew Cherril loved eating. She was one of the few who could eat huge amounts without putting on weight. That was part of what made her such a good air stewardess but it set other women against her.

"But there must be something in her that made Mycroft marry her," Mathilda said thoughtfully.

"Cherril is actually very smart and capable of learning almost anything. Except she never got to study. She became a stewardess because she wanted to see the world. But going around the world shopping with colleagues was not really what she wanted either. I think she has potential."

"I think I'm jealous," Mathilda admitted.

"Jealous? Of Cherril?" Aunty Lee's mind spun. "Hiyah. Don't tell me you also like that Mycroft."

"No, no, no. Of course not. I mean because you seemed to get along so well with her at once. And after I tried so hard to show you I was okay with you and Dad—sorry, I'm talking rubbish."

Sometimes parents did not even realize they had favorites, Aunty Lee thought. And sometimes the favorites themselves did not realize it. Because Mathilda had never given her any trouble, it had never occurred to Aunty Lee that she might feel overlooked. Mathilda changed the subject.

"What are you going to do while your shop is closed, Aunty Lee?"

"I'm going to lunch with the commissioner of police tomorrow and then to a prayer and healing meeting tomorrow night."

"Covering all the bases, eh?"

"You know what I do," Aunty Lee said with a laugh before her voice grew serious. "But you don't know me. Mathilda, ah, you listen to me. I like that Cherril because she reminds me of myself. But you, you remind me so much of your father. Once when somebody saw your photo in the shop and thought you were my daughter I didn't correct her because I wished so much I had a daughter like you."

"Thank you," Mathilda said. Then, after a pause, "Mum."

To Aunty Lee's surprise her throat knotted up and she could not speak as sudden tears welled up in her eyes. Like her brother, Mathilda had always addressed her as "Aunty" with their late father's full approval.

18

Lunch with Commissioner Raja

"I thought this would be a nice change," Commissioner Raja Kumar said. "Since you're not cooking for once, I thought we should have something totally different."

They had been friends for years but Aunty Lee knew better than to ask Commissioner Raja to pull strings and get her kitchen ban lifted. This was Singapore, after all. Tattletale bloggers with camera phones lurked everywhere, eager for material. Aunty Lee had no wish to draw any more attention to her (temporarily) closed café. She knew Raja Kumar would do all he could for her without her having to ask. Aunty Lee usually enjoyed talking to Commissioner Raja. But today she felt uncomfortable. It was the first time she had been a suspect in a police case, no matter how nicely he put it when he asked her to have lunch with him.

They were upstairs (and barefoot) in a little restaurant along Upper Dickson Road in Little India.

"They serve both North and South Indian food and they can prepare dishes for meat eaters and non–meat eaters alike."

Commissioner Raja was no longer as familiar with the neighborhood and its people as he had been when his grandfather had a shop in the area. But he still knew a few of the long-term shopkeepers. As was happening throughout Singapore, fewer and fewer children were going into their families' businesses and more and more of the old medicine shops were being transformed into nail-art boutiques and 7-Elevens.

Floor cushions were provided and it was cool and comfortable in the private upstairs room. It had been a long time since Aunty Lee sat on the floor. She patted the polished floorboards beneath her bent knees and was reminded of long-ago family gatherings where children always ended up sitting on the floor "picnic style" because there were never enough chairs.

"I don't know if you like Indian food," the commissioner said lightly, "but you will after today." Memories of the vegetable curries his late grandmother used to cook and her special-occasion fish-head curry were making him hungry. He wondered whether there would be fish-head curry today, hot and sour and tender.

"Shall we order?"

But Aunty Lee had fixated on his opening comment. "I cook Singapore food. Singapore food is a mixture of Chinese, Malay, Indian, and Indonesian food. And then because of the English we eat sandwiches and chicken puff pie and because of the Americans we eat burgers. My cooking is not limited to what I picked up in my family. Of course I like Indian food. I even cook Indian food!"

Commissioner Raja held up his hands in surrender. "Not here to fight, Rosie. But since I'm buying today, let's have a good lunch. Their mutton biryani sounds good."

"If the mutton they use is from a castrated male sheep, then it should be good. But if it comes from a female sheep killed after it is too old to have any more babies, then it may be tough."

Commissioner Raja debated between chicken and beef for a moment but decided against provoking another information attack. "Ambur mutton biryani," he said to the waitress. The commissioner's ability to make quick, calm decisions under pressure was one of the reasons he was so respected within the force. Singaporeans generally liked having decisions made for them. They much preferred complaining to making decisions on their own. Besides, Raja Kumar was sure Aunty Lee would enjoy the sour, curried *brinjal dalcha* and *raita* of sliced onions mixed with curds and chili tomatoes that made up Ambur biryani.

"Rosie, I don't want to fight with you. You know I can't do anything about the order to close your kitchen."

"I never said I want to fight you, what. Did you invite me for lunch just to tell me that?"

"I just wanted to eat lunch with my old friend, cannot meh?

"You've helped us before. You made us look good," Commissioner Raja said. "I'm asking you for your help again. I know you didn't poison those people but we have to follow procedures."

"If you won't help me reopen my café at least you can help me with this—the newspapers printed a translation of the PRC woman's suicide note." Aunty Lee had come prepared. She took out her reading spectacles and a folded newspaper cutout with yellow highlighter markings.

"The woman wrote to her missing fiancé, 'Because of me you were willing to sacrifice part of your own body.' So clearly the man she was looking for came to Singapore to be an organ donor, right? Have you found any unidentified bodies that you didn't put in the newspapers yet? I am thinking the man obviously came to Singapore to sell his kidney or something. Then the operation must have gone wrong and he died. A man who loved a woman enough to want to sell a kidney to marry her would not just go off without a word to her. Then the illegal organ-donor people just disposed of the body in a reservoir or a construction site or somewhere like that. The point is somebody must have organized it. What if Mabel Sung was talking to organ-donor people to get a transplant for her son and she found out they were illegal and being a lawyer she tried to stop them and they sent somebody to silence her. They probably murdered her and her son as a warning. Criminal gangs are always doing things like that to warn people, right?"

"Maybe in the West," Commissioner Raja said.

"And in the West they probably say it only happens in the

East." Aunty Lee was not discouraged by the police commissioner's tone. "The point is, it must be happening somewhere or people wouldn't be talking about it all the time, right?"

One problem with a mind that worked as quickly as Aunty Lee's was how fast and how far wrong it could go with just a nugget of information, Commissioner Raja thought.

But why not?

"How would they have contacted her?"

"I already thought of that. Through her prayer and healing group. Because all the people there are desperate. Desperate people don't ask too many questions."

"I'm not saying there aren't people here looking for illegal organ transplants. But it's not as easy as all that, you know. You need the doctors, the anesthesiologists, the donors, the facilities—operating theaters, recovery space. You just consider cost and you'll see why people go to Thailand or to India for procedures. And the controls here are so much stricter, the risk is just not worth it."

"If your life is at stake, then of course it's worth it. What do you have to lose?"

Commissioner Raja looked at Aunty Lee's earnest face. Singapore people did not think like that, he wanted to say. Singapore people would think about what people would think of them if they survived thanks to an expensive operation that their family could not pay for (and insurance was unlikely to cover transplants of organs, especially illegal ones). In such cases the medical expenses would most likely ruin them. But instead he said, "You would do it?"

"Not for myself. I'm not interested in letting people cut me up and put funny things in. When my time comes to go I will just go. But if I had a chance to save somebody—"

Aunty Lee was thinking of her late husband. She would have broken any laws she had to if there had been a chance to give him a few more pain-free years. And she could see Raja Kumar's thoughts turning to his lovely Sumathi. Watching as the cancer ravaged her, he had prayed for her to die, to end her suffering. If he had had the power to save her, would the cost—or the law—have stopped him?

It was as though Aunty Lee could read his thoughts. "That's why I keep busy," she said. "But now you all close down my shop, what am I supposed to do?"

"Just don't do anything I have to arrest you for, okay?"

"Are you wearing a wire?" Aunty Lee leaned over the table and whispered.

"No I'm not," Inspector Raja stage-whispered back. "And if I was, whispering wouldn't make a difference. Our devices are very sensitive."

"You said you don't think I had anything to do with poisoning Mabel and her son, right?"

"If I thought you were going around poisoning people's food, would I be sitting here eating lunch with you?"

"Here we are!" Shanti, the hostess, appeared with a tray full of dishes; an assistant who came in behind her was equally laden. "Kaesevan sent you a mix of northern and southern dishes with your Ambur biryani.

"Time out," Commissioner Raja said. "Let's eat."

"I'm going undercover," Aunty Lee said.

Normally Aunty Lee enjoyed spending time with the commissioner. Raja Kumar had ML's way of listening to her go on without feeling any need to comment. And then saying something that showed he had got it. And she enjoyed his company because few other people understood it was easier to lose a life partner after a happy marriage than a difficult one, because it was a loss not warped by regret. But then there were times (like this) when Raja Kumar could be as irritatingly overprotective as the late ML Lee had been. Playing the "man of the world" role, never mind it had always been the women of the world who wrung chickens' necks and scraped the guts out of still-flapping fish.

As they ate, Commissioner Raja explained to Aunty Lee in great detail why she should not get involved in things beyond her control. Despite his admonishments, Aunty Lee enjoyed her lunch.

Commissioner Raja sighed in contentment as he finished his lecture and started on his dessert *laddus*. Nothing could be more familiar than these traditional soft, sweet dessert balls, but even so he paused in surprise after the first mouthful.

"Grated coconut." Aunty Lee had also tasted the innovation. "And spicy pine-nut paste inside, interesting."

They were certainly interesting but Commissioner Raja thought innovative *laddus* should not look like the sweet, safe *chana dal laddus* his grandmother had made . . . and an inexperienced, untrained, self-appointed detective should not look like a sweet, friendly widow.

"So what are you going to do now?" Aunty Lee asked.

He knew she was not asking about his plans for the afternoon.

"We will investigate, following the proper channels. As you say, there may be a connection with illegal organ trafficking. We will follow up all leads, get information from our overseas contacts about organ traffickers, and leave the case open until it is solved. And it will be solved eventually. Either the perpetrators will be caught or they will find that it is not worth the risk to operate in Singapore, and take their business elsewhere."

It was always that way, Aunty Lee thought. As long as criminals stayed out of Singapore, they were not Singapore's problem. The United States was criticized for minding the world's business. But was ignoring everything outside your borders that much better? Given how interconnected everything was, was that even possible?

"I don't think Mabel Sung and her son were killed by illegal organ traffickers," Aunty Lee said.

"I thought you said illegal organ traffickers were involved?"

"Oh yes, definitely involved. But you remember I was there when Mabel and her son were poisoned. I saw Sharon scooping out the chicken *buah keluak* and the rest of the food. She thought she'd bring it up to the house. GraceFaith Ang and Edmond Yong were going up to Leonard's room and she gave them the food to bring. They left it in Leonard's room. He did not eat until Mabel came up to feed him."

"So any of them could have put the poison in the food. Granted. But most likely the perpetrator is still Mabel Sung. No one else had a reason."

"It could have been someone at the party who went up to the house to use the toilet like I did. And we just don't know the reason yet."

"We already checked out all the people at the party. Friends of the family or members of Mabel Sung's law firm. No illegal organ traffickers. And just for argument's sake, if these illegal organ traffickers really exist, what reason would they have to kill Mabel Sung and her son? These people are here to make money from selling harvested organs. They want to keep a low profile, do their business, get their money, and get out as fast as possible without anybody noticing them."

"Exactly. That's why I believe they are around but I don't think they killed Mabel and her son!"

"Mabel Sung knew that Leonard Sung was not going to recover. He was a drug addict who destroyed his health. The woman killed her son rather than watch him suffer."

There was a note in his voice that indicated the discussion had ended. Indeed Commissioner Raja started (not without difficulty) to raise himself off the cushions.

Commissioner Raja waved the problem away. "She must have added the poison to the food before serving it up to herself and her son."

It didn't feel right to Aunty Lee. But enforcers of Singapore law—even one as nice to her as Commissioner Raja—generally did not operate on what didn't feel right to regular citizens. He would have pointed out that she had no proof. He would have thought her not wanting to believe that another old lady could have chosen to kill herself and her son was old-lady squeamishness. So she said nothing. She would think about all the separate parts of the puzzle, and when she managed to put a complete picture together, she would present it to Commissioner Raja

"It's always harder to get up than sit down," Aunty Lee observed. She had somehow got to her feet without trouble and was smoothing down her flared batik pants as she watched her friend struggle to his feet.

"Your men didn't find anything else at all at the Sung house? Even after checking everything? Did they check the house, the grounds, the swimming pool for anything suspicious?"

Finally back on his feet, Commissioner Raja wondered whether genuine police work would ever recover from the effects of television procedurals. "There wasn't much point searching for clues when it was obvious how the poison was administered," he said. "But actually our men did search the whole place thoroughly and they documented the process very meticulously."

"Even the pool filters?"

"Probably. I can go look if it will make you feel better, but I tell you there is nothing to find. Anyway the pool had just been cleaned, so I doubt there was anything."

"Whoever added the poison to my *buah keluak* must have got it from somewhere. If they just cleaned the pool, some kinds of water cleaner can be very poisonous . . ."

Commissioner Raja stretched contentedly and felt a satisfying little burp rise. It had been a good lunch and it couldn't hurt to tell his old friend how close her guess had come. "We found a possible source of the poison. There were containers of Algae Bomb under the food tables, against the wall."

"And just one more thing," Aunty Lee said. "Your officers must have talked to all the people working for the Sungs. There was a PRC woman there. I didn't see her again after Mabel was found. Can you tell me who she is? I just want to make sure that she's all right."

Commissioner Raja gave Aunty Lee a sharp look, almost as though he distrusted her seemingly altruistic motives. "PRC domestic helpers are not allowed in Singapore. The Sungs' two domestic workers are both nurses from the Philippines and they both quit already. The gardener is from Sri Lanka and doesn't speak English. There was no PRC woman there."

"Oh, maybe I was mistaken and she was a guest? I saw her talking to the Sungs' doctor, Edmond Yong, so she may have been a nurse. Yes, she could have been an off-duty nurse. You know nurses and child-care workers always have that bossy exhausted air even when they are not working. If she was a nurse she would know all about poisoning people, right? Did the Sungs have a full-time or part-time nurse to look after their son? He was in quite bad shape, right? So unless they were changing his diaper and bathing him themselves, they would have needed professional help. Anyway, you should find out who she was, shouldn't you?"

Commissioner Raja, however reluctantly, registered her point. She waited while he typed a quick message into his phone. But he put the subject away along with his phone.

"Look, Rosie. I know this must be very difficult for you.

But please leave it to us this time. We'll try to get the inspections done as quickly as possible and your restaurant can open again. I know there is nothing wrong with your kitchens but we have to follow the rules nonetheless, this is Singapore. It is not enough to just do the right thing, we have to let people see we are doing the right thing. Just think of this as a short holiday. In fact, why not go and take a trip somewhere? When was the last time you traveled out of Singapore? Go to England to visit Mathilda. Go and cook all her favorite dishes for her."

Mathilda was always happy to see Aunty Lee. But leaving Singapore now felt like leaving the house with a pot of curry bubbling on the stove. It was not just the curry that might be spoiled. If it burned dry in the pot and caught fire, a whole lot more damage might be done.

"Aren't you people supposed to tell me not to leave the country?"

"Rosie, don't talk nonsense. I told you, you are not a suspect."

"Everybody who was there that day is a suspect. Henry Sung just told me that even he is a suspect."

"When did you talk to Henry Sung?" Commissioner Raja asked sharply.

"We ran into each other at a friend's place. I get the feeling he believes Mabel killed herself but he's too Christian to let himself think it consciously." Aunty Lee broke off with a laugh at the expression on Commissioner Raja's face. "What's wrong? I can have lunch with you but I can't talk to Henry Sung? I'm going to think you're jealous!"

"Rosie, this is all confidential but I think it's better you know than go blundering in deeper. It was Henry Sung who got your restaurant to be closed down. In his words, 'Even if it was an accident you don't want her to poison anybody else.' The man has friends in high places. All retired. But around here the retired judges, retired ministers, are all still connected. There's nothing on paper but they all still have a lot of influence. Their friend has just lost his wife and son. If they can make him feel better by closing you down, they won't think twice. And they are all connected to the people in power now. All it takes is a word. And the second complaint was from his lady friend Doreen Choo. She could not say exactly what she was complaining about, and when we asked her to be more specific, Henry Sung put it all down for her."

Now Aunty Lee understood Doreen Choo's initial discomfort when they had talked. She must have thought Aunty Lee would learn she had agreed to play along with Henry's plan.

"Are you all right, Rosie?"

"I think I need to go to a prayer and healing session."

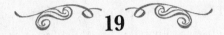

19

Prayer and Healing

Aunty Lee had always prided herself on staying happy by keeping busy. But back at the (sadly closed) café after lunch with the commissioner, it was not easy to find something to be busy with. Nina had already taken care of everything that could be cleaned, sorted, or recycled and was starting to look aimless herself.

"Maybe you should get a dog, ma'am."

"You mean a guard dog? Why? Have there been break-ins again?"

"No, ma'am. But so many of the other maids . . ." Their politically correct employers might call them "domestic helpers" but the women referred to themselves and one another as "maids." "Many of the other maids have dogs to walk in the morning and in the evening. Sometimes they even walk to the playground and have a picnic and listen to music. If you have a dog then I can take the dog and go with them."

"I'm sure you can join them without a dog, Nina."

"If I don't have a dog then people will see and say I am wasting time. They will report me to the police and say I am loitering. But if I got a dog with me then I am dog walking," Nina explained.

It made sense, Aunty Lee supposed, though it was hard on the dogs who ended up standing around while their human walkers talked rather than exercised.

"But what will you do with the dog when the café opens again?"

"We can bring the dog, ma'am. If it is a big dog it will be like a guard dog. And if it is a small dog people will say 'so cute, so cute' and then they will come in to shop and buy things."

"Maybe I should give a party," Aunty Lee said.

"Somebody else dies, we sure kenah arrested."

"Maybe we can't have guests in here, but we can still do outside catering, right?" Cherril said as she entered the shop. She was equally in search of occupation, Aunty Lee suspected. "And we can cook as long as we don't serve. And we can sell food as long as we didn't just make it in the kitchen. We should start making the Christmas and New Year treats and freeze them," Cherril said. "In fact we can sell them frozen. Then people can take home and heat them up and feel that they did their own cooking."

Aunty Lee felt even more fond of Cherril than she usually did, despite a twinge of guilt at the thought of Mathilda. She would make it up to Mathilda some other way. After all, the girl was on the other side of the world. Aunty Lee needed a kitchen companion in Singapore.

"Sorry you got involved in all this. I will understand if you want to pull out, you know."

"Oh, not at all. I'm enjoying it, believe it or not. I like being part of a team. I know it sounds corny, but when I'm doing something on my own I can't get as excited about it. It's very easy to give up and say okay, not worth it, don't sweat the small stuff, just move on to the next job. But like last time when I was part of a cabin crew, it was hard work and there were times when it was really tough and you can hate the people you are working with. But once I put on the uniform and put on the face, then it is like the show is on. I can play the part no matter how tired I am because I know what they expect me to be, so I can be good. And people expect Aunty Lee's Delights to be good also. Don't you know? Once people get you to cater for them, they know that their party is going to be a success. Even if the people there got nothing to talk about, they can always talk about the food. That's why you can't give up."

Unasked, Nina put down a cup of hot lemongrass tea in front of Cherril. And she smiled.

"I got Mykie to look at the injunction again. It only says that you cannot prepare food until the kitchen here has been given the all clear. It doesn't mean that you cannot cook in your house or even in my house, for that matter."

The earnest young woman was trying to cheer Aunty Lee up and boost her morale, Aunty Lee realized. Her preoccupation with Mabel's death must have made Cherril think she was depressed by the forced closure of the café kitchens. As if a little thing like that could get Aunty Lee down, given all the setbacks she had struggled through and triumphed over in more years than Cherril Lim-Peters could imagine! But she was touched that Cherril had tried. And there was Nina watching, uncharacteristically silent. It looked like Aunty Lee had made both Nina and Cherril worried.

"We should use this time to try out new recipes. And see how well things freeze and how to reheat them."

Nina, who had had been listening, nodded approval. "But the freezer is full already. Where to keep all the food you make?"

"I'll bring whatever we make to a prayer meeting I'm going to tonight," Aunty Lee said. "If I don't sell it, it is not counted as business, right? And if the other people are worried about the food they can pray over it before eating, then everybody happy."

At the prayer and healing session that evening Aunty Lee remembered to say it was her knees that were giving her trouble. It was a good choice; she saw other members of the group nodding sympathetically. It appeared Mabel Sung had always led these sessions and now no one seemed willing to take her place. Neither Sharon nor Henry Sung was around. In the end the seven or eight "old fogies," as they called themselves, had a "moment of silence" for Mabel and sat down to sample Aunty Lee's goodies.

Aunty Lee plonked herself next to Doreen and listened as she nattered on. Her chatter was like the drizzle that the southeast monsoon winds brought to Singapore. There was not enough rain to make you stay under shelter or even open an umbrella. The light warm droplets were relentless but so small that you ended up damp rather than wet. Folk wisdom said going out in this kind of rain made people get sick. Aunty Lee, though, believed in vitamin C and germs rather than these superstitions. As Doreen's stream of words continued, Aunty Lee's mind was starting to feel damp. She blinked and shook her head slightly. Doreen paused and looked at her.

"My knees," Aunty Lee said quickly. She changed her expression of polite interest into an exaggerated wince and massaged her knees. Knees were a safe option. Older people were always having problems with their knees, and since there was no practical solution, people were always ready to offer their theories.

Doreen brightened immediately. "You never said you had knee problems!" Her memory, thought Aunty Lee, needed as much help as her corneas.

"You know, with age . . ." Aunty Lee murmured vaguely. "I really don't know what to do."

"Oh, I know, I know. People always tell you, eat this, eat that, don't eat this, don't eat that. Or they tell you to exercise more or they tell you not to exercise at all. I tell you all that is rubbish. You think of your car when there is a part that breaks down. What do you do—you change the part, right? That is the only thing to do. This may sound like science fiction, Rosie, but it's not. I didn't believe it myself until Henry persuaded me to try it."

"You had knee surgery?" Aunty Lee asked, really interested now. She could not recall Doreen disappearing on a "spa retreat" that was the usual cover story for face-lifts and chin tucks.

"Oh no. My knees are still okay, as long as I don't walk too much or stand too long. I'm not like you, Rosie. I don't know where you get the energy to run around all day. You should think about slowing down, you know. Men don't like women who are always running around nonstop. I know you'll say you're not interested in such things, that it's too late, but I tell you—as long as there's life, there's hope. Just the other day I was saying to Henry—"

"Did Henry have knee surgery?" Aunty Lee tried to steer the conversation back onto the course she wanted.

"Henry? What would he do that for? There's nothing wrong with that man's knees. He can play golf all day, no problem. I keep telling him to use those little carts that go around the green. Then I can go around with him and watch him play with his friends. But Henry says he prefers to walk. He says it's the only form of exercise he gets. I mean, that's fine with me. I'm not the sort of woman who has to stick close all the time. Men don't like that kind of woman. You may think you are being loving when you want to spend time together but men see it as being stifled. That's the word they use, 'stifled.'"

Doreen paused, perhaps remembering an unfortunate occasion.

"You were telling me something about knee surgery," Aunty Lee said with a faint touch of desperation.

"Was I? Oh yes. That's right. The surgery. Sharon mentioned it to me the other day. I had been talking to Mabel about it and Mabel must have talked to her. Not knees, corneas."

"Corneas?"

"You know, in your eyes. What you see with is your corneas. I was having so much trouble with cataracts and everything. I had to go and get my cataracts taken out. So terrible having such things growing in your eyes. Makes me think I'm really getting to be an old woman!"

Doreen paused and laughed, giving Aunty Lee a chance to contradict her. Dutifully, Aunty Lee fluttered in: "Doreen, who are you to talk about being an old woman! Don't talk nonsense. Look at you—you're still young!"

"I wouldn't have done the operation otherwise. Other parts not such a big deal. But your eyes, you know . . . Anyway, since I was going to have the cataracts taken out, I thought I might as well get the corneas put in, right? Only one operation, everything done, right? Turns out I still cannot see perfectly. I thought I would be able to see far far, read close close, but no. Still got to wear reading glasses. Thought after all I paid, I would be able to get rid of wearing glasses forever! The operation is not cheap, you know. Of course I complained. I may be getting old but don't think you can cheat me! Mabel just kept pretending not to hear me. I knew she was avoiding me. But that Sharon is a nice girl. In fact she just came and asked me did I want to go and do the operation again. She said since I was disappointed the first time they would give me a discount. I told her that after they botched the first operation they should do it for me this time for free!"

"Are you going to do the operation again?" Aunty Lee asked.

"That's what Sharon asked. I said no. First time cost so much, I still cannot see properly, why would I go through all that whole business again?"

Finally, as Aunty Lee was on the verge of giving up and going home, Henry Sung and Sharon arrived, with Edmond Yong and GraceFaith in tow.

GraceFaith looked around the room and drifted to Aunty Lee's side. "Your first time here? I don't believe you've met Edmond Yong? He was poor Leonard's doctor."

GraceFaith was wearing a silky black dress. Aunty Lee thought it was probably a mourning tribute because Grace-Faith did not look like the sort of girl to depend on a "little black dress." There were flashes of color as she walked. Under the black floating skirt panels there was a bright orange underskirt. GraceFaith could keep up appearances when she had to, but why bother, when there was no point in it?

"Oh yes, I've met him," Aunty Lee said. Then she saw GraceFaith was not listening.

In fact GraceFaith was on edge and displeased about something. She was still efficiently polite. After all, being nice to important old people was one of her greatest strengths and had got her where she was. However once she had anchored herself by Aunty Lee, she ignored her.

Fortunately Aunty Lee's great strength was sniffing out

notes that didn't fit. Anyone can say something tastes good but only an expert nose can tell you why. And that's the only sort of nose that is helpful when things go wrong. Aunty Lee could tell that whatever GraceFaith felt was wrong was anchored in Dr. Yong and Sharon. The two spent most of the evening moving among groups of people as though they were joint hosts. Aunty Lee wondered which of them Grace-Faith was jealous or suspicious of—or was it both?

It looked as though it would be some time before they reached Aunty Lee. She heard several mentions of the Bukit Timah Plaza clinic as several of the group members asked where the new operating theater would be located. Apparently they were as in the dark as Aunty Lee.

"We'll let you know," Sharon said several times. "We're still trying to set things up."

Finally it was Aunty Lee's turn. GraceFaith slipped away as Sharon and Dr. Yong approached Aunty Lee. It was not out of love that GraceFaith was watching them, Aunty Lee thought.

"Doreen says you're having trouble with your knees?" Sharon asked.

"Oh yes. You know how it is, getting old. Very good of you to carry on what your mother started."

Sharon smiled. "I'm just trying to continue what my mother did as she should have wanted." There was a note of sarcasm in her voice that Aunty Lee couldn't understand. Nor could she understand why Sharon was being so nice to Edmond Yong. The last time she had seen them together,

Sharon had seemed to despise the man. "I'm so sorry to hear your shop's been closed down."

"You must understand the family is not blaming you for the tragedy," Edmond Yong said. "But naturally they want to move on and put it behind them as fast as possible. If the police have to do a full investigation it is going to drag on and on . . . you know how these things go. No matter how it turns out, it's not going to bring poor Mabel and Leonard back, right? And knowing Mabel, I'm sure we can all agree that she would want us to carry on with what she started."

He spoke with the condescending fake enthusiasm of someone accustomed to dealing with stubborn preschoolers. The message conveyed was that as long as you did as you were told, you would get candy and be allowed to play with the rest of the group.

Aunty Lee sensed Edmond Yong enjoyed feeling power over people She wondered what hold he had over Sharon.

"Now that I can't work, I might as well use the time to fix my knees. Can you help me?" Aunty Lee asked.

"There is a procedure that should help you, if your problem is what I think it is . . . knee pain when walking and standing for a while—"

"Knee pain all the time!" Aunty Lee interrupted. "Everybody says the only way is to cut off my whole knee and put in some metal joint I don't want. If I got robot knees inside me, then every time I go to the airport the metal detectors beep-beep-beep and they arrest me, then how?"

"It won't be so invasive. Your pain is likely caused by a torn meniscus in your knee. Think of the meniscus as a rubbery cushion that keeps your knee steady. As we grow older the meniscus gets worn and tears easily when you walk or lift things, which leaves the bones of your knee grinding against each other. What I can do is transplant a donor meniscus onto each of your knees. It's very safe, but it's not cheap."

"I got insurance."

"I'm afraid you can't use your insurance for this. It's considered elective surgery," Dr. Yong explained. "But if you can afford to pay, I can guarantee you will find the results satisfactory."

"Well, health is the main thing, right?" Aunty Lee said. "But wait, one more thing. Can I meet the person arranging the transplant? Just to be sure the donor is . . ." She leaned closer and whispered, "Chinese."

"No," Sharon snapped. "You just have to trust us."

Aunty Lee could tell that it was just to spite Sharon that Edmond Yong said, "I will see what I can do. I will come round to your place to see you and discuss details, okay?"

Aunty Lee did not miss the look he gave Sharon Sung. *Look how well I handled things,* it said. But Sharon did not see it. She was watching Aunty Lee and seemed to want to say something.

"Yes?" Aunty Lee said hopefully.

Sharon just shook her head. She was not one to waste words. But Aunty Lee had not given up hope of breaking through to her.

"Sharon doesn't talk much," Dr. Yong said. "Sharon's the

sort of lawyer that only talks when she's paid to talk, right?" He was teasing, maybe even flirting, but Aunty Lee found it offensive. Sharon's face closed up and she said nothing.

Aunty Lee liked Sharon and felt everyone was picking on her because she had not fallen apart with grief after her mother and brother's deaths.

"Sometimes the only way to survive a great shock is by giving your brain something else to work on. Otherwise it just goes round and round—who you've lost, what you've lost, and everything seems pointless. Much better to get on with work and keep yourself busy."

"Everything other than quantifiable, profitable work is pointless to Sharon," Dr. Yong said. "And she tries to turn everything into work."

Dr. Yong reminded Aunty Lee of the Chinese gang she had helped foil. He thought he could intimidate her because she was old and out of touch and frightened by all the things that she did not understand. But like the Chinese gang members, he had underestimated Aunty Lee.

"Thank you," Aunty Lee said meekly. "Young people these days know how everything works."

But it was old people who knew how to work the young people.

"Dr. Yong, ah, can I ask you who was that long-haired Chinese woman you were talking to at the Sungs' house that day?"

"That's rubbish. I don't know what you're talking about," Dr. Yong said very quickly.

He was a bad liar and got angry too easily to succeed at

anything, Aunty Lee thought. Fortunately she was a very good liar. And she knew that sweetened coconut milk could tone down the most fiery chilies.

"Old girlfriend, right? Don't worry. I won't say anything in front of your new girlfriend." She nudged him and tilted her head at Sharon.

Realization and relief and then his old smug look returned. He was flattered and grinned at Aunty Lee. "Cannot kiss and tell, right?"

Sharon looked disgusted.

Aunty Lee knew she had to find out more about the long-haired Wen Ling.

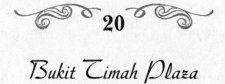

20

Bukit Timah Plaza

Really good cooks probably have dishes that go wrong as often as anyone else. Great cooks have twice as many because they are constantly experimenting with new ingredients and new combinations. Aunty Lee believed she was a great cook, in life as well as in the kitchen. When a dish came out wrong you knew that there was something wrong either with the ingredients or with the way they had been put together. In life, it was people and their personalities who were her ingredients.

Most people cook from set recipes, written down or not. Their dishes are prepared the way their mothers and grandmothers or other cooking idols prepared them, using ingredients as similar as possible.

Aunty Lee often did that too. After all, it was a certain way to get predictable results with familiar dishes. But sometimes it was necessary to work with whatever ingredients were available. In such a case you had to go through your fridge and freezer to examine what you had on hand, what could be best put together to produce a dish at a moment's notice. And sometimes the result was culinary genius. Aunty Lee suspected that this was how the dish that poisoned Mabel Sung and her son had come about.

Mabel Sung must have been poisoned by one of the people at the party that day. They were the ingredients Aunty Lee would be working with. And the person must have had access to Leonard Sung's food tray. After exempting herself, Cherril, and Nina from the list of suspects, Aunty Lee was left with:

- Mabel Sung (suicide and mercy killing of chronically ill son?)
- Leonard Sung (suicide to avoid a long-drawn-out death, accidentally or deliberately taking his mother with him?)
- Henry Sung (same motive as wife for killing son; accidentally killing wife. Or killing wife so he could be free to pursue his relationship with Doreen Choo; accidentally killing son?)
- Sharon Sung (same motive as Mabel for killing brother; accidentally killing mother?)
- GraceFaith Ang (no obvious motive. She had hero-worshiped Mabel and believed that Leonard could be cured.)

- Dr. Edmond Yong (no obvious motive. He was well paid by Mabel to take care of Leonard and there was no sign that Mabel had changed her mind about him. If he had been practicing medicine in Singapore for any length of time, there would be someone who could tell her about him. Cherril had met him previously. And she would visit Bukit Timah Plaza, where his clinic had been before the fire. And an old doctor friend of ML's had a family clinic in Bukit Timah Plaza. Perhaps Professor Koh would remember him?)
- Other members of Sung Law (motive? If any of them had wanted to kill Mabel Sung they need not have waited to do it at a party at her house.)
- Other members of the Sungs' prayer support group, Never Say Die (motive? Anyone upset with Mabel or Leonard had only to leave the group.)
- Domestic help (motive? Again, why wait till the party to carry out the murder?)

Aunty Lee looked at her list. She felt that she had the makings of a satisfying dish in hand but that a main ingredient—a motive—was missing. Was this an impulse killing? To know this she had to find out more about the personalities of the people; for example, who was always losing his temper with bad drivers, who was most aggressive with queue jumpers who took her spot? But still it came back to needing a motive.

This was a *buah keluak* killing; the preparation, the risk, the fragrant black paste that only appealed to the initiated. And it was hard to predict who it appealed to. Mark, for example, did not like *buah keluak* despite his Peranakan roots. But Mycroft Peters with his Anglo-Indian forebears loved the dish. Aunty Lee reminded herself not to make assumptions about the people involved. The problem was she felt she had already done so.

The worst mistakes come from generalizations we don't realize we are making. Aunty Lee decided she had to go more thoroughly into the personalities, impulses, and motives of the people on her list. And she also wanted to find out more about the people who had turned up unexpectedly. Even if they could not have put the poison into the dish, their presence might have triggered a chain of events that landed it there. She was thinking of the long-haired Wen Ling and Patrick Pang's friend Benjamin.

Inspector Salim had requested information from other departments but there was no trace of Benjamin Ng in Singapore or Shanghai or anywhere else.

Sometimes it is harder to see the most obvious cause of problems when you know the people involved. This is not necessarily due to partisanship or prejudice but to the blindness that comes with familiarity. It is the daughter you see every day that you don't notice is growing up and the father asleep in front of the television every night that you don't realize has grown old.

Aunty Lee took a mental step back. If she did not know all these people, if they were all characters on a television drama, who had the greatest motive to kill Mabel Sung?

Aunty Lee settled on Mabel's husband. After all, clichés existed because they were so often true. Henry Sung's motive would be to stop his wife before she lost everything they had. She was on the verge of bankruptcy and Sung Law looked like a lost cause, but with Mabel gone, could he save himself and Sharon? Sharon would have no difficulty finding a job in another company if she did not have her mother and Sung Law weighing her down. And if he sold the house there might be enough left for him to live on. But what about his son? Aunty Lee knew it was far less common for men to kill their sons than their wives. Perhaps Henry had never forgiven his son, Leonard, for throwing away his life and disgracing the family name?

Could Mabel have killed herself and her son? Yes. But Aunty Lee thought she would have done it differently. More decently? No, more privately. Mabel would not have killed herself with her house full of people. But maybe she wanted witnesses to see that she killed herself? She could just have left a suicide note or a suicide video. Or a suicide note like the PRC woman who jumped. Was the closeness in time of the three deaths a link or just a coincidence?

I really wish I could find that long-haired Chinese woman, Aunty Lee thought, but until then she would make the most of her time by visiting Bukit Timah Plaza.

Aunty Lee had not been to Bukit Timah Plaza for some time. The shopping mall was not far from Binjai Park. But it was too far to walk comfortably to yet too close by to be worth getting the car out for. It was not surprising that Aunty Lee had not noticed Edmond Yong's clinic there. But perhaps someone else had.

Aunty Lee had arranged to meet Professor Koh Heng Kiang, an old friend, at his Bukit Timah Plaza clinic. But first she stopped at a bustling little kiosk on the second level to talk to Cosmo.

Cosmo was part of the third generation of his family to run the little Peranakan deli stall with the best *nasi kunyit* outside of Aunty Lee's own kitchen. Rumor had it that Prime Minister Lee Hsien Loong's chauffeur had been seen queuing for Cosmo's *mee siam*. Yes, equality in Singapore meant that even if you were satisfying the prime minister's craving for rice vermicelli in addictively spicy, sweet, sour, shrimpy sauce, you had to stand in line like everyone else.

"Have not seen you around for a long time, sister," Cosmo said when he saw her.

"Been busy, lah." There was a long line and Aunty Lee got straight to the point. "I want to take away some of your *kueh*. Pack for me about half a dozen, can? I heard there was fire here a while ago? One of the clinics in the medical center?"

"Ah yes. Not that nice Dr. Koh's side. You take ten *kueh*, okay? I can pack for you nicely in this box. One of the small clinics on the other side for men who want to look like women and women who want to look like teenagers. You want to try my *bubur terigu*? Made by my sister following my mum's recipe."

"If you can pack for me I want. But ten *kueh* I don't know I can finish or not. Here you are always so full there's nowhere

to sit. When was this fire? Whose clinic, do you know?" Cosmo
always knew everything going on in Bukit Timah Plaza.

"More than a year ago. Dr. Yong and Dr. Sung's clinic, I
think. See, I pack the coconut milk for you separately. The
kueh no need to eat all at once. Can put in the fridge one
week. They are attached to some kind of church, I think.
Always got people praying outside while they are operating inside. See this *oh ku kueh* with mung-bean paste, turtle
shape for long life, and this green *ku kueh*, with *gula melaka*
coconut? I give you two each, okay? You see ten in the box,
just right."

"Okay. Anybody died in the fire? How much do I owe you?"

"Yes, one woman. But don't know who. They said she was a
foreigner working as a prostitute on a social visit pass, came
for plastic surgery then had heart attack. Nobody claimed the
body. Poor thing. Here's your change. Have a blessed day."

Professor Koh's late wife had been one of the women in
Aunty Lee's women's travel group (so much safer than traveling alone and so much easier to shop when traveling without
husbands). Since Eva Koh's death Aunty Lee had kept Professor Koh on her list of recipients for Christmas and Chinese
New Year goodies. Therefore it was only natural that when
Aunty Lee whipped up a batch of *ayam pongteh,* the chicken
and potato stew that Malacca-born Eva had loved so much,
she should bring a large Tupperware of it over to Professor
Koh. That and the cakes from Cosmo would be something
for him to share with his eldest son and his family, who Aunty
Lee had learned he was now living with.

She had also learned that the retired former head of NUH (the National University Hospital) had been chief of surgery when Dr. Edmond Yong left the hospital suddenly.

Though Professor Koh had refused treatment for colon cancer, he looked well enough, and Aunty Lee said so.

"I am well. I suppose as usual they told you to remind me that there's a lot more life worth living and I should let them cut me up and microwave me?"

Aunty Lee suspected part of Professor Koh was touched by the attempts of his family, right down to his grandsons and domestic helpers, to try to get him to accept treatment. But the former surgeon was adamant about not pursuing treatment for his stage-two disease, preferring to wait and see how it progressed. More than 70 percent of people diagnosed would be free of cancer five years after even without adjuvant chemotherapy, and Professor Koh said he would take his chances. "If it goes away, I am well. If it doesn't go away, I see my Eva again sooner."

"She might not want to see you so soon," Aunty Lee pointed out. They had been friends long enough for her to know how much Professor Koh enjoyed talking about his late wife, a subject most other people shied away from.

"She might say you better hang around longer, I want you to take photographs of the grandchildren getting married for me to see!"

"We can watch together from up there." Professor Koh laughed. "But I know you didn't come to see me just to talk about Eva. How can I help you, Rosie?" There was a touch of professional apprehension in his voice. Though his son-in-law and two daughters now ran what was still known as "Professor Koh's Clinic," many older patients preferred to speak to Professor Koh himself when worrying symptoms showed up.

"Do you remember an Edmond Yong? He used to have a clinic around here."

Professor Koh looked at Aunty Lee as though debating whether to ask why she wanted to know. But reticent good manners won out. He answered her question.

"Edmond Yong. His crowning achievement was getting his medical degree. He just stopped working after that. You can tell the really keen ones. They are the ones who are nonstop investigating new methods, new stats, new ways of handling old problems."

"So you don't think much of him?"

"Well, I wouldn't say he was very promising, but workwise, nothing very disastrous. He got into some trouble at the hospital. A patient complained about inappropriate behavior. Said the boy had touched her and made a suggestive comment when the nurse was not in the room. In such cases it's very difficult to tell what really happened. Sometimes people genuinely misinterpret or for whatever reason they have some ax to grind. But the problem is, once a complaint is made, the hospital has to investigate. And then even if you are cleared you have to work under a shadow, very unpleasant. In fact I was chairing the board of inquiry for his case."

"Did it ever happen to you?" Aunty Lee asked, diverting him because she wanted to hear his reflections on the case rather than the factual summary that he might automatically deliver. She was certain he had never fallen under this particular cloud. Her old friend seemed too genial about the subject to have ever experienced it himself.

"Oh no, not me. I was one of the fortunate ones. Remember Eva and I got married even before I finished medical school? After that, with my wedding ring on, even in the wards nobody saw me as a man, just as 'married.'"

That was probably untrue, but the eyes of this man had noticed only one woman since they got together as pre-university classmates, and would not have noticed attention from anyone else. Aunty Lee remembered her late friend and smiled. Professor Koh smiled also, following her thoughts.

"She was always so careful of my health. 'Don't work so hard,' 'Don't eat junk food for lunch,' 'Nobody is going to die if you take one week off to take your children on holiday.' We always thought I would be the one to go first. Male life expectancy, you know. And of course the job was taxing. That's why I always tried to make time for the family. I wanted them to remember me. My brother was only fifty when he got his heart attack. My father, fifty-four. Eva never said so, but after I turned fifty I knew she started worrying. Instead—" He raised a hand and dropped it with a little laugh. Eva had died eight months after being diagnosed with pancreatic cancer. She had been two days away from her sixty-fifth birthday.

"But you don't have any doubt that Dr. Yong was falsely accused?"

This time there was a longer pause. All Aunty Lee's *kaypoh* receptors were primed and on alert as she watched Professor

Koh, waiting for him to speak. He noticed this and laughed at her. But he sobered immediately as he said, "From his past actions, from everything his colleagues said about him, there was no reason to doubt him whatsoever . . ."

"But?"

"But I was uncomfortable. For no good reason, you might say. The nurse had stepped out for a while. It is a rule that there must always be a female nurse present when the doctor is examining a female patient. But in this case the patient had asked for a drink of water in the middle of the examination and the nurse went to get it. She left the door open, which is also a standard procedure, but when she came back with the water it was closed."

"It was the patient who requested the water?"

"Yes. And the patient made no complaint at that point in time. She said she went home and thought about it, talked it over with her boyfriend before deciding to make an official complaint. There was some indication that they had made an attempt to contact Dr. Yong and extort money from him before making the official complaint, so yes, certainly there were gray areas in her story. And there was no conclusive verdict. We labeled it a misunderstanding, sent the woman our sincere apologies, and hoped regardless of whatever happened this would be enough of a warning to Dr. Yong to make sure that nothing like that would happen again—whether misunderstanding or otherwise. I think he was upset that we did not clear him completely, based on his word. Some of these young ones, they are the only one in their family, in their extended family, to get a university degree, maybe the only one from their hometown to become a Singapore doctor, and they get inflated ideas."

Though Professor Koh had not said so, Aunty Lee could see he believed the younger doctor guilty. He did not want her to dig up the old problems because they were over and done with, but neither would he take action to have Dr. Yong reinstated. The unspoken accusation could last far longer than one that was articulated and dismissed.

"What's your interest in Dr. Yong's clinic?"

"An old friend, Doreen Choo, said she had some work done there."

Professor Koh laughed, his relief clear. "She found out that Henry Sung was a partner there, that's why she came. Doreen sucks the life out of men. I know my limits, thank you. I just want a bit of peace. Good luck to Henry! I think one of my girls told me that Edmond Yong borrowed money from Henry Sung to set up his clinic, Beautiful Dreamers. It was an aesthetic-surgery clinic. He must have heard it was the line that made the most money fast."

That must have been when Cherril encountered him, Aunty Lee thought.

"But it's not as easy as that. You look at someone like Woffles Wu. The man approaches his work like an artist and makes the patient feel like a muse and inspiration. Plus he is good-looking himself. And charming, which always helps. You compare that to someone who looks like Edmond Yong and talks like he's selling ponzi shares, who would you trust?"

"So it didn't work?" Aunty Lee didn't like Dr. Yong but she felt sorry for him.

"Plus people here increasingly prefer to go to Korea for treatment. Prices there are lower because there is so much competition. And apparently they don't just fix your nose or your eyes, they can make you look like your favorite K-pop star. But that's all hearsay."

That must have been when he was lured into illegal transplants, Aunty Lee thought.

"But the people who were too sick to travel? I've heard there are ways to arrange to get transplant operations here. But how do they get the donor organs?"

Professor Koh waved a hand, gesturing to the upper floors of Bukit Timah Plaza surrounding the central atrium where they were sitting. "Travel agencies, maid agencies. There are so many of them now. If you pay them enough they will bring in people or parts or whatever you want, with whatever papers you need.

"In compensated donation, donors get money or other compensation in exchange for their organs. This practice is common in some parts of the world, whether legal or not, and is one of the many factors driving medical tourism. Of course it is happening here in Singapore. In fact, given the superior conditions here, it is probably better for both the donors and the recipients that the operations are carried out here. In China approximately ninety-five percent of all organs used for transplantation are from executed prisoners. The lack of a public organ-donation program in China is used as a justification for this practice. It makes you wonder, doesn't it? There's a lot of talk about illegal organ culling but nobody has any proof."

"That woman who killed herself because she couldn't find her fiancé, do you remember? Do you think he's dead?"

"That dead woman's fiancé may still be alive somewhere in Singapore. He's worth a lot of money and he's already paid for. Then again, maybe he just decided to break off with his girlfriend and is working illegally in a massage parlor here."

"Dr. Yong may have been trying to talk Mabel Sung into getting transplants to save her son's life. What if she found out where he was getting the body parts from and he had to kill her?"

"Edmond Yong wouldn't be able to pull something like that off. He was a mediocre student, he would be a mediocre crook. People don't change that much."

Aunty Lee's mind ran over further possibilities. What if Wen Ling had been getting the organs for Mabel's son and Edmond was just the go-between? Like a microwave meal this theory superficially met all the requirements and used all the right ingredients but it did not yet feel like real substance. No. Mabel had not met Wen Ling till the day of the party, the day she died. Aunty Lee was certain of that.

"Edmond Yong wanted to make a quick, big impression on people. That was more important to him than whether he could sustain that impression. I don't think he even planned how he was going to run the clinic. Did he think that he could carry it off by the sheer force of his personality?"

"I suspect he didn't think so far ahead," Aunty Lee said. "I suppose he had fire insurance?"

"It's a requirement here. Regulations. But get this. Immediately after the fire Dr. Yong disappeared back to Malaysia. He didn't even wait to claim insurance here. The Management Committee was trying to reach him. He said, 'Nobody died, so it's no big deal. Let the insurance people fight it out.'"

"Nobody died? I thought the papers said they found a body?"

"Did they?"

Nobody seemed very interested in the dead woman, Aunty Lee thought. Without a name and a story to anchor her, Aunty Lee could feel her own attention slipping away too. She looked up. On the floors surrounding the central atrium, she could see the rows of the shops of Bukit Timah Plaza. The top few floors were crammed with tiny offices specializing in travel and maid agencies. The corridors in front of them full of frightened hopeful young women come to Singapore to work and waiting for potential employers to take their pick. They reminded Aunty Lee of desperate dogs in the adoption pound, pouring hopeful affection on strangers in hopes of finding a home forever. Or worse, they made her think of the "live" seafood in the tanks outside Chinese restaurants. Would anyone report a girl who ran away and died in a fire? Would anyone even miss her?

21

Different People

Edmond was alone in his flat. It was a decent apartment, though too small for him to make the kind of impression he wished to. He was packing up things he would need for a stay at the Sungs' place. This suited him very well, especially as he would have the house to himself for days, perhaps weeks. Henry and Sharon had moved into a friend's place, fed up with the police and reporters lurking outside the gates all the time, and Edmond would be house-sitting as a favor to them. Edmond knew the police were just putting on a show. They had already examined Leonard Sung's bedroom, and since the victims had obviously been poisoned, they had no right to return to the house without a search warrant.

Looking around the rental apartment, Edmond decided he didn't like it, indeed couldn't stand it. He felt trapped and limited by the small rooms, low ceilings, and cheap plywood and plastic furniture provided by his budget-conscious landlord. Instead of taking clothes for a few days, he would pack up everything he had brought down from Malaysia and move out for good. With Leonard gone, he would have to find a new reason to remain at the Sung mansion, but he knew he would come up with one somehow. Dr. Edmond Yong was not one to accept the cards life had dealt him. He knew life was unfair. If he had accepted the hand dealt to him at birth, he would still be somewhere in Kedah working with his brothers in their late grandfather's bicycle shop. Instead he was a qualified medical doctor in Singapore with rich and important connections. Edmond knew that though Mabel Sung had hired him in order to have a doctor looking after her precious Leonard twenty-four hours a day, seven days a week, he had really functioned more as a nursemaid and babysitter. Edmond Yong had not liked Leonard Sung, indeed had often wished him dead. And now, with Mabel and Leonard Sung both dead, it was time for Dr. Edmond Yong to move on to the next stage of the game.

His phone rang. It was another call demanding money. Those people were so shortsighted.

"I was only the contact," Edmond said in Mandarin. "The person you were dealing with is dead. That deal is off. I don't owe you anything. I am trying to make new deals for you, but if you keep chasing me I cannot work." He wanted to hang up on the angry voice shouting at him over the phone but did not quite dare to. He did not fear her threats but he would need her in the future if his grand plan worked out.

Walking around the tiny front room with the phone not quite at his ear, he could hear his neighbors shouting at children to get off their computers, pack for school, and go to bed. Beneath all this blared the arguments, hysterics, and theme music of the current Mandarin-dubbed Korean soap opera. Edmond hated all his neighbors for being so stupid and low class and so concerned about children who would never amount to anything. In their ignorance they had had the cheek to welcome him to their building and to Singapore with offers of introductions to part-time jobs and pretty nieces "just to get you started." As though Dr. Edmond Yong could need help from people like them! He couldn't wait to get rich and show them how much he despised them.

Angry Mandarin words continued spewing from his phone as he walked around the tiny living room. Soon he would be away from them all and alone in the magnificent Sung mansion. He would have all that space to himself and it would be as though he was already living in the style he aspired to. Of course the drawback was that no one would be at the mansion to see him there and be impressed. Well, when he became the official master of such a house, he would have servants around him all the time. His relatives and former neighbors would come to him to humbly beg for favors and money. They would look at his marble floors and his Mercedes-Benzes and finally they would respect Dr. Edmond Yong. And who would be living there with him? Not that social-climbing GraceFaith Ang, for sure. A doctor like himself deserved a doctor's daughter, someone like Sharon

Sung. Edmond was somewhat intimidated by Sharon Sung. But right now she needed his help.

Finally his caller ran out of steam. Edmond said polite good-byes, made polite promises, and immediately after ending the call, pressed the first autodial number on his cell phone.

"Sharon, we have to move things up."

Meanwhile, GraceFaith Ang, alone in her small apartment, made plans for her future. She had never doubted she would get what she wanted—now it looked like success was coming even sooner than she had expected. Soon she would be out of this place forever, out of having to work for a living. No more having to push her way through rush-hour crowds and do her own pedicures.

She looked around her. The small, plain apartment had been home to her since she started work at Sung Law. She felt no attachment to it and had no fond memories of the place. But then she was not attached to the home she had grown up in either. From the start she had known these were temporary stations, no more than stops on her way up to better things. All the furnishings in the small room (one bed, one small table and chair, one built-in cupboard, curtains) belonged to the landlady.

GraceFaith liked expensive clothes and shoes and used only the best makeup, but didn't care about her domicile. At least not here, not yet. After all, no one who mattered would ever see her here. Once she married enough money she would hire the best interior designers to create a beautiful setting for her. Then she would have the best magazines come and photograph her looking casually exquisite in her beautiful home and everyone would realize what classy taste she had.

GraceFaith's dream plans were interrupted by the message bleep on her iPhone. She did not have a landline, so she kept her cell on all the time. It was Sharon Sung. *Call me now.*

At the same time as all this was going on, Patrick Pang was in Benjamin's flat, alone in the apartment he had thought they were going to be so happy together in. Signs of Benjamin were still everywhere. Cleaning because he couldn't sleep, Patrick found a cache of charcoal sticks (for sketching) and cried into them, leaving gray streaks on his hands and face and probably ruining the charcoal. He had to remind himself that despair was not constructive. *Just breathe. Every breath is a triumph. Don't let them destroy you by making you kill yourself.* He didn't even know who was talking to him but he knew it was better than silence and surrender. What was important was that he was alive to listen, and as long as he was alive there was a chance he could change things. He had been keeping himself busy by cleaning till there was nothing left to clean. Perhaps he should take a tip from Aunty Lee and cook something. But what?

Thinking of Aunty Lee made him feel better. Joe and Otto had told him the old woman could solve any problem she set her mind to. And his brother, Tim, seemed to like her, though Tim didn't seem as convinced as Joe and Otto that she could work miracles. Pat pulled out the recipe Aunty Lee had given him. "Don't let yourself get stuck. If something doesn't turn out right, make something else," she had said. He would try.

And if Ben showed up after all, Pat would buy him new charcoal sticks.

While Patrick was contemplating Aunty Lee's recipe, Commissioner Raja Kumar was alone in his office reading an e-mail, then making a call to Aunty Lee on his cell phone.

"So, has Salim told you what he found out about the people on the Never Say Die prayer list?"

"Why should Salim tell me?" she asked.

"Because you gave him the list and asked him to look them up. I thought we agreed we were going to let this die down naturally."

Aunty Lee had the grace to feel embarrassed. "If there's nothing to find, then whether I look or not everything will die down. Anyway, if they want us to pray for people, we should know who we are praying for, right? It is like making investments: you should always check the background first. Anyway, just because a harmless old lady like me is being *kaypoh* I don't see why Salim had to go and complain to you. Because if that woman's missing boyfriend is an illegal organ donor, somebody must be paying for his organs, right? And I ask you, who can afford to pay for something like that? Most likely somebody living around here or across the canal, right? I can read you the list of praying and paying people I gave him . . ." He heard Aunty Lee fumble around for her spectacles.

"It's all right, Rosie. I don't need the list."

"There are people I know recently suddenly got better from having to go for dialysis every week. And they did not go for operation to any of the government hospitals in Singapore."

"Salim didn't complain about you. He just thought I should know what he learned."

"He told you before he told me? When I'm the one who set him on the track? What is wrong with young people these days, no sense of respect!"

"Hey, I'm the boy's boss," Commissioner Raja protested.

"I am also trying to track down the connection bringing the dead man to Singapore. Surely he must have given an address when coming in? Didn't he have to fill in a disembarkation/embarkation [D/E] card? What address did he put in? I asked Inspector Salim to look it up. That handsome boy Timothy Pang is now in Immigration, right? So I asked him to look it up for me."

"He did. The address that the dead man gave was a small Frangipani Inn–type thing. And you know what? The booking was made by Beautiful Dreamers, Edmond Yong's old clinic. According to clinic records, the man was coming to Singapore for a medical checkup but never turned up."

"But his body was not found?"

"No body was found."

And those were not the only results Salim had passed on to Commissioner Raja. In the case of Mabel Sung, fifty-five, and Leonard Sung, twenty-eight, the forensic pathologist reported finding an accidental ingestion of pesticide. A fatal dose of cyanide for humans is 1.5 milligrams per kilogram of body weight and both victims had ingested at least three times that. Death had most likely occurred in minutes. More important, the cyanide in their bodies carried markers that suggested it came from a commercial pesticide product.

There was a short silence on the line after the commissioner mentioned this fact.

"Then it could not have been the *buah keluak*," Aunty Lee said.

And Commissioner Raja knew from her tone that despite all her assertions to the contrary, Aunty Lee had wondered if she had made a fatal mistake.

22

Investigating Sung Law

Aunty Lee surfaced groggily from a dream of trying to find her way to the kitchen through the many rooms of a mansion. She kept finding herself back in the bedroom. Then she was back in bed again and Nina was standing next to her in her nightdress.

"My friend just phoned. She said GraceFaith Ang went back to the Sung Law office. They all left together last night as usual. Then this morning at around five GraceFaith came back by herself. You said you wanted to know right away, right?"

"Right." Aunty Lee sat up. Was it a sign of aging that she found it difficult both to get to sleep and to wake up? "Please tell your friend thank you for me. And give her a small present, okay?"

It was so lucky Nina had a friend working at the 7-Eleven in the lobby of the building where Sung Law had its offices.

"I'm looking for Sung Law." Aunty Lee was in the office lobby in under an hour.

"Take lift to seventeenth floor then turn left."

It was just before eight in the morning. The night security guard, waiting for the morning shift and used to clients arriving at all hours, buzzed Aunty Lee through without removing the phone from his ear.

GraceFaith finally unlocked the door in response to Aunty Lee's persistent knocking and calling after the lift deposited her on the seventeenth floor.

"What do you—"

"Good morning! I saw the light on, so I was sure somebody was already here. Is Sharon here also?"

GraceFaith, expecting a building technician or cleaner, was not prepared for Aunty Lee, who stepped swiftly past her and headed toward the only office with a light on.

It was clearly GraceFaith's office and Aunty Lee saw at once that GraceFaith had not come in early to catch up on her work. The office was a chaos of box files, plastic bags, and papers. On one side of the desk was shoved a heap of desktop decorations with motivational messages and several pairs of high-heeled shoes. GraceFaith was wearing Crocs and looked as though she had been crying. The girl was packing up to leave, Aunty Lee saw.

"Sharon's not here." GraceFaith followed Aunty Lee into the room and sat down heavily on the chair by the door.

Aunty Lee saw an empty Styrofoam cup and plastic salad box in the bin next to it. It looked like the remains of Grace-Faith's dinner from the night before. All this was out of character for such a fastidious girl. GraceFaith was exhausted, Aunty Lee realized, probably dazed from lack of sleep.

"You're packing up your things," Aunty Lee chirruped even more brightly than usual. "Are you leaving the company? I thought you loved working at Sung Law so much. What happened?"

"I got fired," GraceFaith said dully. "What are you doing here?"

"My bill, for the catering." Aunty Lee waved the invoice she had hurriedly scribbled in the car park to serve as her ticket onto the premises should one be needed. "For the party that day. I thought I would save you coming over to the café," she chattered loudly. GraceFaith winced as though her head hurt. "You know they've made us close the kitchen, right? But of course, even with no customers coming in, I still have to pay rent or they will kick me out, so I need the money even more—"

It was not necessary to mention that since Aunty Lee had bought up several shop houses along the row Aunty Lee's Delights stood on, she was her own landlord and hardly likely to evict herself.

"Oh—about the catering bill. Of course. But the thing is—"

GraceFaith had dark circles under her eyes. She had tried to disguise them with concealer but the thick artificial paste only made her look worse.

"It's not that I want to chase you for the payment. But since

I can't open for business, I thought I might as well clear up all my back accounts." Aunty Lee smiled encouragingly at GraceFaith. "Why did you get fired? After big boss died company closing down, is it?"

GraceFaith looked suspiciously at Aunty Lee but the old lady was all busybody curiosity of the most innocent kind. "Well, things are a bit complicated here right now. Not that Mabel left things in a mess—oh no. But handovers are always complicated, right? Now Sharon is the boss and she—"

"She's jealous of having a pretty girl like you on the staff!" Aunty Lee crowed.

"Of course." The jealousy of other females was something GraceFaith took for granted. But in such times of upheaval a little reinforcement was always welcome. "I'm sorry I can't do anything for you. Sharon has frozen all the business accounts, even the petty cash and the charity donations. And she's been letting people go—firing them—people who have been working here for her mother longer than she has! Even me, and I'm the one that's been taking care of all her mother's stuff for her. I offered to stay on until next month, just to explain things to her. I'm the only one who knows how all Mabel's accounts work and even Sharon can't figure them all out overnight. But Sharon said she's cutting all unnecessary expenses. Honestly, I wouldn't stay on even if she wanted me to. Can you believe she called me an unnecessary expense?"

"Change is always difficult," Aunty Lee said in her best old-lady voice. "I'm sure something better will come along. And maybe not even another job—I remember you were getting along quite well with that nice young doctor at Mabel's house that day?"

"Oh, Dr. Yong." GraceFaith shook her head. This was obviously another sore point, though a minor one compared to Sharon. "Previously he used to come in all the time to talk to Mabel. I used to joke with her that he had a crush on her. It wasn't true of course, but Mabel thought it was funny. I think they were discussing plans for her son Leonard's treatment. They didn't want Leonard to know they were talking about him, so they couldn't meet at the house."

"So now the poor boy is dead you don't get a chance to see Dr. Yong anymore?"

"Oh, Edmond has still been coming to the office. But he only talks to Sharon."

"Dr. Yong" had become "Edmond," Aunty Lee noted. And there was a sour note in GraceFaith's voice that Aunty Lee was quick to capitalize on.

"Maybe the young doctor has got a crush on Sharon!" she suggested with a gossipy nudge.

It worked.

"Oh, no way. I think Edmond's trying to get her to pay the bills for Leonard's treatment, what he did for Leonard previously. But good luck to him getting anything out of Sharon! She wouldn't even give a severance package to people who have been working for her mother for over thirty years!"

"Anyway, if Dr. Yong was interested in Sharon he wouldn't have brought his PRC girlfriend to the Sungs' house that day."

Aunty Lee had been wondering how to introduce the subject of Wen Ling. Would GraceFaith respond? And would she know who Aunty Lee was referring to? These days there were so many Mainland Chinese in Singapore, legally and otherwise. It was clear to Aunty Lee from the way GraceFaith twisted her hands and twitched her mouth that she had something to say but was not yet ready to say it. She added a little salt to her spiel.

"In fact I wouldn't be surprised if Dr. Yong is married to that China girl. These days so many men do that. Sometimes I think that's so sad. Not for them of course. I'm sure they will be perfectly happy. But that some Singapore men have got no choice but to look overseas for wives because Singapore girls are too fussy and look down on them."

Aunty Lee was only repeating what women's lifestyle magazines had long trumpeted as the cause for the rising number of unmarried Singapore women. Singaporean men were looking elsewhere in the region for wives because they claimed Singapore women looked down on them. Singaporean women swore such men were only after subservient women who would stay home to produce meals and children. GraceFaith must have heard it before but still she leaped to Dr. Yong's defense.

"That's not true! Not in Dr. Yong's case anyway. I mean he's a doctor, of course he's worth marrying. What he looks like is not so important because you know he'll always have a job and can make a living. Anyway he's not Singaporean, he's Malaysian. He could easily have got his PR and citizenship when he was studying here but he didn't because he would have had to do NS and he said that was a waste of time."

Aunty Lee looked thoughtfully at GraceFaith. She felt

sorry for the girl and there were so many things she could say to her about the qualities that made a man worth marrying. But this was not the time. Neither was it the time to go into why, despite his years in Singapore, Edmond Yong had not applied for the advantages becoming a permanent resident (PR) or citizen would bring him. True, that would have meant National Service (NS) as a medic. And Aunty Lee, of the generation of Singaporeans born before the independence of their country, did not think much of a man who begrudged spending that time.

"There's some kind of business deal Sharon and Edmond are working on. That China woman represents their China partners. Mabel set it up, but now of course Sharon's taken over. I heard her saying that this is worth more than the rest of the firm put together."

Aunty Lee waited hopefully but GraceFaith could not or would not say more. Instead she picked up a coffee mug with a smiley face, considered it, and dropped it in the already overflowing wastebin.

"How is poor Sharon holding up? It can't be easy, losing your mother and your brother so suddenly and in such a horrible way," Aunty Lee said conversationally.

"She's probably depressed. That would explain the stupid things she's been doing. But she won't listen to anybody. Good luck to her! It's not just the firm, you know. The house is also under a double mortgage. They may be kicked out if they can't sort that out."

Aunty Lee had heard rumors of the Sungs' financial

troubles, but it was always nice to have inside confirmation. GraceFaith had returned to her packing and dumping. She obviously thought Aunty Lee was just one more of Sung Law's creditors, and was doomed to disappointment no matter how long she hung around the office.

Aunty Lee could tell from the vehemence with which GraceFaith's "good performance" plaques and birthday cards were being tossed that the girl was distancing herself from the company once so dear to her. It seemed worth risking another nudge for information. She didn't know how much time she had before the rest of the office staff showed up.

"I don't believe that," Aunty Lee said with casual dismissiveness. "Those are just rumors. Mabel Sung was an icon for all women lawyers. How can Sung Law be bankrupt?" She hoped these words would be provoking enough. They were.

"Mabel used company funds to pay for her son's medical expenses. And to cover her contractors and home renovations also. This is a law firm, not some megachurch or NGO where you can say the money was meant to fund your singing career or gold bathroom fixtures."

GraceFaith closed her eyes and shook her head. It was a childish gesture and oddly appealing. Aunty Lee saw the girl was very, very tired.

"You should get some rest. Things will look better after you have something to eat and get some rest."

"Things certainly couldn't look worse."

Aunty Lee only just managed to stop herself from saying "Yes, they certainly can." Instead she said, "You knew Mabel cleaned out her accounts, didn't you? Before she handed things over to Sharon. But Mabel is from the same generation as me. She would have needed someone she trusted to help her with the Internet banking and transfers and onetime passwords and things like that. You helped her, did you?"

GraceFaith's expression didn't change at all. That was what told Aunty Lee she was right. As when a friend of hers set up a nanny cam in her own bedroom to spy on a maid she suspected of bringing men home when she was out. Madam Pang had found nothing wrong on the tapes. But once Aunty Lee had spotted a cockroach on the wall that did not move for five hours, the game was up. No one's face stayed so still unless they were trying to hide something.

"And you put a little of that into your own pocket, didn't you? Even if Mabel suspected, she couldn't complain about you without giving herself away."

"I just thought—what difference could it make? She was using it to pay for equipment and contractors—"

"Was one of them Benjamin Ng?" Aunty Lee asked quickly.

"I don't remember. There were so many. Anyway I didn't take much," GraceFaith said. "I was doing all that extra work for Mabel. I just paid myself transfer fees."

Some people could justify everything they did, Aunty Lee thought. But she nodded. "Sharon is very like her mother, isn't she? And she knew her mother very well. Does she know what you did for her?"

"No—" GraceFaith started to say, then stopped.

"Now Mabel's gone she is going to look for someone to

blame everything on. And you are the one who did all the transfers for Mabel."

GraceFaith started to contradict this, then stopped. "She will."

"Unless of course she's got other things to occupy her," Aunty Lee pointed out.

"Hello. I thought I heard voices." Sharon Sung came into the office. "What are you doing here?"

Aunty Lee realized it was almost seven thirty. Inside the law office, with no windows and artificial lighting, it was easy to disconnect from time in the real world.

"I haven't been paid for the catering," Aunty Lee said with a little-old-lady quiver in her voice. She was going to say she needed the money but remembered in time that she had to appear rich enough to pay for new knees. "I don't want to put my own money into the shop. But now the police say I cannot open the shop and I still got to pay rent—" She hoped Sharon and Dr. Yong had not investigated her finances thoroughly enough to discover she was not only her own landlord but landlord of all the shops along the row where her café was located.

GraceFaith said, "Mrs. Sung prefers—I mean, Mrs. Sung preferred—to pay only after she was satisfied. In this case I don't know—"

"You have no idea how Mabel really ran things," Sharon snapped. "Anyway she's not here now and I'm running things. Write Mrs. Lee a check for the buffet. You ordered it, so you should know how much it cost. I'll sign it."

Despite everything, Aunty Lee felt a fondness for Sharon Sung.

"I like to settle everything up front," Sharon said. "If you pay as you go, it's easier to keep everything straight. And by the way I heard Dr. Yong say he will be meeting you to discuss your knee surgery?"

"Oh yes, Dr. Yong is coming over to my place later today."

Aunty Lee had been trying to come up with a way to get Dr. Yong to agree to talk to her on his own. She was sure she could find out more from him without Sharon (who was, after all, a lawyer) present.

Nina had suggested picking him up, putting him in the trunk of her car, and driving him over to the café without any explanation. After all, if he had been carrying out semi-illegal operations in his aesthetic clinic he was hardly likely to complain to the police. But Aunty Lee didn't think that shoving him into the trunk of a car would make him very amenable to conversation. Instead she phoned Dr. Yong and asked if he could come over for a private consultation. She was an old lady and not comfortable with going to a clinic full of sick people and she had worries about the surgery that she needed to discuss with him. She would of course pay him his standard consultation fee plus his transport costs.

Dr. Yong had agreed.

"I should be getting back." Aunty Lee started for the door, remembering to limp slightly.

"Just a minute!"

GraceFaith hurried out of the office after Aunty Lee to hand her Sharon's check.

23

Edmond Yong Visits

GraceFaith had a good heart, Aunty Lee thought. Aunty Lee liked her practical ambition and willingness to work for what she wanted . . . and for whoever paid. In many ways GraceFaith reminded Aunty Lee of herself and of Cherril. Both young women had started off clever, poor, and wanting to improve themselves. Cherril had focused on learning and had been lucky enough to fall in love with learning and knowledge and with a man who loved both these things and her. What would become of GraceFaith, who had worked on building up her appearance and appeal?

Aunty Lee thought of the last thing GraceFaith had said as she left the office: "Edmond thinks he can blackmail Sharon into marrying him. That's the way he does things. But it's not going to work on Sharon."

"Blackmail with what?" Aunty Lee had asked. But Grace-Faith had already closed the door behind her, leaving it unclear whether she had been talking to Aunty Lee or herself.

As arranged, Dr. Edmond Yong called on Aunty Lee at her house to discuss details concerning her knee surgery. Nina showed him to ML's study, which also served as a library and business room. Aunty Lee was all ready to discuss the pains in her knees and the quality of potential replacement joints, but Edmond Yong seemed more interested in the glass cases housing ML's antique jade and cloisonné collections.

"Are those all genuine antiques?"

"I assume so. My late husband was interested in Chinese and Japanese history."

"They must be worth a lot."

"I imagine they must."

"Did your late husband collect them himself or buy them from suppliers?"

Aunty Lee shrugged, looking bored and uninterested. Truth was, she loved ML's collections but for once had no intention of being distracted from her purpose.

Aunty Lee played her helpless-rich-old-lady card. She knew Dr. Yong would not willingly relinquish his position on the medical adviser pedestal that she had carefully created for him.

"It's very good of you to come. GraceFaith Ang has been so helpful explaining things to me. She knows all about this transplant business. She was also a very good friend of Mrs. Sung and all those praying healers.

"She said they will be willing to help me even if I am not Christian like them. I am willing to go to church and all that, but then some of those Christians are so strict, what if they arrange for me to get that operation and then they want me to take down my husband's photo? I heard sometimes they will do that, you know. It is just for respect, you know. I must always have his photo around because he is not around. But maybe they will say I cannot, it must take down . . ."

Aunty Lee could see that the young doctor was almost squirming in his seat from the desire to jump in and set her right. Graciously she slowed down and turned helpless, confused eyes on him.

"Be careful of her. Grace Ang, I mean."

"GraceFaith? Oh, she is a very nice girl," Aunty Lee fluttered, egging him on. "She is so helpful and she knows so much."

"Yes. That one. She doesn't know that much." Dr. Yong shook his head. "She used to help Mabel. In fact she's being retrenched."

"Oh, why? GraceFaith is such a nice girl." Aunty Lee wondered whether she was laying it on too thick. "She was so close to Mrs. Sung. I thought she would be running things now Mrs. Sung is gone."

"Yes, we gather she thought so too. But not anymore. Anyway, about your knees."

"I had been hoping an old friend of my late husband's could help me. He was a top surgeon. But I left it too late. I saw him just the other day and, aiyoh, his Parkinson's is so bad. The hands shaking all the time. Now even if he says he can help me, how can I believe him? Hiyah. If only with all your transplanting you can transplant new hands for him . . ."

It worked. Dr. Edmond Yong was almost dancing in his seat waiting for her to finish.

"I know who you are referring to—Dr. Henry Sung, right? Yes? I thought so! Dr. Sung is like a sort of mentor of mine. In fact this procedure I'm telling you about? He will be supervising everything. I am just the robot extension, doing what he tells me, though of course I can pretty much handle it on my own. Such procedures are not that complicated. Not like where you are working with a live donor. Here you only have one set of anesthesia and vitals to worry about because the other one is autopilot, you know what I mean?

"Anyway, Dr. Sung doesn't run anything. If that girl told you that, it just shows how little she knows. Dr. Sung doesn't even run his own clinic anymore, he's retired. And he can't operate because of Parkinson's. Honestly you don't want a sixty-year-old man who is shaking like that operating on you no matter how experienced he is. But people like me carry out the actual operations. Dr. Sung just supervises."

"You are one of the surgeons?" Aunty Lee's amazement was all the young doctor could have wanted. "Can I get you some more tea? Something else to eat? My deep-fried sardine-and-onion curry puffs should be ready by now. Some people like them very much. I want you to try and tell me whether you young people will like them or not. Do you think I can sell them in the hospital? NUH now got Mister Bean and Delifrance already, right?" The newly renovated National University Hospital now housed a minimall containing fast-food shops as well as a traditional *kopitiam,* or café.

A touch of the bell brought Nina and the pastries almost instantly. Edmond noticed Aunty Lee did not immediately continue the medical discussion after the servant left. Was the old woman afraid the girl might be lurking and listening or had her mind wandered?

"Actually I wouldn't know. I'm not in the National University Hospital." The crispy, rich pastry melting in his mouth as it introduced the savory, slightly spicy sardine filling distracted Edmond Yong. If curry puffs were sold in heaven, this was what they would taste like.

"So you are in SGH? At Outram Road? Or Tan Tock Seng? Or that fancy building on Orchard Boulevard that looks like a posh hotel . . . Camden Medical. You are operating there?"

"No—no—" It was difficult to answer with his mouth full. Edmond felt he had somehow lost control of the conversation. Aunty Lee was being properly respectful but she wouldn't stop her questions and he couldn't stop eating.

"Chicken and prawn, chicken and potato, and just potato," Aunty Lee announced, pointing at the different curry puffs. "You must tell me which ones you like best. So where are you working now? You are still working as a doctor, right?" There was just the slightest hint of dubiousness in her voice as she said this. As though she was wondering whether she had been taken in by a con man.

"Of course I'm still practicing," Dr. Edmond Yong hastened to reassure her. He felt his reputation (already slightly tarnished, but how could this little old lady know?) impugned by her doubt. Even though at that moment he would have killed for another curry puff, he felt angry with her for daring to doubt him. "In fact there are times when I operate almost every day. Sometimes even twice a day, which is very demanding when you consider how long a procedure takes. It's not just a matter of going in and fixing a fracture or something, you know. This is serious business. But of course that depends on when a case comes up. Right now there's not much going on but I expect things to be very busy very soon. That's why if you are interested in getting your knees taken care of, you should make up your mind soon. Because there is always a long waiting list and there are not that many parts available, if you get what I mean. I will do my best to get you put on the list. Otherwise you may have to wait for months, maybe until next year. I was away for a while, so I'm just starting up again."

"Away where?"

"Korea."

"I always thought one day I must go and visit Korea," Aunty Lee said chattily. "Old lady like me, too old for K-pop but there's all that k-drama and kimchi . . ." She shook her head in awe. "I heard that every house there, they have their own kimchi pots. One day I also want to learn to make kimchi. It is like making our *achar,* right? Except fermented."

"There's so much more to Korea than that. Where I was living—the Wonju campus of Yonsei University, that was way out in the countryside. Yes, I suppose the pop culture was there and the students are probably all steeped in it. But the hills, the forests with pine trees and maple trees—we could be in Europe if not for the paddy fields."

"So you came back to Singapore for how long?"

"As long as it takes, I suppose." Though Dr. Yong didn't say that he had no reason to return to Korea, it was clear that was the case.

"I like Korea."

Edmond Yong looked at her suspiciously but all he saw was a harmless, slightly befuddled old lady offering a plate of steamed yam cubes to him.

"I watch *Big Business and Broken Hearts*." Aunty Lee confirmed this impression by naming a popular Korean soap opera.

Aunty Lee could sense he was about to bolt and stepped in: "I was hoping you could help me if only you were still operating somewhere, but maybe you can recommend someone"— she lowered her voice—"unofficially. Nowadays, with so many rules and regulations, it is so hard to get anything done."

Dr. Yong's whole demeanor changed. Suddenly he was back on familiar ground.

"I see . . . but you still didn't tell me where you work."

"It's a private clinic."

"But can I go and look around first? I am scared of operations, old lady like me, you can understand."

"It's not allowed," Dr. Yong said firmly. He sensed that the balance of power had shifted subtly but he wasn't sure where or how. "It's because of privacy and hygiene and everything. You wouldn't understand. But it's the way it's done."

Aunty Lee looked thoughtful.

"So are you interested?"

"Yes. I think . . . put me down for a pair of knees, okay? But remember, I don't want some old man's knees. I want to be able to walk up and down steps, no problem."

"I promise you. These will be young man's knees. You will be able to go dancing, trust me!"

After Aunty Lee had dutifully laughed at his joke (had he but known Aunty Lee's own two knees were still happy to support her on the dance floor if only she could find someone worth dancing with), she introduced her final piece of bait.

"So then why Dr. Sung cannot show you how to help him?" Aunty Lee was playing the ignorant insistent granny lady for all she was worth.

"Because it's not his hands that are the problem, Mrs. Lee. I don't know how much you know about Parkinson's but it is the big thing old people are always most scared of, right? Parkinson's disease is the result of having too little dopamine— that's a chemical, a neurotransmitter—in the parts of the brain controlling movement. As a matter of fact there has been some research done suggesting that we can do something to help him. The research showed that transplanting brain tissue from fetuses into the brains of people with Parkinson's disease could relieve their symptoms drastically because of a specific type of neuron—that's a brain cell— within the fetal tissue."

Edmond did not expect the old woman to follow all this. It was only meant to confuse and impress her enough to trust herself and her money to his knowledge and expertise.

"Where did they get the fetal tissues from?" Aunty Lee sounded more curious than intimidated.

"Oh, there are always lots from abortions. Don't worry—ha ha—we don't kill any babies."

This was not the time, Aunty Lee told herself, to go into a discussion on abortion. Catholic Nina was already slamming plates around on the other side of the room, even though she was supposed to have been eavesdropping silently.

"The original research was halted, prematurely I believe, because some of the patients developed a different kind of uncontrollable movements and jerking. But this was a very small percentage. If the patients are willing to take the risk, I think we should go on."

"But from where will you get the"—Aunty Lee's voice dropped to a frightened, conspiratorial whisper—"dead baby parts from?"

"You can leave that to us," Dr. Edmond Yong said with genial condescension. "Just let us know what you want done and we will take care of everything. I just want you to look through these papers. Please take note you cannot use your Medisave. You take your time and let me know when you are ready, okay?

"Of course these are not the actual papers you will be signing, those will be drawn up specially for you, depending on your state of health and the procedures you are signing up for. A lot of women feel since we are doing surgery, might as well do liposuction at the same time."

But Aunty Lee, peering confusedly at the papers, did not pick up on this. Edmond Yong didn't think she would actually read them. Old people, he knew very well, had problems with their eyes and their attention spans. In fact he suspected that this old woman had been dragging out their conversation with questions more because she wanted the attention than because she needed answers. He had done a brief course on the psychology of aging and knew that getting attention was important to old folks; he just didn't have the time to spend listening to her. But her financial standing seemed sound enough even though she did not look as though it was.

And he knew that if only he could convince her to go through with the operation, this might be his big break.

The sum indicated was a large one. But Aunty Lee could see that someone in chronic pain would consider it money well spent.

"What is happening with all that poisoning business?" Aunty Lee asked, as though it had just crossed her mind. "Are they still investigating? How long do these things usually drag on?"

Of course Nina had already been dispatched to find out how long such things took. The only answer she had come up with was that it varied with who was involved and how much attention the case received. But Aunty Lee guessed that Edmond Yong enjoyed being consulted as an authority.

"That depends, of course"—he lowered his voice slightly— "and in this case there are complications . . ."

"What complications?"

"The case of your late husband's suspicious death was brought up, so in this case there was a previous poisoning incident."

Aunty Lee looked suitably taken aback. "There was nothing suspicious about my late husband's death!"

"That's because no tests were done, nothing was investigated since your husband was being treated for cancer. But someone clearly remembers a family member, possibly the daughter of the deceased, saying at the funeral wake that it was impossible ML Wong could have died of a heart attack because he never showed any previous signs of heart trouble."

Aunty Lee was stunned. She had never been accused—at least not to her knowledge and certainly not by Mathilda—of having anything to do with her beloved ML's death. As for the improbability of a heart attack, hadn't Aunty Lee said so herself? Despite ML's cancer, none of them had expected a sudden heart attack. Indeed the family member who Dr. Yong's source was quoting was more likely Aunty Lee than Mathilda! Aunty Lee had done her utmost to make sure the wake had all the dignity due to ML's life and memory, but she had been so distraught that she could barely remember it. "Yes," she had said in response to many condolences. "Yes, it was fast. But after surviving all the cancer treatment, how could he suddenly die of a heart attack when he had never had heart problems before?" Indeed dear Mathilda had repeatedly and patiently reminded Aunty Lee that ML's heart had likely been weakened by the cancer and the chemotherapy.

Aunty Lee started to tell the young doctor this, but stopped when she saw how intently Edmond Yong's attention was fixed on her, his lips slightly parted in an unconscious smile of anticipation. He suddenly reminded Aunty Lee of herself in the middle of a delicate cooking procedure such as frying *kueh pie tee* shells or "top hats." The oil had to be at just the right temperature, the brass mound coated in just enough rice-flour batter of just the right consistency to make the crispy little shells one by one . . .

Dr. Edmond Yong was coating her in lies and insinuations, Aunty Lee realized, and dipping her in hot oil, expecting to easily crush and crumble her.

Aunty Lee shook herself. She reminded herself to look confused and anxious. "Oh no," she said faintly.

"You see, everybody has complications," Dr. Yong said smoothly. He was already certain he could make this old woman do whatever he wanted but he went on adding to her fears because he enjoyed it.

"And on the business side also, since your kitchens here are being investigated, it's only right that all your products already on sale in supermarkets should be recalled, just in case. And consumers with previously purchased bottles of your *sambal* or *achar* should be warned. The public always gets angry when product information is not made available to them, so it's only right that they are warned there may be something wrong with the Aunty Lee's Delights line of products."

Edmond Yong felt confident and smoothly authoritative. All the marketing and self-help guides he had studied were paying off. He had a good product, knew his target market, and had an offer in hand that she could not refuse.

"All Sharon's friends tell her that she should call for a full investigation but she told them that there was no point.

After all, no matter what they find out, it would not bring her mother and brother back. I'm sure you will agree that that's the best course."

"Of course," Aunty Lee said cautiously and curiously. "So what do you want me to do?"

"We just need you to agree that it was your chicken *buah keluak* that was responsible for what happened. Of course with all your deepest regrets for the tragedy and all that blah blah blah. But basically, that all this was a careless accident on your part, that you are sorry, and it won't happen again, and that's that. Case closed. We can all move on and stop wasting so much time."

"Are you trying to blackmail me?" Aunty Lee asked with some interest.

"No, of course not. I'm only saying that since nothing can be done for them now, the best thing we can do is contain the damage, right?"

"So you want me to say that it was my fault that two people died?"

"I'm just saying that it will all blow over faster."

"But then the real killer—if there is one—will get away? Of course that's assuming that they didn't kill themselves. But if they did, the police investigation will find that out."

"The police." Edmond Yong snorted. "They will find out what they're paid to find."

"You cannot talk about Singapore police like that," Nina said.

Edmond was startled. He had not noticed her come into the room, but she was standing by a door he had not seen before, between two of the display cases. "In the Philippines everybody knows the police are always trying to do a lot of reforms, Aquino is trying to make them do reforms, but they are still corrupt. Here you try to offer the police a bribe to escape fine, you get arrested—double fine!"

Aunty Lee noted that however Nina treated Salim to his face, she defended his back fiercely. That was a good sign if only Aunty Lee could find some way of letting Salim know. But cheering Salim up was not a top priority for Aunty Lee right then and she filed the thought away for future reference.

"What is it, Nina?" was all she said.

"Madam, the gardener is asking if you want him to cut down the rambutan tree branch over your porch, otherwise the next time strong wind comes, sure kenah."

"No. Those branches got a lot of fruit just turning yellow. Those can be very sweet."

"Maybe dangerous, madam."

"Going to turn yellow then red then ripe already. Tell him don't worry."

"I will tell him to keep an eye on it," Nina said darkly as she exited.

Edmond Yong ignored the interruption, forgetting Nina as soon as the door closed behind her.

"You don't want your husband's two children asking questions about his death, do you?"

Hearing her late husband referred to still gave Aunty Lee a slight jolt. Especially here in what had been his favorite room.

"Nobody asked questions."

"And you don't want them to," Edmond Yong said. "Because you know how things work. If you say anything to anybody about this knee surgery, people will hear the rumors about your husband's death. Everybody will know this is the second time somebody died after eating your cooking. Rumors are enough to destroy you. It will be good-bye to your business, to you, everything. For your own sake you don't want that to happen, right?"

Was Edmond Yong really trying to threaten her into silence? Aunty Lee was reminded of a gang of Chinese con artists that conned old women into handing over their jewelry to be cleansed of bad luck. If they told anyone then bad luck would be doubled on their families. Apparently this scam had worked successfully in the Chinatowns of several American cities where the aging Chinese women were isolated from their new countrymen and their Americanized children. Unfortunately for the scammers, in Singapore they had run into Aunty Lee buying dong gu mushrooms in Chinatown. It was one of the cases that had made Inspector Salim look good.

Now Edmond Yong was trying to intimidate her the same way, and Aunty Lee felt a thrill of realization. "Of course!"

"Mrs. Lee, do you understand what I'm saying?"

Apparently she had not looked intimidated enough. Aunty Lee did her best to look flustered and confused.

"You want me to say my food poisoned those people. So what do you want me to do after that, close down?"

"Oh no, of course not! Aunty Lee's Delights is a household name! All I am saying is admit one mistake, the family says no hard feelings. Take a break until all of this blows over.

While you're resting, let me fix your knees for you. When you get back to work you will feel so much better. No more pain when you are standing all day in your kitchen. You may feel so good that maybe you'll even take up aerobics or jogging—ha ha!"

It was that little laugh that made Aunty Lee decide she detested this man the same way she detested the little smiling faces that people used to end unpleasant text messages, like "We read over your menus and find they are not suitable for us :)." That smiling icon was confusing. Aunty Lee was never certain whether it meant "I'm joking" or "I'm happy" or "I'm just smiling at you for no reason even though I never smile at anyone I meet in person." Now the unpleasant young man was transposing the most annoying part of text messages into real life.

"And you'll perform the operation yourself?"

"I'll take very good care of you. You'll be better taken care of than you would be in any hospital, believe me. It will be personalized care specially tailored to your needs."

"What guarantees do I have that it will work? What if I pay through the nose for this procedure and my knees end up worse than ever?"

"Oh, don't worry. Once we take you on as a patient, we guarantee that you will be happy with the results. Of course you will have to be reasonable. There is a possibility, I will admit that—no operation can be one hundred percent guaranteed—that is, there is a possibility you may not be satisfied with the results immediately. But if you are patient we will keep going until you are happy with how it feels. That is what I can guarantee you. And for sure you will be better off in many ways than if you decide against doing the procedure. Are we agreed?"

"Just one more thing—but this is important. I want to know where you get the body parts from. I heard Indian prisons sell dead bodies of rapists and drug addicts to medical schools to teach anatomy. I don't want you to put some Indian drug addict's cartilage in my knees. Are you sure you are using Chinese people's body parts?" Aunty Lee tried to look prejudiced and racist.

Another smirk from Dr. Yong. Apparently he anticipated such racism.

"Remember that China woman you asked about at the party that day? She's not my girlfriend. She's a business contact. She is the one who can guarantee the body parts are hundred percent Chinese."

By now Aunty Lee was walking her guest/blackmailer out of the front door. She hoped he would not notice there were no trees, rambutan or otherwise, near the porch of her house and wonder at Nina's message. Fortunately his phone rang, even as he said: "Don't worry, Mrs. Lee. You can leave everything to me."

He glanced at the ID and ignored it. There was a bleep as a text message followed. What it said made Edmond autodial someone and shout: "What shit are you talking! How can the power be off?"

Aunty Lee could hear a woman's voice on the line, also shouting, but could not make out her words. She heard enough to tell it was English—not Wen Ling, then.

"What's happening?" Aunty Lee asked eagerly, but she had been forgotten.

Edmond stumble-ran across the driveway with the phone still clamped to his ear. He dropped his keys before he could unlock his car. His hands were shaking too hard to drive and he sat for a moment, ignoring the man in a long-sleeved T-shirt and broad-brimmed sun hat trimming the hedge beyond. He dialed again.

"What the hell did you do?"

Aunty Lee walked to her "gardener" in time for them both to hear Edmond shout, "They turned off the power supply at the house. Everything. You're supposed to keep everything running!"

Though Edmond Yong was not paying any attention to them, Aunty Lee and Salim remained apparently engrossed in the bougainvillea hedge till he had backed out of the driveway and the car disappeared in the direction of the main road.

"The police force not paying you enough, is it?"

"Nina was worried. She doesn't trust that man. She said you were alone in the house, thought he might try to drug you or kidnap you or something."

Aunty Lee was touched. She was touched too that the officer had taken Nina—or Edmond Yong—seriously enough.

Back in the library, they found Nina had already thrown out the remaining puffs (a sign of clear displeasure). She said to Aunty Lee, "You are not seriously going to let that man go anywhere near your legs!"

Aunty Lee did not answer. She had returned to her favorite seat facing the portrait of ML Lee above the serving hatch through which Nina had listened to the interview with Dr. Yong. What would ML have thought if he, instead of Nina, had been listening?

"Did you hear that young fart call me 'old people'?" Aunty Lee demanded of the portrait. "And imply people think I poisoned you?"

ML Lee smiled out of his portrait, saying nothing. He might have found a replacement for his deceased first wife in Aunty Lee but she had no intention of replacing him.

She had been sitting there for almost an hour by the time Salim and Nina returned.

"How are your legs feeling?" Nina asked Aunty with exaggerated sweetness.

"I am feeling much better," Aunty Lee replied. "I think maybe I will go out tomorrow and join that gym your friend works at."

"I don't like that man. I don't like him coming here."

"Because he threatened me? I don't think he's going to do anything. He just wants to scare me because he wants to work with me. Some people think fear is only way to make people behave."

"And he says our food no good but he keeps on taking and eating. All the time he is talking he is eating. But, madam, if you suspect Dr. Yong, how can you even think about going for operation under him?" Nina wailed. Her Filipina accent was always exaggerated when she was upset.

"Of course I'm not going to go for the operation. I just

want to find out more about how they operate. I suspect Edmond Yong has been working with illegal organ transplants. Maybe Mabel Sung found out about it. She may have been tempted to get them to heal her son if the prayer and faith healing didn't work—or maybe she did ask them and it didn't work and she was going to tell on them, so they had to silence her and get rid or her son because he was evidence of the illegal surgery!"

"Ma'am, nowadays with postmortems and everything, you still got evidence, what."

"Yes, but this is Singapore. They give you a quick look-over, find out what you died of, then poof, you're cremated. Next thing you know you are a pile of ashes inside a nice pot in the columbarium. No way anybody can open up the pot and find out what kind of previous operations you had!"

Nina, with her nursing training, had more faith in hospital records than Aunty Lee did, but it was no use talking to her boss in one of her superspeed moods.

Salim, who had changed back into his uniform, held up his phone now.

"Power company says power supply to the Sung house was terminated till further notice by the owner's request. Same thing with the water supply. So it can't have been Sharon Sung that called Edmond Yong just now if she asked for the power to be cut off."

Aunty Lee thought about it. She couldn't prove it but she felt the first call had been from Sharon. It had probably been GraceFaith who had instructed that power and water to the house be cut off. This was not entirely surprising given that no money was coming in and Sharon and Henry Sung had moved out. And GraceFaith would not have minded making Edmond Yong a little uncomfortable.

But why had Edmond's caller been so upset? Had he someone in the house with him? Someone caught in the middle of a hot shower perhaps? No. It was more than that. She had seen shock, fear, rage, and loss in Edmond Yong's reaction to news of the power cut to the empty house.

"He had something in the house," Aunty Lee said to Salim.

"We checked through the whole house that day," Salim said. "There's nothing there."

24

Anne Peters

It was not the gym that Aunty Lee headed to the next morning. She had woken up with the sense that she was missing something.

"Where are you going so early?"

"For a morning walk. Walking is good for the health. That's why they build so many parks for us. You even see ministers walking around when there is no election coming. It must be good."

"What are you up to now?" Nina asked suspiciously. She sounded like one of those harried domestic helpers trying to keep hyperactive children out of trouble. "You want me to make egg for your breakfast?"

"I have to deliberately meet someone and make it seem

like a total coincidence. Not very easy these days," Aunty Lee said. For a moment she thought wistfully of the fresh food markets of the past. In those days you knew where you were likely to find people, whether they preferred freshly caught fish, freshly cropped vegetables, or chickens slaughtered on demand. Walking around the market, you could get your day's food, news, and exercise at your own pace.

"I'm taking my phone with me. If that GraceFaith sends me anything, you phone me right away, ah!"

Anne Peters was out walking Tammy, her sweet-natured "Singapore special." Mycroft had brought the mongrel puppy home for his mother after she had not left the house for three months following his sister's death. Now she walked with Tammy two, three times a day. And when she was home, the dog stayed devotedly by her side. There were definitely different ways of healing, Aunty Lee thought.

Tammy greeted Aunty Lee with her customary delight. Tammy was always overjoyed to see everyone. After Tammy had licked and nuzzled Aunty Lee and had her head scratched, Aunty Lee continued walking with Anne Peters as Tammy returned to the joys of sniffing the trails of dogs gone by.

"Something on your mind, Rosie?" Anne Peters looked mild and gracious. But people who knew the family believed Mycroft's Queen's Counsel brains had come from her.

"Mabel Sung. Mycroft mentioned that you used to know her quite well."

"He told you Mabel tried to match her Sharon to him, I

suppose. Poor boy. He never recovered from that. But I told him he should be flattered. Obviously his qualifications overcame any qualms she had about his being Indian."

"You think Mabel was racist?"

"Actually no. Not more than any average member of a majority race. I think Mabel tended to classify people by how useful they could be to her."

"You knew Mabel Sung before she became a big-time lawyer. You probably knew her better than most people. Do you think Mabel could have killed herself and her son?"

They walked on for a while in silence after this, led by Tammy's nose and curiosity.

"I think Mabel would be willing to kill someone else to save her son. But I don't believe she would kill herself."

"Leonard was always her favorite, wasn't he?"

"Oh yes. The boy was a holy terror but he could do no wrong in her eyes. Sharon was too like Mabel herself. She was just an extension of Mabel. I always felt that Leonard was the other side of Mabel, the wild side that she never got the chance to explore. But I always got the feeling that there was some of that wild side in Sharon too, only it never got the chance to come out."

"Sharon seems very focused on taking care of her mother's legacy," Aunty Lee said. "I would say she's trying to prove herself except I don't know who she is trying to prove herself for."

Anne Peters laughed ruefully. "Daughters can be difficult. For years my Marianne thought Mycroft was my favorite because I kept pushing her to do better, to try harder. All along she was the one I was thinking of. I knew Mykie would be all right somehow. No parent will admit it, but good children can be a bit dull.

"But compared with Leonard Sung," she continued, "I would take a dull child anytime. For years Sharon must have seen her brother as Mabel's favorite. Their parents spent a lot of money sending Leonard away to college in America. They gave him an allowance, paid for his expenses, his apartment, his car. Sharon got her law degree at the National University of Singapore on a scholarship. Yes, of course they would have paid for her fees and her books, but that was nothing compared to what they spent on her brother and Sharon would have taken that for granted. She didn't even move into the college dormitory because her mother said she would be more comfortable at home.

"When Leonard dropped out of school and got mixed up with bad company, his parents didn't know what to do. They got him into another college, he dropped out again. They went over to talk to him, they sent friends to talk to him, but as Henry said, it was only after Sharon made them stop sending money to him that he finally came back to Singapore. And by that time he was already sick."

"Sharon must have thought it was very unfair that her parents took her doing well for granted but made such a fuss over Leonard," Aunty Lee said. "I heard her telling people at the prayer and healing meeting that since what happened to Leonard was his own fault, it was ridiculous that people were putting so much effort into praying him better."

"You went to prayer and healing meeting?" Anne Peters asked.

Aunty Lee nodded. "Mabel called when ML first got diagnosed." She was only prevaricating a little.

Anne Peters nodded. "I've had a heart problem for some years. IE, infective endocarditis. I was told that since I have a damaged valve, the infection could have come from something as basic as bacteria introduced through a scratch on my gums when chewing or flossing. Anyway it didn't kill me, I carried on with my life. Then this absurd, odious little man came and tried to convince me to pay the earth to get a transplant. He implied my poor dead daughter's memory would be destroyed if I didn't pay up. Plus I would get a brand-new healthy heart valve. Can you believe it? I told him to get lost and if I ever heard from him again I would call the police."

"Why didn't you call the police?"

"I thought he might have got his information from Mabel Sung. I didn't want to get her into trouble with the police. And to be frank I didn't want to drag up poor Marianne again. You know what the papers can be like. I know what it's like to worry over a child. I didn't want to cause Mabel more trouble. Rosie, you're not being blackmailed into doing something, are you?"

"Oh no," Aunty Lee said with perfect honesty.

"Don't you agree it's easier to forgive people who wrong you on impulse than people like that man who plan it? I don't understand people like that. Is it worth it?"

"My helper Nina always says, if we are all parts of the same body, some people are ingrown toenails and should be cut off."

This got a smile from Anne. "She's Catholic?"

"I believe so."

Anne nodded, as though this helped her decide which folder to file the observation under. Poor woman, Aunty Lee thought. She was still trying to find meaning in her daughter's death.

"Have you seen Henry since?"

"He seems a bit lost without her. I suspect Mabel made all the decisions for them."

"Some men are like that." Anne Peters smiled. "As long as everybody knows they own the car, they don't mind being driven around by a chauffeur."

"But in his case it was true, wasn't it? Mabel was the one running the successful law firm. Henry was semiretired. Because of his Parkinson's, he couldn't operate anymore."

They had reached the gate of the Peters house by now. Anne unlatched it.

"I don't know about that. There were rumors of trouble in paradise for a while. Apparently Henry was angry about how much money Mabel had spent on Leonard. Many men just aren't very good around sickness."

"You're not saying Henry would have done something—"

"I'm not saying anything," Anne said firmly. "Except I would advise you to stay away from Mabel's schemes. I know she's dead but you don't know what tangled webs she's left behind. And there's Sharon, you said she's taking over the law firm?"

"She's trying to save it, I think."

"The problem with Sharon is she's too much like Mabel. No matter what, she would always have been either a shadow or a competitor. She never had a chance while Mabel was alive."

"And now?"

"Now I suppose she'll carry on where her mother left off and do whatever Mabel would have."

Back home, Aunty Lee could not decide whether she had learned a lot or nothing at all. There was the shape of something vitally important in the mass of details that Anne Peters had shared with her but she could not figure out what it was.

She sat down on her bed. She could hear Nina operating the vacuum cleaner in one of the other rooms. She was glad both that Nina was in the house with her and that she was not in the same room. She wanted to process the teeming thoughts in her head in private. But since her loss of ML, her fear of being alone had grown. How had this happened? Rosie Lee had always thought of herself as the strong, independent one. Now she felt she would rather be dead than alone. What was going to happen to her when Nina left to go home?

Aunty Lee shook her head. This was still part of the grieving process, she told herself. It could go on for years. She was lucky because having time to grieve was a luxury. Some women who lost their husbands had to worry about feeding themselves and their children. How would she have coped with feeding five, six, seven little Rosies and MLs? Aunty Lee had to laugh at herself and the image this conjured up. Now Mark and Mathilda were independent and she only had to look after herself. The least she could do was stay healthy and happy. She knew the best way to do that was by staying active.

But now Aunty Lee's Delights, which was supposed to take care of that, had also been taken away from her.

The photographs in the bedroom were some of Aunty Lee's favorite portraits of ML. Their wedding portrait held pride of place over the bed. They had not gone through all the traditional marriage ceremonies but Aunty Lee was wearing the phoenix collar and *kebaya* that had been worn by ML's mother as well as by his first wife. It had made her feel accepted by them as well as by ML (who was looking at her instead of at the camera). Well, one good thing about being alone was that ML was not around to worry about her.

Aunty Lee could finally understand offering food to the dead. In households with family altars, samples of all the best foods were ceremonially offered to dead ancestors. As a Western-educated child whose parents and grandparents were all alive, it had seemed a waste to the young Rosie. Now that loss was a permanent part of her life, she saw that the custom was less a matter of superstition than of wanting those you loved most to share your experiences. Doing this doubled your pleasure because you got to see things through their eyes. Aunty Lee preferred feeding the living. Still, she shared all she had learned that morning with ML and felt better.

ML Lee had been so fond of his little wife. Where any other man would probably have been irritated, ML Lee had been entertained. But then Aunty Lee, with her knack for understanding people (through the way they ate, she said) had probably known him better than anyone else. She realized the vacuum cleaner had been silent for a while. When she looked around Nina was peering through the half-open door.

"Madam, you want hot tea?"

"No thank you, Nina."

"Madam Cherril telephoned just now. Said when you come back please phone her."

Much as she liked Cherril, Aunty Lee was reluctant to break away from her contemplative mood.

"In a moment. Thank you, Nina."

An unexpected parcel from GraceFaith arrived by courier. There was also a note from GraceFaith saying Henry Sung could not have poisoned his wife because GraceFaith herself had been with him from the time the first tray was dropped till she went into Leonard's room and found Leonard and Mabel dead. Aunty Lee put aside that little nugget to chew on later. It was the papers GraceFaith had sent that caught her attention now. For once Aunty Lee felt out of her depth. And she was going to ask a big favor. She picked up the phone.

"Raja? Can you trust me?"

"Rosie, what are you up to?"

"I want to pass Salim something to investigate privately. No, never mind where I got it from. Let him decide what he wants to do with it. If it works out there will be plenty of other evidence and no one will bother where the information came from. If nothing comes of it, no one need know."

"Rosie, you are as bad as Mabel Sung."

"I couldn't wait, I wanted to tell you right away." Cherril dashed in through the French doors from the lawn. "People on TV who keep secrets always end up dead. I managed to talk to Wen Ling. Or someone else like her. Same difference. Online on a Chinese health forum site promising people genuine Chinese organs and blood transfusions. I said I wanted to know if the body parts my aunt was getting are Chinese body parts and I wouldn't pay unless I knew for sure. This person wrote they only deal with organs from healthy Chinese people. She's very big on health and she is vegetarian. We talked for some time and now I'm feeling a bit bad for lying to her. But not too bad. I told her I had a vegetarian friend—Carla—in Shanghai. In a different world we might all have been friends and business partners. Isn't it crazy?"

Aunty Lee looked at ML's picture. If all the information she had been looking for was coming through, why did she feel so strongly that she was missing something? But the first thing to do was to pass on the information GraceFaith had given her.

"Nina, ask Salim to come by and collect something. And I think he should hear what Cherril said too. In fact call him now. I want to talk to him, fast-fast! Or no—wait. Phone him quick and pass me the phone!"

"Yes, Aunty Lee?" Salim did not sound surprised. "The commissioner said I should—"

"Yes, all that later. Now quickly tell me, your people didn't check the pool house at the Sungs' place right?"

"It's a sterile space, they couldn't go in. But they checked the camera monitors. There's nothing inside except equipment."

"Oh my goodness, you people so *goondu*. Don't you watch

TV? I got inside information, just get inside there somehow. Send the mosquito-check people in. Those guys can get inside everywhere, not like you policemen."

"At least tell me what you expect us to find."

"Just go look, Salim. Quick, quick, quick!"

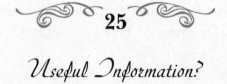

25

Useful Information?

Sergeant Panchal was at the Binjai Park bungalow by noon.

"Mrs. Rosie Lee, you were at the Sung Law offices early this morning before the office opened. Why?"

"I was only trying to get my money. Mabel Sung never paid me for catering the party at her house. I went there to look for Sharon Sung because she wasn't returning my calls. I needed her help about an urgent matter. The security guard let me in because he knew that Miss Ang was still in the office and I said I might as well talk to her. Why are you asking? Did somebody complain about me being there? Was it Sharon Sung? GraceFaith can tell you that I just went and talked to her for a little while and left."

"Miss GraceFaith Ang is missing. Her employer, Miss Sung, says some confidential company documents are also missing and suspects that she took them. She believes Miss Ang may have passed them to you when you were in the office."

"Why would she do that? What company papers is she talking about?"

"If you don't mind I need you to come down to the station to answer some questions. And I will need to search your premises for Miss Sung's company documents."

"Nina, call Salim."

"Inspector Salim is away on a case," Staff Sergeant Panchal said. She had been looking forward to this meeting since Sharon Sung reported the theft of her company documents and named Mrs. Rosie Lee as the prime suspect. "It is a very important case and he cannot be contacted. I am in charge of this investigation."

To SS Panchal's surprise Aunty Lee seemed oddly pleased to hear this. "Of course I'll come with you. Can I change first? And can I finish my lunch? I have low blood pressure. If I don't eat, my blood sugar drops and I faint and fall down. Or can I call for my doctor to come and meet me at the police station?"

Panchal, who had expected defiance and resistance, was disconcerted by her apparent victory.

"Oh. Of course. I will wait for you."

"Why don't you join me for lunch?"

"No. I'm on duty. And I already ate."

"Then why don't you come back after two?"

But though Aunty Lee dressed herself up, Panchal did not come back.

"All the cars are out," Nina reported. "And not just our

station. Plus all the 'on standby' got called in. Must be fire or terrorists somewhere. Otherwise unless it is National Day or Formula One why do they need so many police for?"

Aunty Lee had an idea but did not voice it even to Nina. She would wait and see. There was nothing on the radio news or in the evening papers and no word from Inspector Salim on what he had done with Aunty Lee's documents.

Salim came by the house much later, looking very tired. Nina had been worried about him and covered up her anxiety by attacking.

"Did you come to check whether we closed the shop or not? If I go to the shop to clean, will you arrest me?"

"If people complain, we have to investigate," Salim said. "Can I come in?"

"Even if it is your own people? You say Aunty Lee is like your family. Even if you know she would never do something like that, you must close her down? If you never trust anybody like that, then how can anybody ever trust you?" Nina sounded so furious that Aunty Lee was almost afraid for Salim.

"As long as I am paid to do the job, I must do the job following the rules. If I cannot do the job anymore, then I quit the job first and then I help my people. Do you want me to quit?"

"You can help us a lot better by staying where you are," Aunty Lee said quickly. "Did you manage to do anything with the papers I passed you?"

Nina understood Salim was only doing his job. She was not angry with him for that. Indeed she was not angry with him but she was angry and she could not be angry with Aunty Lee and there was no one else around.

Luckily Salim understood. Or even if he did not understand, he was wise enough and fond enough of her to not take notice. It made Nina feel bad to know she was taking advantage of his good nature. But telling him to go away because as long as he was around she would be nasty to him, would that be better or worse?

"It looks like Dr. Yong was the one responsible for bringing the donor in," Salim said. "He was the one liaising between the PRC suppliers and the Singapore customers."

Customers, thought Aunty Lee. It sounded like they were shopping for human organs at an online supermarket.

"It looks like Dr. Yong took the live donor on consignment. He may have agreed to pay them on delivery but there is no sign he did. Payment from Mabel Sung for Leonard Sung's operation covered less than half the cost. Dr. Yong is someone who has trouble coming up with his monthly rent. We think he was planning to raise the rest of the money and a profit by selling the rest of the live donor's organs. Then when Mabel and Leonard died there was no money and no patient."

"We need to get in touch with Dr. Edmond Yong. I don't think he realizes what kind of people he is dealing with. They can be dangerous. Aunty Lee, do you have any idea at all how to reach him?"

"I wouldn't worry about him if I were you," Aunty Lee said grimly. "I suspect Dr. Yong can take care of himself! What about Henry Sung? And Sharon?"

"Henry Sung says he didn't know anything about it. That

doesn't seem very likely but there's nothing to prove otherwise. And the daughter—Sharon Sung isn't saying anything.
All the documents in the office are in Mabel Sung's name, so
technically Sharon is not involved either."

"And what was GraceFaith Ang's role in all this?"

"Small time. It looks as though she has been pinching
money from the company. But it's hard to tell what she took
and what Mabel Sung took." Salim paused. "I believe you vis-
ited Sung Law and spoke to her yesterday?"

"I did."

"After you left, Miss Ang emptied out what was left of the
Sung Law accounts and instructed that the power and water
supply to the Sung house be cut off. And of course to the
pool house. You already knew what we were going to find
there, didn't you? Anyway, once the power was cut off, the
body died."

"He was already dead, wasn't he?"

"He was technically alive but it is unlikely he could have
been revived."

Aunty Lee felt relieved. "So his body is not worth anything
to anybody now?"

"Sentimental value to his family, but apart from that, no."

Alive, Zhao Liang had been worth a minimum wage but
little more. Semi-alive he had been worth millions of dollars
of transplant organs. Now dead, he was worth nothing. But
perhaps GraceFaith's act would give his family closure.

"Do you know where GraceFaith Ang is?" Aunty Lee could
not help being concerned for the self-possessed, perfectly
turned-out young woman.

"I would certainly like to talk to her if she shows up."

But GraceFaith had her money and was probably too smart to show up on his radar for a good while. Aunty Lee could see her somewhere in the Maldives. Or more likely buying herself a house in Australia. Aunty Lee hoped she would hear from her again.

"Sir? Yes, I'm at Mrs. Lee's house now," Inspector Salim said in reply to the call that came in at that moment. "I will be back there in under half an hour. Sir, we are still waiting for the search warrant for Dr. Henry Sung's house but we checked the outdoor areas for, er"—he coughed—"mosquito breeding sites and we found the body. The body has been transported to NUH for examination. I will get back to you once we get any results. International Affairs has come in to assist. They assigned Timothy Pang because of the PRC links uncovered. No, sir, I did not. I believe he requested the assignment for family reasons."

Aunty Lee had been listening to the one-sided exchange with fascination till Salim cut the connection.

"How is Commissioner Raja?"

"He said you were talking about illegal organ-transplant syndicates from the start, ever since the body of the dead PRC woman's fiancé was not found. And he said I should have remembered that in Singapore the Lees are always right, and that means Lee Kuan Yew and Aunty Lee."

26

Illegal Organ Traders Caught

The *Straits Times Online:*
International Illegal Organ Traders Nabbed!

Officers of the Singapore Police Force, acting on information from the public, have cracked an international organization dealing in illegal organ trading. Apparently the organization has been transporting live donors from China around the region and especially into Singapore via a network of maid agencies and travel agents. The ring is thought to have been dealing in most cases with transplants of nonessential organs. Large sums of money and at least sixteen individuals are thought to be involved. Unfortunately any surviving donors appear unwilling to come forward for fear of prosecution.

The police and the Health Ministry are looking into cases of supposed "miracle" cures.

Evening Drive Time Buzz:

It looks like things were going well for the illegal organ traders for years—if you look at what people are willing to pay for a Lamborghini or Lexus, it almost makes more sense to pay for a cornea or kidney, doesn't it? Anyway, apparently things changed when local lawyer Mabel Sung let it be known she was willing to pay anything for a live donor heart for her precious son. Yes, a heart! Have a heart, lady! We can all get along reasonably well minus a few platelets, minus a few liver cells, but without a heart? Did she not realize what she was asking for or did her mother love drive her to murder? It's almost enough to make me forget the traffic report . . .

Inside Health Weekend Special:

At the time Mabel Sung and her son, Leonard Sung, died, everything was ready for her son's operation. It appears Mabel Sung had paid her PRC contact half the costs up front and was to pay the remaining amount following a successful transplant. A medical consultant had been preparing Leonard Sung for the procedure, feeding and hydrating him to stabilize his condition.

According to Staff Sergeant Timothy Pang, Head of the Special Task Force on Illegal Organ Trading, a kidney transplant operation in China costs around $70,000, a liver transplant around $160,000, and a heart transplant over a million dollars. For the sake of comparison, he pointed out that in the United States a kidney transplant starts at $100,000, a liver transplant at $250,000, and a heart transplant at

$860,000. Given the relatively low cost of Chinese organs, China is currently a major provider of underground organs for transplantation surgery to other countries.

Speaking to our *Inside Health* reporter, Staff Sergeant Pang said, "The PRC organ traffickers brought 'donors' into Singapore as tourists or domestic workers. These were poor, healthy people from China. They were given a deposit on a kidney, say, a sum that seemed immense to them but is minuscule compared to what the body parts bring in. These donors believed that once they were paid for the donated kidney, the money would be enough to start them off on a new life. We believe this is what happened in previous cases but none of the previous donors have been willing to come forward. However, in this case the request was for a donor heart. The donor believed he was donating a kidney and the first payment was made according to the agreement. His trip to Singapore was paid for by the client. But after that the donor, Zhao Liang, aged 23, was kept unconscious on life support until such time as his heart could be transplanted into Leonard Sung. It is believed the rest of his organs were then to be sold to the highest bidder."

Aunty Lee was, of course, fascinated by all the stories. She had long since discovered that online news sites carried far more juicy details—and put them out sooner—than she could get from the official newspapers, and Nina was kept busy supplying her with all the latest speculations and details.

"These people are saying it's not so terrible because otherwise those people would be carrying drugs in, they are so desperate for money. And in that case it is a death penalty anyway, so . . . but it is terrible, right? They say Singapore is stupid to make such a big fuss. After all, the family gets compensation, probably more than they could earn in a lifetime."

"I don't think we are making such a big fuss. It is terrible," Aunty Lee said, "and I think we should make a big fuss about the death penalty here too. That's what they used to do in China, right? Sentence people to death and then use their organs for transplants? Here we sentence people to death for carrying drugs for other people and don't even use their organs!"

The death penalty was one of Aunty Lee's favorite rants, but at the moment there were more interesting wrongs to focus on while slicing mushrooms for drying.

"They say this is the first case in which Singaporeans were involved. Do you think that's true?"

"Until they find out some more cases, it must be true, lor."

It was also reported discreetly in the press that one Dr. Edmond Yong was helping the police with investigations. By this time everyone agreed that Mabel Sung had contacted Edmond Yong to get a living heart donor for her son, Leonard. Aunty Lee was certain that she had thought of it first. If only certain authorities had paid more attention to her instead of investigating her kitchens, things would have been resolved far more quickly. It was Edmond Yong who had arranged for the living donor to be kept on life support on the Sung property, in the locked pool house, which the police investigators had so irresponsibly overlooked. Other people on the Never Say Die waiting list had been in need of parts from the same donor, but Mabel Sung refused to let any other transplants take place until after her son was taken care of. Fortunately this made them more disposed to speak out against her and they did. The scheme might have worked, but when the power supply to the Sung property and pool house was cut off so was the life supply system and the living donor turned into a corpse.

Aunty Lee wondered whether GraceFaith had known the consequences of cutting off the power supply to the house. She had no doubt at all that this had been Grace-Faith's doing. And even if the girl had only made the call to spite Sharon and make things difficult for Edmond Yong in the Sung house, she had ended up sabotaging the whole of their grand moneymaking scheme. Something about that made Aunty Lee think of how Mabel and Leonard had been almost casually poisoned. But Aunty Lee could not imagine GraceFaith deliberately doing something to provoke Mabel Sung as Sharon had.

And Aunty Lee could find no mention in all the papers (even the Chinese ones that Cherril was delegated to scour) of what had become of Wen Ling, the China woman responsible for the local organization. Her contacts at various maid agencies and travel centers could only give the phone numbers they had reached her at, numbers that were no longer in use. They had only done what they were told, they said. And she had not yet paid them.

"It's all about money, isn't it?" Cherril said. "If only people had enough money they wouldn't do things like that."

Neither of her companions agreed with her.

"Singaporeans think there's never enough money!" Nina said as she thumped a huge plastic carrier of string beans onto one of the tables.

"Mabel Sung was trying to save her son," Aunty Lee said from behind her pile of papers. "Once Mabel Sung found out about the illegal transplants, she became fixated on getting a new heart for her son. A parent would do anything to save the life of a child. But . . ."

Nina heard her change of tone and looked worried.

"But what?"

"But why would they kill her?" Aunty Lee demanded.

"The case is over, bad people are in prison or out of the country. Everybody is happy. Why worry?"

"She must have found out about the illegal transplants last year and discovered a way to link them to the Never Say Die people," Cherril said. "That was brilliant actually. If people wondered why they were suddenly healthy, they could say the praying works miracles. Mycroft says it's not like it is in India, where a kidney transplant operation runs for around as low as five thousand dollars and they get medical tourists from the West all the time. I was surprised Mabel didn't bring her son to India for the operation, but Mycroft says people here are prejudiced. They don't trust the doctors there or they think that if the organs come from Indians they must be dirty."

Her husband, Mycroft, an ethnic Indian, looked embarrassed. He had taken to walking over to the shop with Cherril when she came in on weekends. He said it was because he needed the exercise but Aunty Lee suspected he was being a protective husband and his need for exercise would fade away now the murderers had been brought to justice. But had they?

"She was a racist, elitist woman but there was no reason for them to kill her," Aunty Lee said.

Aunty Lee's mind was already elsewhere. The illegal transplant business had required a lot of planning and organization. If the same people had branched out into murder, they would have to had put in a lot of careful advance planning, like the amount of preparation that went into making chicken *buah keluak*. But the deaths of Mabel and Leonard Sung did not feel like that sort of murder at all. They felt like impulse murders. Ingredients like the *buah keluak* and Algae Bomb and the food tray all coming together were like the sort of dish that just fell into your lap. Like when a husband went fishing and came back with a huge *garoupa* or a net full of plump *kembong* and you happened to have a sack of charcoal and a bag of salt. Then no planning was needed at all. All you had to do was grab and gut the fish and get it onto the grill as fast as possible. Because you could take your time to decide who to call to come over to dinner later, but without enough freezer space the whole point was being able to kill and gut a fish fast.

That was the kind of murder it felt like to Aunty Lee. Not one that had been planned for a long time but one that had depended on chance uniting motive, opportunity, and a calm killer.

"I should go and talk to that Dr. Yong again," Aunty Lee said thoughtfully. Any or all of the others, tired and stressed by recent events, would have told her to drop it. But at that moment Mycroft was asking Cherril if she felt ready to return home and Cherril was teasing Nina for *gayuma* recipes because with the right Filipino love potions on the drinks menu, people might be persuaded to fall in love with the shop as well as with each other. Aunty Lee took their silence for agreement.

But it wasn't until she was back in her house that evening that Aunty Lee got the chance to pursue her inquiries further. Nina had firmly refused to discuss a case she considered closed and settled on clearing fallen leaves out of the driveway drain gratings, something she had been dying to do for weeks. Aunty Lee retreated to her living room. She was feeling low and dissatisfied, both tired and restless at the same time. The room felt unpleasantly empty and even the portrait of ML failed to comfort her. Perhaps she should get it reframed? But then the reframing of pictures and redecorating of houses was precisely the kind of pointless *tai-tai* busyness Aunty Lee hoped to avoid.

Aunty Lee told herself she was only feeling bad because her case and her shop were both closed. But once the paperwork was done, they would reopen and everything would be back to normal. But even there, what was the point? Wasn't that just more aimless busyness? She even had her doubts about why the PRC gang would have wanted to kill Mabel Sung. Was she just another bored old woman matchmaking corpses and motives?

Perhaps she should take up tai chi in the park with all the other old aunties . . .

"Rosie!"

Aunty Lee turned and saw the only (live) man capable of making her feel better right then standing at the French doors that opened from her living room to the lawn.

"Nina told me you were back here, so I thought I would come round this way and join you."

Raja Kumar had taken off his tie and rolled up his shirt-sleeves in an attempt to look casual.

"Please come in," Aunty Lee said, all thoughts of tai chi immediately forgotten. "I thought you were out of the country. I called your office a few times but every time they said you were busy or in meetings, so I thought for sure you went off to Indonesia or Vietnam on some hush-hush business."

"This is an unofficial meeting," Commissioner Raja said. "I just happened to stop by on my way home and ran into you when you just happened to be here."

"That's an easier story to believe if you set it in my shop than in my house!"

"You can open your shop again anytime. Your paperwork is cleared. Salim will bring it over to you tomorrow once it is stamped and recorded. You won't be inconvenienced again by this whole kitchen investigation nonsense. You'll have seen from all newspapers that you were right. There were more than minor discrepancies in the accounts at Sung Law. From the look of things they are in serious trouble. And Mabel Sung's personal accounts are just as overextended," Commissioner Raja said. "Everything was going to collapse sooner or later no matter what happened. That might make the suicide theory easier to believe. Mabel had bankrupted her company and her husband trying to find a cure for her son, but Mabel's son was not going to recover. It was only a matter of time before he died and Mabel lost everything."

"Mabel and Edmond Yong must have arranged with the Chinese employment agencies for a donor who thought he was coming to donate a kidney. The Chinese agency who brought him in was not paid in full till after the operation—"

"They must charge a lot. Did you see how much Mabel Sung took out of her accounts?"

"Edmond Yong must have persuaded her they could more than make up for it by selling off the poor bugger's other body parts. He was never going to make it to the wedding he was selling a kidney to pay for. Dr. Yong was quite happy to make money on the side with a kidney or cornea transplant, but it must have been a jump for him to agree to do a transplant that would kill the donor."

"So you've arrested him?" Aunty Lee asked eagerly. "Make him tell you who his China contacts are and who else is involved. The transplant scheme was still going on after Mabel died. Henry and Sharon Sung must be involved somehow."

"We don't have proof of that yet. We have to wait and see what Edmond Yong gives us."

"I wish I could talk to him," Aunty Lee said. Commissioner Raja made a point of not hearing her.

"And I thought you would like to know that given Leonard Sung's state of health and Mabel Sung's probable state of mind at the time of her demise, they are writing it up with weight on the mercy killing/suicide angle."

Aunty Lee could see Commissioner Raja thought this was good news for her. If the unofficial official view was that

Mabel Sung had indeed killed herself and her son, that meant Aunty Lee and her catering business were off the hook.

But convenient as it was, Aunty Lee could not believe it. If Mabel had killed herself and her sick son after her live donor transplant scheme crashed, then it would have made sense. But before, with all the plans for her son's operation in place, why would Mabel have killed her son and herself? And there was as little reason for the illegal organ traders to kill them.

"What about the woman who was organizing things from the China side? Wen Ling?"

"Wen Ling has probably moved all her operations out of Singapore, at least temporarily. It's too profitable a business to give up. And as they get richer they can buy into legitimate businesses, probably in the West."

"Actually that's not so different from what our ancestors did," Aunty Lee said.

As soon as Timothy Pang opened the door, the senior officer—Sergeant Yap? Sergeant Yeo?—rose to his feet to acknowledge him. "Sergeant Pang. Good of you to come. Your brother came to offer us a statement."

"I want to clear Benjamin's name," said Patrick. "I want the papers to print that they were wrong. They were saying all kinds of things about him. That he was part of some illegal business and set the fire to cover his tracks and then disappeared."

"Come with me first," Timothy said firmly. "I'll take care of it."

A small ungenerous part of him wondered whether he was

going to be spending the rest of his life taking care of his younger brother. Maybe the years that Patrick had spent not talking to him had not been so bad after all.

Patrick protested—he wanted to see the statement he had given the police, he said. He wanted them to remove Benjamin Ng's name from whatever suspects list they had put it on. He went on talking even as his brother tried to genially erase any record of his visit without making it look like any kind of a cover-up.

"I have to be sure you don't say anything to incriminate yourself," Timothy Pang said.

"Maybe you should both hear our current report on Benjamin Ng," Sergeant Yeo Seng Meng suggested respectfully. Timothy hesitated but the sergeant gave a small nod.

"Benjamin Ng was commissioned to design a home ICU and operating theater for the Sungs. He put it down to the eccentricities of rich people wanting to prolong their lives beyond death. This was completed before the fire at the Beautiful Dreamers clinic and Benjamin Ng did not make the connection then. Notes subsequently found in his apartment and handed over to us reveal that Ng became suspicious after the fire when the intensive-care-unit equipment, like the bedside monitor and dialysis pumps he had been sourcing for the home ICU setup, were offered to him cheap without purchase history or guarantees. His notes include records of serial numbers verifying this. His research linked these items to those supposedly destroyed in the fire at the Beautiful Dreamers clinic. Ng asked Edmond Yong about this but did not get a satisfactory answer. This was before the suicide death of the PRC girl. He suspected only that Dr. Yong was involved with arson for insurance and was trying to make extra money by forcing him, Pang, to buy back the same equipment that had supposedly been lost in the fire."

"What happened to him after that is anybody's guess," said the other officer.

Patrick listened quietly to these words. "So you don't have him down as a criminal."

"No. Quite the opposite. He was one of the first to suspect there was something funny going on. I just need you to sign a receipt for the notebooks you brought in."

Edmond Yong was released on bail.

His body was found the next morning dumped at a Downtown Line station construction site.

"It will cause work holdups and delay the station opening," Nina said when the news came over the radio. "That man was always a troublemaker. You want to read the online reports?"

"Such a waste." Aunty Lee sighed, moving to where Nina was priming her iPad to STOMP, Singapore's "citizen journalism" web portal.

"You think it is a waste? That man who is supposed to be a doctor saving lives goes around killing people and you think it is a waste?"

"It is a waste I didn't get to talk to him," Aunty Lee said with dignity. "Now he is dead and I still don't know what happened."

But it was a waste, Aunty Lee thought. She had not liked Edmond Yong and she felt sorry for him because not only his death but his life had been a waste.

27

What Next?

Aunty Lee got her kitchen license back. Everything had returned to normal, but as Aunty Lee told the portrait of ML by the wine room door, she was not yet satisfied,

"The China gang had every reason to keep Mabel Sung and her son alive as they had not yet got all their money. And Mabel had every reason to stay alive because her son had not yet got the transplant!"

However, everyone else was satisfied, including Mark, who came by to congratulate her on the reopening, then disappeared into his precious wine room.

"You can still come back to visit, you know. Even after you sign the business over to Cherril," Aunty Lee said when he finally emerged to join her and Selina for tea.

"Not if she returns all the stock to the distributors. Wine

doesn't travel well, you know. It was not easy getting all the bottles here in good condition. And I don't know whether Cherril knows enough to take care of them even if she keeps them here."

Mark looked like a disappointed small boy, Aunty Lee thought.

Selina said nothing. Aunty Lee could tell she was also trying to get Mark to sign the forms that would complete the handover. For once, Selina and Aunty Lee were on the same side. And vague, gentle Mark, whom each of the women suspected the other of bullying, was defying them both.

"It's most important to decide what kind of dish you are preparing, and for who," Aunty Lee said as Mark sat down beside his wife. "That doesn't depend on the ingredients because your ingredients can always be adjusted."

"Like chili-pepper ice cream. And we saw squid-ink-and-octopus ice cream in Japan." Mark snorted with laughter. "Sel said she wouldn't eat it if they paid her."

"*Sambal* ice cream would be interesting, especially in hot weather. Maybe *sambal ikan bilis* ice cream . . . Nina, remind me to follow up on this ice cream business when all this fuss is over, okay? But what was I saying . . . oh yes. What kind of dish. What motive. Someone must have had a reason for killing Mabel Sung. If we can find out who had reasons, then it will be easier to find out who did it."

"Money," Mark said. "It's always about money, isn't it? The root of all evil and all that?"

"Love," suggested Selina. "Jealousy, infidelity . . ." Aunty Lee hoped that Mark was paying attention.

"Damage control," said Cherril from the sink, her hands in a tub of pineapple chunks, "so a situation doesn't get worse. Or revenge. Maybe Mabel Sung did something to somebody years back and they waited until now to get back at her. Or maybe Mabel knew some secrets about somebody and they had to shut her up because they are running for MP or something."

Aunty Lee hoped Cherril wasn't speaking from experience. The very proper, ultrarespectable Mycroft Peters did not seem the sort to have secrets about anybody. But then neither did he seem the sort of man to marry a former air stewardess, so there were obviously depths to him.

"Salim says sometimes people kill to protect other people," Nina said. "Like to protect their children or their parents."

"Mabel Sung probably killed her son to protect him," Selina said. "Better to get it over quickly than a long drawn-out death costing a lot of money. And then she killed herself because she couldn't live with the thought that she killed her son. Anyway I have to go. I have a hot-yoga class," she said. "I know, some people say that it's satanic and all that, but for me it's just exercise. Mark, have you discussed everything you want to? You want to just sign the papers now then you won't have to come back?"

"Sel likes hot yoga because she can sweat without exercising too hard," Mark said with a snort of laughter that no one joined in. "I should just help Aunty Lee sort out this mess she got herself into first. Wouldn't be fair to desert a sinking ship."

That was most unjust, Aunty Lee thought. She never created messes. Indeed, a goodly amount of her time was spent clearing up the messes made by other people. Very few people understood that if you wanted to do a good, thorough cleanup of something, you had to dig right down deep, turn it inside out if possible, and shake out all the debris that had accumulated. It was the same whether you were tackling a store cupboard, an old handbag, or some-body's life. And then you untangled and cleaned up the contents and replaced them in an orderly fashion.

Aunty Lee's kitchen sometimes looked as though she cooked in a state of chaos. But the chaos was only on the surface and always temporary. Everything in her kitchen had a place and reason for being there.

"I'm sure the police are looking into that," Selina said. "You should all just leave it to them and Aunty Lee. After all, you don't want to get into any more trouble, right?"

Aunty Lee reminded herself that Selina probably meant to be helpful and supportive. It was not the woman's fault that her voice made her sound bossy and condescending. Besides, it was a good suggestion. Aunty Lee was never surprised by good suggestions, taking them as part of the natural flow of life. What surprised her was that the suggestion came from Selina.

"You're getting a real investment," Mark said. "There's a bottle of Mouton Rothschild 1945 in there. When my ship comes in I'm going to buy it back from you. It is an amazing Bordeaux—you just look at its color."

"I know," Cherril said quietly. "Why don't you buy it now? Then we'll have a bit more space here and you'll have your wine."

"It's only here on consignment, you know," Mark said. "It's not yours until it's paid for. Until then it's better not to move it more than we have to. When I've set up a space at home to store it properly, I'll buy it directly from Grand Heds and take care of all the paperwork for you."

"You mean you'll cut us out of the deal. You just want us to store it for you until you're ready to bring it home," Cherril said.

"Of course you're welcome to sell it if you can find anybody willing to pay fifteen thousand dollars for a bottle of wine."

"I'm thinking of selling it online," Cherril said. "I've been following Wine Bots and Bids online and I think it won't be a problem. In fact, if I run some kind of competition to generate interest, I'll probably get even more for it."

"You can't do that. That's so . . . low."

"That's why I can," Cherril said. "I'll need some way to authenticate it first, though. They say online that this is one of the most faked wines on the market. Are you checking the online market for it, Aunty Lee?"

Cherril was only teasing Aunty Lee, who generally left digital research to younger eyes. But Aunty Lee's absorption in her phone while business was being discussed was unusual. "Something wrong?" Cherril added when Aunty Lee did not answer immediately.

It took Aunty Lee some effort to pull her thoughts back

into the room. "No. I just got a message from somebody. Nothing urgent."

No, what Aunty Lee had just learned from Commissioner Raja's text had no place in the middle of a petty business discussion. And all discussions of business profits suddenly felt petty to her.

Benjamin Ng's body had been found, caught up by bottom-fishing trawl nets in Indonesian waters just south of Singapore's maritime border, still locked inside the trunk in which it had been thrown into the sea.

28

Party Revelations at Aun

Aunty Lee's Delights had been closed for less than a week but it was announcing its reopening with a party. This event had been spearheaded by Cherril because Aunty Lee, who loved parties and had never needed an excuse for throwing one, had been surprisingly subdued until it struck her that Henry and Sharon Sung must be invited.

"Just to show no hard feelings, you know? And they will have to come, to show us there are no hard feelings on their side. Otherwise I can sue them for slander, all the terrible things they went and said about me and my cooking!"

Though not fond of the Sungs, Cherril could see the PR sense in this. " 'The Grand Reopening,' do you think? 'Deadly Special Declared Not Deadly' night."

Nina did not think it a good idea. "Why throw a party? One week we don't earn money, now want to waste more money. And then you invite these no good people that try to sabo us!"

"It's like doing a warm-up," Cherril said. "After being closed, this will give us a chance to start up again. And if anything doesn't work we'll find out now and they can't complain because they're not paying. Think of them as our guinea pigs."

"What for feed pigs," Nina said.

Cherril was right, of course. And Aunty Lee knew it was always easier to put things in order (whether in your kitchen or in yourself) when you had a party to look forward to. She had another more important reason for wanting to have the party, which she kept to herself.

That other reason was why Aunty Lee was so preoccupied the evening of her reopening party. She had returned home to shower after cooking all morning and afternoon and was dressing with more care than usual. And it was good that she had her scheme to occupy her mind, because she could feel the malaise of uncertainty that had descended on her during the shop's closure threatening to return.

Nina was still busy with preparations in the shop kitchen, so Aunty Lee talked to the tiny photo portrait of ML (smartly casual in a green polo T-shirt) on her dressing table: "Even I don't think it's a good idea, so I don't need you to tell me so. But I cannot just sit back and do nothing. I know what you will say: if everybody else is happy with how things turned out, why can't I be happy? But I know inside me—inside here—" Aunty Lee thumped her chest. She was wearing one of her cooking outfits but she had added a few gold chains, which jangled most satisfyingly.

ML's portrait remained benign. Why wasn't he around to tell her what to do or what not to do like he used to do? Even though she had never listened to him, hearing his thoughts always helped.

"And that poor boy. I mean Timmy Pang's brother. So handsome, so unhappy. Is not fair, right? I wanted Raja to bring him over to see me after they told him about finding his friend's body. But he said nobody bothered to inform him. The police just sent an e-mail to their contacts in Malaysia to inform his family there and ask them to make arrangements. Can you imagine? If you died and nobody bothered to inform me?"

Aunty Lee's only comfort was that Timothy Pang might have broken the news to his brother before he heard on the news or read in the papers that his partner's body had been found. And she knew Patrick Pang had expected the worst even as he could not help hoping for a miracle.

Aunty Lee had invited Commissioner Raja and Inspector Salim to drop in. And she had asked Doreen Choo to bring Henry and Sharon Sung along, "Just to show there's no hard feelings. Please tell them I particularly want them to come because I have something to say in Mabel's memory that I know they will want to hear.

"I just want to ask them a few questions, find out what really happened," Aunty Lee said to the portrait on the wall. "No harm asking questions, right? And no harm finding out what really happened even if Raja Kumar can't do anything about it. I just want to know." ML looked genially noncommittal. What would he have said if he were alive? Aunty Lee knew he would have told her not to get involved.

For a moment Aunty Lee felt totally alone in a totally pointless universe. Why bother cooking chicken curry and catching murderers and exercising to lose weight when at the end of it all you wound up dead and not caring about anything? If ML had been alive he would have said "low blood sugar" and made her fix a snack for herself (and for him too, since she was doing it anyway). A toasted-banana-and-peanut-butter sandwich had been one of ML's favorite treatments for existential angst when they first met. And it had worked.

"Eating doesn't solve anything," Aunty Lee had protested. But over the years she had come to see the wisdom in ML's point of view. Eating might not solve anything except hunger and low blood sugar. But eating well put you in better shape to handle all the problems you encountered. Except loneliness, perhaps. Though she knew it didn't make sense for her to be lonely with a party to host.

"I'll let you know how it goes later," she said to the portrait. "I have to do this. Not for Mabel Sung and her son, not even for my reputation, but for that poor boy Benjamin Ng and all the others who got used and hurt." The portrait was unresponsive but the certainty that it would be there when she returned was a small anchor in the uncertain evening ahead and Aunty Lee clung to it.

Back at Aunty Lee's Delights, Cherril was singing as she rimmed glasses in lemon juice and salt and Nina—

"Eat this, madam," Nina said, handing her a banana. "Today you did not eat proper lunch and when people come you will not eat proper dinner. Afterward you go fainting, Boss sure say my fault."

Aunty Lee ate the banana. "Thanks, boss," she said to ML's portrait.

"Okay, I brought them," Doreen Choo whispered to Aunty Lee as soon as she arrived. "What's the big occasion? What are you planning?"

Doreen Choo's sleeveless gray silk blouse with gold embroidery worn over dark maroon pants and bejeweled sandals showed off her slimness. As always, her hair was carefully arranged (and spray-fixed) into artful curls, her eyes mascaraed and drawn up at the corners with china-doll ticks, and the glossy sheen on her lips matched her shimmering pants. As always, she made Aunty Lee wish she had dressed up more. But then her T-shirt, yoga pants, and Hello Kitty apron with all its pockets was the perfect outfit for cooking in. Nina, in an identical apron, hurried past with a bag of ice and a carton of orange juice.

"I'm not planning anything other than dinner," Aunty Lee said vaguely. "What would you like to drink? Cherril has come up with some new health drinks. You said you brought Henry and Sharon? Where are they?"

"Right behind me—" Doreen turned and looked vaguely around. "Oh, no, thank you, dear. Could you make me a martini?"

"Of course," Cherril said, and disappeared into the wine room.

"It's probably that girl that's slowing them down," Doreen said crossly. "She's always standing around doing things on her phone. Even when we sit down to eat a nice dinner, she's staring into that phone of hers. 'Playing games?' I asked her nicely once. I was just trying to make conversation. She almost bit my head off. 'This is work!' she said. I don't know what work she can be doing. I thought Sung Law is supposed to be on shutdown now. Like the American government.

"You see it more and more these days," Doreen continued after getting her drink. "These young girls. Study so hard to become doctors and lawyers and become so intense and high-strung that they cannot live a normal life, cannot get married. What kind of life is that?"

"What does Henry think?"

"Oh, Henry is a typical man. He doesn't think any-thing—ah, here they are now. Our guests of honor are here!" Doreen called, and waved like a schoolgirl. Henry Sung looked embarrassed but pleased. Doreen knew her men, Aunty Lee thought. Henry would probably have resisted if he had been ordered to come or begged to come to a party. But as a "guest of honor," he turned up like royalty visiting his subjects. And he had brought Sharon with him. Sharon was clearly unhappy to be there. Cherril offered her cock-tails, moctails, doctails, fresh-squeezed juice, and was turned down. Her father did not seem to notice. Sharon had prob-ably sulked her way through adolescence and beyond till her

family took sulking for her natural state. Doreen had commandeered a whiskey sour for Henry and they had sat down
with Commissioner Raja, who had been sitting with an un-
touched glass of orange juice since arriving.

"You must be glad you finally got hold of the PRC gang—
read about it in the papers, good job!" Aunty Lee said to him
as she came by to check the new arrivals were all provided
with drinks.

"Thanks."

Commissioner Raja had a feeling Aunty Lee was up to
something. He also knew it was no use telling her to stop it
when he did not know exactly what she was up to. "Stop cooking? Stop eating? Stop what?" he could imagine her saying.
He had been invited to dinner as an old friend to celebrate
the reopening of Aunty Lee's Delights and the closing of
the illegal organ trading, but he had turned up to keep an
eye on things. He suspected Inspector Salim was there for
the same reason. Neither of them was in uniform and the
younger man had greeted him with a bland casual friendli-
ness, which gave him away. Salim always had a touch of earnest formality about him. His casual manner indicated he
considered himself undercover rather than off duty.

Salim was torn between watching and worrying. Sitting at
the table, he looked a little bored and as if he were thinking
of nothing at all. The only thing that gave away his actual
state of mind was that he was not eating. He accepted everything he was offered with thanks and pushed it around
on his plate. He drank only water, straight out of the plastic

bottle. If Aunty Lee hadn't been feeling much the same way as he was, she would have felt offended.

Mark and Selina arrived late, as usual, Selina explaining to the room at large how busy they were.

"We should go," Sharon Sung stood up and said. "Thanks for inviting us. Now we've all sat down together and agreed no hard feelings, we can all get on with our lives, right?"

Doreen and Henry were still eating. Henry shoved another heaping spoonful into his mouth and started to stand up but Doreen put a hand on his arm. "We're still eating, Sharon. You can let your father finish his dinner, can't you?"

"We can get something somewhere else. We've put in our appearance. Everybody's said what they have to say, so let's go."

"So rude, some people," Selina remarked to the ceiling.

"Actually I haven't said what I invited you all here to say," Aunty Lee said. Commissioner Raja caught her eye but said nothing. Stopping Aunty Lee was like trying to stop ice melting, he thought. It's going to happen anyway, you just try to put the bucket in the right place.

"I found out that Henry Sung and Sung Law are both on the verge of bankruptcy because Mabel mortgaged everything to get money for Leonard's illegal organ transplant."

Henry issued a weak denial that was ignored. Sharon, still on her feet, listened in silence. Her expression said she was going to sue the pants off this meddling old woman once she got the chance.

"Sharon tried to save the law firm by selling off parts of the living heart donor Mabel brought in but had not yet paid for. The man was being kept alive on the life-support system created for Edmond Yong by Benjamin Ng. Ben Ng thought he was creating a future life-support system for Leonard Sung. When he learned the truth, that one man was being murdered to save another's life, he was upset. Edmond Yong told the PRC gang this and Ben disappeared.

"Meanwhile," Aunty Lee went on, "Sharon thought Mabel was finally giving her all the recognition she deserved when she was made partner. As a full partner in Sung Law, she believed she would effectively be running everything because Mabel was increasingly devoting all her energy and attention to her son and the prayer and healing group.

"But Sharon found out that not only was Mabel not interested in the company anymore, she had destroyed it. Sharon, you found this out the night before your celebration party when you went through the company accounts and found out about the enormous amounts Mabel had been drawing out, didn't you? That's why you spent the night there going over the facts again and again.

"You confronted your mother when you finally got home. What did she say? Did you tell your father what you found out? What did he say? If we can just clear up what really happened to your mother, then we can all move on."

If this had been part of an episode on a television murder series, this was the point at which Henry Sung or his daughter would break down and confess, right in time for the closing credits.

Instead Henry sat staring at Aunty Lee with his mouth open, seemingly incapable of speech.

"What are you taking about!" Doreen cried out. "Mabel was not that kind of woman at all. She was responsible. She knew how to make money and run companies and heal people! Mabel would never go bankrupt. Tell her, Henry!" In her excitement she thumped Henry on the arm.

Henry Sung closed his mouth. He turned to Doreen and the cold venom in his eyes shut her up immediately.

Aunty Lee felt a strong sense of anticlimax. Once Doreen started babbling, there would be no confessions. Commissioner Raja felt a strong sense of relief. The worst that could come of this was a libel suit, he thought. He picked up a chicken wing. In times of stress and times of relief, a spicy buffalo wing was a great comfort.

"Are we supposed to fake outrage and storm out?" Sharon Sung said. Her voice was steady, controlled, and icily amused. "If you've finished, we're leaving now. Come on, Dad. Doreen can stay if she wants."

Henry Sung rose, shaking off the hand Doreen had tentatively placed on his arm.

"Thank you for coming," Aunty Lee said. Her mind was spinning. She was sure she had guessed the facts but she had misjudged her criminals. If she could just try another approach—her hostess autopilot kicked in at this point. "But you didn't eat much. I pack up some food for you to take home with you."

"No thank you."

"There's so much here, don't waste. Can keep in the fridge for up to one week—"

"Stop it!" Sharon snapped. "Nobody wants your stupid

food!" People stopped talking and turned to stare. Aunty Lee also stared, feeling a twinge of delight that she had managed to provoke a genuine response from the young woman.

Without another word Sharon Sung turned and walked out, followed by her father.

"I'll just take a quick look in the wine room if you've finished." Mark seemed oblivious to any tension. Perhaps he had chosen the best path after all.

29

Post-Party Problem

It was late by the time Aunty Lee stood on the walkway just outside her shop waving as the dark green Volvo drove off. After Henry and Sharon left with Doreen, the party had lightened up considerably.

Commissioner Raja had stayed to see Aunty Lee's last guests leave. Even though Aunty Lee had not shared her little plan with him (or even admitted she had a plan), he had been curious to see if anything came of it. But even if her gambit had failed, everyone had had a pleasant evening and left full of good food. There were far worse ways to end a day.

Nina still had not appeared.

"Nina, come, let's go. We can come in and clean up to-morrow."

Nina did not answer.

Aunty Lee decided Nina must have got tired of waiting for her and started cleaning up the kitchen. Once Nina got into her cleaning zone, she could lose all sense of time. Aunty Lee knew how that felt. It was like what people described in running marathons—you were in a zone beyond tired but you kept going. And then afterward, when you looked over your clean kitchen or clean house, it was all worth it. Because you had pushed your body beyond its comfort level and accomplished something.

Either that or she would find Nina poring over one of the books Salim had given her. Despite everything Nina said to the contrary ("You are full of crazy dreams," "Whoever heard of a Mat lawyer in Philippines or Pinoy lawyer in Singapore!"), all the signs showed Aunty Lee that the young woman was dreaming along the same lines—even if she didn't realize it yet herself. Nina might mock Salim's dreams but she kept the stack of books he had given her. That was another problem brewing, Aunty Lee thought as she went back into the café. She would do all she could to help Nina of course, but—

But Nina was kneeling on the floor in front of the kitchen sink with her arms behind her, beside the legs of Henry Sung, who was sitting on a chair.

"Nina, what—are you all right? Henry, you're still here? I thought you left long ago!"

"It's all your fault. If you didn't come nosing around, everything would be all right."

Sharon Sung was standing behind the kitchen door, which she now closed. And Sharon was holding Aunty Lee's favorite

Korin Suisin High-Carbon Steel Gyutou chef knife to Aunty Lee's only (and therefore favorite) throat.

"Please be careful with that!" Aunty Lee said. "That is a carbon steel blade that can slice through a two-centimeter-thick pumpkin shell as though it is tofu!"

"Oh, now you're scared, are you? It's about time but it's too late now."

"That is not a stainless-steel knife, you know. It will tarnish if you don't rub it with oil after washing it. The cloth I usually use for that is over there by the sink, behind Nina. Nina, are you all right, girl?"

Nina nodded silently. She looked scared but otherwise unhurt.

Aunty Lee's mind seemed to have jammed. All she could think of was that the whirring from the wine cooler room's air chiller was unusually loud. The door had probably been left ajar again. Customers seldom realized they had to turn the lock after leaving the room to close it properly. This had always annoyed Mark, who worried more about the temperature of his precious wine than about someone getting locked inside the cooler room by accident.

Aunty Lee shifted her attention away from the wine cooler room. The kitchen door leading to the back alley was also standing open.

"You left and came back through the back door?"

"Which I made sure to unlock. I thought those people would never leave!"

"You should not have come back."

Sharon laughed, shaking the knife point against Aunty Lee's neck. Aunty Lee winced at the sensation rather than from pain as the blade's svelte point slid smoothly through her skin and drew blood.

"Sharon! Be careful!" Henry Sung spoke for the first time. "Blood, your fingerprints, these days everything is dangerous. Be careful, girl!"

Sharon ignored her father. "I want the bills you took. The ones you stole when you went to see GraceFaith in the office that night."

"Did I?" Aunty Lee looked as though she was trying to remember. "I went to see her in your office, yes. But you gave me a cheque for the catering already, so no more bills."

"The electricity bills. Mabel's payment records. She was a fool to keep them in the office. Just now you said GraceFaith gave you something important when you saw her."

"GraceFaith has relatives in Hong Kong. She told me she knows somebody that can get me the secret recipe for Tian Tian XO sauce."

"Don't talk rubbish."

"It's not rubbish. It is a very special sauce they never sell outside the restaurant and their employees have to sign contract saying they will not reveal the secret ingredient."

"Anyway, that doesn't matter now."

Aunty Lee was counting on Sharon's patience running out before she had meandered through her old-lady stories. A lifetime in the kitchen had taught her that impatience always made people careless. The problem was, Aunty Lee had no idea how to take advantage of this until . . .

"Sharon, I really didn't mean to kill your mother and brother, you know," Aunty Lee said piteously. She turned to look at Henry Sung, ignoring a second knife prick.

Sharon laughed. She pushed Aunty Lee roughly, making her fall onto the ground next to Nina.

"Dad, did you hear that? This stupid old fool thinks we're after her for killing Mabel and Lennie!"

Henry Sung studied Aunty Lee, who tried to look like a helpless old woman struggling to get up.

"My leg—"

"Aunty, what happened to your leg?"

"My leg so pain. I don't know what happened—"

"Shut up, both of you. And stay down there." Sharon paced around the kitchen, still holding the knife.

"Don't trust her," Henry Sung said. Sharon ignored him. Aunty Lee thought that was a good sign, though she had no idea how to make use of it. She fluttered to Henry: "Henry you mustn't be angry with me. I am so sorry. I swear I would never have done anything to hurt Mabel on purpose. But you know what *buah keluak* is like . . ."

"I know you didn't kill Mabel. I killed Mabel," Sharon snapped. She was clearly annoyed that Aunty Lee was paying more attention to Henry than to her.

Aunty Lee managed to look suitably shocked. "But you were telling everybody that I poisoned your mother!"

"And you went around saying you didn't and making trouble. If you had just shut up everything would have been fine. And then now you turn around and say you thought you poisoned her all along. You stupid old woman." Sharon laughed again. She sounded tired, Aunty Lee thought. She was probably very tired. That was not good. Tired people were often irrational and self-destructive. And in this case likely to be destructive of others too. "If you had just kept your loud mouth shut, everything would have been all right.

"I put the Algae Bomb powder in Len's *buah keluak* before making Edmond bring it up to the house for him," she went on. "I only meant to make him sick, really sick for once. To pay him back for lying around and making everybody run around doing things for him all the time. And I thought if Edmond ate it and got sick too, it would serve him right. He was so greedy, always sneaking around and pinching things. How was I to know that it was poisonous enough to kill people? It's supposed to be for swimming pools, for goodness' sake. And how was I to know my mother would go up to eat with him? She never ate with me. Anyway, it was her own fault. I'm not sorry."

"You are saying you accidentally killed your brother and your mother," Aunty Lee repeated as though she was slow-wittedly trying to understand this. Actually she was thinking fast of ways to distract Sharon, though she was not sure what good it would do. All the shops in the row were closed and no one would be coming around till midmorning. Nina was frowning with a faraway look in her eyes. Aunty Lee hoped she had not been hit in the head. And Henry Sung did not look surprised to hear that his daughter had murdered his wife and son.

"Sharon, if you tell people it was an accident, I'm sure they will understand."

Sharon shook her head at Aunty Lee's stupidity. "It turned

out to be the right thing to do. It was the only thing to be done. Now, without Leonard draining us, I can start over with a clean slate and save the company. And you and your maid are going to help us."

Henry Sung was shaking his head. But he had been trained all his life to obey his wife without question and now that she was gone he obeyed his daughter.

"Mabel set up the whole system. We just have to use it better than she did. People need healthy organs, we can give them healthy organs—for the right price."

"You want to take and sell our organs?"

"Not yours, old woman. We can use Nina as the donor body. And we are going to set things up here so that everybody thinks that Nina killed you and disappeared with all your money. This way we get rid of you and nobody's looking for her. Or rather, everybody will be looking for her as a criminal. Isn't that brilliant?"

The girl was so desperate for approval, Aunty Lee almost felt sorry for her. "But why—"

"Don't talk to her. She's mad," Nina said. Almost casually Henry Sung smacked her hard on the side of her head and she fell against Aunty Lee.

"Ow—my arm—twisted—" she moaned.

Henry Sung laughed. He was not a nice man, Aunty Lee thought. He probably kicked dogs when he thought nobody was watching. She put an arm around Nina and helped her sit up.

"Anyway, you don't know anything," Sharon said. "You don't even know why I'm not sorry I killed my mother!"

"Why aren't you sorry you killed your mother?" Aunty Lee asked obligingly. What she had felt in Nina's hand made her even more eager to distract Sharon and Henry. "Mabel was such a good woman. Such a dedicated lawyer and devoted mother." She had heard so many people say this over the past couple of weeks.

Henry Sung nodded. "God rest her soul," he said automatically.

Sharon stared at him. Aunty Lee could not tell whether the expression in her eyes was directed at her father or at the soul he spoke of.

"You have no idea what I had to put up with!" Sharon said. "Nobody knows. People fawned over her and she thought she was the Virgin Mary and the Second Coming all rolled up in one. And all the time I was the one staying back in the office doing all the work that she took on, just to look good. And did she ever say thank you? Did she even acknowledge who was doing all the real work? Ha! All she said was 'You're late again' and 'Can't you wear some makeup or something. People will think you're one of those butch lesbians.'"

"Girl, I'm sure nobody thinks that you—"

"Shut up, Dad."

Henry Sung shut up, as he had been shut up by his wife throughout his married life.

"I thought Mabel making me partner meant she was finally realizing how much I'd done for her. I thought she was finally remembering she had two children, not just one useless son. I asked if I could look at the private company files and she said 'why not?' and left. Idiot that I was, I was actually pleased. I thought that showed how much she trusted me. But the truth is, she just didn't care anymore.

"Mabel only made me partner because she was washing her hands of Sung Law. She dumped it on me like she dumped everything she couldn't be bothered with.

"I started reading her stuff and I couldn't believe it. I went through all her back files and ended up staying on in the office the whole night. It was all there. Sung Law was going bankrupt. You didn't know that, did you? Nobody knew except Mabel. That was the last straw. She didn't make me partner because she was proud of me. She just wanted to wash her hands of it, so she dumped it all on me. She told GraceFaith she was going to announce her retirement at the party and then she was going to cash out her insurance. She already got GraceFaith to make an appointment with the insurance people. Mabel was going to take Len on a holiday with the money that was left after his operation. Can you believe it? The firm is broke, we're losing the house, and she's showing him holiday brochures?

"Sung Law was mine, my inheritance. Everybody knew that. I worked for it, I earned it. And Mabel totally ruined it before handing it to me. What's more, she had a second mortgage on the house. You didn't know that, did you, Pa? There was even a note to herself, a reminder to tell me she was going to retire to look after Len, but she still forgot to tell me. She systematically stole from the firm, drained it to pay for Len's medical expenses, then put me in charge to take the blame when things fell apart."

"Poisoning her with my *buah keluak* wouldn't help you keep your law firm or your house," Aunty Lee managed to interject.

"I told you I only wanted to make Len throw up because the only thing that my mother minded was her precious Lennie feeling bad. She died because she shared Leonard's food, though she never shared mine."

"So she died because of your brother, Leonard," Aunty Lee said. Henry Sung glanced at her suspiciously but the old woman was looking sympathetic, as though she understood what parents had to put up with. "But your poor brother couldn't help being sick. Liver failure is a terrible thing. I had a friend who was on liver dialysis for two years and poor thing, she—"

"Bullshit!" Sharon snapped. "Don't you see? My fool of a brother did it to himself. My parents paid a ton of cash for him to study in the States because he didn't qualify for Uni here, but instead of getting a degree, he got addicted to heroin. That's why his heart was failing, that's how he got AIDS."

"Long-term heroin use causes infection in the heart lining and valves," Henry told Aunty Lee, "and HIV can be transmitted on needles. Lennie was never one of those gays."

Sharon snorted.

"Of course not," Aunty Lee said soothingly. Then, as though by natural thought progression, "What happened to Benjamin Ng? He helped design the ICU and operating theater at your house, right?" Aunty Lee asked.

"He was stupid. He thought it was an end-of-life facility for Dad and Mabel and he was so proud of it. His job was done, finished, but of course that idiot Edmond hadn't paid him because he didn't have the money and apparently Benjamin Ng came back to check something or change something and saw the body on life support."

"You mean the dead man from China."

"He wasn't dead. That's the whole point. He was a live donor. Anyway, Edmond freaked out. Benjamin Ng was threatening the deal, and if the deal didn't go through there would be no money for anybody."

"So Edmond Yong killed Benjamin Ng?"

Sharon shrugged. "He's an idiot. He panicked and hit his friend on the head, then dragged him into the pool and drowned him. I only found out about it later because he got the PRC people to get rid of the body, and Wen Ling, his PRC contact, charged Mabel for it."

And that had been the end of Patrick Pang's friend. Aunty Lee wondered if Patrick would ever recover.

"But all that was nothing to do with me," Sharon said. "Mabel was a fool to trust Edmond Yong. She should have dealt directly with Wen Ling like I did. In less than one week I set up Mabel's system much better than Mabel did. Even Wen Ling said I was much better at it than my mother. Everything was working out fine and then that fool GraceFaith went and sabotaged everything. But the equipment is still there even if the body is dead. We just need a new live donor."

Aunty Lee did not like the sound of that. "And Edmond, did you kill Edmond too?"

"Again, nothing to do with me. After Wen Ling met me, she decided it was much better working with me than with

Edmond. Frankly Edmond was only good for babysitting my brother. He probably couldn't even have done the transplants."

"My friend Doreen Choo said Edmond Yong did her transplants."

"I did Doreen's transplants," Henry Sung said. "They went very well. She was very pleased. I'm the one who did them. The boy was just a robot. My robot hands. I told him exactly what to do and he still had trouble. We need to find a better doctor."

"But when you found out your mother was making money off the organ transplants—" Aunty Lee began.

"It wasn't about the money!" Sharon snapped. "If Mabel had thought more about money, we wouldn't have got into such a mess. She was rehearsing for Len's heart transplant. She didn't want to take any risks with him. She took risks with everything else but not with her precious son!"

"I told Mabel that God was testing us by asking us to sacrifice Leonard," Henry said. "If only we trusted God, it would be all right. God would send a ram to be sacrificed instead. But Mabel tried to act on God's behalf. She tried to provide the sacrificial ram herself. And now they are both dead."

"Shut up, Dad," Sharon Sung said.

"But that's over now," Aunty Lee pointed out gently, "and nobody is blaming you for anything. Why not just forget it and move on?"

"Move on with what? There's no money left, why can't anybody see that? But Mabel's transplant setup works, even if she was too stupid to see that. We can easily make back enough to save the firm, save the house."

It was all about money after all, Aunty Lee thought. For some people it always was—money and pride, because money was the only thing they valued enough to be proud of.

"I'm doing this for my mother, don't you see? I'm going to make sure people remember her as the founder of Sung Law. And as my mother."

"Wen Ling wanted to be paid for the organs your brother needed before the transplant operation, didn't she?" Aunty Lee asked. "That's why Dr. Yong brought her to the house the day of the party, to meet Mabel and prove they were rich people who could afford to pay. They agreed that Wen Ling would take the house if Mabel didn't come up with the money."

"Mabel would never have let her have the house," Henry Sung said. "She would have come up with something. She always did."

"How, by burning it down too." As Aunty Lee said this she realized she should have made that connection long ago. That was how Dr. Yong's debt-laden clinic had been disposed of.

"Father wanted to just turn off the power, let the man die, and get rid of the body. But then how were we going to pay for the mortgage on the house, etc.? That body was money. And we had already paid for it in a way."

"You'll have to find another doctor," Aunty Lee said, "and the police have got the PRC gang."

"So we'll find another doctor. Not a problem. There are tons of doctors from India complaining online that they have medical degrees but Singapore won't let them practice here. My father can supervise the operations. And who needs the PRC gang? I just need to find another living donor."

"No—"

"Not you, old woman."

Aunty Lee did not like the way Sharon looked at Nina.

"People will ask questions," Aunty Lee said. A small part of her brain warned her to keep quiet and be terrified because this madwoman was going to kill her and Nina. But if that was true she had nothing to lose. "People saw you here today."

"Everybody who was here saw us leave," Sharon retorted. "And Doreen will swear we were at her house all night."

"Nowadays," Aunty Lee observed, "forensic pathologists can take one look at dead bodies and tell how the people were murdered!"

Nina might laugh at Aunty Lee's passion for crime shows imported from America, but Aunty Lee was certain some of their technology had to be founded on fact.

"She's right, you know," Henry Sung said. "Girl, maybe we should just—" He made a vague gesture that Aunty Lee could not interpret. But Sharon was not to be stopped.

"Just do nothing like you've been doing nothing all your life? If you had stopped Mabel's mad schemes, we wouldn't be in this mess now. So just keep your mouth shut. Have you got the needles?"

"Now?"

"No, next week. Or maybe next month. Just get them, will you?"

As her father went to obey her orders Sharon turned back to Aunty Lee, "Of course they can do all the tests on you they want. And of course they'll find out that you were murdered—by your maid, who stole all your money and disappeared. Mark and Selina will get your house and money like they've always wanted and everybody will live happily ever after."

Aunty Lee's attention was drawn again to the slightly open wine room door. Had she heard something or was it wishful thinking? Her eyes moved to the portrait of ML Lee on the wall by the wine room door. ML Lee smiled, benignly protective. ML would not like her killed in front of him by these people, Aunty Lee thought. This reminded her that she did not want to be killed by these people.

"Dad, what are you doing? Give me that!"

"What is it?" Aunty Lee asked, pleased (and surprised) to find her voice quite steady. She could be scared later. Right now she had to make sure she had a "later."

"Digoxin," Henry Sung said with a trace of professional pride. "Digitalis is no longer the first choice of treatment for congestive heart failure, but nobody will be surprised if you have a heart attack due to digoxin overdose."

"I thought you were going to make it look as though Nina killed me. Where would Nina have got hold of digoxin?"

"Nobody is going to worry about that," Sharon said. Almost mesmerized, Aunty Lee watched her tilt the syringe and depress the plunger to expel any air.

"People will ask." Henry put a hand on Sharon's wrist. "Raja will ask questions. You don't know how much trouble that man made about closing this place. He refused to believe Rosie Lee could have poisoned anybody accidentally or on purpose. He said he would sooner believe his own mother was a murderer. I had to get a former cabinet minister and former president of SINDA to put pressure on him before he gave in. And then he tried to resign. Over a simple kitchen closure!"

"Why SINDA?"

"The Singapore Indian Development Association. All the important Indians and those who want to get anywhere are members. But I tell you, if anything happens to this one, Raja Kumar is going to dig into it. And nowadays they can run tests to show what people died of." Henry shook his head.

Dear Raja Kumar, Aunty Lee thought. He had got himself into trouble for her and not even told her about it. Aunty Lee felt bad. But she would thank him if she got out of this alive.

And Henry Sung?

"You're not already taking digitalis, are you?" Sharon asked Aunty Lee.

"No. My heart is very healthy. Checkup last week showed no problems at all," Aunty Lee said brightly, though she had not been for a medical checkup for years, not since her husband died.

"Dad, you are so stupid sometimes." Sharon slammed the syringe onto the counter, snapping the needle. Aunty Lee winced. But how Sharon handled sharp objects was the least of her problems right then.

"You're such a hopeless case! Why did you pick that of all things?" Sharon shouted at her father.

"Why are you shouting at me? You are the one that told me to get something that would kill her fast! Anyway you should just leave her here and start a fire. Then even if they run tests it will show she died of smoke inhalation after being knocked out. Then they will blame it on the maid. Especially if the maid disappears with all her money. We should find what money she has here and take it. And from the house also. You should go there and take the maid's clothes and passport to show that she ran away after killing her boss."

"There might be a fire alarm?" Sharon said. "Is there?"

"Of course," Aunty Lee said. "Kitchen regulations." She looked at the kitchen she was so fond of . . . the storage cubicles specially designed for her dried goods, spices, and oils . . . the neat stacks of scraped but unwashed plates.

"She's bluffing," Henry Sung said. "Where's the fire alarm, do you see it anywhere? In these small places they never bother. Plus in a kitchen with all the cooking and burning and smoke inside and all the smokers with their beer outside, if she really had a fire alarm it would never stop ringing. Just tie her up, start the fire, and we get out of here with the servant."

Aunty Lee said nothing. But she was offended by the suggestion of smoke and burning in her kitchen. Still, it was better to feel offended than scared.

"Tie her up with what?" Sharon looked around the kitchen space. "I already used the *ketupat* raffia to tie up the maid."

"Or just lock her in. There must be a toilet or something.

Nobody will be able to tell whether the door was locked from the inside or the outside. They will think that she locked herself in to escape from the maid and the maid started the fire and ran away."

Aunty Lee did not say anything but she threw a long, shifty glance in the direction of the wine room. Sharon's eyes lit up.

"In there!" Sharon pulled Aunty Lee to her feet and started dragging her toward the wine room.

30

Hot Save

One advantage to being of a certain age is that people expect you to be physically weak. Aunty Lee stumbled feebly and fell against the wall of storage cubicles containing jars of spices and oils.

Sharon Sung backed into the wine room, pushing the door open with her shoulder as she pulled Aunty Lee away from the counter she was steadying herself on.

"Come on, hurry up. Damn, the light in here's not working—"

The crash of breaking glass and Sharon's cry of pain startled Aunty Lee. But not so much that she forgot Henry Sung, who left Nina to see what had happened to his daughter. Aunty Lee twisted open the jar she had grabbed (with some exasperation at Nina's strong fingers that had twisted it shut).

"Henry," Aunty Lee called out, "over here!"

Automatically Henry Sung turned to Aunty Lee. She threw the contents of the jar in his face.

"Hey, what—" the old man cried out, startled. He wiped down his face with his hands, his eyes tearing. Then he screamed, "It's burning me!" He reeled away, bumping into a table and knocking over a chair before collapsing to his knees, moaning and sobbing. He would not be making any more trouble for a while.

Aunty Lee hurried to the wine room, then stopped cautiously at the door. Should she just lock it and call for help?

"Madam! Madam!"

"Nina, wait. I have to find that crazy girl!"

"Untie me first, madam!"

"She said the light inside is not working. I think a bottle fell down and hit her on the head. But just now I thought I heard someone inside. And why was the door open, did you open it?"

"Madam, untie me!"

Now Aunty Lee definitely heard someone in the wine room, "Who's there—Cherril, is that you?"

"Hi, Aunty Rosie." It was Mark. "There's nothing wrong with the light. I unscrewed the bulb. I was inside when they came in through the back and I didn't want to interrupt, so I just kept quiet—"

"What did you do to Sharon?" Aunty Lee asked Mark. "Where is she?"

"I just hit her with a bottle. On the side of her head. She's somewhere on the floor. I don't think she's really hurt, but there's glass—and wine—all over the floor so I'm not sure."

"You came to take more bottles, right?" Nina turned on him. Being threatened by death had a way of making your employers less frightening. "You are the one who took the bottles and then Madam Silly blame me! Because you don't want to pay Madam Rosie and Madam Cherril!"

"Oh, Mark." Suddenly Aunty Lee was teary and trembling with relief. It seemed to her that ML's portrait seen over Mark's shoulder was smiling with relief too. "Your father would be so glad you are exactly as you are!"

Mark put his arms around her and gave her a big hug. "I heard what Sharon said about Selina and me wanting Dad's stuff. It's not true."

Aunty Lee's "Selina?" was slightly muffled by Mark's comforting shoulder.

"No. Not all the time, anyway," Mark admitted. They both laughed.

That was when Inspector Salim kicked open the kitchen door and rushed in. Once he saw Nina, he stopped and took a deep breath.

"If this was some kind of joke, I'll kill you myself," Salim said to Nina.

At least she looked glad to see him, Aunty Lee thought.

"What took you so long?" Nina demanded. "I left my phone on for so long the battery is dead!"

After Salim released her from a most inappropriate but totally satisfactory hug and went back to his car to radio for support, Nina kept watch with a pair of lethal-looking rotary barbecue skewers while Aunty Lee tied the dazed Sharon's hands behind her with bamboo and reed strings that were soaked and rinsed and all ready to tie up bundles of *nonya* rice dumplings. Modern cooks used raffia, but anyone who had ever struggled with knotted bamboo and reed twine knew their tenacity. It seemed unnecessary to tie up Henry Sung. He was sitting on the floor against the wall, moaning, with tears running down his face, and ignoring the confused stream of mumbled complaints and commands coming out of Sharon.

"What did you do to my father? Help him! Call an ambulance! Dad, don't just sit there—do something! You better let us go or I'm going to sue you until you wish you are dead! Oh God, my head hurts."

"What did you do to him?" Mark asked. "Is he going to be all right?"

"Naga king chili oil," Aunty Lee said. "My best home-dried and fried chili-oil concentrate." Two or three drops of the prized oil was enough for most dishes. A liquid potent enough to burn careless fingertips . . . even now Aunty Lee winced at the thought of what it could do to the eyes and lips.

"Nina, take some coconut milk from the fridge and rub on his face." Coconut was an all-purpose salve, working especially well to soothe chili burns.

"Salim is back. I can see the car. I go and talk to him first."

"You knew exactly what Wen Ling's people in China were doing, didn't you? You put them in touch with people willing to pay for transplant organs and they were supposed to pay you enough to save your house and the law firm."

"It would have worked too, if you hadn't come nosing

around. It was good for everybody. We could have saved a lot of people's lives!" Henry Sung wailed.

"And what about that poor man?"

"That poor man had no job, no money, no prospects. He could have been hit by a car and killed and it wouldn't have made a difference to anybody on the planet. He was willing to sell a kidney for money and people die on the operating table all the time. We gave his family compensation money, more than he would ever have earned if he survived," Henry Sung said. "Alive he was worth nothing."

Aunty Lee decided it would not hurt to let the man burn a while longer. She put away the coconut milk.

"Maybe you should take out an ad in the papers," Mark said to Aunty Lee, "telling people there was never any poison in your *buah keluak*, that a murderer who wanted to cover up killing people to make money off illegal organ transplants framed you and your restaurant."

That sounded too complicated even for Aunty Lee. Singaporeans didn't like complications around their food or in their food. Besides . . .

"Newspaper advertisements cost a lot of money," Nina said, coming back in.

Things were getting back to normal, Aunty Lee thought. "We'll just open and see if anybody comes," she said.

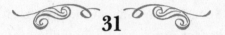

31

Open for Business

"Well, the crowd in here is not bad tonight," Mark said. He had finally completed the transfer of the wine business to Cherril Peters.

Being hailed as a hero suited him. Aunty Lee had made much of the fact that Mark had saved her life, and no one asked why he had sneaked back into the shop. Selina must have known. After all she had been waiting in the car outside. But she didn't say anything either.

Aunty Lee's Delights was full of customers again.

Not only were people coming back, they were all ordering Aunty Lee's Deadly Special, the chicken *buah keluak*, and taking photos of themselves "risking" their lives.

"They are crazy," Nina said. But these were paying customers, so she said it indulgently.

As far as Aunty Lee was concerned, a traditional dish had been given a new lease on life and that had to be good.

Aunty Lee's Delights was extra-safe that night too, because the very police officer who had kicked in the back kitchen door leading to the alley was stationed by it, well supplied with the best samples of what the busy, happy cooks thought were their best dishes.

Of course another reason Salim was more comfortable in the kitchen was that his big boss, Commissioner Raja, was in the main restaurant and seemed determined to stay until he saw Aunty Lee safely home.

"You don't have to play security guard here all night. If you can't eat any more you should go now," Nina told him as she saw his appetite flagging.

"Of course Salim can eat more!" Aunty Lee swept by, depositing a dish of gelatinous blue rice cakes by him as she passed. "We haven't fed him for days!"

"I surrender." Salim laughed helplessly. "But I don't want to hurt her feelings."

"She will be happy that you are full," Nina promised. "But I will pack the *pulot tai-tai* cakes up for you to bring home. The butterfly pea flowers for the coloring came from the old vines behind the police post, your Sergeant Panchal helped collect for us. She is not too bad when she not trying to show off for you. You can give your mother for breakfast, they will last two, three days."

Salim did not try to digest all Nina's information at once, but he accepted the blue cakes along with a container of *kaya,* or coconut jam, for dipping them in. "Thank you. My mother likes homemade *kaya* very much. And speaking of my mum, she wants to meet you."

"What?"

"Come for lunch at my mum's place this Sunday."

"No, Salim."

"Nina, we are alive. We should take full advantage of being alive before it is too late. I keep thinking, if Mark had not been there—"

"Salim, don't—"

Nina knew that if she had died, Salim would have grieved in a most genuine and romantic way and everyone would have pitied him and left flowers and candles for her. But alive, they would get very little sympathy or support. Restrictions on foreign domestic workers marrying were severe. And as a police officer, Salim must be only too aware that many of Singapore's laws and restrictions equated "racial harmony" with "Chinese majority," and "traditional values" with "Christian morality."

"It's just a lunch. My mum knows you are always cooking for me. She wants to cook for you."

Nina wavered. "I have to check with Aunty Lee first."

"Don't worry. Giving domestic workers their day off is mandatory now, remember? If Aunty Lee won't let you come, I'll arrest her!"

"Mycroft's here," Cherril said when the café was almost empty.

Mycroft had asked Cherril to wait at Aunty Lee's Delights

till he came to walk or drive her home. It was probably safer for a woman to walk alone along the well-lit housing estate streets of Singapore than almost anywhere else in the world, but Cherril was smart enough to be appreciative. And Aunty Lee had made up a bento-box dinner for Mycroft.

"Any news? Have you had your dinner yet? We packed up something for you in case. Just some leftovers. Do you know what's going to happen to Sharon Sung yet?"

"No I haven't had dinner," Mycroft admitted. "Oh, thank you—I was going to get some cup noodles at home—"

"This is much better for you than cup noodles," Cherril said. "Why don't you eat it here and tell us what you heard? Aunty Lee won't mind waiting a little while, right?"

Aunty Lee, all agog, had already set up a serving place for Mycroft and plunked herself down across from it. "Cherril, sit down so that Mycroft can eat and tell us. Raja, don't pretend you're not interested. Come here and listen to what happens to murderers after your people bring them in!"

Both Henry Sung and his daughter, Sharon, had been charged with murder, attempted murder, and a host of other things Cherril dismissed as unimportant. Given they all paled in importance next to the attempted murder of Aunty Lee, Aunty Lee agreed.

Mycroft said that Henry Sung had been calm, even genial. He smiled, waved, and told reporters, "Her mother could probably have got us off with no problem, but now we'll have to wait and see what's going to happen. I don't have as much influence as people think." Henry Sung did not seem to feel any remorse for what he had done.

"It could be part of his defense. He'll probably say his late wife was responsible for everything and he and Sharon were only trying to cover up for her."

Asked about Mabel and involvement in the black-market organs, Henry had said, "You people don't understand about Mabel. She did it for our son. Any parent would do that. If it was your son who was dying, maybe you would be able to understand."

He could not grasp that other people had lost their children because of his wife's actions. Perhaps people other than family were not quite real to him.

"I suspect he still thinks he and his friends can smooth everything over once public interest has died down. But that's not going to happen. GraceFaith came to testify at the preliminary hearing. Sharon started shouting and screaming she was going to kill her and had to be taken away," Mycroft said.

"Most people learn they can't have everything their way all the time when they are children. I think it's a lesson easier learned when young," Aunty Lee said.

"Mabel Sung was in much deeper trouble than anyone guessed. But she was such a forceful personality that nobody thought to question her. The people in her law firm, the members of her prayer group and her family had been under her leadership for so long that questioning her would have seemed like an act of treason to them. That's why until Sharon went through the books, no one knew that Mabel had got Sung Law into serious financial trouble. What made it worse from Sharon's point of view was that Mabel had borrowed against her house as well as the company. If Mabel was declared bankrupt they would lose the house, their reputation, everything."

"Everything was all right until Mabel Sung was careless enough to let Sharon find out what was happening," Cherril observed. "If she pulled off the organ scam she would have had more than enough money pay back everything and to rescue the house and the law firm."

"I don't think it was carelessness." Aunty Lee said. "The problem from the start was that Mabel Sung and Sharon never understood each other. To make it worse, they thought they did.

"My stepdaughter, Mathilda," she continued, "told me how competitive Sharon already was back in her school days. If Sharon couldn't be the best at something, she had to put it down and show that it wasn't worth doing. But it wasn't her teachers or her peers that she was trying so hard to impress. What Sharon really wanted was to get her mother to notice her.

"It was only after she was made partner that Sharon discovered her mother had been putting more than prayer into Leonard's recovery. His drug use had damaged his heart. Because of his HIV-positive diagnosis, it was unlikely Leonard would be considered for a heart transplant in Singapore no matter how much money his family threw into the system. Which is probably why Mabel started to look outside the system. By then Leonard wasn't well enough to travel, so she had to find a way to bring a donor into Singapore—and someone and someplace to perform the operation.

"That night Sharon learned that Mabel had ruined the law firm—which she considered her birthright—to try to save her sick son's life. That's what drove her to put the Algae Bomb powder into Leonard's food. And almost by accident she killed her mother too."

"So Sharon killed them?" Commissioner Raja could remember Sharon Sung as a skinny girl in a school uniform.

"I don't think she meant to. But after she did it, I don't think she minded. You know, accidents upset some people terribly. They run over a dog by accident and feel so guilty they kill themselves and leave all their money to the SPCA. Of course that's a bit extreme, but I don't think Sharon Sung felt anything except that she had got away with it. And it would have got easier with practice," Aunty Lee said. "Like with killing chickens. So it's a good thing you stopped her."

"*You* stopped her," Commissioner Raja said. "It's hard to believe. On the surface they were such decent, law-abiding people. It just shows how little you can tell."

"According to Mabel, the laws necessary to maintain social order are not the same as God's laws. To her that meant she had a God-given right to save her son by any means that did not upset the social order. Sharon is very like her mother. She felt her mother had cheated her, so she was entitled to get what she wanted as long as she didn't get caught."

"I can't believe old Henry Sung went along with it," Aunty Lee said.

"Henry Sung always let his wife run him. He only did as well as he did because of her. If he had married someone else, he might have spent his whole life working in a government hospital and living in a semidetached house. Mabel was always the energetic driving force. But Henry Sung liked being rich and comfortable, and once Mabel was gone, Sharon was his only hope of maintaining that lifestyle. Henry spent most of his life doing what his wife told him. It was easy for him to switch to obeying his daughter's orders, no questions asked."

"She could have killed you," Commissioner Raja said feelingly. Death could come so quickly and almost easily, but with irreversible consequences, and Aunty Lee, caught up in the thrill of figuring out the ingredients that had gone into producing killers, seemed to be forgetting this. "Sharon Sung would have killed you if she could. You might be dead now. Think about that."

Aunty Lee thought about it.

"I want to serve crab cakes at my funeral," Aunty Lee said. "Made with fresh pepper crab meat inside a light batter pastry. I can make them in advance and freeze them and all Nina will have to do is put them in a deep fat fryer. But I haven't made them yet, so I'm glad I'm not dead yet."

Raja Kumar looked at her with some exasperation, but Aunty Lee was not just being facetious. She had just realized that the heavy cloud of misery that had hung over her for so long, carrying the conviction that everything she did was pointless, had evaporated.

"That poor China man and poor Benjamin Ng are still

dead for nothing. But poor Patrick came with Timmy Pang tonight, so at least the brothers are eating together now. You know, we may offer food to remember the dead, but funerals and feasts are for the living, do you know what I mean? People must go on eating together to remind themselves why life is worth living."

"And you will go on feeding us." Raja Kumar laughed. He almost added "from beyond the grave," but stopped himself. "We should go. Mycroft and Cherril have already gone and Nina and Salim are waiting to lock up."

"You see?" Aunty Lee took a moment to say to the portrait by the wine room as she picked up her handbag. "I told you things would work out all right."

ML Lee, as tactful in death as in life, did not contradict her.

Acknowledgments

So many wonderful people helped me make this book happen. I would like to thank Priya Doraswamy, my magical agent, Rachel Kahan, my wonderful editor, NaNoWriMo-er (the insanely wonderful milieu which helped me get the first draft down), the Magic Spreadsheet (which guided me through rewrites), the Artist's Way Circle (which told me I was a writer before I was one), KanbanFlow (which provided work-life balance), Bouchercon-ers (who made me believe I could do a second book), and all the great people at William Morrow/HarperCollins who did the real work of making this book happen: Trish Daly, Joanne Minutillo, Alaina Waagner, Jennifer Hart, Liate Stehlik, Joyce Wong, Austin Tripp, David Wolfson, and Sarah Woodruff.

Insights,
Interviews
& More . . .

Meet Ovidia Yu

Kar-Wai Wesley

OVIDIA YU is one of Singapore's best-known and most acclaimed writers. Since dropping out of medical school to write for theater, she has had more than thirty plays produced in Singapore, Malaysia, Australia, the United Kingdom, and the United States, including the Edinburgh Fringe First Award–winning play *The Woman in a Tree on the Hill*.

The author of *Aunty Lee's Delights* and *Aunty Lee's Deadly Specials* and a number of other mysteries that have been published in Singapore and India, Ovidia Yu received a Fulbright Fellowship to attend the University of Iowa's International Writers Program and has been a writing fellow at the National University of Singapore. She speaks frequently at literary festivals and writers' conferences throughout Asia.

Despite her writing career, when she is recognized in Singapore it is usually because of her stint as a regular celebrity guest on Singapore's version of the American television game show *Pyramid*. ‿

Reading Group Guide to *Aunty Lee's Deadly Specials* by Ovidia Yu

1. Aunty Lee loves her kitchen, which is "small enough to get around quickly but there was space to fit in friends. She always felt that the bonds formed while cooking together ran deeper than those formed merely eating together." What role does cooking play in your friendships and family life? How do you think cooking together encourages bonding?

2. Aunty Lee likes buffets because she learns about people by watching how they pick items off the buffet table. What might your buffet approach say about you to Aunty Lee's sharp eye?

3. The traditional *buah keluak* dish ends up at the center of the whodunnit. Why does Aunty Lee continue to prepare such a labor-intensive dish when many don't seem to appreciate its intricacies?

4. Mabel Sung claims to hate Peranakan food in the novel, and it seems that sometimes a line is drawn between traditional, local fare like *buah keluak* and more modern. What does this say about Singaporean culture? What do the different characters reveal about themselves in the way they respond to Aunty Lee's food?

5. Singapore's strict social codes play a role in the novel with many characters facing legal challenges to their relationships: Nina's status as a foreign domestic worker and Patrick Pang's sexual orientation. How do the characters in *Aunty Lee's Deadly Specials* participate—or not—in these codes? What is Aunty Lee's take on the matter?

6. There is a complex web of moral and legal issues around the illegal organ donor ▶

3

trade in the novel. Aunty Lee asks, "even if you have the organs, how does the law decide who gets them? It's like playing God. Throw a dice, pick at random. As long as the people can pay." Where do you think the members of the Never Say Die prayer and healing group would fall in this debate? Do you sympathize with Mabel Sung's attempts to try to save her son—even at the cost of another's life?

7. Appearances are very important in the world of *Aunty Lee's Deadly Specials*, from displaying family income to "appropriate" clothes to surgically enhanced or repaired bodies. Are appearances deceptive? How does Aunty Lee use people's needs to maintain appearances to her advantage?

8. Among the shops at Bukit Timah Plaza are offices for travel and maid agencies, "full of frightened hopeful young women come to Singapore to work and waiting for potential employers to take their pick. They reminded Aunty Lee of desperate dogs in the adoption pound . . . Or worse, they made her think of the 'live' seafood in the tanks outside Chinese restaurants. Would anyone report a girl who ran away and died in a fire? Would anyone even miss her?" Singapore's underclass of undocumented workers plays a large role in the plot of *Aunty Lee's Deadly Specials*. How do the characters in the novel view these immigrants? How is this similar or different from the way immigrants are treated in your home country?

9. Despite their differences, Cherril and Mycroft are one of few examples in the novel of a happy couple, especially compared to Mark and Selina or the dysfunctional Sungs. Why does Aunty Lee think their relationship works? What made her own marriage with ML Lee so satisfying?

10. GraceFaith Ang, like Edmond Yong, is an unabashed social climber who cares only about her own success, but it is her action that breaks the case wide open, while Edmond only digs deeper into his crimes. Why do you think GraceFaith gave Aunty Lee the documents and shut down the Sungs' donor scheme? Was it her conscience? Or something else?

11. Healing through grief is a theme in the novel: Anne Peters walks her dog three times a day, while Aunty Lee stays busy, makes food, and solves mysteries. Yet even cheerful Aunty Lee still grieves: "Now that loss was a permanent part of her life, she saw that the custom [of offering food to the dead] was less a matter of superstition than of wanting those you loved most to share your experiences." Because she has experienced loss, she feels compassion for Patrick Pang after his partner's death. Does your culture or family have customs around the grieving process? In what ways have you or those you know learned to heal?

12. Commissioner Raja confesses at the end of the book that he was worried the Sungs might kill Aunty Lee. She, of course, takes this as a cue to reflect on what food might be served at her funeral, saying: "We may offer food to remember the dead, but funerals and feasts are for the living. . . . People must go on eating together to remind themselves why life is worth living." Do you agree with Aunty Lee's pragmatic outlook on life and death? What food would you have served at your funeral? ❧

Read on

Aunty Lee's Easy Candlenut Chicken Curry

(Because when in a hurry, any curry is better than none.)

Buah Keluak can be difficult to find, even if you don't believe it's deadly. But a good alternative is the candlenut (the small round nuts also on the cover of this book). Aunty Lee loves the way candlenuts give a nutty, slightly bitter flavor to a curry mix. If you can't buy candlenuts where you live, you can always substitute macadamias.

Ideally the rempah curry mix would be pounded by hand, but for now, use your food processor. If you use fresh (deseeded) chilies and turmeric instead of chili powder and turmeric powder, good for you—they go in the blender too.

This will make enough to feed four adults or two ravenous teenagers.

Chicken

1 onion (preferably red), peeled and chopped
1 pound chicken cut into even-sized chunks
2 potatoes, peeled and cut into chunks
1 cup chicken broth (or water and a bouillon cube)

Rempah Curry

5 candlenuts (or macadamias)
2 cloves garlic
Half an inch of peeled ginger
2 teaspoons curry powder
2 teaspoons coriander powder
2 teaspoons cumin powder
1 teaspoon chilli powder
2 teaspoons turmeric powder
1 teaspoon vinegar

Add a little oil as you blend the ingredients in a food processor to a smooth paste

Salt (approximately half a teaspoon)
Freshly ground black pepper
1 tablespoon sugar (the secret ingredient)
1 cup coconut milk

Heat a little oil in a frying pan and fry the chopped onion. Add the blender paste and fry that, too, until it darkens and becomes fragrant.

Add the chicken and stir fry until the chicken is coated with the curry paste. Add the potatoes. Stir in the chicken broth, salt, pepper, and sugar. Let simmer on low heat for 15 to 20 minutes. After the liquid is reduced, stir in enough coconut milk to the consistency you like (soupy or just saucy) and simmer for about 5 minutes more. Taste and adjust the seasonings.

Serve with bread or rice and Aunty Lee's Amazing Achar! ⌒

Cherril's Ginger Lemongrass Doctail

"Why you want to call them duck's tails?
What have they got to do with ducks?"

"Not ducks, Aunty Lee. You know, like cocktails
and mock-tails, only these are healthy, like a doctor
would recommend, so we call them doctails. I'm
using green tea, barley water, soy milk, and brown
rice tea as bases for the freshly juiced fruits."

This recipe makes 4 cups. (Two to drink right away, and two to put in the fridge to be chilled for later.)

5 cups water
An inch of fresh ginger root, peeled and chopped
3 big stalks of lemongrass (or 5 little ones) including
   the juicy white bulbs, washed and chopped
Honey to taste

Bring the water to a boil in a pan. Add the chopped ginger and lemongrass and turn the heat down to simmer for at least 5 minutes. Stir in the honey to taste. Strain and serve.
   Aunty Lee prefers her Ginger Lemongrass drinks served hot, but you'll find it delightful either way.

According to both traditional Chinese medicine and traditional Malay jamu, ginger has many healing and balancing properties, including the ability to warm the blood and soothe the digestive system. ❧

Aunty Lee's Guide to All Things Singapore

Her favorite places to check out for food, shopping, and everything in between!

Aunty Lee's Favorite Food Spots in Singapore

Food courts and hawker centers are the best introduction to Singaporean food because they offer the widest variety of foods. As a general guideline, food courts are mostly air-conditioned, whereas hawker centers are not.

BEST PLACE FOR FIRST-TIME VISITORS

The Food Republic on Level 3 of VivoCity
The decor here evokes the good old-fashioned hawker streets with wooden stools and tables, but with air conditioning, clean toilets, and clearly marked prices. And it is handy if you're going across to Sentosa. Aunty Lee recommends their thunder tea rice, butterfly fritters, and egg pratas . . . and the *kueh tutu* (coconut and peanut).

BEST PLACE FOR BREAKFAST OR LUNCH

Tiong Bahru Market is the best place for an authentic heartland breakfast or lunch. It's best not to risk trying to have dinner there, as most of the stalls close once they are sold out for the day, usually by mid-afternoon. Aunty Lee likes the *chwee kueh* there—*chwee kuehs* are tiny savory rice cakes served with a topping of preserved radish and eaten with chili sauce.

BEST SPOT FOR LOCALS

Lau Pa Sat (meaning "old market") is what the locals call Telok Ayer Market. Unlike Tiong Bahru Market, you don't want to get here too early. The stalls inside the pavilion are open all day, but every evening around 7 P.M. the road outside is closed off for the satay stalls to set up. Lau Pa Sat dates back to the time of Singapore's founder, Sir Stamford ▶

Raffles. Aunty Lee recommends the barbecued prawns and octopus.

Aunty Lee's Favorite Shopping and Spots in Singapore

1. **Kampong Buangkok**. Singapore's last "kampong" or village. This is what Singapore looked like when Aunty Lee was growing up, with zinc roofs and red mailboxes and open doors. It makes Aunty Lee nostalgic for the calm and quiet (except for birdsong and insect buzz) of old Singapore. But she doesn't visit often because despite their openness, these are people's private homes and lives.

2. **Indri Collection in People's Park Complex**. They have a large collection of ready-made Peranakan embroidered *kebaya*s and batik sarong skirts (and batik shirts for men). Indri is really more a stall than a shop, and doesn't have a unit number. It's on Level 1 of the People's Park Complex, just off the central atrium and next to the security guard counter. (And if you make it there, Aunty Lee suggests you take a quick detour to the basement food court of People's Park Complex to try their noodles.)

3. **Arab Street**. One of Singapore's oldest and most beautiful mosques is found here. Sultan Mosque was built in 1826 by Sultan Hussein Shah of Johor. If you wish to enter the mosque, and are not appropriately dressed, robes are provided. Arab Street is a rich bazaar-style mix of cafés and shops dating from the 1950s selling textiles, carpets, and souvenirs. Aunty Lee also recommends Haji Lane around the corner, where pre-war shop houses showcase the latest up-and-coming fashion designers.

4. **The German Girl Shrine and Chek Jawa on Pulau Ubin.** Pulau Ubin is Singapore's second

largest offshore island, but completely different from Sentosa. The German Girl Shrine, also known as the Barbie Doll Shrine, is a yellow hut beneath an Assam tree. Legend has it that it commemorates a German girl who fell to her death in a granite quarry during World War I and some believe she brings good luck. Chek Jawa is Singapore's only surviving multiecosystem site—sandy beach, rocky beach, seagrass lagoon, coral rubble, mangroves, and coastal forest—and protected from development until 2012. Now, in 2014, its time may be running out.

5. **And finally, the Mustafa Centre in Little India (Syed Alwi Road).** This is a huge department store that sells everything from refrigerators, jewelry, tea towels, and mobile phones to plasters and painkillers. In operation since 1971, it is open twenty-four hours a day, every day (including Chinese New Year) and also has a foreign currency exchange. Aunty Lee suggests you take a look around Little India while you are there and explore the ayurvedic medicine shops, fortune tellers, henna tattoo artists . . . and of course sample the roti prata, thosai, dhal, and kebabs!

Aunty Lee's Top 5 Food Favorites

1. **Katong laksa** with homemade barley water. Fierce debate rages in Singapore over the most "authentic" *katong laksa*. It consists of rice noodles served in a rich, spicy gravy with fish cake, prawns, and cockles and garnished with laksa leaf.

2. **Kaya toast** with soft eggs. A delicious sweet coconut jam. Kaya toast and eggs are a standard breakfast set available all day at most "kopitiams" or corner coffee shops.

3. **Fish head curry**. The head of a red snapper stewed in a sweet and sour tamarind curry with okra and eggplant and ginger flower buds. ▶

Aunty Lee's Guide to All Things Singapore
(continued)

This is best eaten with fingers off banana leaves but also tastes good with cutlery.

4. **Kueh lapis**. Multilayered, multicolored, traditional steamed cakes made of glutinous rice flour, coconut, and sugar. *Kueh lapis legit* is made of layers of rich batter, each spread over the previous layer and grilled separately, creating the brown lines in the buttery cake.

5. **Tau suan**. A sweet hot dessert soup made of split mung beans and flavored with *pandan* (screw pine) leaves. Though widely available at dessert stalls, this is a favorite comfort food . . . and full of protein and soluble fiber. It's healthy as well as delicious! ⌒

Don't miss the next book by your favorite author. Sign up now for AuthorTracker by visiting www.AuthorTracker.com.